Table of Co

Prologue

Bibliography

Prologue

For most of my adult life, I have wanted to write a book about ghosts one day. Now that I have partially retired from my career as a Civil Servant, I finally find myself with some time on my hands – so here goes!

People who have asked what I am going to do with all this new found freedom tend to look slightly bemused when I respond – "I'm finally going to write my book!" The inevitable follow up question of "what sort of book?" is followed by a variety of responses when I say "a ghost book". Most people give a slightly glazed over, perplexed look as they respond, "you mean like a ghost story, right?" as if they are slightly worried about my sanity.

When I explain that no, it will be referencing the tales and myths as well as the "true" ghost stories of an area, some are downright dismissive and rapidly change the subject, some are politely curious, but an excited few are immediately keen to share their own experiences of the weird or the inexplicable that has happened in their own lives. And I am always fascinated to listen…

But regardless of their initial reaction, almost everyone goes on to ask me, "Do you believe in ghosts then?"
Ah, now there's the question.

When you really start to think about that subject, you can never truthfully answer with just an immediate "yes" or "no". You need to start by finding out what the other person's perception of the meaning of the word "ghost" actually is, before you start agreeing or denying that you believe in the same thing that they do.

Are they thinking of the spirits or souls of our dearly departed, watching over us as we go about our daily lives, waiting and hoping for their chance to communicate with us?

Or are they thinking of rattling chains, headless horsemen, and wailing grey ladies? Or ephemeral shadows flitting through the night, only half glimpsed?

Or maybe they're thinking of orbs, or angels, or daemons, or the film series "Paranormal Activity"… everyone's perception of the meaning of that simple word seems to be different and I guess is probably rooted in a combination of their own cultural or spiritual belief system, possibly coupled with some personal or third hand experience.

If anyone has been daft enough to hang around in conversation with me this far, they still often want to know what my personal stance is. I was brought up as an atheist. Curiously though, and I suspect mostly due to availability and proximity, I spent my formative years attending a Church of England School which was attached to the local cathedral in Bury St Edmunds, UK and where the whole school attended Prayers every Wednesday morning. Although our mother gained permission for my sister and I not to have to take part in this, we actually preferred not to be singled out from our classmates and dutifully attended every Wednesday. I learnt some strange aspects of religion there – not least of which was that half of the children, although nominally religious themselves and considering themselves so, preferred once the first prayer was over not to return to a seated position but rather to remain kneeling on the floor behind the pews – where we would play "jacks"[1] for the rest of the service…

All my life I have had a healthy dose of curiosity about me, and these religious visits did at least inspire me to read the Bible to see what all the fuss was about. I read it all the way through. Cover to cover. Even all the bits about "begetting" which went on for pages.

---

[1] A game involving a small bouncing ball and five little star pointed metal devices.. You had to toss them out and pick them up in a sequence whilst catching the bouncing ball in between…

I read it again in my early teenage years, but this time admittedly because I had just read Von Daniken's "Chariot of the Gods"[2] and got pretty cross and adamant whilst reading it that he was in fact misquoting and quoting out of context from the Bible in his arguments.

I have remained atheist despite my reading, and so don't have a set religious view on what happens to us after death.
So I guess, really, the way to sum up all you need to know about my thinking on ghosts is – I don't really know what I think. But I'm not just going to take someone else's word for it. I do confess to quite liking the description of ghosts ascribed to the ghost hunter Tom Corbett by the authoress Diana Norman:

> *"He does not bother to lay traps for ghosts, try to trip them up with wire or take photographs of them with infra-red equipment because he dislikes wasting his time. You cannot, he says, prove ghosts to anyone who has not experienced them and does not want to believe in them. Ghosts cannot be put on the witness stand, or have their fingerprints taken. They are completely proof against proof."*

That something odd is "out there" I have absolutely no doubt. I've heard it. I've seen it. I've even smelt it sometimes. For one period of our childhood, my sister and I had to put up with what is usually referred to us a poltergeist: in our case it was a really annoying and sometimes frightening experience.

Annoying when it moved things around (sometimes in plain view) and frightening when in the dead of night it would make loud banging and crashing noises, or bang loudly on the bathroom door which you flung open in annoyance to find no-one there...

---

[2] Chariot of the Gods – Erich Von Daniken – Souvenir Press 1968/1970

I've seen smoke-like animals on several occasions which disappear like mist on the wind, and I have heard sighs and my name called out from an empty room, and this makes me sure that "something" is out there.

But just what is "it" – what is that "something"?
You see – that's the part that bugs me. What are the wraiths and mists and sounds, and objects moving that people experience? And why do some people seem to experience it a lot in their lives, some just that weird elusive once, and others never at all? That's what keeps me endlessly fascinated. And ultimately, that's what leads me to want to share this fascination with you.

I decided to write my first book (ha! There's ambition for you…) about the ghosts of Marston Vale, since Marston Moreteyne is where I live. I've left in the locations where people were happy to do so, but I have changed all of the names of individuals except historical figures.
I hope you enjoy.

I'm happy to have your feedback – or hear your own tales of the weird – if you wish to email me on wa-1400@outlook.com.

Ruth Roper Wylde
January 2017

Chapter 1
The village of Marston Moreteyne (or Moretaine if you spell it that way) and the area of Marston Vale

Marston Moreteyne has a more modern spelling of "Moretaine", and the village is definitely a bit schizophrenic about it, with modern road signs spelling it the new way, but older signs or business names etc. having it the old way. A few years ago, the Post Office wrote to us all asking us to decide once and for all how we were going to spell it as they were fed up, but I think opinion was pretty much split 50/50, so nothing ever seemed to come of that.

The village lies about fifty miles or so north of London in the UK, in the gently rolling countryside of Bedfordshire, around ten miles west from the county town of Bedford and thirteen miles east from the city of Milton Keynes.

The village is nestled just below the edge of the geographical feature known as "The Greensand Ridge", in the lowest part of an ancient valley formed when Bedfordshire was a sea in the Lower Cretaceous period. The valley itself, the area known as "Marston Vale" and which this book loosely covers, is bounded by the Greensand Ridge to the South, the hills (on top of which lie Cranfield with its small airfield) to the North, the M1 motorway to the West, and the suburbs of Bedford itself to the East.

Within the valley are the villages of Wootton, Stewartby and Lidlington, as well as several even smaller hamlets such as Upper Shelton and Wood End. There are at least five lakes in the valley, the largest of which are Stewartby and Brogborough.

The earliest historical reference to Marston is from 969A.d. and in the late 1990's excavations for the new "Millennium Park" country park found remains of a Saxon village. St Mary's church, in the village, certainly appears to have had a much earlier main entrance facing south east than the one it has now, and its tower is exceptionally unusual in that it lies separate from the body of the church itself, and may even be the remains of a former motte and bailey castle.

Marston Moretaine is actually home to some of the most easterly of standing stones in Great Britain, and these three stones were originally known as either "The Devil's Jump stones" or the "Devil's toenails". One of them is still in situ if you know where to look. It can be hard to find, since it isn't very tall or impressive.

There are several versions of the myths surrounding these three stones, which are covered in more detail later on. Moreteyne Manor, which was built in the early 16th Century, still stands in the village and is now a popular and beautiful wedding venue and restaurant, with its Tudor architecture and picturesque moat. It was owned and occupied by the Snagge family for around two hundred years, before being sold in 1739 to the Duchess of Marlborough. It remained then in the Spencer family until 1811, when it passed to the Allington family.

The Duke of Bedford bought it in 1873 and converted it into a farmhouse, removing the magnificent oak panelling to Woburn Abbey, where it still remains today.
It is perhaps not surprising then, with at least a thousand years of history, that there should be tales of ghosts and things that go bump in the night all across this ancient vale.

Cranfield

Cranfield sits on top of one of the hills which bound Marston Vale.

Renowned now for its university and small airfield, Cranfield seems to have been inhabited since at least 969 a.d, as it was mentioned in a document listing the boundaries of Aspley Guise as "Cranfeldinga dic". Certainly in 969 a.d. it was listed as a Manor when Alwyn the Black died and bequeathed it to the Abbot and convent of Ramsey.

There is a beautiful old church in Cranfield, parts of which date back to the middle of the 13th Century.
There used to be a huge manor house called Cranfield Court built in the 1860s with amazing little towers and fancy gables, but it was demolished only seventy years or so later in the 1930's or so – which seems an astonishingly short life span for such a magnificent building. My own *house* has stood for a longer period than that. Today only Lodge Road remains with the former entrance Lodge to commemorate its existence, and the former servant's quarters which were converted into a private dwelling.

Lidlington

Lidlington appears to have gone through quite a series of name changes through its long history. In around 1086 it is listed as Lilincletone, and seems to have moved through various spellings such as Lutlingeton, Lytlington and Lytlyngtan before arriving at its present day spelling.

The original church had to be replaced due to damage caused by unstable foundations and so the current church building was funded by the Duke of Bedford in the late 19th century. The church is now actually converted into private luxury dwellings, but retains its picturesque outside structure.
There are remains of old hamlets still scattered around the village, such as Thrupp End. Thrupp end is listed as Thorp End as recently as the earliest prints of the Ordnance Survey from the early 1800's.

There are still some partial remains of the moat which once surrounded Goldington Manor house visible in one of the fields between Lidlington and Marston Moreteyne. Records show that the property belonged to the Abbess of Barking, and was held by the Goldington family from the 15th Century or possibly earlier. With Goldington Road in nearby Bedford and Stoke Goldington village over by Milton Keynes, it seems the family had quite extensive influence over the area. The site of Goldington Manor is now designated as an Ancient Monument, and lists a deserted medieval village visible still from aerial photography (try Google Earth – the outlines are quite clear), complete with two moated residences. Within the moats lie evidence of fish ponds and even of a sheep wash. This may well be the reason behind the name Sheeptick End which is one of the roads leading out of Lidlington.

It is believed there are still some remains of an Anglo-Saxon burial mounds near the village, and a coin dated 275 a.d was once discovered, which suggests settlement going even further back than the mentions around the time of the Doomsday Book.

The steep hill which Lidlington clings onto is believed to be "The Delectable Mountains" from the tales "A Pilgrims Progress", and legend has it that author John Bunyan, when preaching in Lidlington, would ride his pony down the hill but never back up it – preferring instead to choose the longer route round through Millbrook.

The village also suffered the double murder, in January 1809, of Mr James Crick, a dairyman, and his housekeeper Rebecca. Both had their throats slit, and Rebecca was found at the top of the stairs in the house, whereas Mr Crick's body was found a couple of fields away: with two sets of footprints leading to it showing he had walked along with his murderer in the snow. Curiously, although boxes and chests at the house had been broken open and strewn about, a considerable sum (in those days) of £50 was found to have been left intact in one of the opened chests.

Kempston Hardwick

Kempston Hardwick was originally one of the small hamlets associated with Kempston, and originally when Kempston Town and Kempston Rural were designated in 1896 it was listed as within the Kempston Town boundary. Today, it actually lies within the modern boundary of the parish of Stewartby.

There was a priory belonging to the Knights Hospitaller here from 1279 a.d to 1489 a.d. Once Henry VIII came along with the Dissolution, the property, now called the Manor of Hardwick, was bestowed upon the Longe family in 1540 a.d. and was apparently also moated. The main road through the hamlet is still called Manor Road to this day.

Millbrook

Millbrook is mentioned as a manor in the Doomsday Book, and was part of the Ampthill and Clophill manors at various stages in its history. Although unclear just how far its history goes back beyond the 11th century, there was mention of a monastic cell there linked to St Albans and founded by Nigel de Wast.

By the late 13th century the Knights Templar owned the Manor of Millbrook.

Its church, the Church of St Michael, stands in an unusual position, being so high on the hill and overlooking the surrounding Vale. Parts of the building date back to the mid-14th century.

Stewartby

Stewartby is the new-comer to the area. It was built in 1926 to form homes for the workers at the London Brick company.

There are still some of the brickwork chimneys standing, and they are a familiar landmark now in the area. It was originally called Wootton Pillinge, but was renamed Stewartby in honour of the Stewart family who were instrumental in developing the brickworks.

Upper and Lower Shelton

These were hamlets originally which lay in proximity to Marston Moreteyne itself. Upper Shelton has been separated from the main body of Marston Moretaine now by the advent of two by pass roads – the original single carriageway bypass and then the later dual carriageway A421.

The manor of Nether Shelton is listed in 1562, and Albert of Lorraine was listed as having a manor there in 1086. The priory of Caldwell had properties listed there in 1536 as within **Wootton Shelton, alias Upper Shelton**. However, at the Dissolution, these properties passed into Royal custody before eventually being passed into the hands of private families in 1560.

Wootton

Wootton is first mentioned in the Doomsday book and there were a number of Manors associated with it. One was held by the Knights Hospitallers in the 13th Century, as it is recorded that a criminal took refuge in their chapel.

The church at Wootton was bestowed to Newnham Priory by Simon de Beauchamp in 1166 a.d.

It can be seen from these various potted histories just how far back settlements within this valley go: at least as far back as Anglo Saxon times and very possibly much earlier.

The rest of the book seeks to list both some of the legends and some more modern tales of the weird and wonderful that pertain to this valley.

Chapter 2

Arundel Road, Marston Moretaine

Arundel Road is a development of pleasant modern houses with pretty gardens in a quiet enough area for young families to raise their children.

One such young family lived at one of the properties for a few years when their children were growing up. The children in particular were wary of one of the bedrooms which always had a rather strange "feel" to it, and which they would claim contained something scary living under the bed which they referred to as "the scary man". Later on, they started referring to it as "the funny man".

At first, the adults in the house dismissed such childish fantasies, but after a time it became apparent that something was not quite "right". Footsteps were often heard emanating from areas where no living person was currently present, and these could be heard by children or adults alike.

Then, one warm summer's evening, the lady owner recalls that something particularly peculiar happened to her. She was lying in bed, not yet asleep, and because it was such a warm summer's evening, she had the windows open and an electric fan situated in such a way as to be pointing straight at her as she attempted to get some sleep despite the heat.

Suddenly, the soothing flow of cooling air completely ceased, causing her to her to sit up in bed and look over at the fan, thinking that something must have gone wrong with it such as perhaps a blown fuse.

To her amazement, and then almost immediate consternation, she could see that the fan was still running and was still functioning normally – but the air flow it produced was failing to reach her, just as if *something* was standing directly between her and the fan.

Understandably terrified at the thought of something apparently solid enough to block the flow of air so effectively, and yet at the same time remain utterly invisible to the human eye, she dived under the covers and hid there trembling until whatever "it" was went away and normality seeped back into the room.

On another occasion the lady was at home when she noticed that the door which led from the house into her back garden was standing open. The garden itself had no other form of entry into it, either via the house or through the fence surrounding it.

She thought little of the matter, assuming some breeze had popped it open since she was alone in the house and the children were upstairs in bed at the time, and simply closed it and locked it to make sure it couldn't open again.

She went upstairs and enjoyed a relaxing bath without giving the matter another thought. Much later in the evening, she returned downstairs, and much to her consternation found the garden door standing open again!

Worried, she checked around to ensure there were no intruders, and again carefully shut it and locked it, this time testing her actions to make sure she wasn't inadvertently making a mistake.

She continued to busy herself around the house as she was waiting for her partner to return from work, and a short while later when she came downstairs again she found to her horror that although the garden door was standing firmly shut and locked as she had left it, the front door was now standing mischievously open!

When her partner came in from his late shift a while later, he came upstairs to where she was readying herself for bed and complained that he had just had to shut and lock the garden door, because she had obviously left it open when she came upstairs…

She told him what had been happening all evening, and explained that it most certainly was not her who had left the door open. They talked about it for a little while, as he was understandably a bit sceptical, and so together they decided to go downstairs and check on the doors again.

This time, they found that the garden door was still shut – but was no longer locked. Her partner, now convinced, was absolutely adamant that he had indeed locked it before coming upstairs to complain.

Some months after this incident, the lady awoke suddenly in bed one night, unsure at first as to what had startled her awake. As she sat up and looked around the room, however, she immediately noticed a young boy standing near to her bed. From their relative positions she could actually only make out the top half of his body in the dimly lit room, but she gained an impression in those few seconds of looking at him that he was dressed in what she thought of as Victorian style clothing and that he looked very neat and pristinely attired.

She remembered him having a round face and big brown eyes, and there seemed no reaction from him to her scrutiny before he was suddenly, and inexplicably, just "not there" any more.

Burridge Close, Marston Moretaine

A lady living in Burridge Close reports that on occasion her pet cats will suddenly drop into a defensive crouch. They seem to be reacting to a threat that only they can see: and they act as if whatever they have noticed has really spooked them. They never used to behave like this at their previous address. She herself has never seen or felt whatever it is they are reacting to.

Beancroft Road

As Beancroft Road winds its way out of the village and towards Cranfield, it passes Drapers Farm on the left and Beancroft Farm on the right. Still a working farm to this date, the buildings have an ancient heritage and were in their day separate manors: the remains of the ancient moat is still present and still happily occupied by ducks (and sometimes the owner's dogs having a cooling swim) at Beancroft Farm.

When a teenager, the farmer and his brother were walking back towards the main farmhouse at Beancroft, having finished their work late. As they approached Beancroft Lane in the dark, they heard the sound of a rushing horse, and something large rushed past them. Even today, the farmer cannot fully articulate what it was that rushed past them in the dark – he says it was more that he sensed it was a horse and rider rather than clearly heard or saw it.

Whatever it was, it thoroughly spooked the two of them, and they took off running for home. Beancroft Road is not so very far, as the crow flies, from Wood End, which makes an entry in a later chapter with its ghost rider and horse – so there may well be a connection there.

Brogborough – The Round House

Perhaps one of the strangest buildings in the area, the Roundhouse stands on the hill by Brogborough overlooking the Vale. Despite its name, it was actually a completely foursquare building with a strangely tall central stack of four chimneys, and an external first floor door with stone steps leading up to it. Some people have said that it got its name from an internal central round hallway.

Now completely derelict, the house was originally built in the 17th Century and was a stronghold during the Civil War which was held by Colonel Okey, one of the regicides who signed the death warrant of Charles 1. He paid dearly for his treason, being hung drawn and quartered at Tyburn.

Through the next couple of hundred years, the property became a farm house, but was taken over by the Hudson Bay Company in the early 1900s, and the farm was used as a teaching farm demonstrating Canadian farming methods. Eventually falling into disuse, the house was used as a hostel for workers employed in the Brickworks just after the Second World War, and in its very latter days there were two women living there alone whom some folk thought were rather strange.

It was gutted by fire in August 1993, and from then until the present day the building has been slowly collapsing.
There are vague stories of how it was haunted through all those centuries by the sounds of Civil War fighting.

Chapter 3

Cranfield – Buttercup Lane

Supposedly in 1969 two men walking along Buttercup Lane in Cranfield watched a legless and armless torso wearing a large hat drift down the lane. The said it was about two meters tall and changed colour from white to black. The trouble I have with this report is I can't find a Buttercup Lane in Cranfield and a lifelong resident I asked has never heard of it either… email me if you know where it is or where it used to be?

Cranfield – Court Road

One tale tells how a man murdered his wife and daughter in one of the old cottages on Court Road after believing that his wife was being unfaithful. The tale tells how the screams can still be heard today. I haven't found any records of a murder in Cranfield, which might mean this is either a very old story, or an urban myth.

Cranfield – Crane Way

There is a legend that the ghost of an old lady sat at the side of the road spinning can be seen on Crane Way late at night. The last sighting seems to have been sometime in the 1940s, when the father of one current resident of Cranfield used to have to walk home very late from his night shift at work.

This particular night was an ordinary night, just like any other, but as he walked along he suddenly caught sight of the ghost sitting there spinning… and hurried home at a much faster pace. He didn't really like talking about what he saw but would sometimes be coaxed into telling the tale in the years that followed.

Cranfield – Lodge Road

The Lodge on Lodge Road is actually all that remains of the once splendid Cranfield Court. One legend says that sometimes the ghost of a mad monk can be seen running backwards and forwards on its roof – but doesn't give any explanation as to why he might be doing that.

Cranfield – nearby farm

In summer 2016, a local workman was working on a farm just outside of Cranfield, in a small gated field where he was working with chainsaws and a petrol strimmer for the day. He had parked his works van in the entrance to the field, where the gate stood open. It was a warm day with hardly a breeze to lift the heat, so he often returned to the van to get a drink of water, since his work was quite heavy labour. Not once did the gate so much as stir.

However, at the end of his working day, he packed his tools into his van and went to reverse out of the gateway. As he did so, the gate suddenly swung violently shut with such force that it actually hooked itself into the handle of his driver's side door – and partially ripped the handle from its mountings, breaking the mechanism inside the door as it did so.

Immediately the gate, completely unharmed, swung back to its original position and returned to its hitherto state of perfect stillness.
And still not a breeze stirred the air…
A few swear words did though, once the driver realised the damage done and the cost.

Cranfield

One Cranfield resident explained that his family had lived in Cranfield for over 50 years, and encountered many a spook, but usually of the "cold feeling" in the night type variety.

One particular evening in 1996, the resident's mother, "Karen", was sitting quietly in the room she referred to as the pantry, busily working on her crochet.

Suddenly the door swung shut, effectively trapping her in the room, since it was the only means of entrance or exit.
She became concerned that it was not just the result of a passing breeze, as she straight away could hear noises in the adjoining kitchen, and was immediately afraid that there were intruders (of the flesh and blood kind) in her house.

Being somewhat cautious in nature, and wanting to know what she might be up against, she applied her eye to the keyhole of the door to see if she could work out how many intruders there were.

She can still describe perfectly all these years later what she saw that day. The cutlery drawer in the kitchen was rhythmically opening and closing all by itself, and each time it did so, it shook the cutlery within sufficiently enough for it to make the faint metallic rustling noises that had alerted her in the first place.

A moment later, one of the kitchen chairs pulled sharply away from the table – just as if some unseen hand had pulled it out in order for someone to seat themselves.

Karen waited for a full five minutes in complete silence, unable to account for what she had just witnessed. When she was certain there was no more activity, she carefully opened the pantry door and stepped warily out into the kitchen. Even as she did so, the chair which had been pulled away from the table jolted suddenly, as if someone had hastily stood up from it.

Karen herself has always insisted to her family that she believes the ghost to be one Mr Walker, who used to teach her when she was a very young child. Her reasoning behind this, is that on another occasion, she came downstairs to start her breakfast, and found a framed photograph of her classmates from some time in the 1950s inexplicably damaged. There were two large cracks across the glass of the framed picture, and the two cracks met in a cross directly over the face of Mr Walker.

On another occasion, in 1997, Karen left a plate of left over sausage rolls out on the counter, amongst other plates of similar finger foods. She had held a buffet that evening to celebrate the engagement of her best friend, and intended to clear the debris away in the morning.

When she came to clear everything away, she found the plate of sausage rolls were nowhere to be found. She did have a small Shih-Poo dog at the time (a cross between a Shizhu and a poodle), but there was no way a dog of its small stature could have reached the counter where the food was stored. There was of course the possibility of rodents, but there had never been any sign of such, and none of the other plates of food were touched.

This would probably never have stuck in her mind as an occurrence, if it weren't for the fact that it actually heralded the beginning of a pattern of behaviour. Whenever sausage rolls were bought and placed in the cupboard, they would invariably have disappeared the next morning, complete with whatever packaging they were in. Nothing else was ever disturbed – only the sausage rolls – which tends to belie the presence of rodents unless they were of a particularly choosy kind. Perhaps Mr Walker used to enjoy sausage rolls..

Cranfield - Hartwell Farm

In Bachelor's Agricultural Survey published in 1813, it reported that there was a well at Hartwell Farm in Cranfield which could cure sore eyes due to the high iron content in the water, and that it had once been a Holy Well held in high esteem.

Cranfield – Rectory Lane

There is a legend that a ghostly funeral cortege complete with black plumed horses is sometimes seen passing through Cranfield as a harbinger of death.

Many years ago, the father of one Cranfield resident was walking home from his night shift, and passing where the old Rectory used to stand before the newer houses were built, he had to stand aside while a coach and horses all dressed in sombre plumage pulling a hearse trundled solemnly by.

He didn't think much of it until he got home, when his wife, who customarily would wait up for him, pointed out the unlikelihood of a hearse operating at 2am in the morning!

Drapers Farm - Beancroft Road.

At one time in the recent past, the farm had an old grain drying system which had to be turned off following a certain sequence of buttons: failure to do so (or any sort of power failure) would result in catastrophe as the mechanism would run out of its prescribed sequence and force grain to back up and cause blockages. This could be very time consuming to sort out and was something the workers would avoid at all costs.

It was a matter of chagrin to the farm workers that quite frequently, the dryer would apparently manage to switch itself off late at night before the grain was properly dried, and without the help of human hand.

Yet whenever it did this, it seemed to manage to switch itself off *in sequence* – so that no harm was done and no grain backed up and blocked the channels.

Much more recently, in 2016, one of the workers in the units at the farm turned up at 5.30am to start his day, as was his usual habit. Since he was always the first to arrive, it was always he who unlocked the door to the workshop and switched all the lights on.

On this occasion, as he stepped through the door he had just unlocked, he saw the figure of a man hurrying away from him up the stairs.

Thinking he had surprised an intruder, he rushed after the figure, following it up the stairs to (quite bravely) confront whoever it was. When he reached the upstairs of the workshop however, he found not a living soul up there. And there is no other way of exiting that level other than the stairs he had just rushed up. At that point it also occurred to him that the only way into the building was through the doors he had **just unlocked** himself…

Chapter 4

Hillson Close, Marston Moretaine

One of the houses along Hillson Close is said to be haunted, and a couple of people have mentioned that it might be the one which used to be the village bakery – but there seems to be very little detail other than that. There is certainly some mention of one of the properties in that road having had an exorcism carried out in the 1980's to try and lay a restless spirit.

Houghton House

Although not strictly within the Vale, this beautiful old ruin with its ghosts which stands high on the Greensand Ridge overlooking it, deserves a place in this book.

Houghton House is a Grade I listed building and is owned by English Heritage. It is completely free to visit, and is a stunning ruin today with spectacular views and relatively close free parking.

The house was built in around 1615 for Mary Sidney Herbert, the Dowager Countess of Pembroke. Unfortunately she died only six years after its completion, not long before her 60th birthday.

In 1624 the house passed to the Bruce family, and then finally to the Fourth Duke of Bedford in 1738. The fifth Duke then stripped the house of its furnishings and removed its roof, and thus the slow decay into the ruins that stand today began. Conservation work was undertaken in 2006 to preserve and maintain safety at the site, and there are some informative history boards installed for the interest of visitors. It is also thought that the house was the inspiration for House Beautiful in John Bunyan's allegory The Pilgrim's Progress.

There are reports that as you walk around the house, there will be shadows of people that flit around just in the corner of your eye – never quite substantial enough to focus on. There is also supposed to be the ghost of a young girl that can be seen standing in the doorway waving.

The ghost of a knight on a horse is said to gallop sometimes down the tree-lined entry – but other sources attribute this haunting to Ampthill Great Park just nearby, not to the House itself.

In 1915, a lady walking along the lane leading up to the house distinctly heard the sound of a coach and horses rushing up behind her. Terrified that she was about to be struck by the fast moving vehicle, she flung herself out of its way into the hedge – only to hear the sound rush on by her with absolutely nothing to be seen. One cannot help but wonder what she would have seen or felt had she actually stood her ground.

In July 2012 a paranormal investigation group called Totally Haunted from Hampshire conducted an overnight vigil with digital recording equipment, and picked up the sounds of objects being thrown, a woman's sigh, and a faint voice saying "get out". They also picked up the sound of footsteps.

They revisited the site in September 2013. Once again, they heard the sounds of stones being thrown and the sound of footsteps. This time the weather was less helpful than the first visit since it was quite a windy night, which affected what their equipment was able to distinguish from natural sounds. They have a website if you want to hear the clips of what they captured from each investigation[3].

Another investigator, Chris Halton, visited the site in 2010 and also captured an EVP of a voice swearing at him, and another allegedly saying "be later" and then "turn it out, I turned it down".

---

[3] totallyhaunted.co.uk

EVP stands for Electronic Voice Phenomena, and is a tool investigators often use of having a digital recorder running which then captures the sound of voices or other sounds which the investigators did not hear with their own ears. Chris also caught a glimpse of one of the shadow figures which are said to flit around the ruins.

Chapter 5

Jubilee Cottages, Marston Moretaine

As Station Road leaves the village of Marston Moretaine heading towards the next village of Lidlington, it passes a single row of properties, which are grouped together in small terraces of four, so that the outside two are semi-detached properties, and the middle two are fully terraced. These are Jubilee Cottages, and they were built in the 1930's as homes for families of the men who worked at the brickworks, which used to abound all through this Vale.

Jubilee cottages boast quite large gardens with open countryside views to the front and to the rear – but at least one of them allegedly has a more sinister view inside.
Locals tell of how the ghost of a young girl is sometimes seen in one of the cottages, and how on occasion a black "shadow figure" is seen to walk through the lounge.

Jubilee Cottages to the Church – pathway

At one end of the row of cottages, there sit six semi-detached houses which were built at roughly the same time, and which were for the managers at the brickworks. In between them and the first of Jubilee Cottages is a concrete pathway which runs across the two fields behind the buildings to the church (known as Church Piece and Redlands fields).

Several years ago, some metal detectorists working in the two fields with the permission of the local farmer found several Jacobean coins and a small decorative Jacobean jewel.

Local legend also has it that a gentleman making his way home along this path late one night, having imbibed maybe one or two more beverages than he perhaps ought, briefly saw and heard the sounds of a bloody battle raging across the fields. You can't help but wonder if that was why the field got the name of Redlands.

Certainly the English Civil War of 1642 to 1651 seems to have generated more than one tale of ghosts in this area so that is always a possible candidate for scenes of fighting. There are no actual battles listed for this area, but it's very likely skirmishes will have taken place up and down the country. There were battles listed for Cropredy, Brentford, and Newbury: so it is not impossible that troops could have been crossing this little corner of England passing between those points.

Lidlington – London Brick Houses

Partway between the villages of Lidlington and Marston Moreteyne, there stands an isolated row of houses which were originally built by the London Brickworks to house its workers. They lie close to the rail line, and to the site of some of the brickworks which are now flooded and form a small fishing lake called Marston Pit which is run by Ampthill Angling Club.

One of the houses seems to host an extra visitor. Around 2010 or so, the current occupier would often awake at night with a feeling of being watched, and as they opened their eyes they would see a shadow just walking out of their bedroom door.

Elsewhere in the house a shadow of a small person or a child is sometimes seen moving about, but never seems to interact in any way.

Chapter 6

Manor Road, Marston Moretaine

Some of the properties on Manor Road (itself named for the nearby Moreteyne Manor, which still stands) were originally of a very flimsy "pre-fabricated" type of build from the mid-1970s, and many have had extensive work done on them over the years to bring them up to more modern and robust specifications.

One family moved into such a house on Manor Road in 2011, and decided that it needed complete renovation. Part of the reason for this was that the new lady owner, whom we shall refer to as Cathy, could not help but feel overwhelmingly sad every time she walked into the house – and it seemed feasible that brightening the home up would dispel such feelings since she could not pinpoint where her misgivings were coming from. The couple spent the first two weeks of their occupancy stripping all the walls right back to bare plaster, in preparation for creating their dream home.

Despite the noise of their renovation efforts during those two weeks, they couldn't help but notice that they could clearly hear the sounds of children running up and down the stairs, and assumed it was noise from the adjoining house. This added to the worry Cathy felt: were they going to have to suffer noisy neighbours as well as a depressing atmosphere in this new home?

However, she pushed on, determined to overcome the problems since the family needed this new home, and really there was no specific issue with the house. Although, she admitted to herself, it did start to get a little annoying that the children they could hear seemed to be allowed to run around at all times of the day – and even during the night.

It was only after some months of living there that they began to realise that there was something not right about the sounds they so frequently heard. For a start, the neighbours appeared to be perfectly pleasant with well-behaved children. And as Cathy's boyfriend pointed out – surely children wouldn't be running up and down during school hours, and in the middle of the night? Gradually they came to realise that the sound did not emanate from next door at all… and that actually they could not find any rational explanation for it whatsoever. It became a feature of their lives that they just learned to live with.

The following summer, Cathy happened to be alone in the home, so whilst using the bathroom facilities had left the door slightly ajar since there was no need for privacy with no one else home. She heard the sound of one of her pet cats coming up the stairs, so she opened the door a little wider and called to it, but no cat showed up. Thinking nothing of it, she finished in the bathroom, and then as she passed the window she noticed both cats out in the garden, happily sunning themselves on the lawn. She has no explanation for what it was she had clearly heard coming up the stairs.

In 2013, her young son Jamie was born, and it was noticeable that there was some escalation in the activity from that point forward.

At first, Jamie was a very quiet baby, but at around six weeks old he seemed to become very animated, crying all through the night and constantly scratching at the back of his own neck. He continued to be quite agitated at bedtime as he grew older, and when he was nine months old his mother recalls him screaming hysterically and pointing at the corner of his bedroom ceiling shouting "Boo! Boo! Nanna!" In his limited vocabulary at that age, a "Boo" meant something scary…
It also came to his mother's notice that the toys which were bought for Jamie would sometimes seem to switch on all by themselves.

One afternoon at around half past four, she sat on the bottom step of their stairs, just taking a quick breather from her chores. As she sat there, she heard a squeak and a distinctive click – the bedroom door was opening by itself! There were no other doors or windows open to cause a draught. Slightly puzzled, but shrugging it off, she stood and continued bustling around the house putting everything straight. As she passed by the bottom of the stairs again a couple of minutes later, the bedroom door suddenly snapped shut with a resounding bang above her.

Then for a period, the activity seemed to extend its attention to the electric lights in the house. Every time they left the home, the family would make sure all the lights were off – but when they came home inevitably one of the lights would have turned back on again. At the same time, they would always leave all the upstairs doors shut when they went out to stop the cats making too free with their leisure time, but when the family returned home, again the doors would be standing open. Often it was just the bathroom door, but sometimes it would be the master bedroom door, or even both at once.

As time went on, Cathy became more worried about the activity, and so her mother, who practices the craft of Reiki, performed a blessing on the house for her. This appeared to calm things for a while, but eventually after a couple of months the effect seemed to wear off, and the activity began to escalate again.

On one evening, the hatch in the loft kept banging, so her partner went to investigate, only to see it lift up and drop back in place as if someone was trying to open it. There was no wind that night which could have explained it.
They would hear the sounds of pebbles being thrown at the windows – and sometimes it seemed like the sound came from within the room – not from the outside. Cathy describes how the house never really felt uncomfortable – other than the sadness she had felt pervading it when they first moved in. She was always just left with the vague feeling that someone was trying to get her attention.

Her daughter Kate once saw the shadow of a person standing on the landing, and sometimes heard some-one calling her name when she was trying to sleep.

When he was still little, Jamie would say that he had seen a rabbit hole at the top of the stairs and had been through it, and that there were monsters in there.

Once they had lived there some time, and had made friends with all their neighbours, they were told that a previous inhabitant of the house used to be known as "the witchy lady". She was rumoured to be doing "mad stuff" in the house, and there was even some sense that she might have opened a portal to another world or another dimension.

Sometimes things around the house would be moved – and this was even after the family no longer had any pet cats who could have taken the blame. For instance, one time Cathy walked in to the unoccupied kitchen to find crumpets (a bread based toasted snack) arranged in the middle of the kitchen floor… yet no-one else was home who could have done it.

Eventually Cath allowed a paranormal investigation team to come in, who tried both E.V.P (Electronic Voice Phenomena) and took E.M.F (electro-magnetic field) readings. High levels of E.M.F in a building are known to slightly scramble the electrical signals in the human brain, making us feel slightly uneasy and as if we can see something moving out of the corner of our eyes: sometimes this can be the explanation for an apparently paranormal occurrence.

It certainly does not explain the banging doors and reticent light switches though.
Either way, their findings were relatively inconclusive and did not make much difference to the house and its activity.

Marston Moretaine – address unknown

One former resident of the village wrote to say that the house she used to live in had the sound of people running up and down the stairs regularly disturbing the family, although there was never anything to be seen. It would be interesting to know if this house was actually the same one in Manor Rd (see above) or the one next door, or a different property entirely.

She always felt that their ghost had a fascination with the television, since the set would regularly turn itself on or off or the volume would suddenly increase or decrease. On the odd occasion, it was actually possible to see the buttons on the remote control depressing by themselves, as if being operated by an unseen hand.

Millbrook – Station Lane

Station Lane runs, not surprisingly, from Millbrook station, around past what is now the Millbrook Proving Ground, and up to Millbrook itself. Legend has it that the lane is haunted by the ghost of a notorious highwayman who terrorised the area, known as Galloping Dick. In life, he apparently made his home in the sandpits near Millbrook – but it is not clear from that description where the sandpits were – since the brickwork pits (Rookery Pit being the nearest) are much younger than tales of highwaymen. It is possible they were the area listed as "Blacklands" on the earliest Ordnance Survey maps. Galloping Dick is said to gallop his horse still all along this lane – and like any self-respecting highwayman ghost, he is of course headless….

Other tales attribute the ghost of the highwayman to Black Tom, who is more often said to frequent the Midland Road area of Bedford.

It's said the sound of galloping hooves can also be heard from Sandhill Lane, and one resident also recalls a tale about a spectral coach and four that runs through Millbrook.

Millbrook – Black Shuck

A Black Shuck is an integral part of British Folklore, and for the most part seems to be found in Norfolk, Suffolk, Essex, and strangely, Devonshire myths. They are said to be huge supernatural black dogs, sometimes with glowing red eyes There are instances of them appearing elsewhere in the country – and Marston Vale is one of those areas – specifically around the area of Millbrook.

It is entirely possible that the tales originated with the Vikings and their tales of Odin's black War Hound. The word itself, Shuck, might be from a dialect word "shucky" which meant shaggy or unkempt. Conversely, it might originate from the Anglo Saxon word "Sceocca", which meant "demon".

The legend for Millbrook says that a young lady encountered a Black Shuck many years ago in the lanes around Millbrook which was described as being as big as a calf and with terrifying glowing red eyes. So disturbed and unhinged was she by her encounter that she died of shock three days later.

Millbrook – St Michael and All Angels Church

In the mid 1800's the tombs of William and Mary Huett were disturbed during works being carried out in the building. For some years afterwards, it was claimed that the church was haunted by the sounds of spectral groaning coming from the disturbed tombs. Another source claims there was also the sounds of whipping. Eventually, the pastor decided enough was enough and reburied the tombs…but it was still some years before the sounds finally died away fully.

Millbrook – A507 Woburn Road

Although the A507 is actually just outside the geographical area this book covers, since these tales pertain to Millbrook (which it passes) I have included them for completeness' sake.

One night a mother was walking along the footpath beside the A507 on Woburn Road, when a small pile of stones suddenly rose in the air and proceeded to fly about in all directions – a little like a swarm of granite bees.

On another occasion, a man walking along the road saw a strange light emerge from the hedgerow which followed him for a short distance before just as suddenly disappearing.

Yet another lady walking there saw a large indistinct, dark coloured shape leap over the hedge and land in the middle of the road without making a sound, where it promptly disappeared from view.

These sightings are very close in location to the supposed manifestations of both Galloping Dick and the Shuck and it is possible there is a correlation between all of it – but people are interpreting what they see and hear a different way according to the time period they came from and the prevalent theories at the time.

That doesn't account however, for the story of the chap who climbed a stile along a footpath close to this stretch of road – and suddenly found himself nearly 7 miles away in Clophill! So, word of warning, be a bit careful where you walk your dogs around there…

Millbrook – The Rectory

Now a private residence, there is a legend that whilst the Rectory was the home of the Reverend Ben Cotton, his daughter awoke in bed one night to find the figure of a monk bending over her as she lay sleeping.

She assumed it was just her father in his robes checking up on her, and drifted back to sleep – only to discover later that he had not been in to her room at all that night.

Chapter 7

Old School House, Marston Moretaine

The Old School House is currently a nursing home, now renamed the Village Green Care Home. Part of the building is a much older building which would have been the village school in years gone by. At one point in its history it was used as a private residence, and it is during this period that one older resident, who lived there when a child, recalls the property being haunted.

St Mary's Church Marston Moretaine

St Mary's Church in Marston Moretaine is a particularly beautiful old building, and boasts the rather rare attribute of having its tower separate from the main building of the church itself.

Built in the 14th Century, the church stands in the middle of its own peaceful graveyard, with the church tower off to one side and a good few yards away from the main body of the building.

The tower's origins are not fully clear, but it seems likely that the base of it might originally have been part of a fortified motte and bailey structure. Motte and Baileys were an old English defensive structure, consisting of a single tower surrounded by a ditch or moat, known as a fosse. The style of building came originally from Normandy in France, and was brought over to England with William the Conqueror in 1066. Hundreds of them were built in England over the next few decades, but from around 1100 onwards they started to fall out of favour as better, stone built castles replaced them. The tower incorporates a rather strange feature in that it has an archway built into the wall which can only be reached using a long ladder.

When the entrance for the new "Millenium Park" wildlife and country park was in construction, quite close to where the church stands, the remains of an Anglo Saxon village were found, which perhaps strengthens the idea of a motte and bailey being built to protect the village: the Anglo Saxon era was technically brought to an end by the Norman invasion, but obviously villages and homesteads would have continued on regardless of whomever happened to be in power at the time.

The church itself also boasts a very fine "Doom" painting on the walls above the chancel arch. A doom painting is one which shows the story of the Last Judgement: when everyone's soul is judged at the end of the world and is either allowed to ascend to heaven, or cast forever into the fiery pits of hell.

The tomb of Sir Thomas Snagge and his wife inside the church itself features very fine carved effigies: and legends of her supposed haunting activities are detailed in the Woodend chapter of this book.

So the site of the church is probably around a thousand years old, and it's not surprising with that antiquity that it comes complete with legends and ghost stories attached.

Some of the oldest legends associated with the church are those concerning the separation of the tower from the church. One story says that when the good townspeople were trying to erect their church, the devil kept coming along every night and moving their tower. Eventually they drove him off, but as he jumped down and sprang away in three giant leaps, he left one of his toenails behind on each leap, in the form of the three small standing stones which used to be situated in a straight line running away from the site of the church. These were called the Devil's Toenails in this version of the legend.

There is another version of this legend which says that the devil actually tried to carry off the tower completely, but finding it too heavy to carry abandoned it after just a few short steps.

Other legends also concern these three standing stones, one of which can still be seen today if you go through the gateway opposite Jubilee cottages into the Millennium Country Park and turn immediately to your right. Follow the hedgerow along to the first corner, where you will find the stone still standing in the corner, often overgrown by tall grass (it's not a very tall standing stone!) It doesn't seem to be very clear where exactly the other two stood, but some say that one used to stand in the corner of the field called Church Piece just by the recently replaced white bridges, and possibly the third within the church yard itself. These two seem to have been lost over the centuries however.

These standing stones were also often called "The Devil's Jump Stones" or just "The Devil's Jumps", and I have heard them referred to as "The Leap Stones".

This last name perhaps derives from the other legend about how these stones came to be placed: but there are two actual versions of that legend that I have come across too.

One version says that three naughty schoolboys were playing truant from Sunday School and decided to amuse themselves by going out into the fields to play the ancient game of "leapfrog" in the fields by the church. Leap frog is a simple game where one participant bends over, placing their hands on their knees to brace, and the other runs up and jumps over them, placing their hands in the small of the back of the first and spreading their legs as they jump – much in the way modern athletes might jump over a pommel horse. Apparently their antics caught the attention of the Devil himself, who decided to punish them for their lack of piety and care for their souls, by turning them into stone.

Another version says it was four young men playing the game when "in their cups" (drunk) and that they did not realise that the fifth player who joined in their game was actually the devil, who leapt over each player, turning them to stone as he went, and carried the last screaming down to hell with him in a pit that opened up...

Interestingly, the house built on the site of what used to be a coaching inn serving the village which was called "The Three Jumps" – or in some histories "The Leaps" - suffered an underground water leak in the driveway a few years ago. When the contractors dug down to effect the repairs they came across the very old stop-cock which would have belonged to the pub.

The churchyard itself is also said to be haunted by the figure of a monk, although there seems to be little detail of actual sightings. The monk is also said to haunt the grounds of the nearby rectory. Further stories are told of shadowy figures seen moving about in the church tower or next to it.

One lady was walking her dogs through the churchyard in the early 1990's, coming back from the fields where they had had their last romp of the day, one February afternoon just as the light was starting to fade. It was turning distinctly chilly, and she had put both dogs on the lead before starting to hurry home to get in the warm and start thinking about preparing an evening meal.

She was suddenly brought to an unexpected halt by both dogs stopping dead in their tracks. Both dogs were mongrels, but one was quite collie like in appearance, and was very good at protecting his mistress when he perceived that people coming near were in some way threatening or not to be trusted. Over the years she had learned to trust his instincts, since with the majority of people he was friendly and polite, greeting them with wagging tail and lolling tongue.

On this particular day, as the dogs suddenly stopped, she recognised in the low growling coming from the collie that he thought he could see someone approaching her that he didn't like the look of. This made her feel particularly apprehensive, since after all, she was alone and it was starting to turn dark quite quickly, and if there was someone hanging around in the shadows the dog was probably right in sensing that they were up to no good.

Feeling nervous, she stood still for a moment and carefully looked around her to see if someone was lurking in the shadows. She couldn't see anyone, so tried to set off again to hurry home. However, it quickly became apparent that both dogs were actually fixated on one particular large gravestone. She took a good look at it as she dragged the growling dogs past – but there was no-one hiding behind it. At least, no-one living…

There is also a legend that during the English Civil War some cavalier soldiers were trying to hide from the roundheads and utilised an ancient tunnel that apparently used to run from the church to the nearby rectory. Unfortunately, the roundheads discovered their hiding place, and rather than enter into yet another pitched battle in the very bloody war, hit upon the simple idea of sealing the two ends of the tunnel: leaving their victims to die a slow and tortuous death of starvation and dehydration. Legend says that on windy days, you can still hear the sound of drumming from below the ground.

Station Road, Marston Moreteyne

One of the properties in Station Road suffered a catastrophic fire in the late 20th Century, in which sadly the old gentleman died asleep in his armchair in the front room – probably from smoke inhalation, and probably by a smouldering fire caused by a dropped cigarette. His wife, who was bedbound and suffered dementia, survived him. As she was unable to care for herself without her husband by her side, she was taken into care and left the property standing empty and partially derelict for some years before it was eventually purchased and renovated in the late 1980's.

During that time, it is said that people walking down the footpath by the property would often see the face of the old man peering out at them from the windows – even though the house was unoccupied and badly fire damaged.

The current owner has never seen the old man, but occasionally things in the house seem to move around of their own accord and with no real explanation. This was particularly the case with a packet of cigarettes which seemed to disappear in the front room over the space of a couple of minutes from being tossed onto the sofa in there, which then reappeared some months later sitting neatly on the sofa arm with the lighter placed on top: identifiable because they weren't actually a brand the owner actually normally smoked and only had the one packet of…

There has also been the phantasm of a small black cat on the driveway, which ran between someone's legs as they went to get into their car one afternoon in broad daylight, and dashed out towards the road – but faded away like smoke in the wind even as the astonished person looked on.

Salford to Cranfield Road

Late one night in July 2009, a driver was returning home to Marston from a night working. As they came along the road from Salford, the headlights of the car briefly picked out the strange sight of an apparition with no legs or head visible, seemingly floating in the road and wearing what appeared to be a scarlet tunic which was covered in blood stains.

The vision was only picked out by the headlights for a moment, but not surprisingly the witness was in no way inclined to turn the car around and go back to look for whatever it was they had briefly glimpsed.

Chapter 8

The Thrift – Wood End

The Thrift is a wonderful patch of ancient woodland situated on the hillside below Cranfield and down onto the valley floor, to the hamlet of Wood End.

Much of the land adjoining it was purchased by the Marston Vale Community Forest and planted with new trees to form new areas of woodland such as Rectory Wood or Strawberry Hill. There are landscaped pond areas, hard-core paths and wooden benches throughout the new areas of woodland, making it a very pleasant location for all the family to enjoy. The older parts of the Thrift itself remain natural woodland – hard to access in some places but easy walking across ancient leaf mould or ancient grassed over trackways called "rides" in others.

It is another area that the redoubtable Lady Snagge is said to ride through, but there are also some rather more modern tales to be told of the atmospheric glades.

One such story is that of the people that can sometimes be seen walking ahead or to the side of you as you walk through the wood – glimpsed quite clearly but momentarily through the trees. Just as suddenly they disappear completely with no trace whatsoever and no sound to mark a real live human tramping away into the distance.

One dog walker saw another lady walking on the other side of one of the small brooks or ditches that run through the woods, who was wearing a bright blue anorak and had a small white dog trotting along beside her. The tree cover was quite thin there, so for a moment or two she was in plain view as the dog walker's own dogs bounded happily over the little stream to go and greet the other dog – only to stand casting around in perplexity on the other side of the bank when suddenly there was no sign of the other walker or her dog.

On another occasion, Linda, a professional dog walker, was walking her charges through the woods, as she did very often due to her particular line of work.

Suddenly, as she walked along enjoying the solitude and fresh air, she stumbled over an exposed tree root and started to fall forward with that horrible feeling of realising there was nothing to grab on to in order to save her from the inevitable fall and probable skinned knees.

In that split second of starting to fall, someone suddenly grabbed her arm from behind and pulled her sharply backwards, giving her enough assistance to allow her to arrest the forward momentum and regain her balance.
Heart thumping with the adrenaline of the "near miss" she turned to thank her benefactor – only to find that there was no-one there at all.

Many other people have mentioned feeling a "presence" there in the woods.

One local countryman was out one day shooting pigeons some twenty years or more ago. He was intending to shoot as the pigeons came home to roost for the night, and so had entered the woods in the latter part of the afternoon and had quietly sequestered himself on a shooting chair on the very edge of the woods overlooking the fields, where he could watch as the light slowly faded away and the birds start to fly home to their roosts, but where he was effectively just hidden under the canopy of the trees and scrub. Every shooter knows that it is best to take up position some time before the light fades, and then sit very quietly and wait, since if the pigeons see the movement with their incredibly keen eyesight from across the fields, they will simply fly somewhere else to spend the night.
This means that a patient hour or so is spent letting the wildlife acclimate itself to the human presence sitting quietly amongst it, and for everything to gradually return to its usual buzzing and rustling as the fauna of the woods go about their daily lives.

As he sat there listening to the sounds of the wood resume behind him, and patiently scanning the skies in front of him, he suddenly became aware that all sounds of life around him had ceased, and a preternatural silence had descended: he describes it as feeling as if everything around him were suddenly holding their collective breaths waiting for something to happen.

This sudden silence and watchful feeling were so alien to the experienced hunter, that he found himself slowly and carefully reaching for his gun which lay on the ground beside him in an almost instinctual reaction of self-preservation.

As he did so, he heard a low feline growl behind him. Stunned at the completely unexpected sound (since he was well versed with badger, fox and dog sounds and knew this was different), he carefully turned to look – and saw two huge cat's eyes staring at him through the bushes and scrub behind him, from just a few feet away within the wood itself. He grabbed for his gun and fired a shot into the air – and whatever it was turned and slinked away through the brush.

To this day he is sure he encountered some sort of big cat, perhaps escaped from a collection or zoo somewhere. He is also sure that on that day, he wasn't the only one doing a spot of hunting and probably had a narrow escape.

Also many years ago, very late one night, a father and son were returning from Cranfield to Marston on their push bikes after a night out at the pub.
Since it was a calm, dry, bright moonlit night, they decided to cut their journey short by riding down through the fields and pathways into the Thrift, then out onto Wood End Lane and home to Marston that way, rather than following the road down Cranfield Hill and onto Beancroft Road.

Neither of them cared to speak about it very often after that night, but they were both certain that for a time, as they cycled through the actual woods, they were followed by a glowing orange orb which bounded after them as if with some sort of intent. They had of course both had a drink at the pub, but they remained certain that this night, something very strange had happened.

More recently, a little over ten years ago, two local men were sitting on the edge of The Thrift as dusk fell as it curves around the corner of Wood Field on the hillside. They were hoping to shoot a few rabbits, but were actually sitting chatting companionably and staring out across the view of the valley spread out before them.

As they looked across the valley to the low hills of the Greensand Ridge on the opposite horizon, movement in the sky caught their eye.

Something was tumbling down through the sky, and whatever it was seemed quite large. It seemed to be roughly over the site of what is now Lockheed Martin, but then belonged to Huntings Engineering.

More than a little puzzled they watched with amazement as whatever it was fell – and their amazement was caused because actually, they could not see whatever "it" was.
The best description they have been able to give was that it was similar to the special effects used in the film "Predator", where the alien attackers camouflaged themselves by using a cloaking technology that reflected the background and could only be seen by distortions in the imagery as they moved.
So it was with whatever was falling through the summer sky that evening – it was causing a sort of prism effect distorting the light around it as it fell, but no actual object could be made out.

The encounter last only a couple of moments, but they have never been able to offer an explanation for whatever it was they saw.

And finally for the Thrift, another hapless dog walker had an alarming encounter there, when walking back down the wide gravel bridle path towards her car, which was parked in the small car park at the end of Wood End.

This is quite a wide path way – enough for several people to walk along side by side, and so the tree canopy does not meet overhead there. The path is bounded on either side by ditches which in places are very deep, forming steep sided gullies. On one side, the woodland of the Thrift itself stretches away, whilst on the other there is only a thin belt of trees on the edge of land which currently belongs to Shanks and McEwan.

As she strolled along, she came within sight of her car a couple of hundred yards ahead, and started to reach for her dog lead and car keys. As she did so, she became aware of a loud thrashing sound coming towards her at speed in the canopy of the woodland trees and stopped to look behind her and upwards, startled by the sudden commotion. Even as she did so, a strange hooting ululating cry came from the tops of the trees from within the woods, and her dog came running to her clearly disturbed and afraid of the noise. She says that the sound put her in mind of a troop of monkeys or apes coming through the trees the way you sometimes hear them on wildlife programmes on the television, hooting and howling as they came.
Seriously alarmed, she started to turn to make a dash for her car, but in the same moment another loud noise burst into the air in front of her – and a Black Hawk Helicopter Gunship came screaming into view over the trees from the other side of the car park in front of her, flew overhead and away towards Cranfield – flying low and making a lot of noise as they often do over this particular bit of airspace.

The sudden appearance and noise of the helicopter seemed to frighten off whatever was behind her, because just as swiftly as it had come, the sound of thrashing tree canopy and hooting turned and rushed away again back into the woods and very quickly faded from hearing.

The entire encounter probably lasted less than a minute, she thought, but it was an awfully long time before she would walk in the Thrift again.

Wood End – land now covered by Shanks and McEwan

Before the modern day landfills were built, there used to be an ancient farmstead there. It was accessed by an ancient track which bisected the route of the modern day A421, rather than by the lane which still runs down to Wood End.

The oldest Ordnance Survey map shows a farm roughly in that area called Moat Farm – but it is hard to tell if that is in the right location with no modern landmarks to go by, and with the fact that the geography of the map does seem a little distorted compared to modern boundaries.
One older resident of the village, Ken, now deceased, used to live there as a teenager: this might have been in the late 1950's.
His son recalls him telling the story of something very strange that happened there when he was home alone one day. Being so rural, and with only Ken himself home, the house was practically silent that afternoon. Suddenly, the silence was broken by the sound of a loud slap – Ken though it sounded like the slap of leather on flesh. The slap was followed by the sound of someone crying out in pain, then agitated voices, followed immediately by the ringing of swords clashing in a fight.

He could not make out what the voices were saying, but showing remarkable bravery for a teenager home alone, he followed the noises to the area of the house they seemed to be emanating from: which happened to be the very oldest part of the building.

To reach that part of the building he had to walk down a dim passageway which ended in an old wooden door with a very ancient wooden latch. This was operated by pulling upwards on a piece of string to move a lever. As he put his hand on the latch mechanism, all the sounds of fighting swords ceased, and an eerie silence ensued. He flung the door open, but there was nothing to be seen and nothing was out of place. He was never able to explain what it was he heard that day, and it was never repeated as far as he knew.

Wood End Lane

The lane itself at Wood End is said to be haunted by the apparition of a headless horse and rider galloping madly down the road.

The legend concerns Lady Elisabeth Snagge, whose effigy lies in Marston Church, alongside that of her husband Sir Thomas Snagge. He was a member of parliament, and a wealthy landowner, who owned a few properties, but was resident at Moreteyne Manor in the village.
In the legend, it is said that Elisabeth Snagge was riding down the lane at speed one night having visited her illicit lover at Brogborough, when she was decapitated by a rope strung across the lane by some footpads, who then mercilessly robbed her body of its jewellery and finery before slipping off into the night.

Since then it is said that sometimes she can seeing riding pell-mell down the lane, without her head, but other times it is just the sound of galloping hooves late in the might, or even the sensation of a horse swishing past at speed.

One historian has said that in reality it was unlikely to have been Lady Elisabeth Snagge, as she had seven children by her husband and then outlived him by 43 years – which would put her a dowager in her eighties when she apparently took a nocturnal ride to meet a lover – which seems a little far-fetched even for a quite sprightly octogenarian. There were plenty of younger Snagge women over the next hundred years, but I couldn't find a record of one being decapitated or murdered by thieves.

Nevertheless, over the years the ghost has been reported[4] – and does it really matter who it was if you were to be confronted with that when walking or driving down that lane…

It is possible however, that whoever she was, the ghost no longer rides, as I did find one reference that the Rector of Cranfield was called to the lane and put the ghost and her steed to rest with the use of bell book and candle.

Alternatively, it's possible this is actually connected to the ghost heard on Beancroft Road mentioned earlier.

Wootton – The Chequers Inn

There are stories that bar staff serving behind the counter see a customer in the corner of the bar patiently waiting out of the corner of their eye. When they turn to serve the customer, there is no one actually there. Sometimes glasses have fallen inexplicably from the shelves, but landed intact on the floor. Some have attributed to the ghost to the time when the pub was a coaching inn, and state that the ghost is that of a groom who stumbled and fell under the wheels of a coach – and who died from the injuries he sustained.

---

[4] See also – Beancroft Road, Chapter 3

Wootton – Fields Road

In 2002, when Fields Road joined up with the old A421 without the benefit of a bridge and roundabout, before the new dual carriageway was built, a driver came around one of the bends to find a woman dressed all in black stood in the middle of the road, straight in the path of his car.

Terrified that he was going to hit and injure someone, he slammed his brakes on so hard and came to such a screeching halt, that the car behind collided with him. The collision was not too serious however, as it turns out the second driver had also seen the woman – and also hit his brakes: thus gaining a split second of extra time and enough leeway to avoid him colliding with too much force with the car in front.

The difficult part however, was that there was absolutely no sign whatsoever of the woman they had both reacted to. One telling of the tale says that the woman actually approached the driver of the first car and asked him if he was alright before disappearing.

Bibliography

Haunted Britain and Ireland Richard Jones New Holland Publishers
The Encyclopedia of Ghosts and Spirits Rosemary Ellen Guiley . Facts on File inc.
www.Lidlington.org
Damien O'Dell – 2013 Paranormal Bedfordshire
Totally Haunted Paranormal Investigation – *totallyhaunted.co.uk*
Chris Halton – Haunted TV – Youtube – Haunted Houghton House 2010
www.paranormaldatabase.com
Bedfordshire Libraries – Daniel Stannard 2006
Central Bedfordshire Virtual Library – Historic Buildings
The way we were – John Taylor
Haunted Bedford – William H King

VENOM

CARNAGE UNLEASHED

VENOM®: CARNAGE UNLEASHED

First published in Great Britain in 1996 by Boxtree Limited, Broadwall House, 21
Broadwall, London SE1 9PL. Copyright © 1996 by Marvel Characters, Inc. All rights
reserved. All prominent characters appearing herein and the distinctive names and
likenesses thereof are trademarks of Marvel Characters, Inc. This book is sold
subject to the condition that it shall not, by way trade or otherwise, be lent,
resold, hired out or otherwise circulated without the publisher's prior consent in
any form of binding or cover other than that which it is published and without a
similar condition including this condition being imposed upon a subsequent pur-
chaser. No part of this book may be printed or reproduced in any matter without
the written permission of Marvel Entertainment Group, Inc. A CIP catalogue entry
for this book is available from the British Library.

ISBN: 0 7522 0322 3

10 9 8 7 6 5 4 3 2 1

B☐XTREE

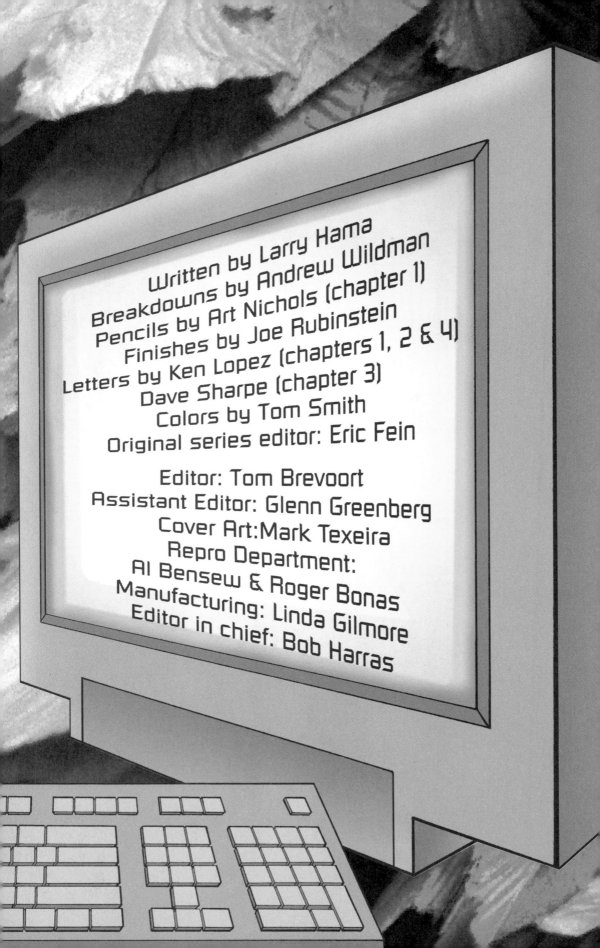

Written by Larry Hama
Breakdowns by Andrew Wildman
Pencils by Art Nichols (chapter 1)
Finishes by Joe Rubinstein
Letters by Ken Lopez (chapters 1, 2 & 4)
Dave Sharpe (chapter 3)
Colors by Tom Smith
Original series editor: Eric Fein

Editor: Tom Brevoort
Assistant Editor: Glenn Greenberg
Cover Art: Mark Texeira
Repro Department:
Al Bensew & Roger Bonas
Manufacturing: Linda Gilmore
Editor in chief: Bob Harras

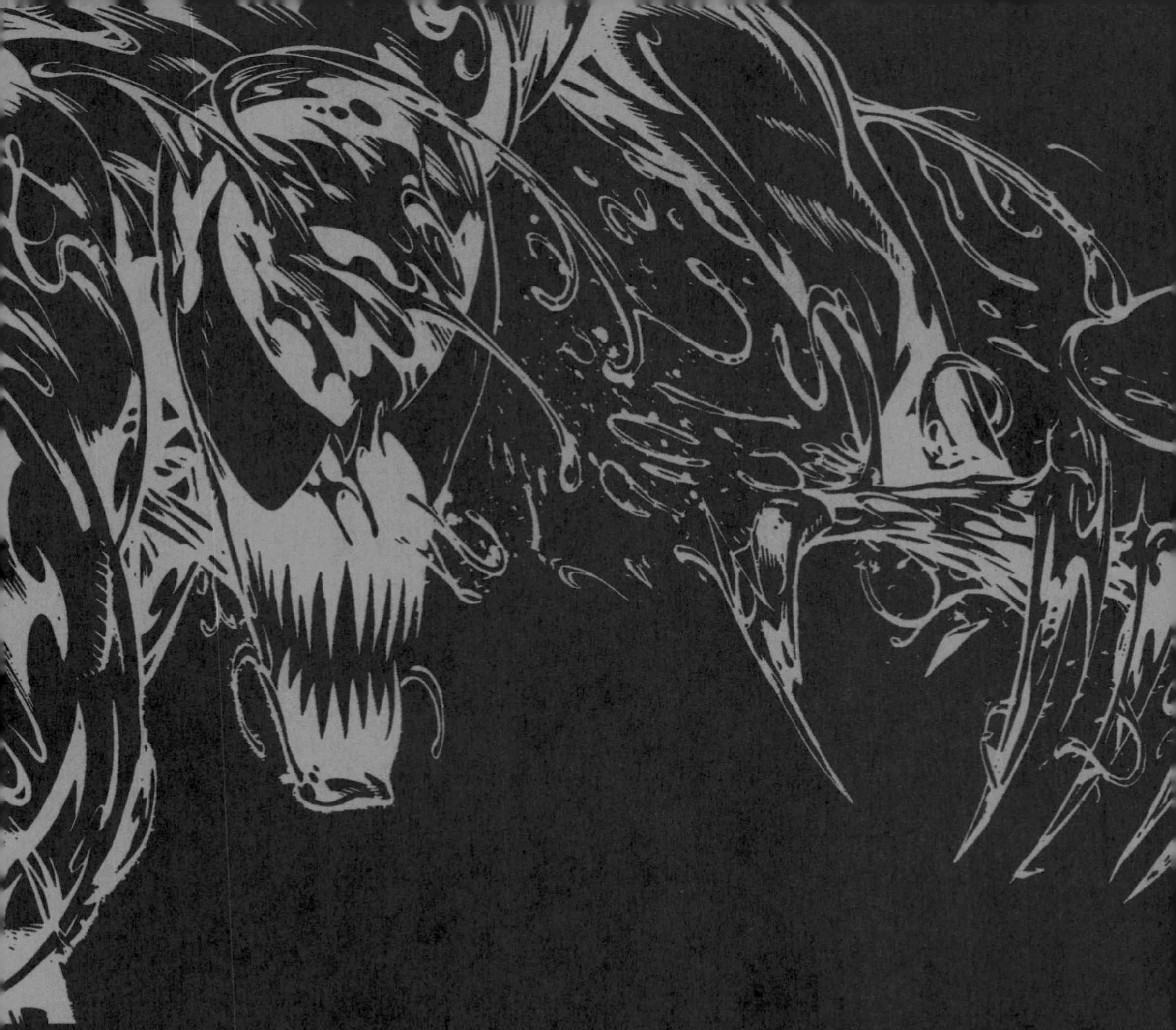

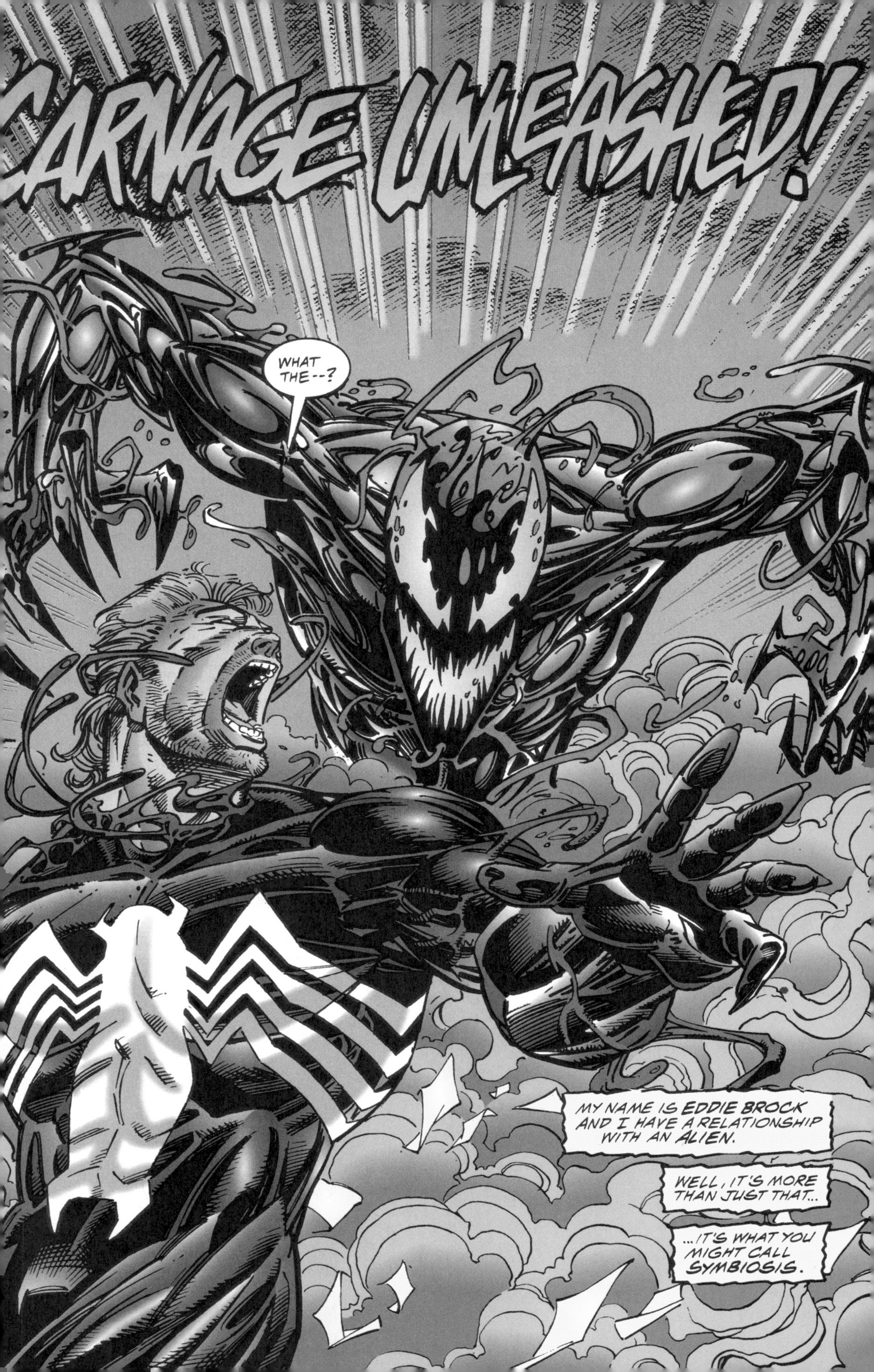
CARNAGE UNLEASHED!
WHAT THE--?
MY NAME IS EDDIE BROCK AND I HAVE A RELATIONSHIP WITH AN ALIEN.
WELL, IT'S MORE THAN JUST THAT...
...IT'S WHAT YOU MIGHT CALL SYMBIOSIS.

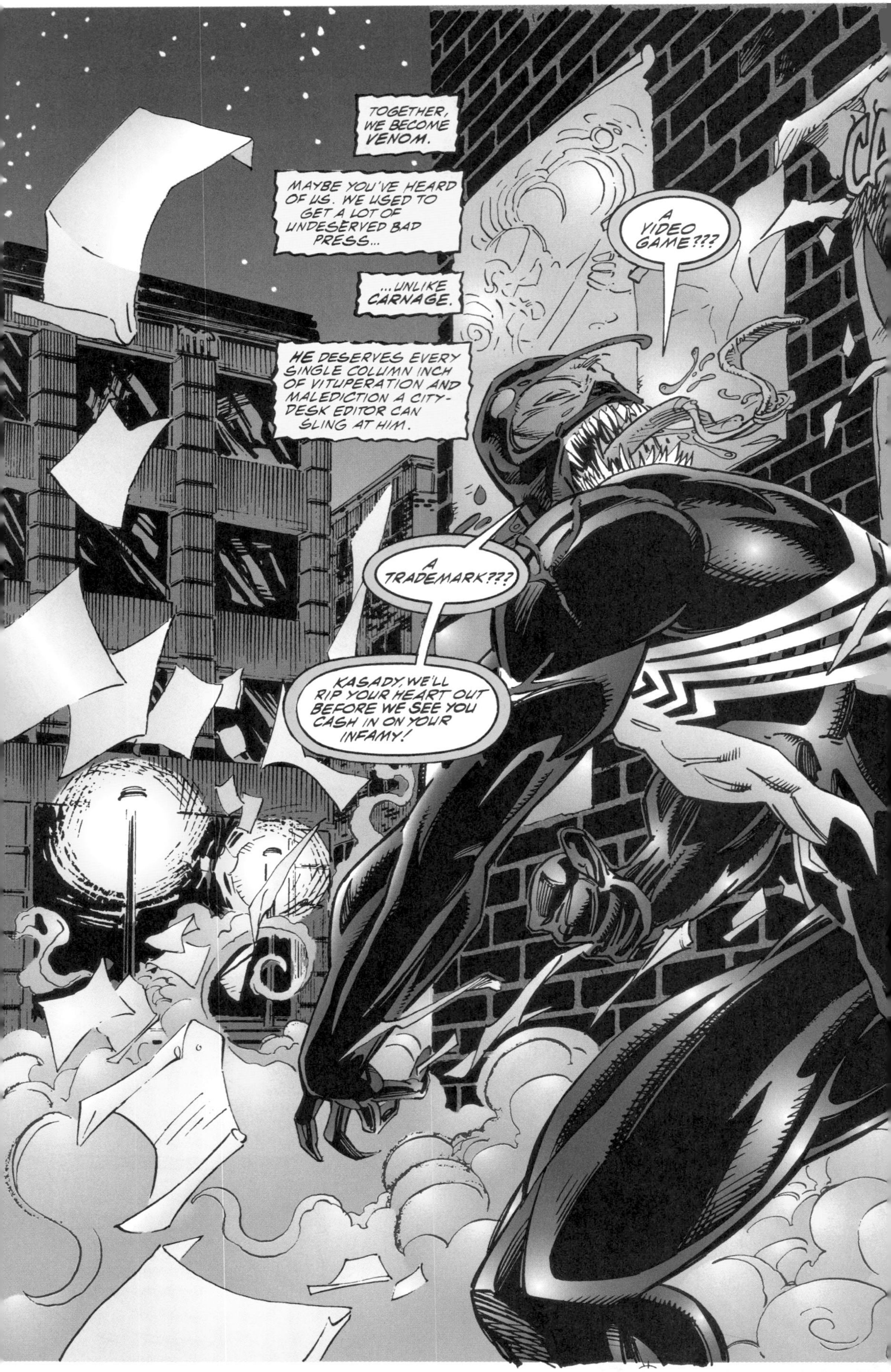
TOGETHER, WE BECOME VENOM.
MAYBE YOU'VE HEARD OF US. WE USED TO GET A LOT OF UNDESERVED BAD PRESS...
...UNLIKE CARNAGE.
HE DESERVES EVERY SINGLE COLUMN INCH OF VITUPERATION AND MALEDICTION A CITY-DESK EDITOR CAN SLING AT HIM.
A VIDEO GAME???
A TRADEMARK???
KASADY, WE'LL RIP YOUR HEART OUT BEFORE WE SEE YOU CASH IN ON YOUR INFAMY!

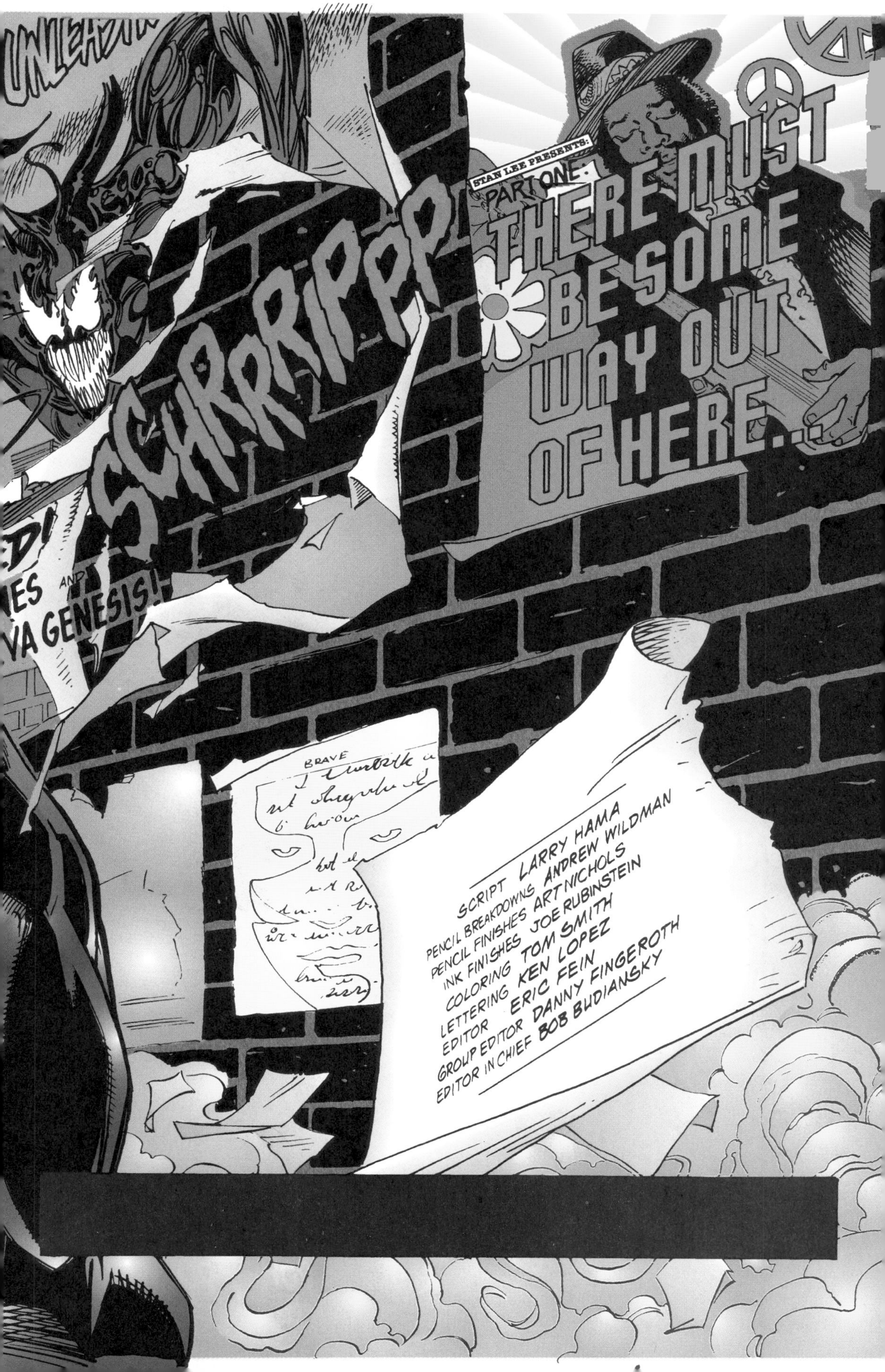
SCHRRIPPP!
STAN LEE PRESENTS:
PART ONE:
THERE MUST BE SOME WAY OUT OF HERE...
SCRIPT LARRY HAMA
PENCIL BREAKDOWNS ANDREW WILDMAN
PENCIL FINISHES ART NICHOLS
INK FINISHES JOE RUBINSTEIN
COLORING TOM SMITH
LETTERING KEN LOPEZ
EDITOR ERIC FEIN
GROUP EDITOR DANNY FINGEROTH
EDITOR IN CHIEF BOB BUDIANSKY

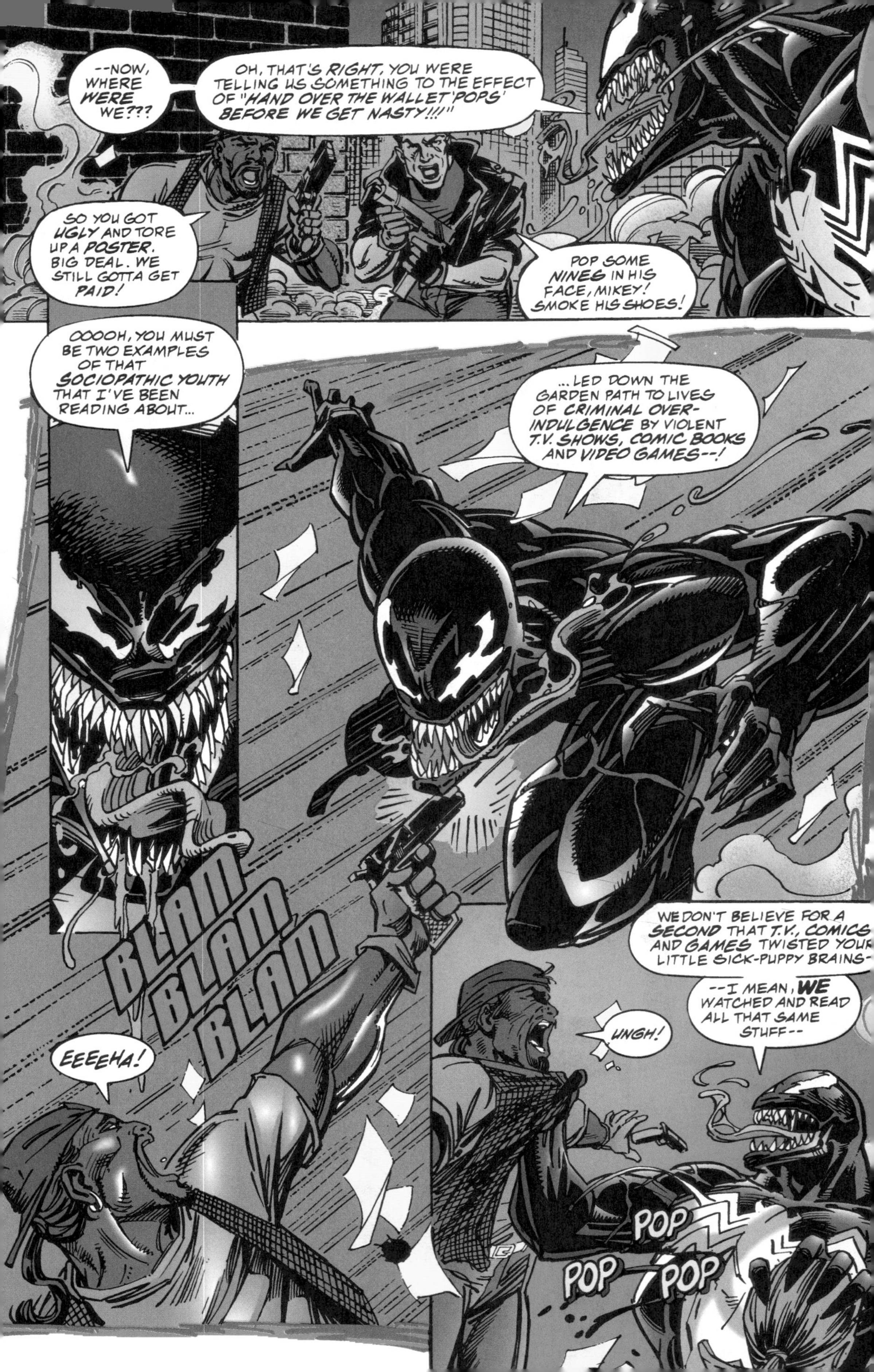
--NOW, WHERE WERE WE???
OH, THAT'S RIGHT, YOU WERE TELLING US SOMETHING TO THE EFFECT OF "HAND OVER THE WALLET 'POPS' BEFORE WE GET NASTY!!!"
SO YOU GOT UGLY AND TORE UP A POSTER. BIG DEAL. WE STILL GOTTA GET PAID!
POP SOME NINES IN HIS FACE, MIKEY! SMOKE HIS SHOES!
OOOOH, YOU MUST BE TWO EXAMPLES OF THAT SOCIOPATHIC YOUTH THAT I'VE BEEN READING ABOUT...
...LED DOWN THE GARDEN PATH TO LIVES OF CRIMINAL OVER-INDULGENCE BY VIOLENT T.V. SHOWS, COMIC BOOKS AND VIDEO GAMES--!
BLAM BLAM BLAM
EEEEHA!
WE DON'T BELIEVE FOR A SECOND THAT T.V., COMICS AND GAMES TWISTED YOUR LITTLE SICK-PUPPY BRAINS--
--I MEAN, WE WATCHED AND READ ALL THAT SAME STUFF--
UNGH!
POP POP POP POP

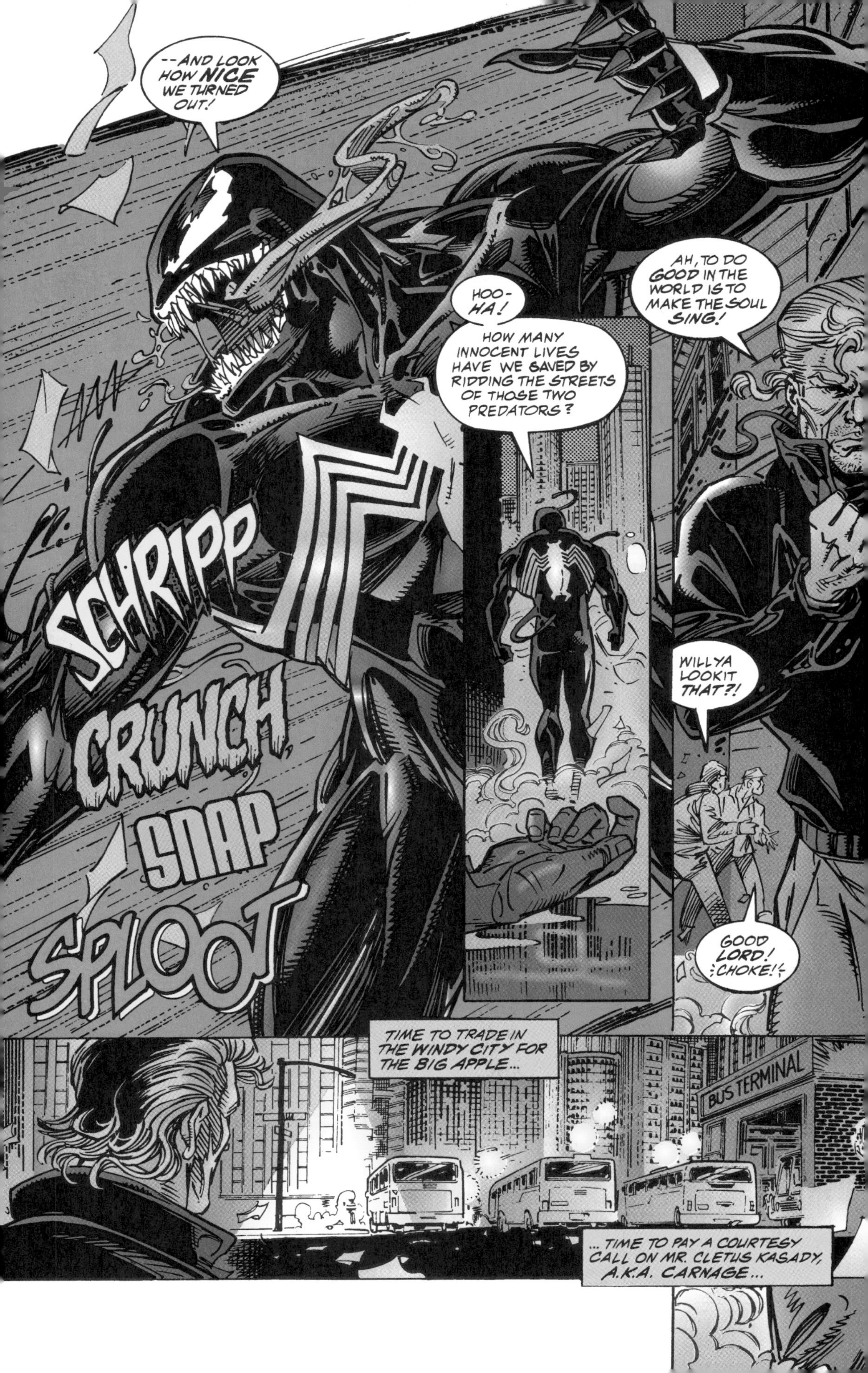
--AND LOOK HOW NICE WE TURNED OUT!
SCHRIPP
CRUNCH
SNAP
SPLOOT
HOO-HA!
HOW MANY INNOCENT LIVES HAVE WE SAVED BY RIDDING THE STREETS OF THOSE TWO PREDATORS?
AH, TO DO GOOD IN THE WORLD IS TO MAKE THE SOUL SING!
WILLYA LOOKIT THAT?!
GOOD LORD! CHOKE!
TIME TO TRADE IN THE WINDY CITY FOR THE BIG APPLE...
BUS TERMINAL
...TIME TO PAY A COURTESY CALL ON MR. CLETUS KASADY, A.K.A. CARNAGE...

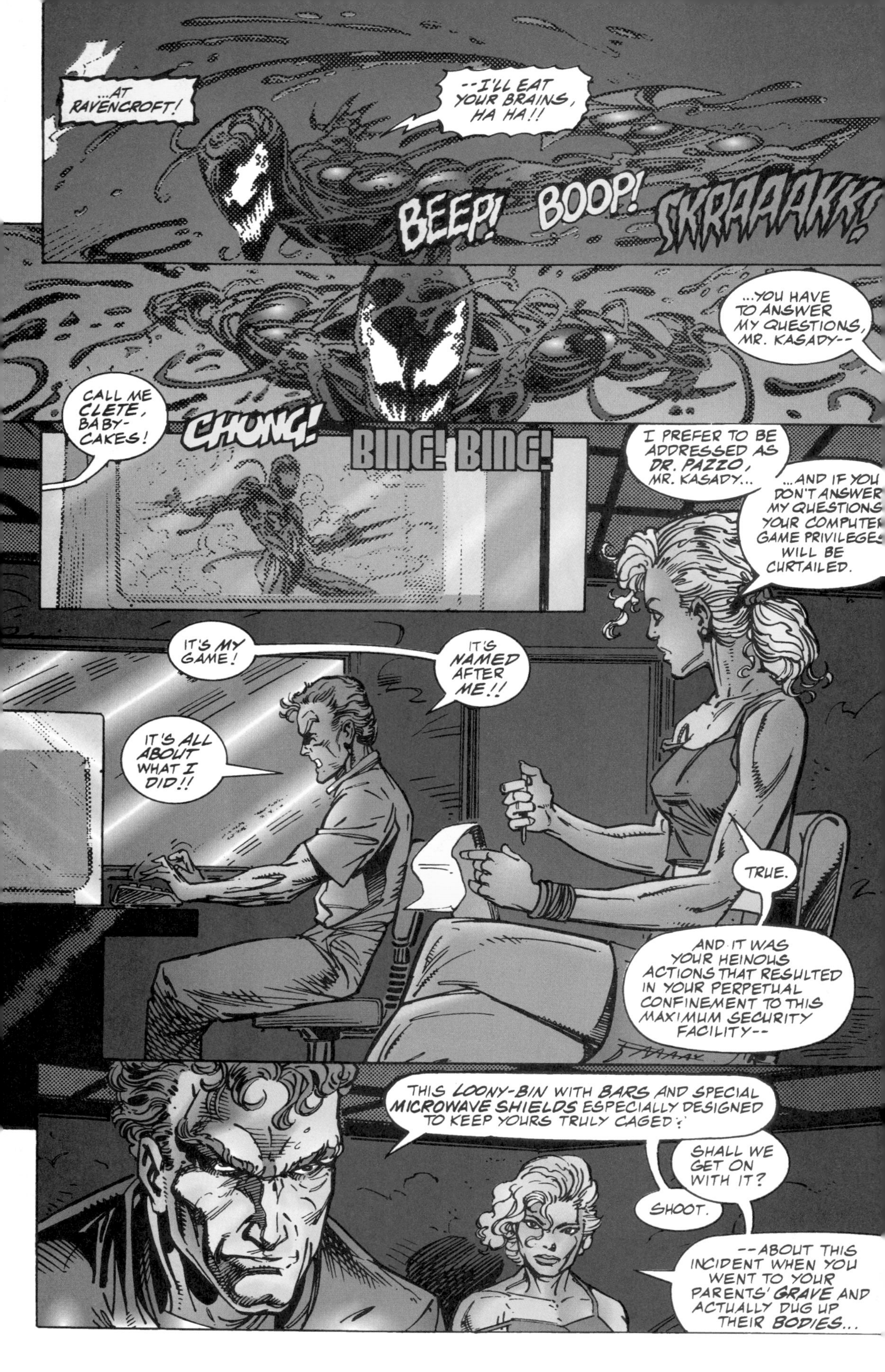
...AT RAVENCROFT!
--I'LL EAT YOUR BRAINS, HA HA!!
BEEP! BOOP! SKRAAAKK!
...YOU HAVE TO ANSWER MY QUESTIONS, MR. KASADY--
CALL ME CLETE, BABY-CAKES!
CHONG!
BING! BING!
I PREFER TO BE ADDRESSED AS DR. PAZZO, MR. KASADY...
...AND IF YOU DON'T ANSWER MY QUESTIONS YOUR COMPUTER GAME PRIVILEGES WILL BE CURTAILED.
IT'S MY GAME!
IT'S NAMED AFTER ME!!
IT'S ALL ABOUT WHAT I DID!!
TRUE.
AND IT WAS YOUR HEINOUS ACTIONS THAT RESULTED IN YOUR PERPETUAL CONFINEMENT TO THIS MAXIMUM SECURITY FACILITY--
THIS LOONY-BIN WITH BARS AND SPECIAL MICROWAVE SHIELDS ESPECIALLY DESIGNED TO KEEP YOURS TRULY CAGED?
SHALL WE GET ON WITH IT?
SHOOT.
--ABOUT THIS INCIDENT WHEN YOU WENT TO YOUR PARENTS' GRAVE AND ACTUALLY DUG UP THEIR BODIES...

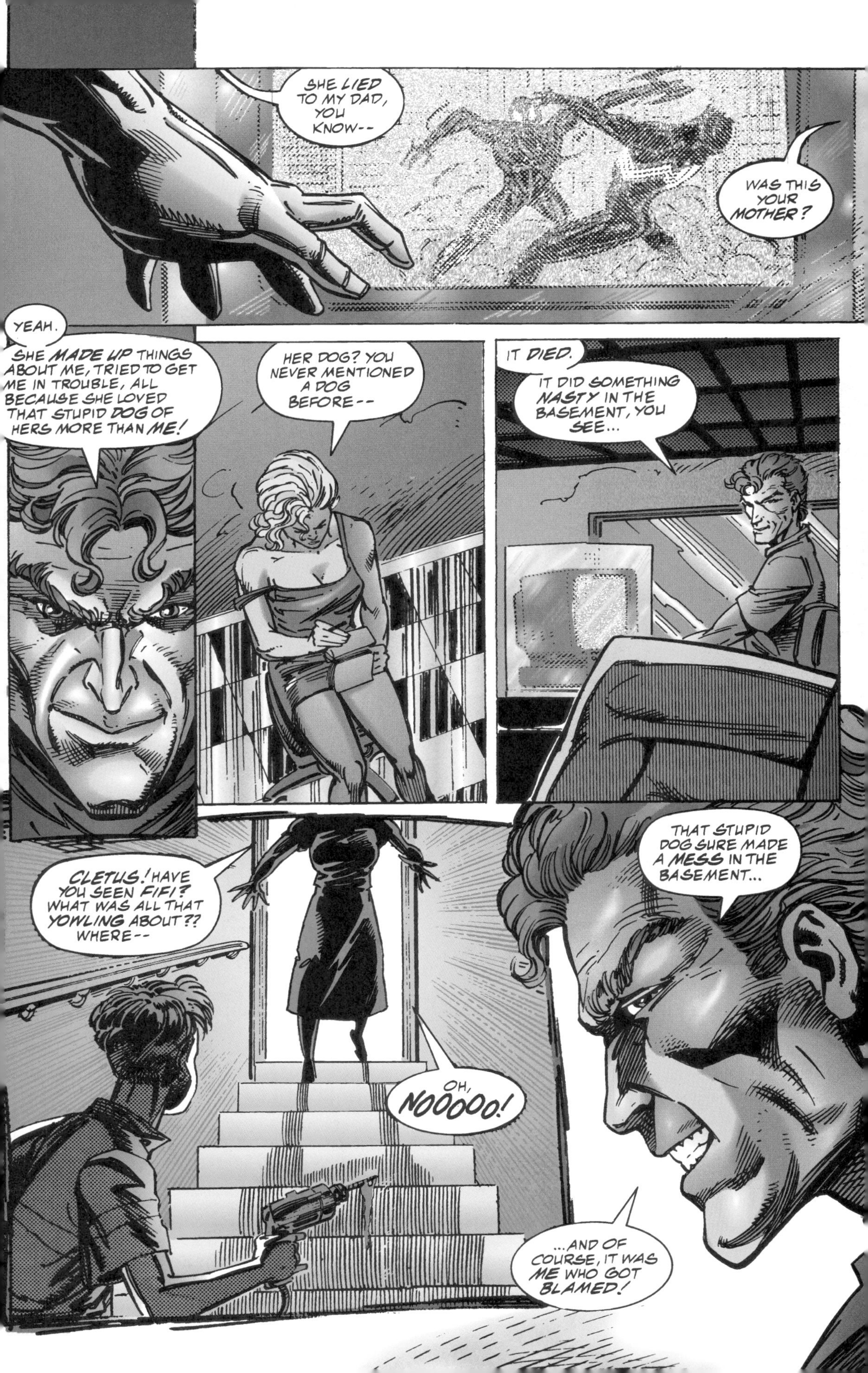
SHE LIED TO MY DAD, YOU KNOW--
WAS THIS YOUR MOTHER?
YEAH.
SHE MADE UP THINGS ABOUT ME, TRIED TO GET ME IN TROUBLE, ALL BECAUSE SHE LOVED THAT STUPID DOG OF HERS MORE THAN ME!
HER DOG? YOU NEVER MENTIONED A DOG BEFORE--
IT DIED.
IT DID SOMETHING NASTY IN THE BASEMENT, YOU SEE...
CLETUS! HAVE YOU SEEN FIFI? WHAT WAS ALL THAT YOWLING ABOUT?? WHERE--
OH, NOOOOO!
THAT STUPID DOG SURE MADE A MESS IN THE BASEMENT...
...AND OF COURSE, IT WAS ME WHO GOT BLAMED!

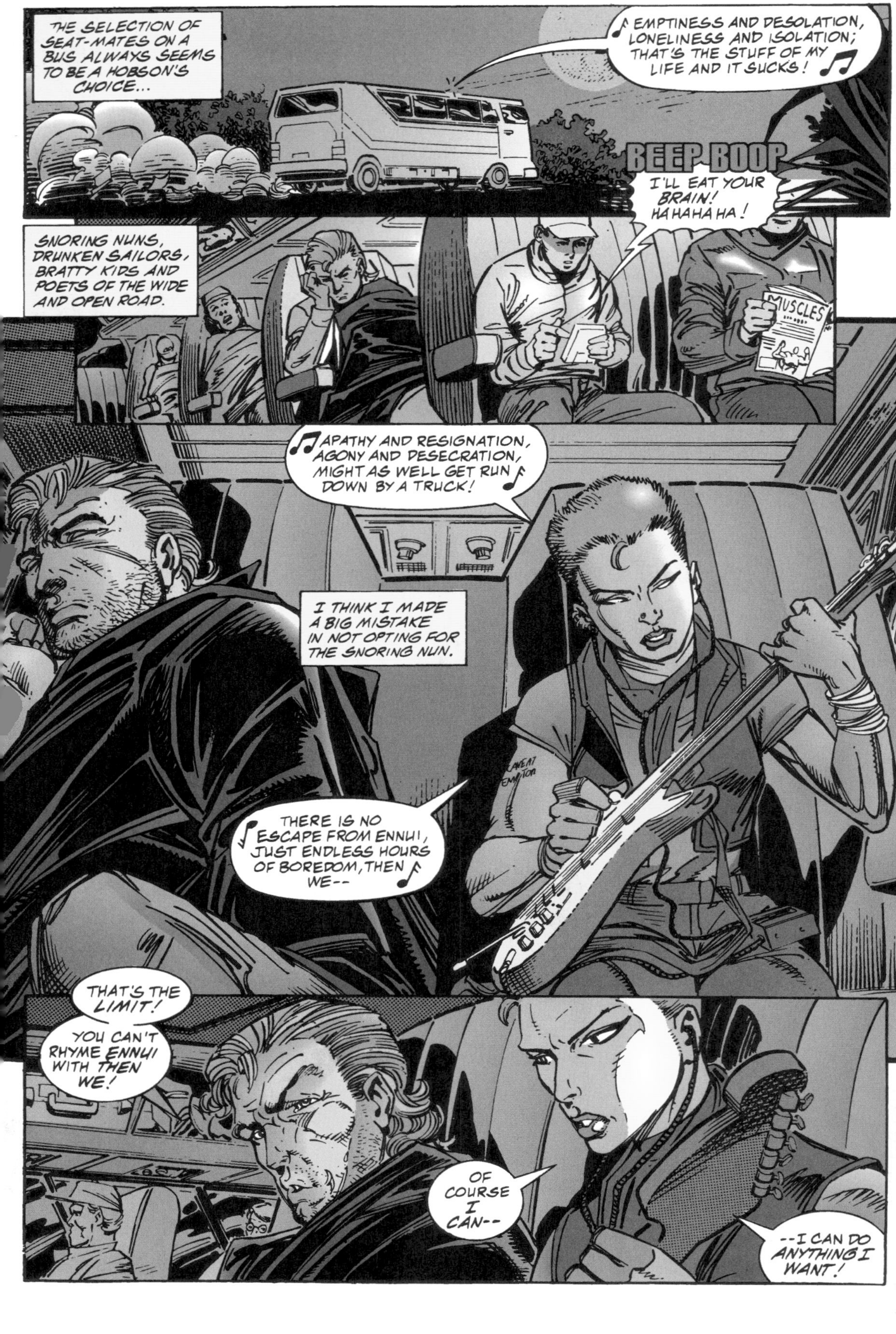
THE SELECTION OF SEAT-MATES ON A BUS ALWAYS SEEMS TO BE A HOBSON'S CHOICE...
EMPTINESS AND DESOLATION, LONELINESS AND ISOLATION; THAT'S THE STUFF OF MY LIFE AND IT SUCKS!
BEEP BOOP
I'LL EAT YOUR BRAIN! HA HA HA HA!
SNORING NUNS, DRUNKEN SAILORS, BRATTY KIDS AND POETS OF THE WIDE AND OPEN ROAD.
MUSCLES
APATHY AND RESIGNATION, AGONY AND DESECRATION, MIGHT AS WELL GET RUN DOWN BY A TRUCK!
I THINK I MADE A BIG MISTAKE IN NOT OPTING FOR THE SNORING NUN.
THERE IS NO ESCAPE FROM ENNUI, JUST ENDLESS HOURS OF BOREDOM, THEN WE--
THAT'S THE LIMIT!
YOU CAN'T RHYME ENNUI WITH THEN WE!
OF COURSE I CAN--
--I CAN DO ANYTHING I WANT!

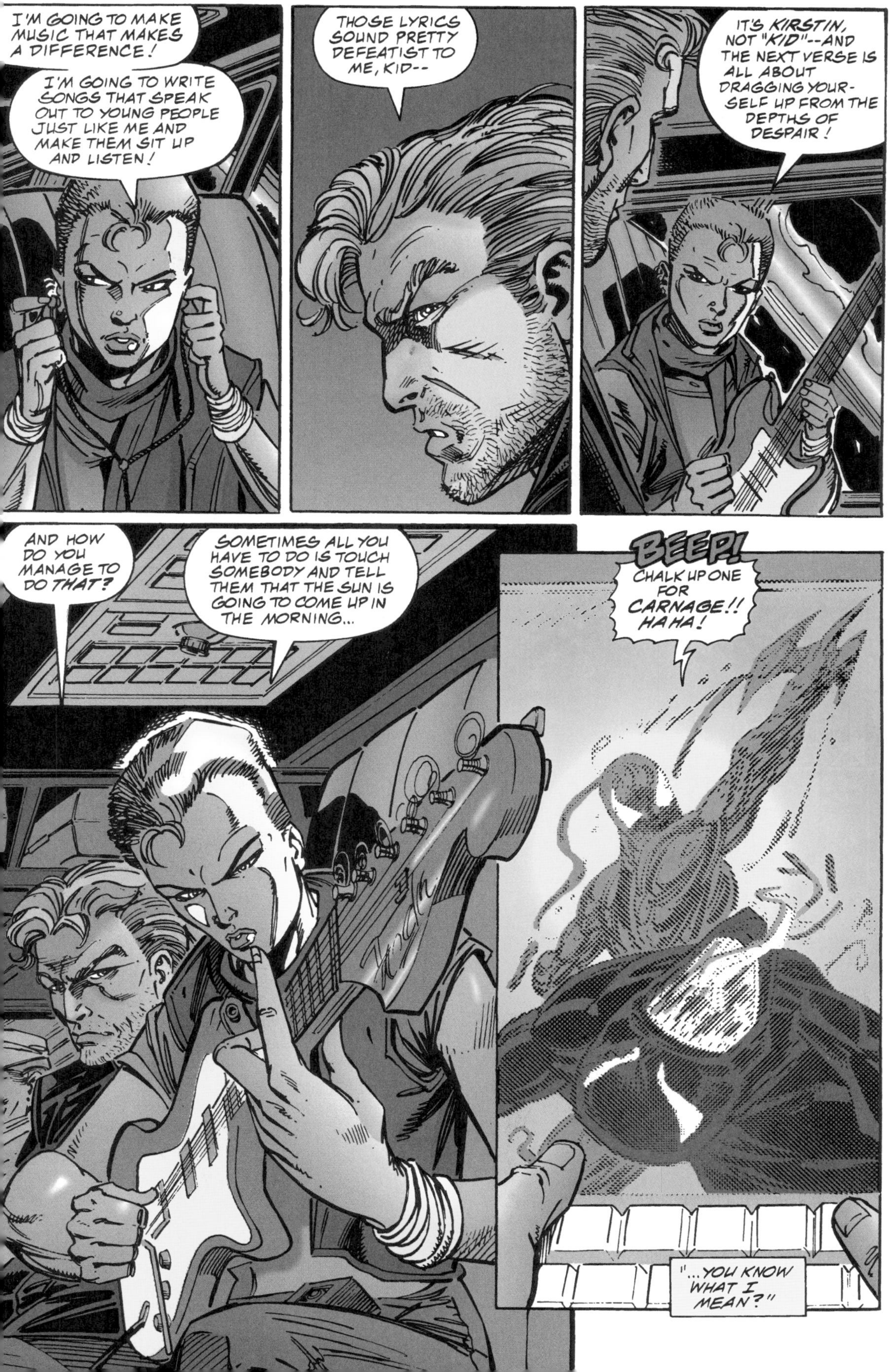
I'M GOING TO MAKE MUSIC THAT MAKES A DIFFERENCE!
I'M GOING TO WRITE SONGS THAT SPEAK OUT TO YOUNG PEOPLE JUST LIKE ME AND MAKE THEM SIT UP AND LISTEN!
THOSE LYRICS SOUND PRETTY DEFEATIST TO ME, KID--
IT'S *KIRSTIN*, NOT "*KID*"--AND THE NEXT VERSE IS ALL ABOUT DRAGGING YOURSELF UP FROM THE DEPTHS OF DESPAIR!
AND HOW DO YOU MANAGE TO DO *THAT*?
SOMETIMES ALL YOU HAVE TO DO IS TOUCH SOMEBODY AND TELL THEM THAT THE SUN IS GOING TO COME UP IN THE MORNING...
BEEP!
CHALK UP ONE FOR CARNAGE!! HA HA!
"...YOU KNOW WHAT I MEAN?"

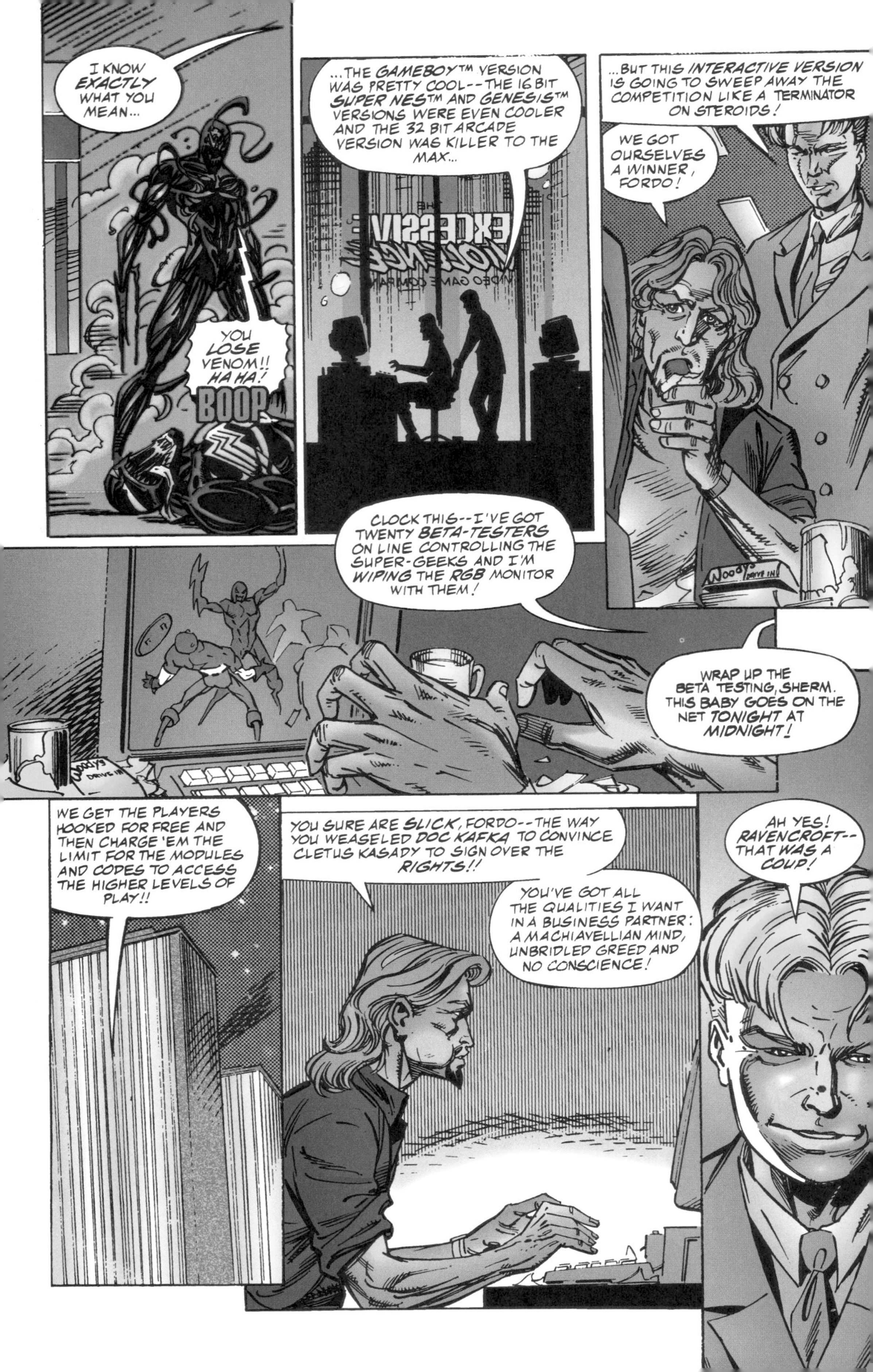

I KNOW EXACTLY WHAT YOU MEAN...
YOU LOSE VENOM!! HA HA!
BOOP
...THE GAMEBOY™ VERSION WAS PRETTY COOL--THE 16 BIT SUPER NES™ AND GENESIS™ VERSIONS WERE EVEN COOLER AND THE 32 BIT ARCADE VERSION WAS KILLER TO THE MAX...
...BUT THIS INTERACTIVE VERSION IS GOING TO SWEEP AWAY THE COMPETITION LIKE A TERMINATOR ON STEROIDS!
WE GOT OURSELVES A WINNER, FORDO!
Woody's DRIVE IN
CLOCK THIS--I'VE GOT TWENTY BETA-TESTERS ON LINE CONTROLLING THE SUPER-GEEKS AND I'M WIPING THE RGB MONITOR WITH THEM!
WRAP UP THE BETA TESTING, SHERM. THIS BABY GOES ON THE NET TONIGHT AT MIDNIGHT!
WE GET THE PLAYERS HOOKED FOR FREE AND THEN CHARGE 'EM THE LIMIT FOR THE MODULES AND CODES TO ACCESS THE HIGHER LEVELS OF PLAY!!
YOU SURE ARE SLICK, FORDO--THE WAY YOU WEASELED DOC KAFKA TO CONVINCE CLETUS KASADY TO SIGN OVER THE RIGHTS!!
YOU'VE GOT ALL THE QUALITIES I WANT IN A BUSINESS PARTNER: A MACHIAVELLIAN MIND, UNBRIDLED GREED AND NO CONSCIENCE!
AH YES! RAVENCROFT--THAT WAS A COUP!

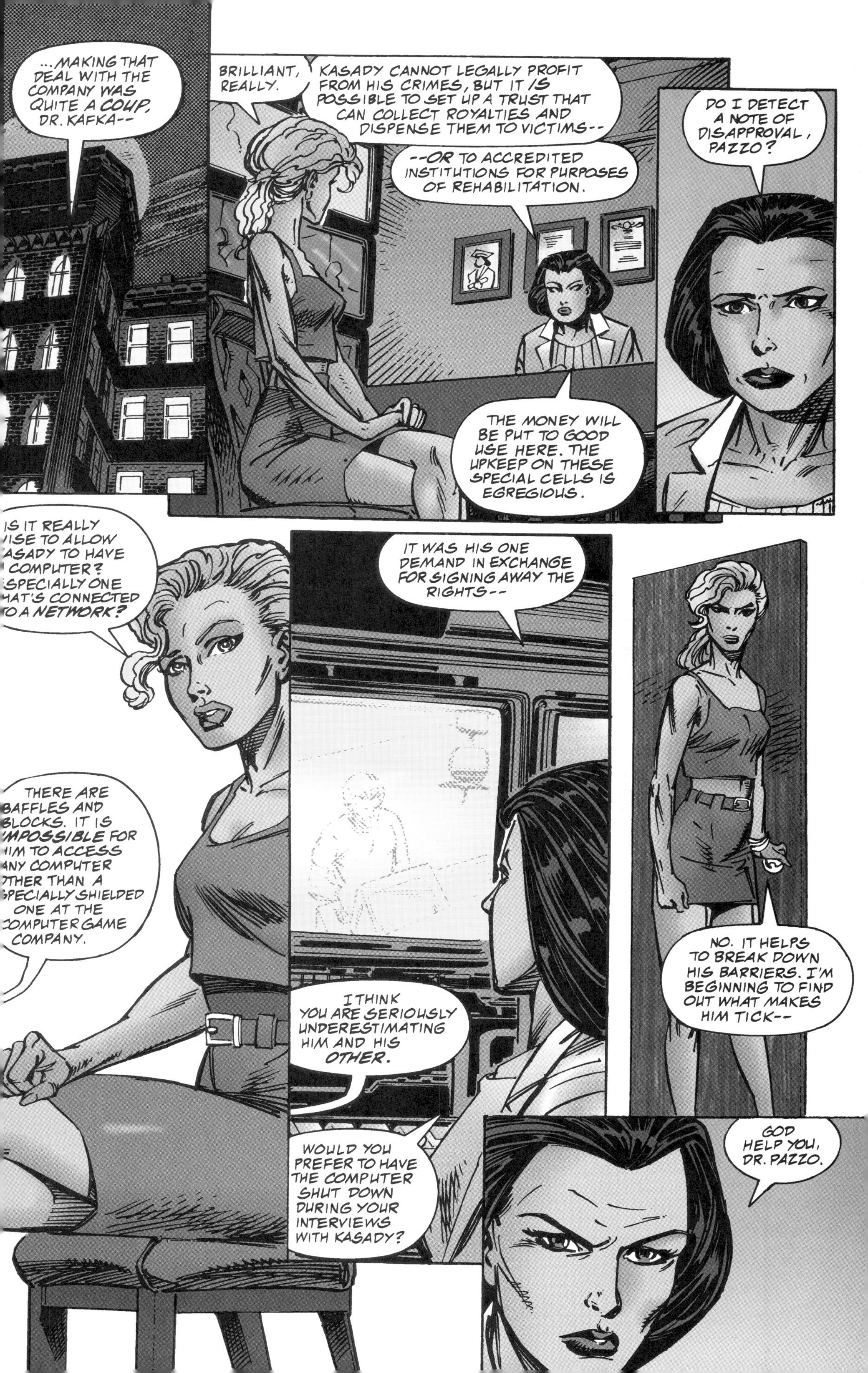
...MAKING THAT DEAL WITH THE COMPANY WAS QUITE A COUP, DR. KAFKA--
BRILLIANT, REALLY.
KASADY CANNOT LEGALLY PROFIT FROM HIS CRIMES, BUT IT IS POSSIBLE TO SET UP A TRUST THAT CAN COLLECT ROYALTIES AND DISPENSE THEM TO VICTIMS--
--OR TO ACCREDITED INSTITUTIONS FOR PURPOSES OF REHABILITATION.
THE MONEY WILL BE PUT TO GOOD USE HERE. THE UPKEEP ON THESE SPECIAL CELLS IS EGREGIOUS.
DO I DETECT A NOTE OF DISAPPROVAL, PAZZO?
IS IT REALLY ISE TO ALLOW ASADY TO HAVE COMPUTER? SPECIALLY ONE HAT'S CONNECTED O A NETWORK?
IT WAS HIS ONE DEMAND IN EXCHANGE FOR SIGNING AWAY THE RIGHTS--
THERE ARE AFFLES AND LOCKS. IT IS MPOSSIBLE FOR IM TO ACCESS NY COMPUTER THER THAN A PECIALLY SHIELDED ONE AT THE OMPUTER GAME COMPANY.
I THINK YOU ARE SERIOUSLY UNDERESTIMATING HIM AND HIS OTHER.
WOULD YOU PREFER TO HAVE THE COMPUTER SHUT DOWN DURING YOUR INTERVIEWS WITH KASADY?
NO. IT HELPS TO BREAK DOWN HIS BARRIERS. I'M BEGINNING TO FIND OUT WHAT MAKES HIM TICK--
GOD HELP YOU, DR. PAZZO.

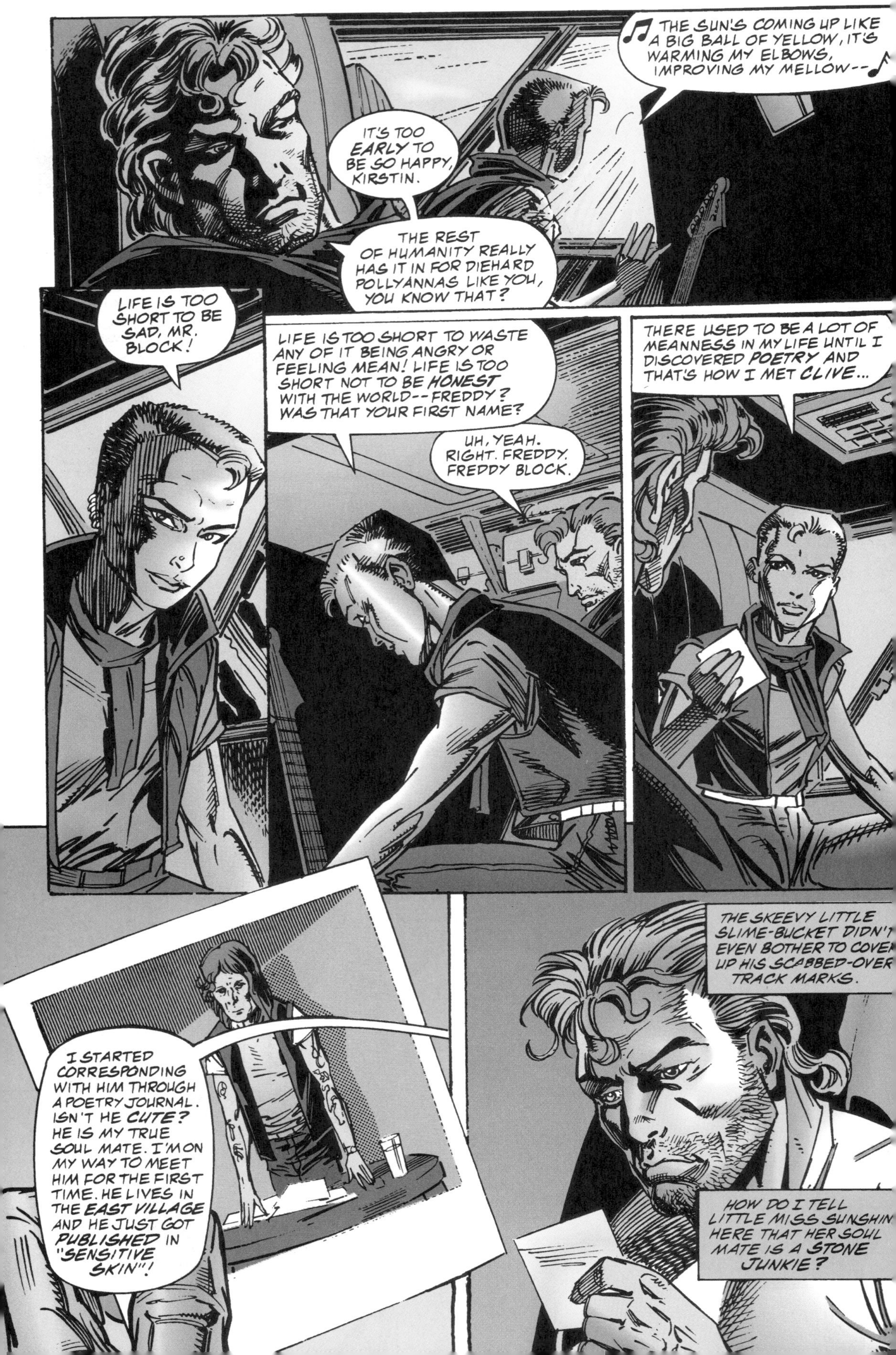
♫ THE SUN'S COMING UP LIKE A BIG BALL OF YELLOW, IT'S WARMING MY ELBOWS, IMPROVING MY MELLOW-- ♪
IT'S TOO EARLY TO BE SO HAPPY, KIRSTIN.
THE REST OF HUMANITY REALLY HAS IT IN FOR DIEHARD POLLYANNAS LIKE YOU, YOU KNOW THAT?
LIFE IS TOO SHORT TO BE SAD, MR. BLOCK!
LIFE IS TOO SHORT TO WASTE ANY OF IT BEING ANGRY OR FEELING MEAN! LIFE IS TOO SHORT NOT TO BE HONEST WITH THE WORLD-- FREDDY? WAS THAT YOUR FIRST NAME?
UH, YEAH. RIGHT. FREDDY. FREDDY BLOCK.
THERE USED TO BE A LOT OF MEANNESS IN MY LIFE UNTIL I DISCOVERED POETRY AND THAT'S HOW I MET CLIVE...
I STARTED CORRESPONDING WITH HIM THROUGH A POETRY JOURNAL. ISN'T HE CUTE? HE IS MY TRUE SOUL MATE. I'M ON MY WAY TO MEET HIM FOR THE FIRST TIME. HE LIVES IN THE EAST VILLAGE AND HE JUST GOT PUBLISHED IN "SENSITIVE SKIN"!
THE SKEEVY LITTLE SLIME-BUCKET DIDN'T EVEN BOTHER TO COVER UP HIS SCABBED-OVER TRACK MARKS.
HOW DO I TELL LITTLE MISS SUNSHINE HERE THAT HER SOUL MATE IS A STONE JUNKIE?

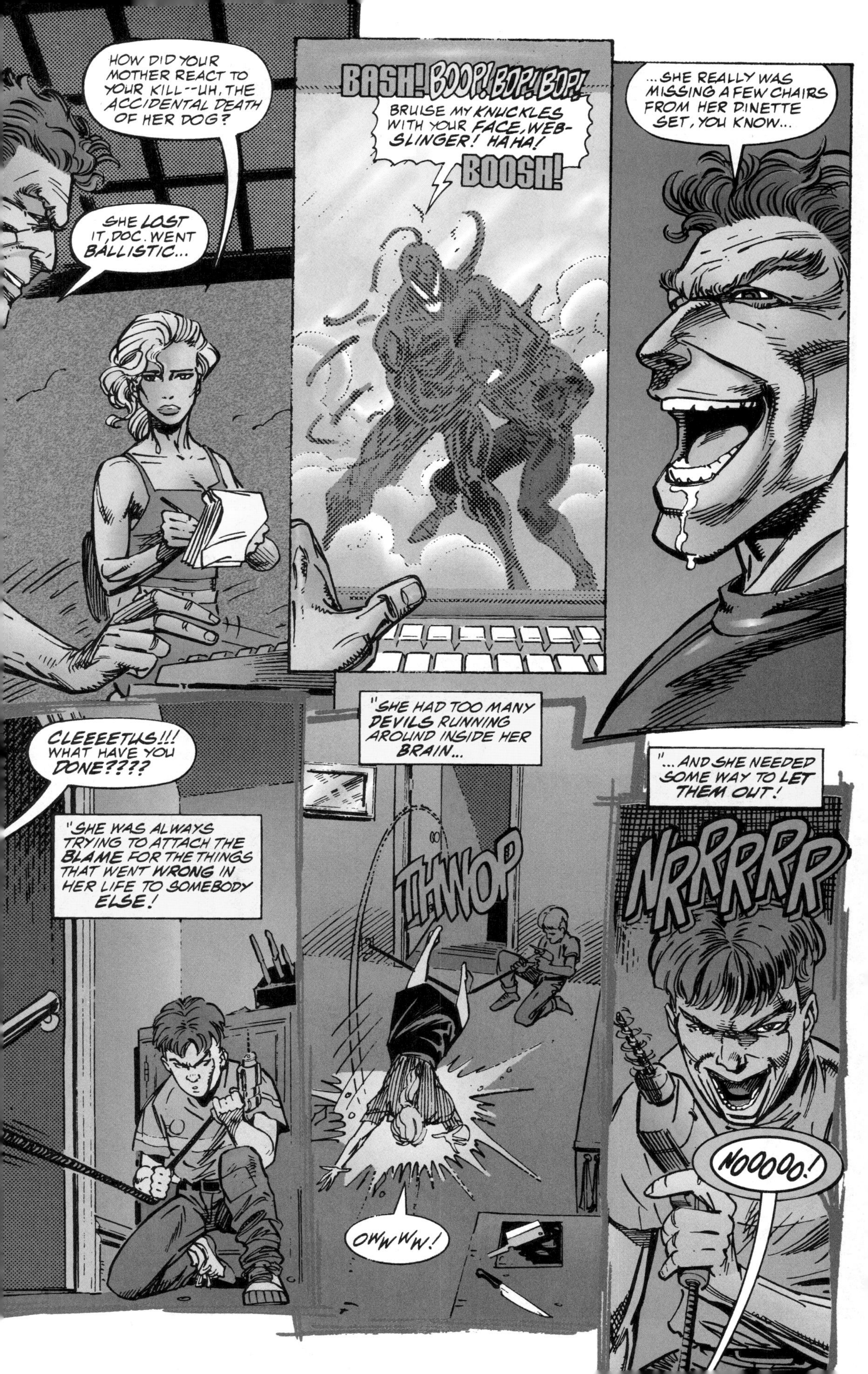
HOW DID YOUR MOTHER REACT TO YOUR KILL--UH, THE ACCIDENTAL DEATH OF HER DOG?
SHE LOST IT, DOC. WENT BALLISTIC...
BASH! BOOP! BOP! BOP!
BRUISE MY KNUCKLES WITH YOUR FACE, WEB-SLINGER! HAHA!
BOOSH!
...SHE REALLY WAS MISSING A FEW CHAIRS FROM HER DINETTE SET, YOU KNOW...
CLEEEETUS!!! WHAT HAVE YOU DONE????
"SHE WAS ALWAYS TRYING TO ATTACH THE BLAME FOR THE THINGS THAT WENT WRONG IN HER LIFE TO SOMEBODY ELSE!
"SHE HAD TOO MANY DEVILS RUNNING AROUND INSIDE HER BRAIN...
THWOP
OWWWW!
"...AND SHE NEEDED SOME WAY TO LET THEM OUT!
NRRRRR
NOOOOO!

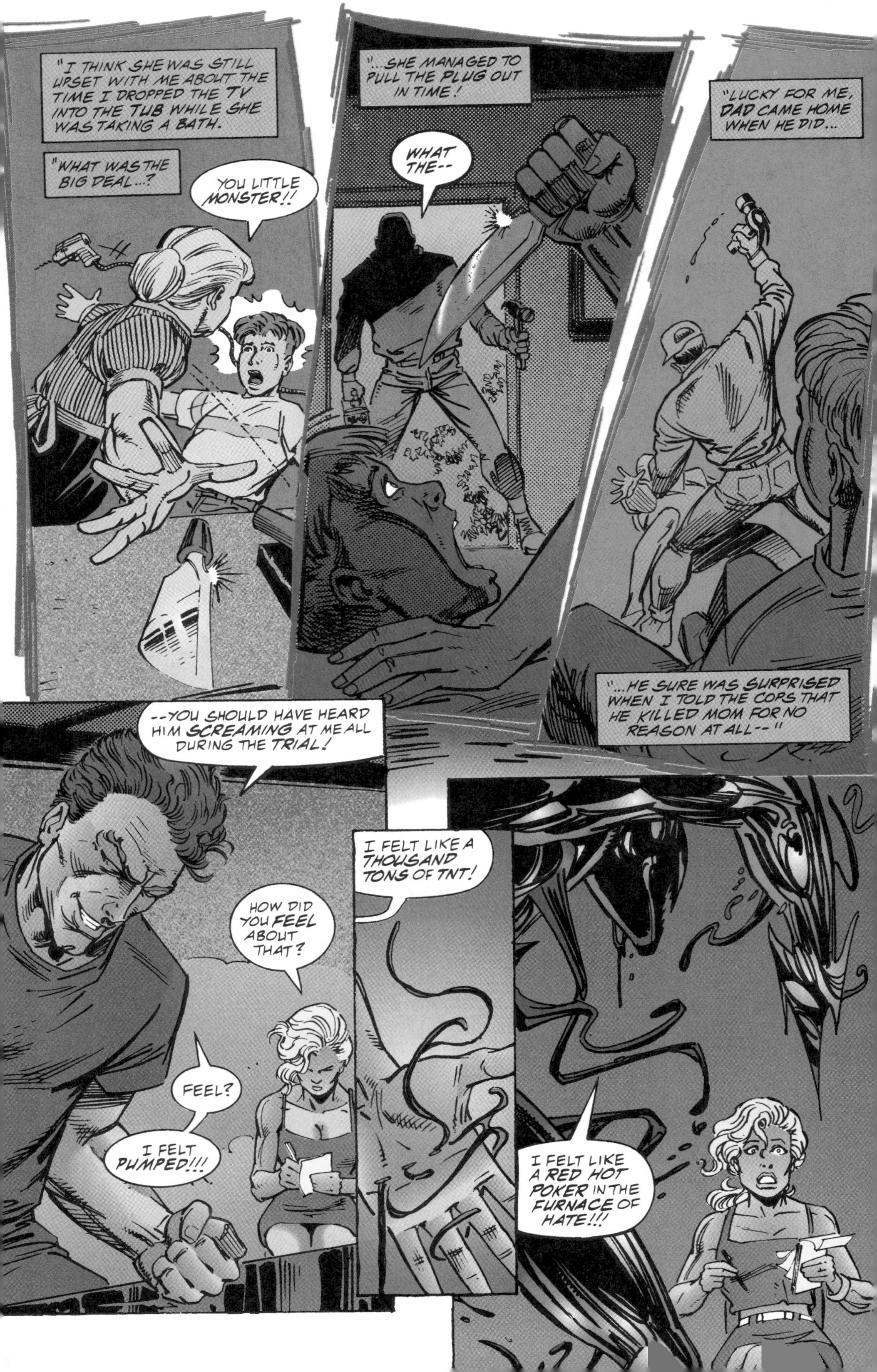
"I THINK SHE WAS STILL UPSET WITH ME ABOUT THE TIME I DROPPED THE TV INTO THE TUB WHILE SHE WAS TAKING A BATH.
"WHAT WAS THE BIG DEAL...?
YOU LITTLE MONSTER!!
"...SHE MANAGED TO PULL THE PLUG OUT IN TIME!
WHAT THE--
"LUCKY FOR ME, DAD CAME HOME WHEN HE DID...
"...HE SURE WAS SURPRISED WHEN I TOLD THE COPS THAT HE KILLED MOM FOR NO REASON AT ALL--"
--YOU SHOULD HAVE HEARD HIM SCREAMING AT ME ALL DURING THE TRIAL!
HOW DID YOU FEEL ABOUT THAT?
FEEL?
I FELT PUMPED!!!
I FELT LIKE A THOUSAND TONS OF TNT!
I FELT LIKE A RED HOT POKER IN THE FURNACE OF HATE!!!

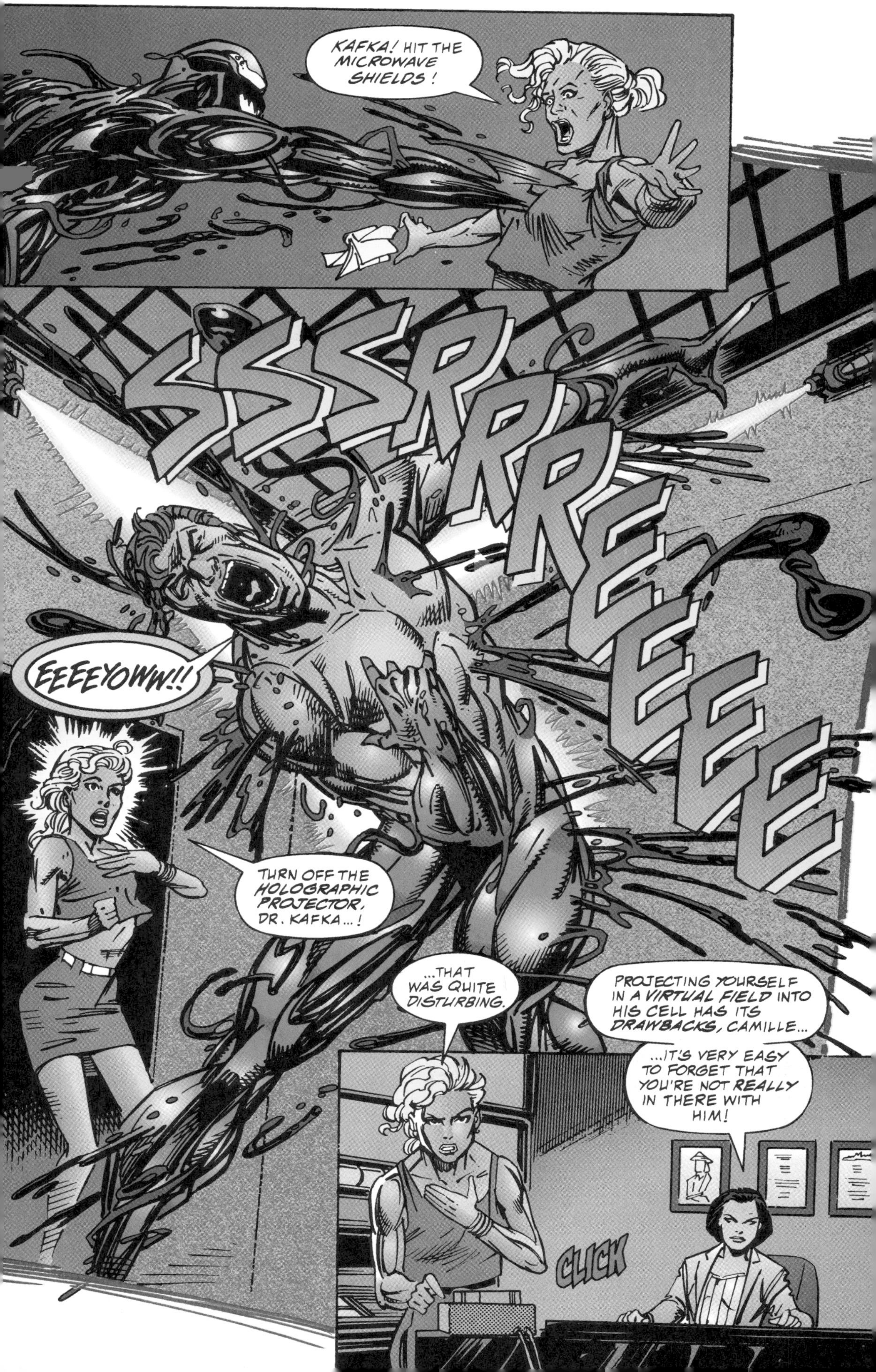
KAFKA! HIT THE MICROWAVE SHIELDS!
SSSRRREEEEE
EEEEYOWW!!
TURN OFF THE HOLOGRAPHIC PROJECTOR, DR. KAFKA...!
...THAT WAS QUITE DISTURBING.
PROJECTING YOURSELF IN A VIRTUAL FIELD INTO HIS CELL HAS ITS DRAWBACKS, CAMILLE...
...IT'S VERY EASY TO FORGET THAT YOU'RE NOT REALLY IN THERE WITH HIM!
CLICK

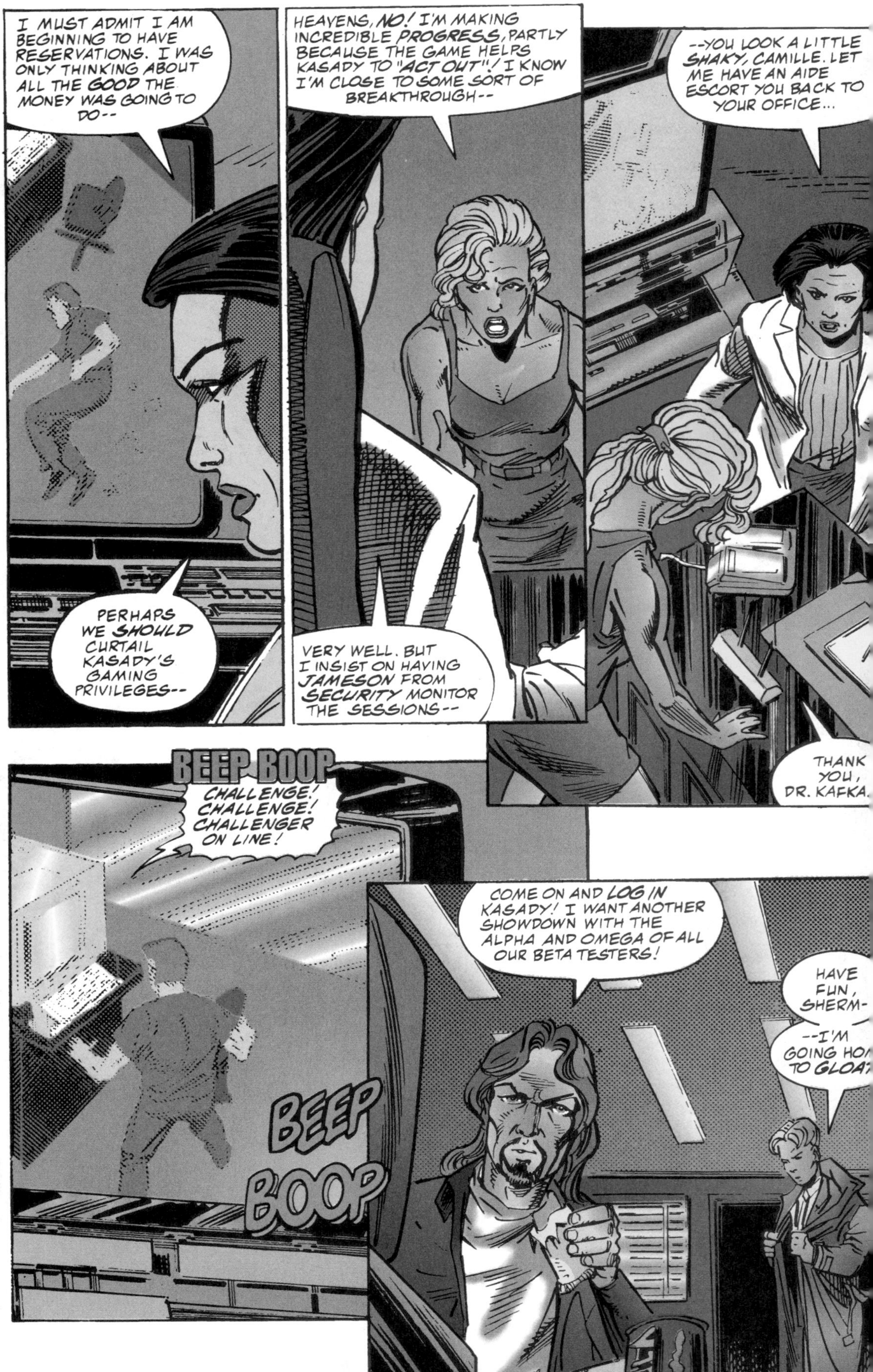
I MUST ADMIT I AM BEGINNING TO HAVE RESERVATIONS. I WAS ONLY THINKING ABOUT ALL THE GOOD THE MONEY WAS GOING TO DO--
PERHAPS WE SHOULD CURTAIL KASADY'S GAMING PRIVILEGES--
HEAVENS, NO! I'M MAKING INCREDIBLE PROGRESS, PARTLY BECAUSE THE GAME HELPS KASADY TO "ACT OUT"! I KNOW I'M CLOSE TO SOME SORT OF BREAKTHROUGH--
VERY WELL. BUT I INSIST ON HAVING JAMESON FROM SECURITY MONITOR THE SESSIONS--
--YOU LOOK A LITTLE SHAKY, CAMILLE. LET ME HAVE AN AIDE ESCORT YOU BACK TO YOUR OFFICE...
THANK YOU, DR. KAFKA.
BEEP BOOP
CHALLENGE! CHALLENGE! CHALLENGER ON LINE!
BEEP
BOOP
COME ON AND LOG IN KASADY! I WANT ANOTHER SHOWDOWN WITH THE ALPHA AND OMEGA OF ALL OUR BETA TESTERS!
HAVE FUN, SHERM-
--I'M GOING HO
TO GLOA

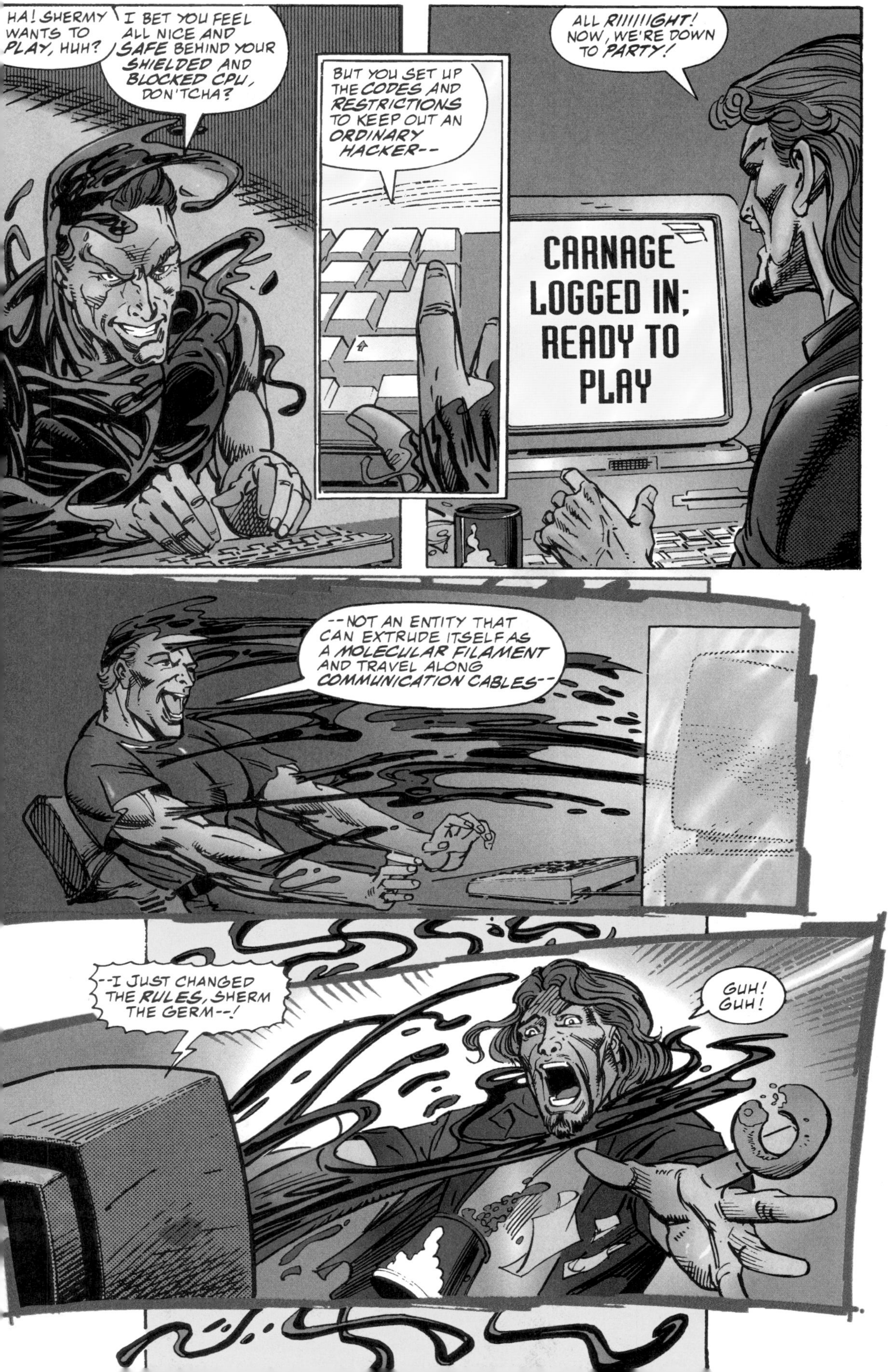
HA! SHERMY WANTS TO PLAY, HUH?
I BET YOU FEEL ALL NICE AND SAFE BEHIND YOUR SHIELDED AND BLOCKED CPU, DON'TCHA?
BUT YOU SET UP THE CODES AND RESTRICTIONS TO KEEP OUT AN ORDINARY HACKER--
ALL RIIIIIIGHT! NOW, WE'RE DOWN TO PARTY!
CARNAGE LOGGED IN; READY TO PLAY
--NOT AN ENTITY THAT CAN EXTRUDE ITSELF AS A MOLECULAR FILAMENT AND TRAVEL ALONG COMMUNICATION CABLES--
--I JUST CHANGED THE RULES, SHERM THE GERM--!
GUH! GUH!

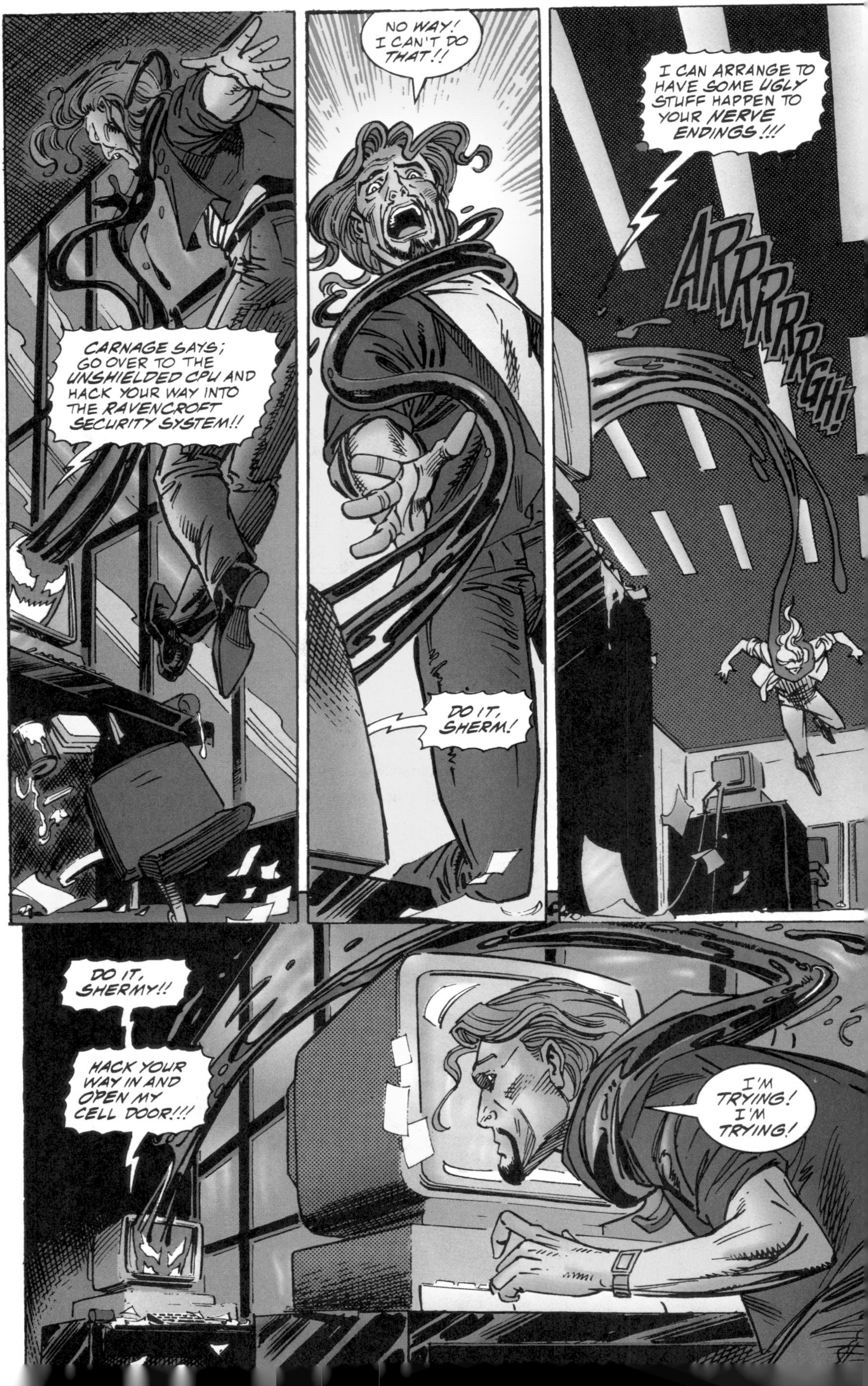
CARNAGE SAYS; GO OVER TO THE UNSHIELDED CPU AND HACK YOUR WAY INTO THE RAVENCROFT SECURITY SYSTEM!!
NO WAY! I CAN'T DO THAT!!
DO IT, SHERM!
I CAN ARRANGE TO HAVE SOME UGLY STUFF HAPPEN TO YOUR NERVE ENDINGS!!!
ARRRRRRGH!
DO IT, SHERMY!!
HACK YOUR WAY IN AND OPEN MY CELL DOOR!!!
I'M TRYING! I'M TRYING!

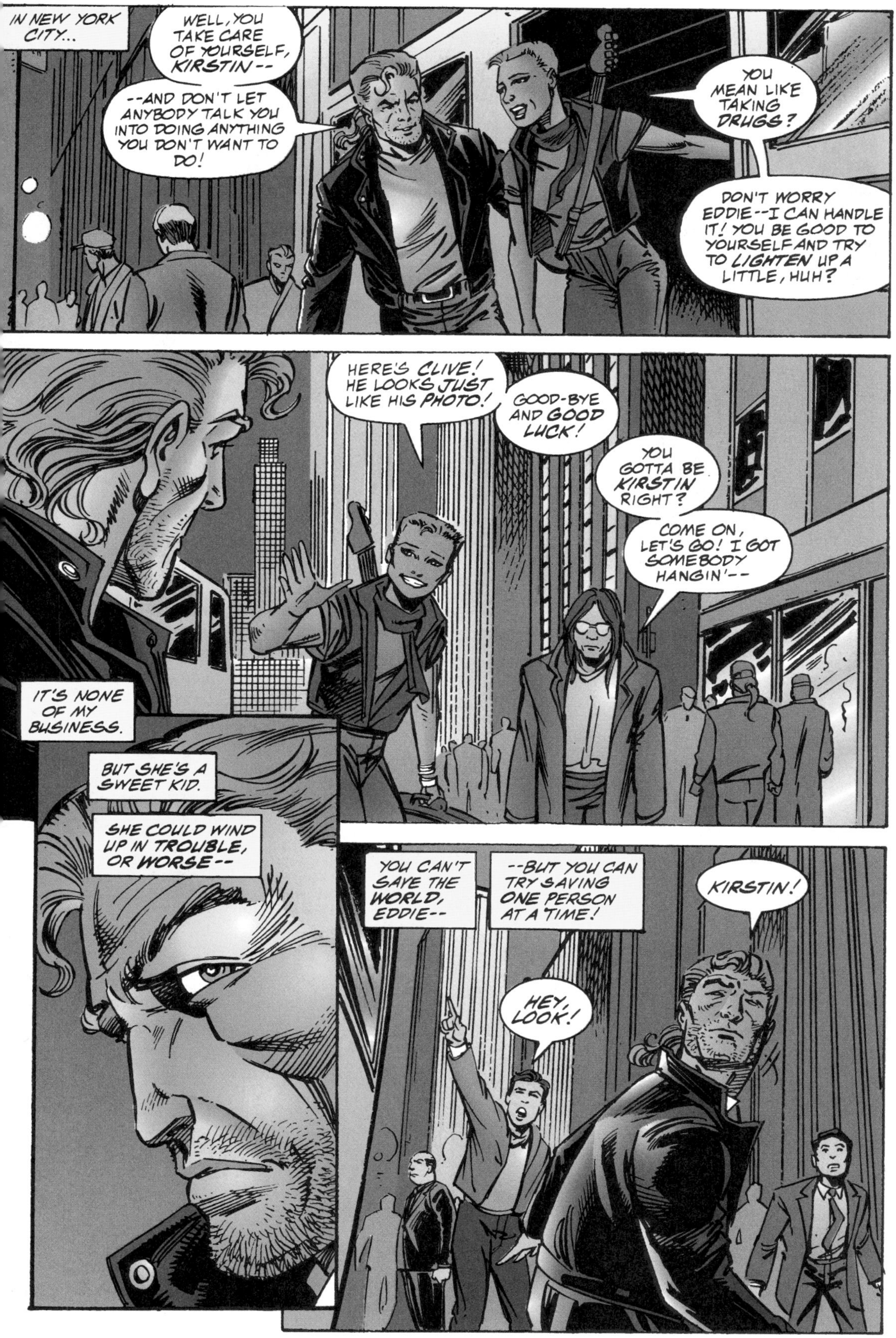
IN NEW YORK CITY...
WELL, YOU TAKE CARE OF YOURSELF, KIRSTIN--
--AND DON'T LET ANYBODY TALK YOU INTO DOING ANYTHING YOU DON'T WANT TO DO!
YOU MEAN LIKE TAKING DRUGS?
DON'T WORRY EDDIE--I CAN HANDLE IT! YOU BE GOOD TO YOURSELF AND TRY TO LIGHTEN UP A LITTLE, HUH?
HERE'S CLIVE! HE LOOKS JUST LIKE HIS PHOTO!
GOOD-BYE AND GOOD LUCK!
YOU GOTTA BE KIRSTIN RIGHT?
COME ON, LET'S GO! I GOT SOMEBODY HANGIN'--
IT'S NONE OF MY BUSINESS.
BUT SHE'S A SWEET KID.
SHE COULD WIND UP IN TROUBLE, OR WORSE--
YOU CAN'T SAVE THE WORLD, EDDIE--
--BUT YOU CAN TRY SAVING ONE PERSON AT A TIME!
KIRSTIN!
HEY, LOOK!

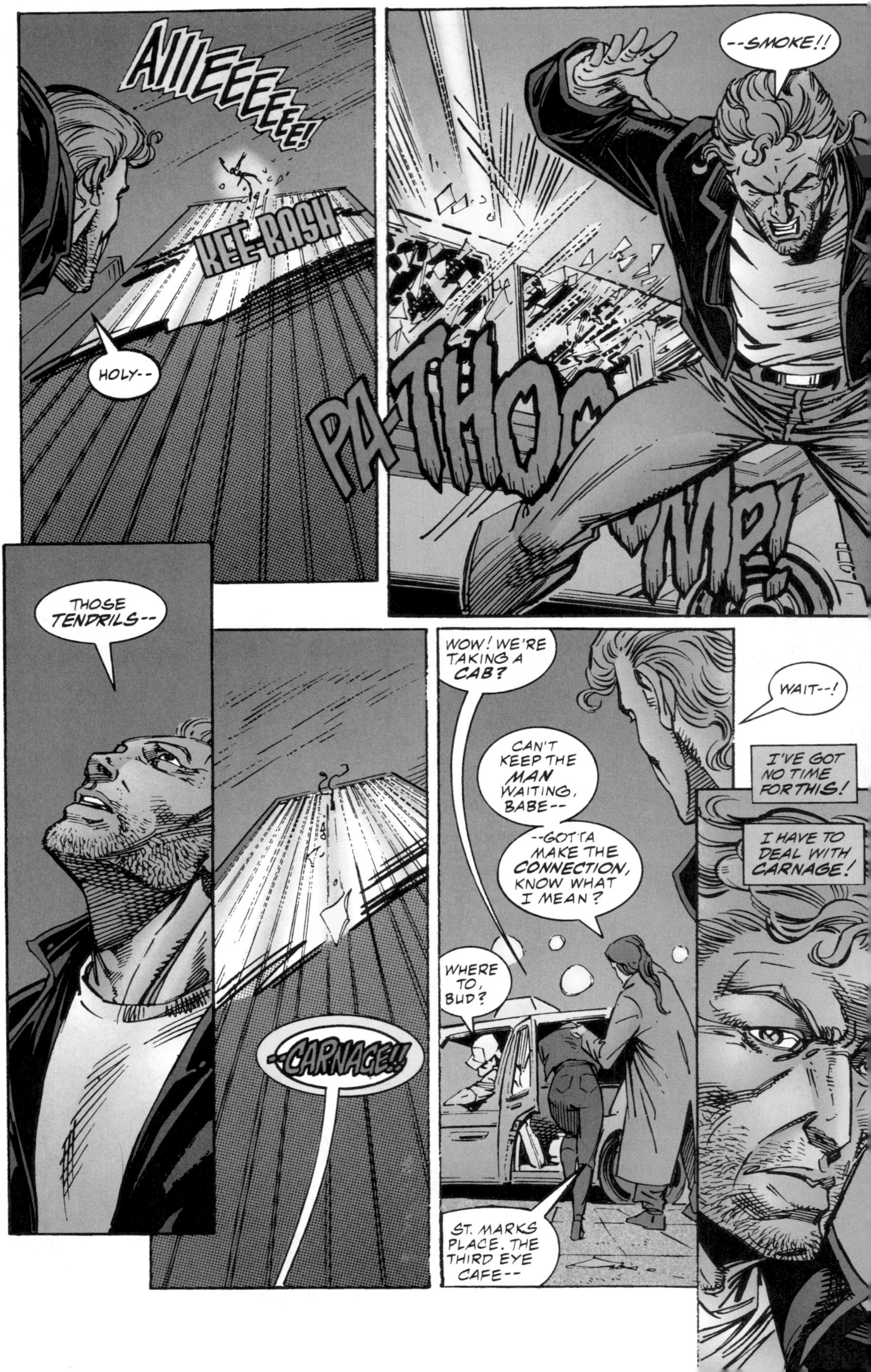
AIIIEEEEEE!
KEE-RASH
HOLY--
PA-THOOOMP!
--SMOKE!!
THOSE TENDRILS--
-CARNAGE!!
WOW! WE'RE TAKING A CAB?
CAN'T KEEP THE MAN WAITING, BABE--
--GOTTA MAKE THE CONNECTION, KNOW WHAT I MEAN?
WHERE TO, BUD?
ST. MARKS PLACE. THE THIRD EYE CAFE--
WAIT--!
I'VE GOT NO TIME FOR THIS!
I HAVE TO DEAL WITH CARNAGE!

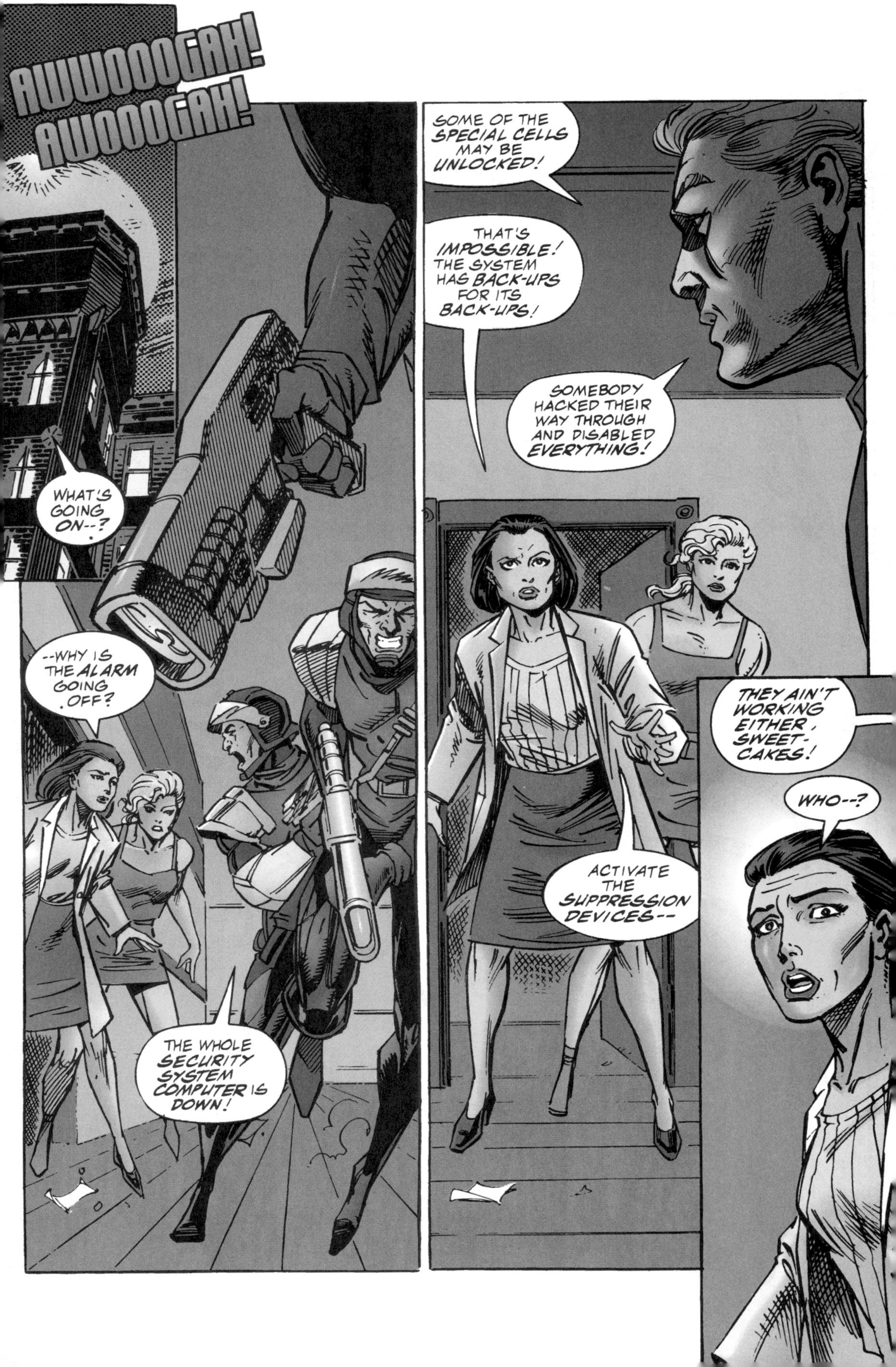
AWWOOOGAH! AWOOOGAH!
WHAT'S GOING ON--?
--WHY IS THE ALARM GOING OFF?
THE WHOLE SECURITY SYSTEM COMPUTER IS DOWN!
SOME OF THE SPECIAL CELLS MAY BE UNLOCKED!
THAT'S IMPOSSIBLE! THE SYSTEM HAS BACK-UPS FOR ITS BACK-UPS!
SOMEBODY HACKED THEIR WAY THROUGH AND DISABLED EVERYTHING!
ACTIVATE THE SUPPRESSION DEVICES--
THEY AIN'T WORKING EITHER, SWEET-CAKES!
WHO--?

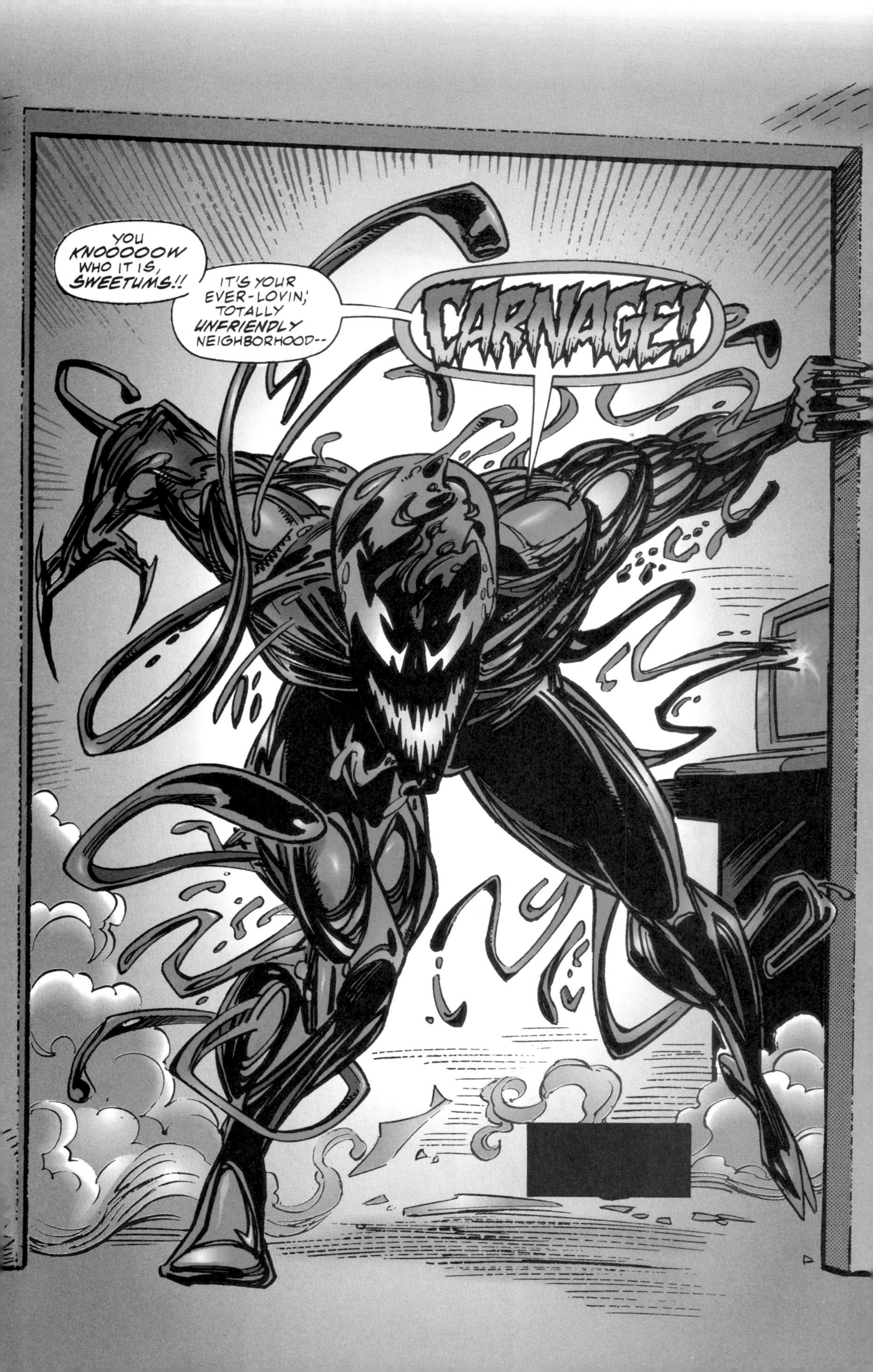
YOU KNOOOOOW WHO IT IS, SWEETUMS!!
IT'S YOUR EVER-LOVIN,' TOTALLY UNFRIENDLY NEIGHBORHOOD--
CARNAGE!
[redacted]

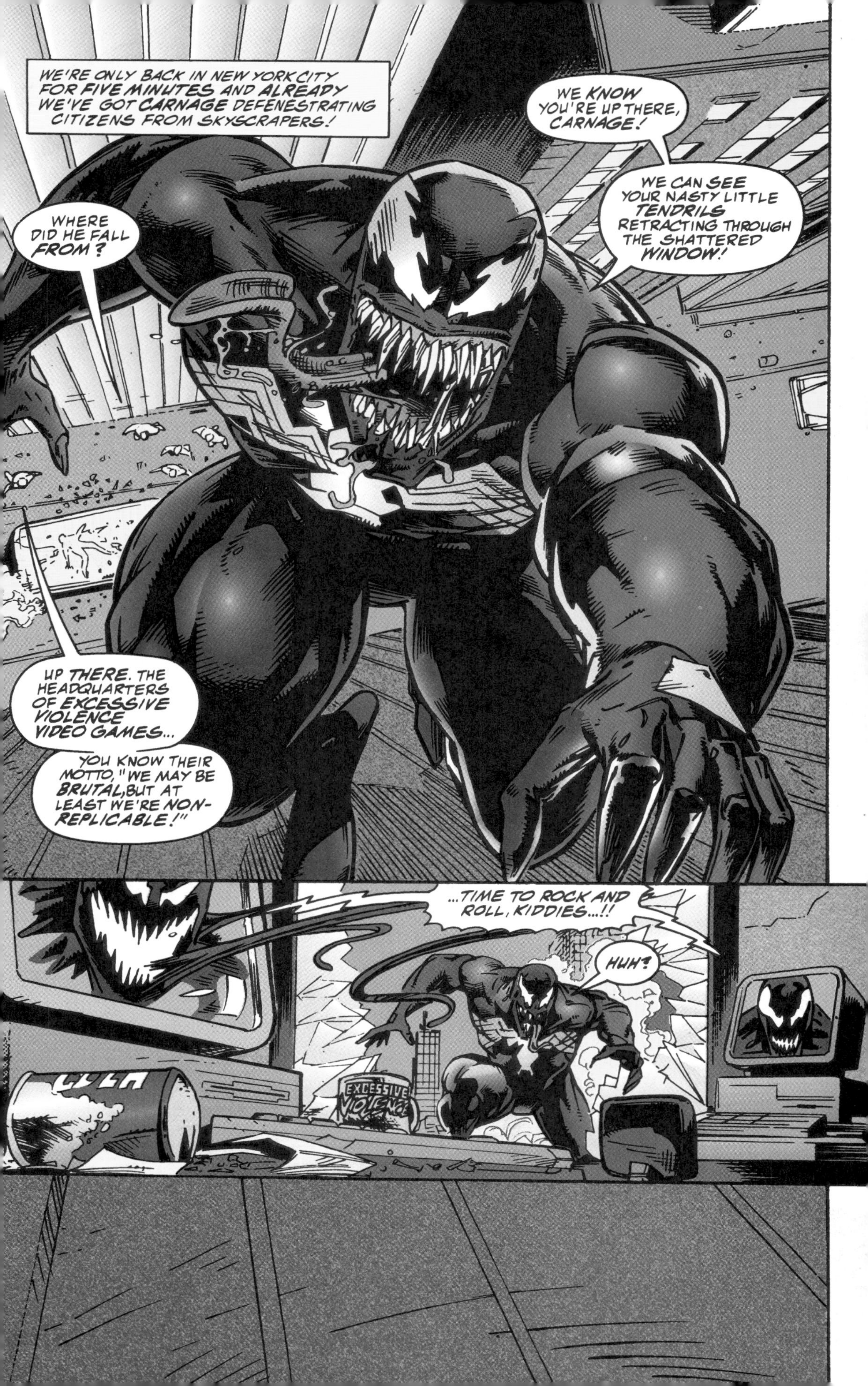
WE'RE ONLY BACK IN NEW YORK CITY FOR FIVE MINUTES AND ALREADY WE'VE GOT CARNAGE DEFENESTRATING CITIZENS FROM SKYSCRAPERS!
WHERE DID HE FALL FROM?
WE KNOW YOU'RE UP THERE, CARNAGE!
WE CAN SEE YOUR NASTY LITTLE TENDRILS RETRACTING THROUGH THE SHATTERED WINDOW!
UP THERE. THE HEADQUARTERS OF EXCESSIVE VIOLENCE VIDEO GAMES...
YOU KNOW THEIR MOTTO, "WE MAY BE BRUTAL, BUT AT LEAST WE'RE NON-REPLICABLE!"
...TIME TO ROCK AND ROLL, KIDDIES...!!
HUH?
EXCESSIVE VIOLENCE

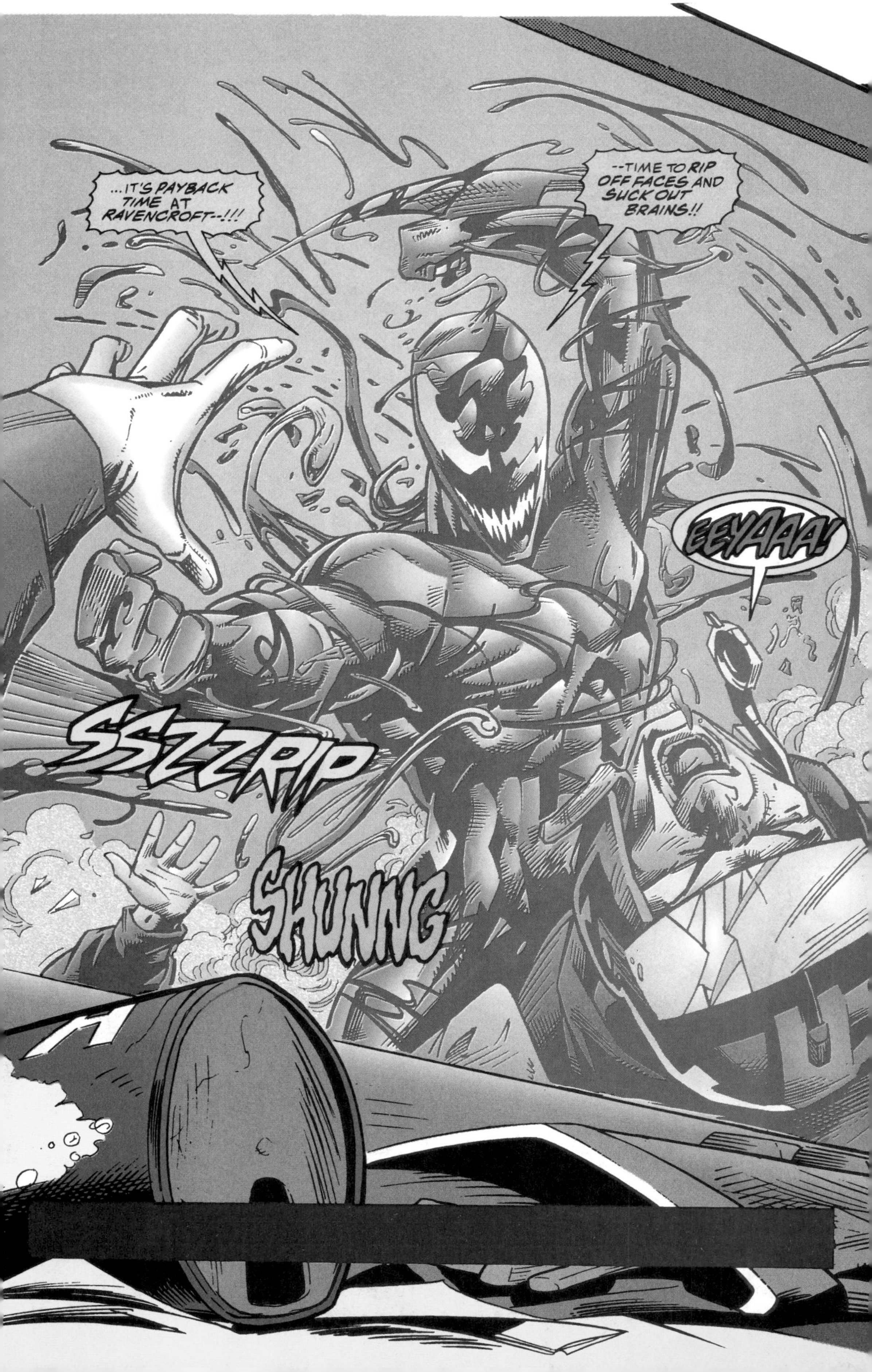
...IT'S PAYBACK TIME AT RAVENCROFT--!!!
--TIME TO RIP OFF FACES AND SUCK OUT BRAINS!!
EEYAAA!
SSZZRIP
SHUNNG
[redacted]

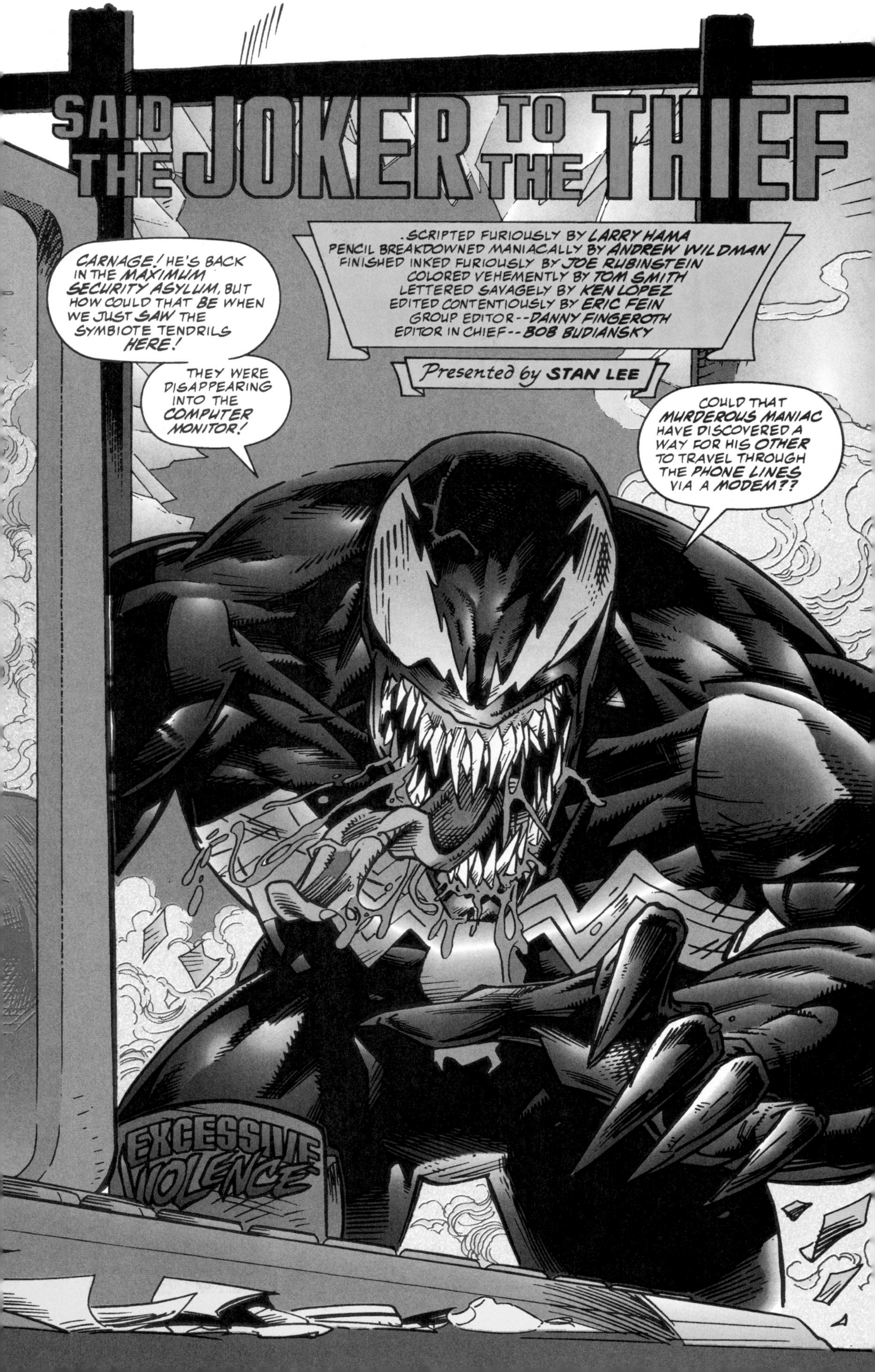
SAID THE JOKER TO THE THIEF
CARNAGE! HE'S BACK IN THE MAXIMUM SECURITY ASYLUM, BUT HOW COULD THAT BE WHEN WE JUST SAW THE SYMBIOTE TENDRILS HERE!
THEY WERE DISAPPEARING INTO THE COMPUTER MONITOR!
.SCRIPTED FURIOUSLY BY LARRY HAMA
PENCIL BREAKDOWNED MANIACALLY BY ANDREW WILDMAN
FINISHED INKED FURIOUSLY BY JOE RUBINSTEIN
COLORED VEHEMENTLY BY TOM SMITH
LETTERED SAVAGELY BY KEN LOPEZ
EDITED CONTENTIOUSLY BY ERIC FEIN
GROUP EDITOR--DANNY FINGEROTH
EDITOR IN CHIEF--BOB BUDIANSKY
Presented by STAN LEE
COULD THAT MURDEROUS MANIAC HAVE DISCOVERED A WAY FOR HIS OTHER TO TRAVEL THROUGH THE PHONE LINES VIA A MODEM??
EXCESSIVE VIOLENCE

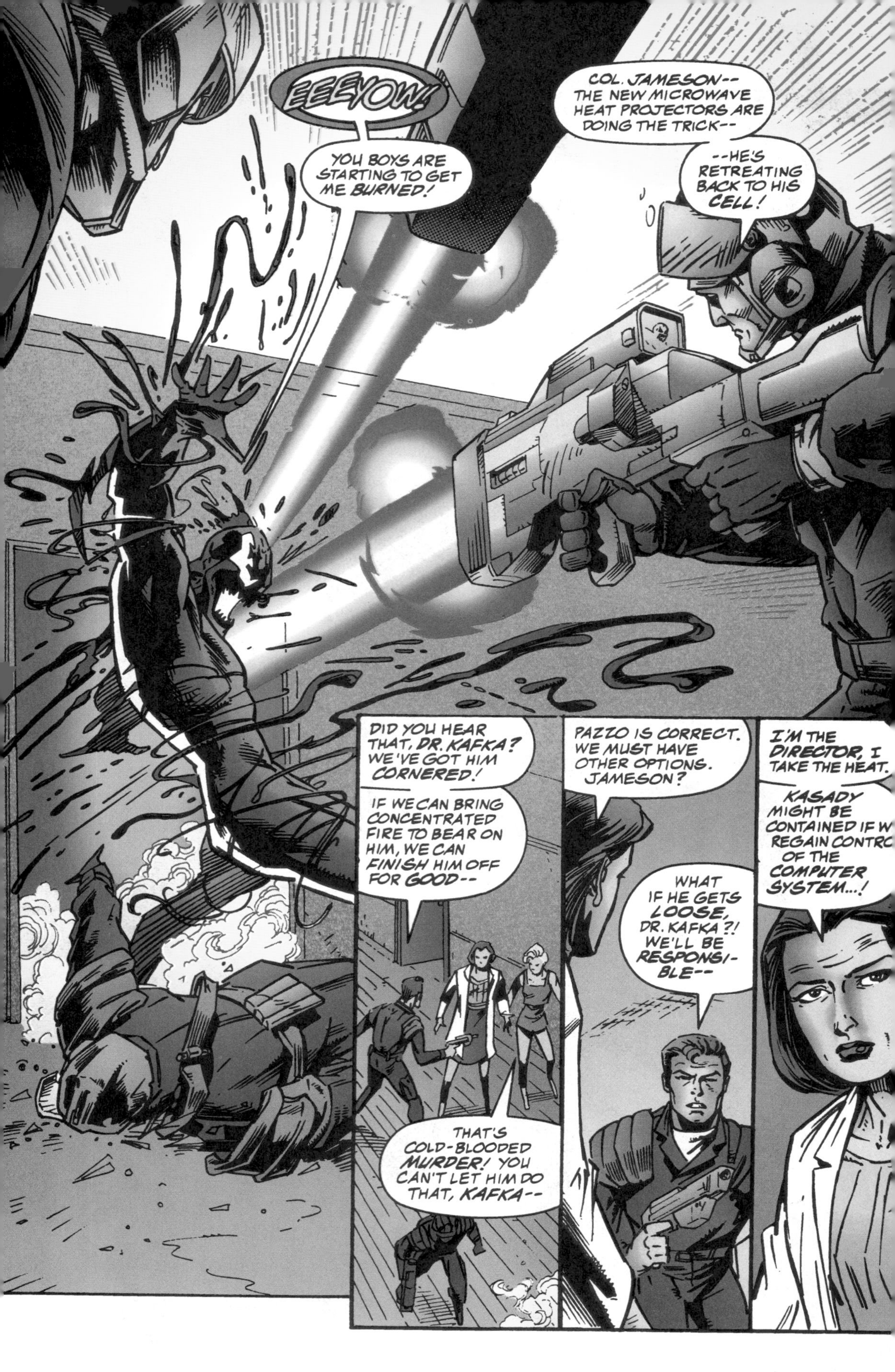
EEEYOW!
YOU BOYS ARE STARTING TO GET ME BURNED!
COL. JAMESON-- THE NEW MICROWAVE HEAT PROJECTORS ARE DOING THE TRICK--
--HE'S RETREATING BACK TO HIS CELL!
DID YOU HEAR THAT, DR. KAFKA? WE'VE GOT HIM CORNERED!
IF WE CAN BRING CONCENTRATED FIRE TO BEAR ON HIM, WE CAN FINISH HIM OFF FOR GOOD--
THAT'S COLD-BLOODED MURDER! YOU CAN'T LET HIM DO THAT, KAFKA--
PAZZO IS CORRECT. WE MUST HAVE OTHER OPTIONS. JAMESON?
WHAT IF HE GETS LOOSE, DR. KAFKA?! WE'LL BE RESPONSI-BLE--
I'M THE DIRECTOR, I TAKE THE HEAT.
KASADY MIGHT BE CONTAINED IF W REGAIN CONTRO OF THE COMPUTER SYSTEM...!

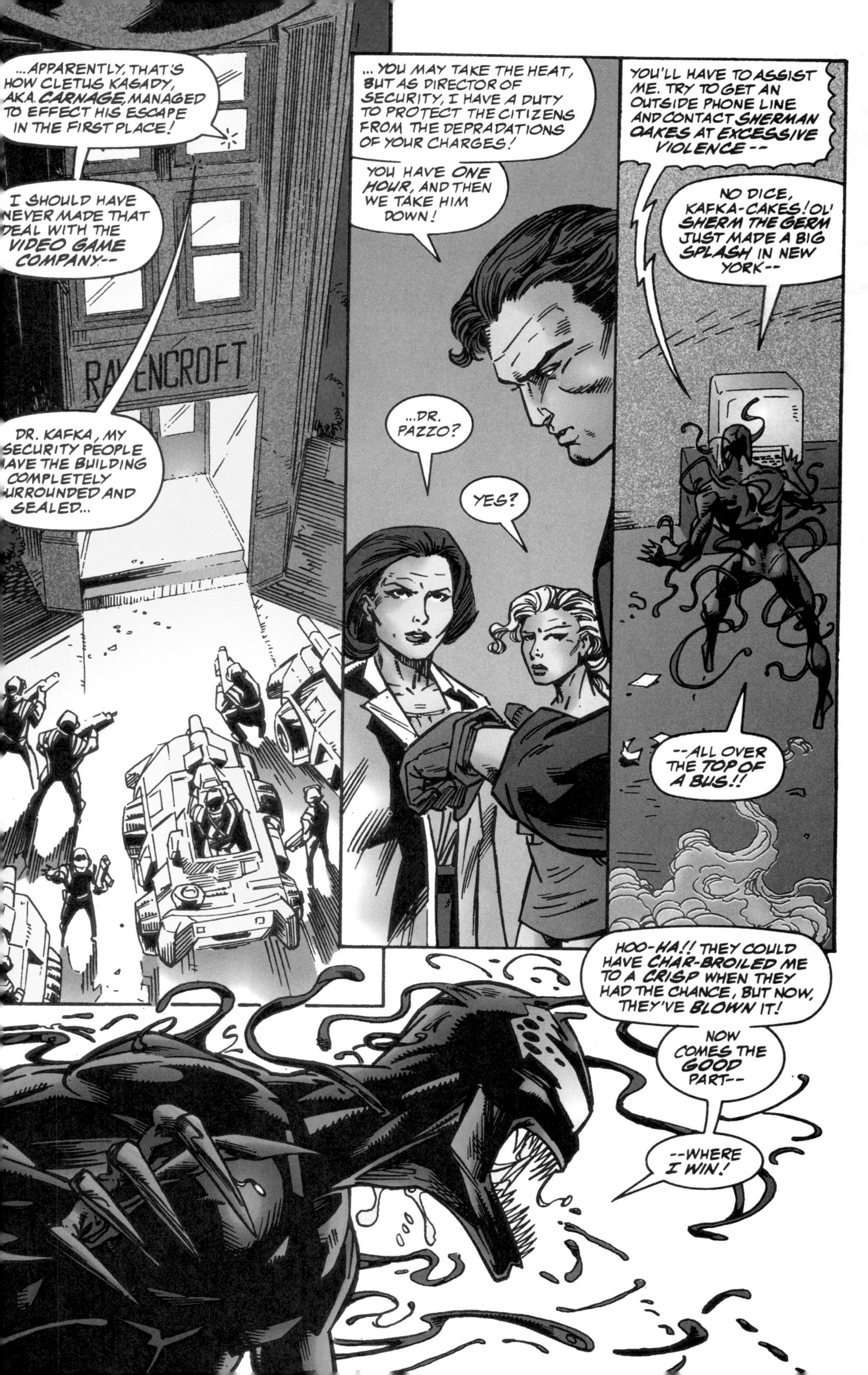
...APPARENTLY, THAT'S HOW CLETUS KASADY, AKA. CARNAGE, MANAGED TO EFFECT HIS ESCAPE IN THE FIRST PLACE!
I SHOULD HAVE NEVER MADE THAT DEAL WITH THE VIDEO GAME COMPANY--
RAVENCROFT
DR. KAFKA, MY SECURITY PEOPLE HAVE THE BUILDING COMPLETELY SURROUNDED AND SEALED...
... YOU MAY TAKE THE HEAT, BUT AS DIRECTOR OF SECURITY, I HAVE A DUTY TO PROTECT THE CITIZENS FROM THE DEPRADATIONS OF YOUR CHARGES!
YOU HAVE ONE HOUR, AND THEN WE TAKE HIM DOWN!
...DR. PAZZO?
YES?
YOU'LL HAVE TO ASSIST ME. TRY TO GET AN OUTSIDE PHONE LINE AND CONTACT SHERMAN OAKES AT EXCESSIVE VIOLENCE --
NO DICE, KAFKA-CAKES! OL' SHERM THE GERM JUST MADE A BIG SPLASH IN NEW YORK--
--ALL OVER THE TOP OF A BUS!!
HOO-HA!! THEY COULD HAVE CHAR-BROILED ME TO A CRISP WHEN THEY HAD THE CHANCE, BUT NOW, THEY'VE BLOWN IT!
NOW COMES THE GOOD PART--
--WHERE I WIN!

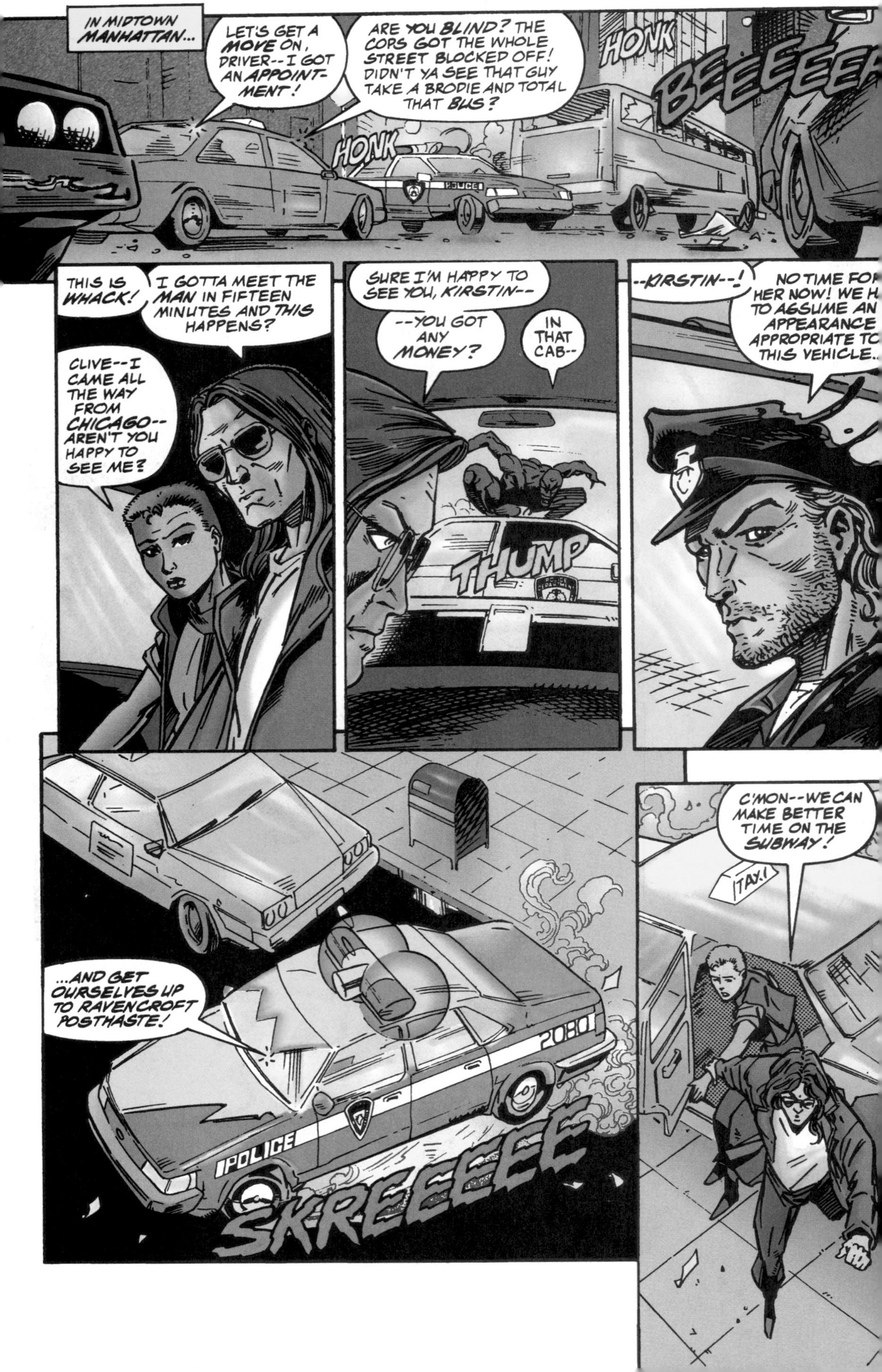

IN MIDTOWN MANHATTAN...
LET'S GET A MOVE ON, DRIVER--I GOT AN APPOINT-MENT!
ARE YOU BLIND? THE COPS GOT THE WHOLE STREET BLOCKED OFF! DIDN'T YA SEE THAT GUY TAKE A BRODIE AND TOTAL THAT BUS?
HONK
HONK
BEEEEEE
POLICE
THIS IS WHACK!
I GOTTA MEET THE MAN IN FIFTEEN MINUTES AND THIS HAPPENS?
CLIVE--I CAME ALL THE WAY FROM CHICAGO--AREN'T YOU HAPPY TO SEE ME?
SURE I'M HAPPY TO SEE YOU, KIRSTIN--
--YOU GOT ANY MONEY?
IN THAT CAB--
THUMP
--KIRSTIN--!
NO TIME FO HER NOW! WE H TO ASSUME AN APPEARANCE APPROPRIATE TO THIS VEHICLE..
...AND GET OURSELVES UP TO RAVENCROFT POSTHASTE!
2080
POLICE
SKREEEEEE
C'MON--WE CAN MAKE BETTER TIME ON THE SUBWAY!
TAXI

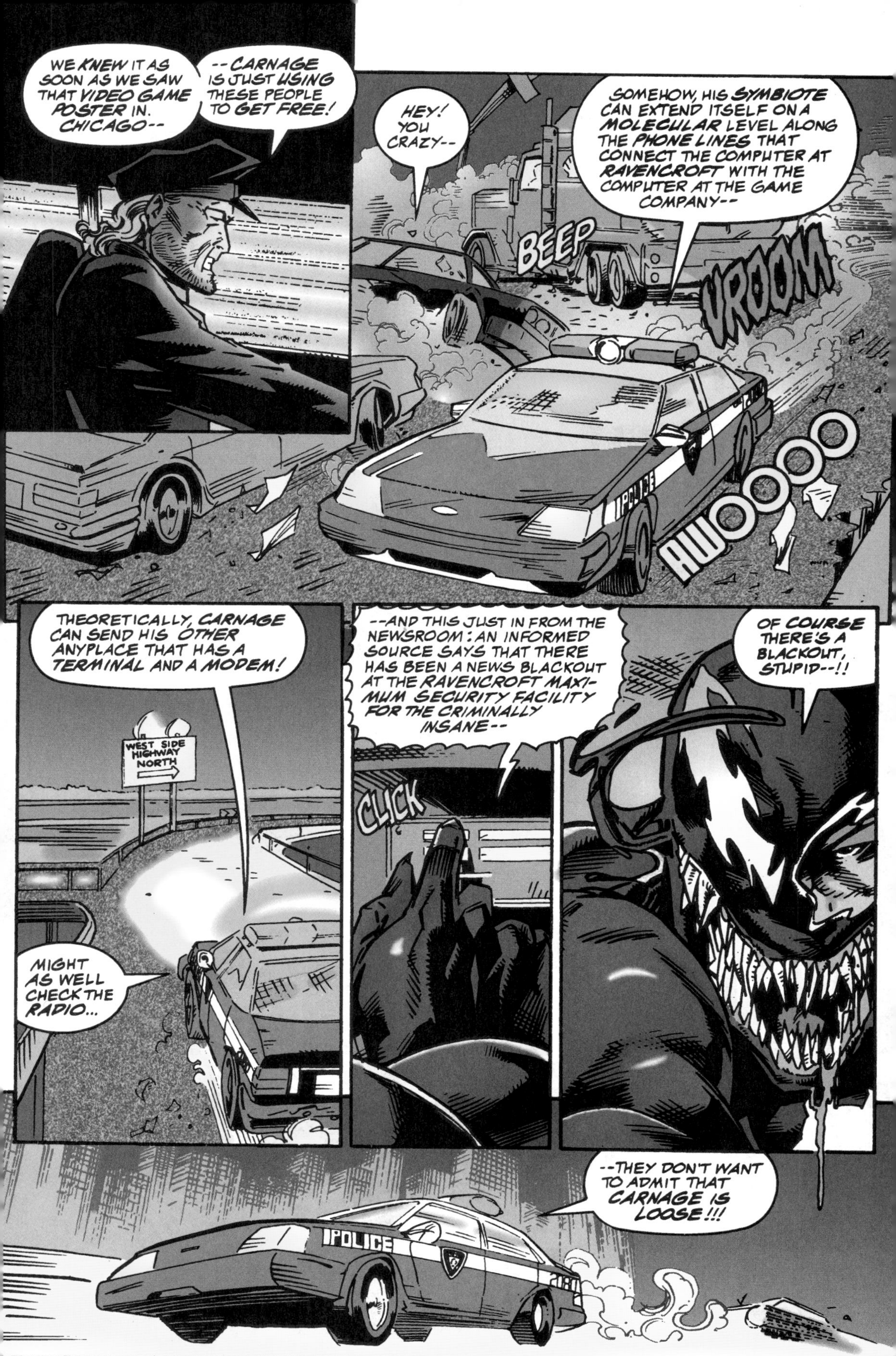
WE KNEW IT AS SOON AS WE SAW THAT VIDEO GAME POSTER IN. CHICAGO--
--CARNAGE IS JUST USING THESE PEOPLE TO GET FREE!
HEY! YOU CRAZY--
SOMEHOW, HIS SYMBIOTE CAN EXTEND ITSELF ON A MOLECULAR LEVEL ALONG THE PHONE LINES THAT CONNECT THE COMPUTER AT RAVENCROFT WITH THE COMPUTER AT THE GAME COMPANY--
BEEP
VROOM
AWOOOOO
THEORETICALLY, CARNAGE CAN SEND HIS OTHER ANYPLACE THAT HAS A TERMINAL AND A MODEM!
WEST SIDE HIGHWAY NORTH
MIGHT AS WELL CHECK THE RADIO...
--AND THIS JUST IN FROM THE NEWSROOM: AN INFORMED SOURCE SAYS THAT THERE HAS BEEN A NEWS BLACKOUT AT THE RAVENCROFT MAXI-MUM SECURITY FACILITY FOR THE CRIMINALLY INSANE--
CLICK
OF COURSE THERE'S A BLACKOUT, STUPID--!!
--THEY DON'T WANT TO ADMIT THAT CARNAGE IS LOOSE!!!
POLICE

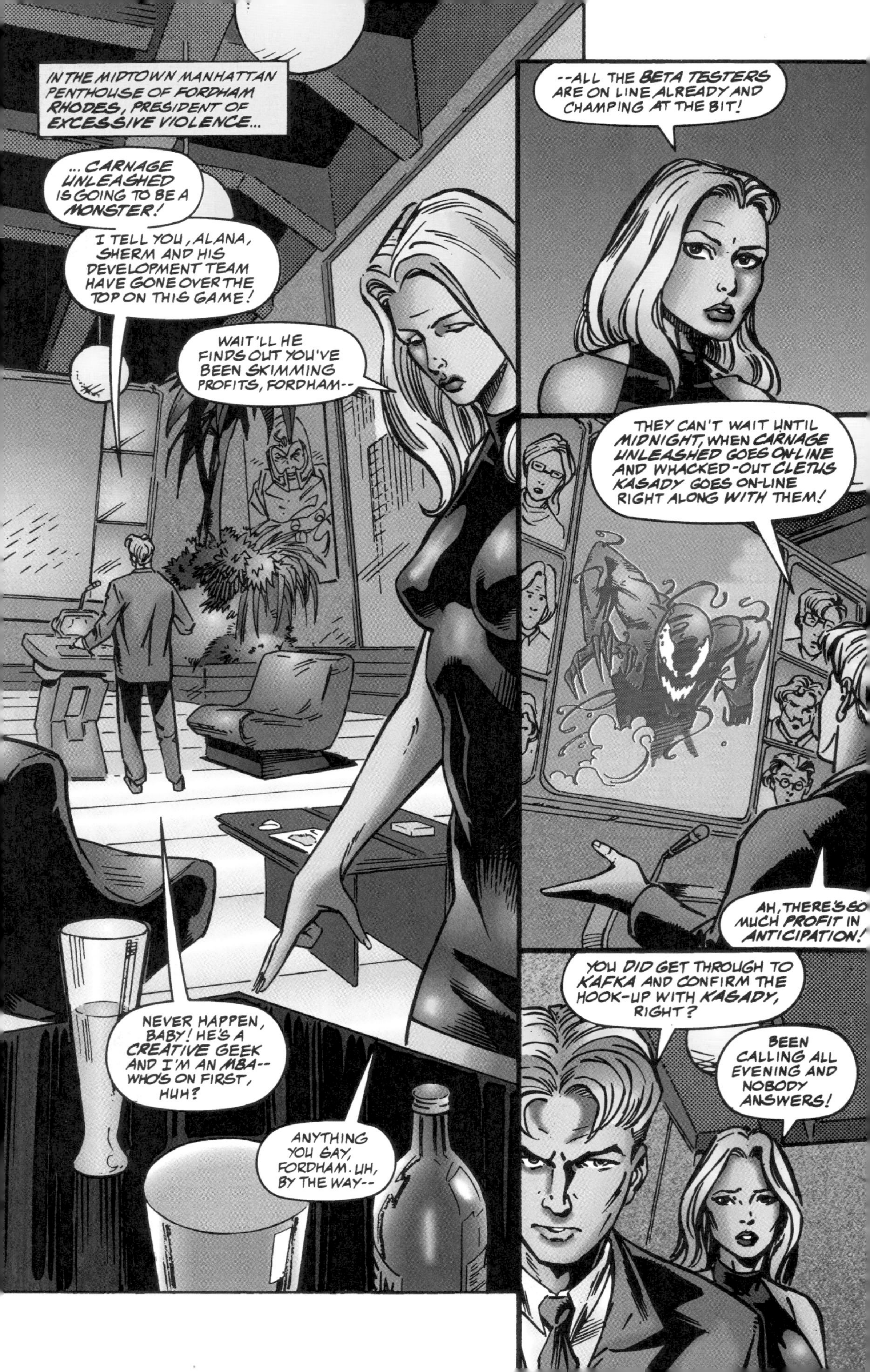
IN THE MIDTOWN MANHATTAN PENTHOUSE OF FORDHAM RHODES, PRESIDENT OF EXCESSIVE VIOLENCE...
...CARNAGE UNLEASHED IS GOING TO BE A MONSTER!
I TELL YOU, ALANA, SHERM AND HIS DEVELOPMENT TEAM HAVE GONE OVER THE TOP ON THIS GAME!
WAIT'LL HE FINDS OUT YOU'VE BEEN SKIMMING PROFITS, FORDHAM--
NEVER HAPPEN, BABY! HE'S A CREATIVE GEEK AND I'M AN MBA-- WHO'S ON FIRST, HUH?
ANYTHING YOU SAY, FORDHAM. UH, BY THE WAY--
--ALL THE BETA TESTERS ARE ON LINE ALREADY AND CHAMPING AT THE BIT!
THEY CAN'T WAIT UNTIL MIDNIGHT, WHEN CARNAGE UNLEASHED GOES ON-LINE AND WHACKED-OUT CLETUS KASADY GOES ON-LINE RIGHT ALONG WITH THEM!
AH, THERE'S SO MUCH PROFIT IN ANTICIPATION!
YOU DID GET THROUGH TO KAFKA AND CONFIRM THE HOOK-UP WITH KASADY, RIGHT?
BEEN CALLING ALL EVENING AND NOBODY ANSWERS!

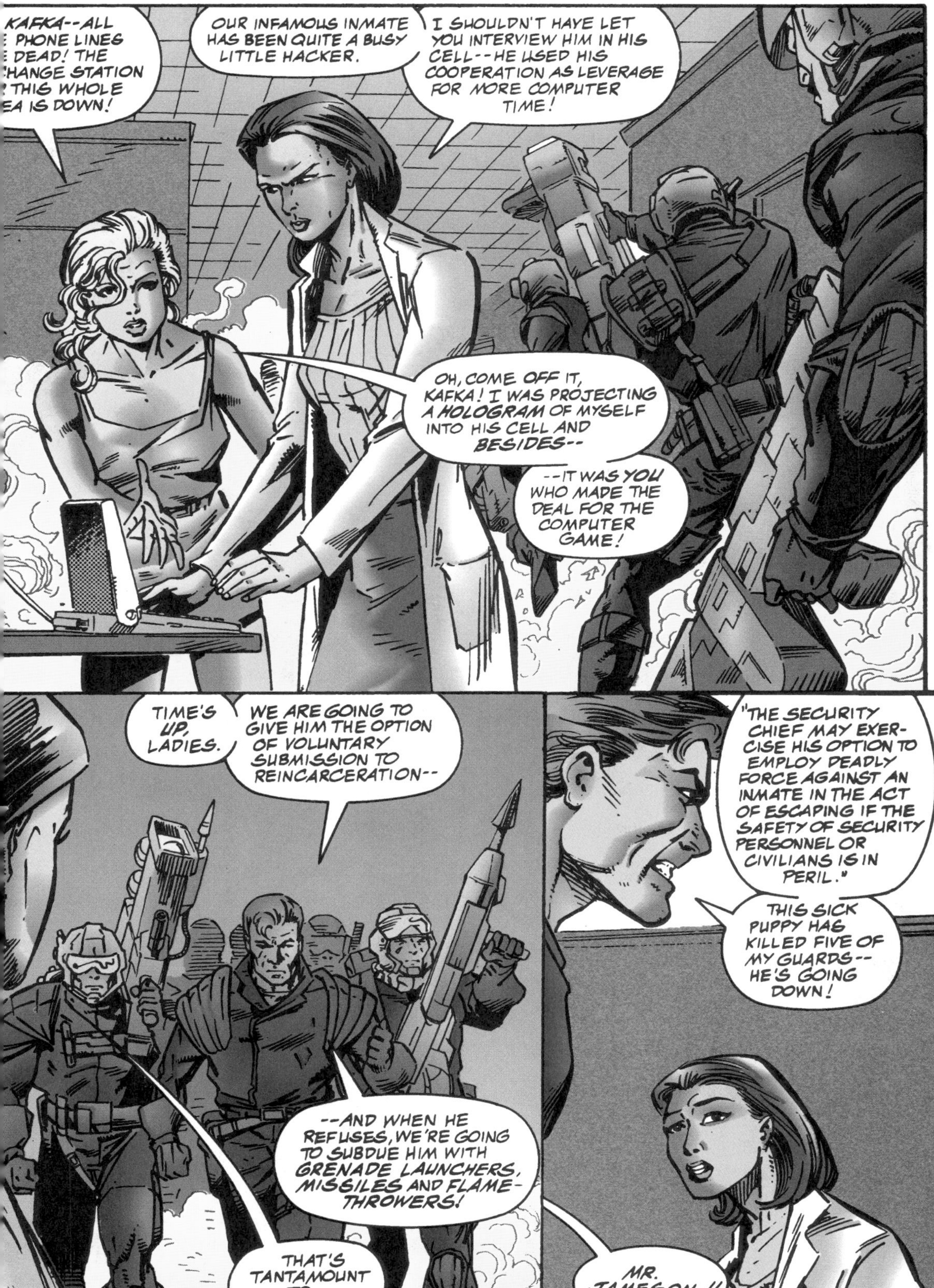
KAFKA--ALL PHONE LINES DEAD! THE HANGE STATION THIS WHOLE EA IS DOWN!
OUR INFAMOUS INMATE HAS BEEN QUITE A BUSY LITTLE HACKER.
I SHOULDN'T HAVE LET YOU INTERVIEW HIM IN HIS CELL--HE USED HIS COOPERATION AS LEVERAGE FOR MORE COMPUTER TIME!
OH, COME OFF IT, KAFKA! I WAS PROJECTING A HOLOGRAM OF MYSELF INTO HIS CELL AND BESIDES--
--IT WAS YOU WHO MADE THE DEAL FOR THE COMPUTER GAME!
TIME'S UP, LADIES.
WE ARE GOING TO GIVE HIM THE OPTION OF VOLUNTARY SUBMISSION TO REINCARCERATION--
--AND WHEN HE REFUSES, WE'RE GOING TO SUBDUE HIM WITH GRENADE LAUNCHERS, MISSILES AND FLAME-THROWERS!
THAT'S TANTAMOUNT TO MURDER!
"THE SECURITY CHIEF MAY EXERCISE HIS OPTION TO EMPLOY DEADLY FORCE AGAINST AN INMATE IN THE ACT OF ESCAPING IF THE SAFETY OF SECURITY PERSONNEL OR CIVILIANS IS IN PERIL."
THIS SICK PUPPY HAS KILLED FIVE OF MY GUARDS--HE'S GOING DOWN!
MR. JAMESON--!!

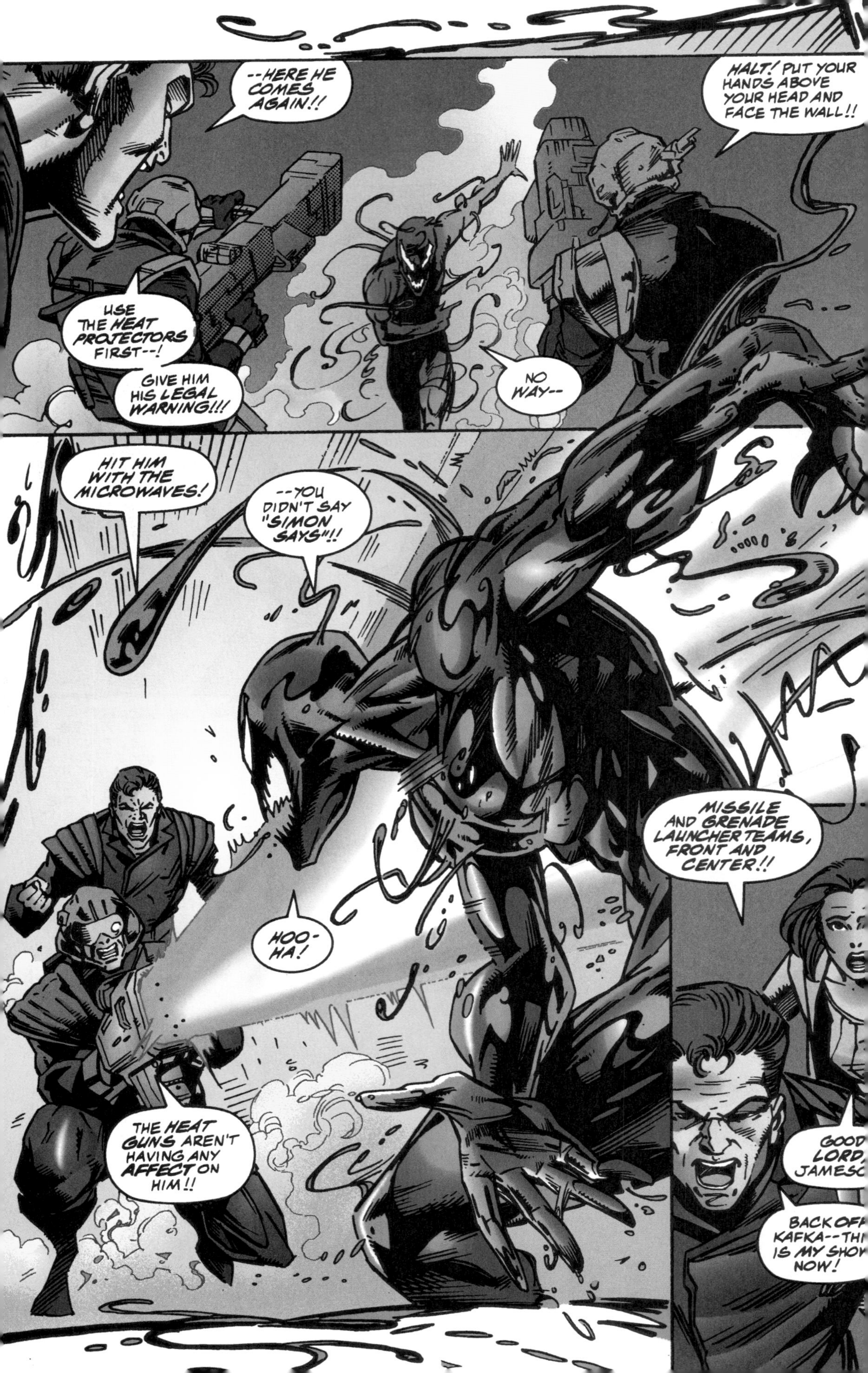
--HERE HE COMES AGAIN!!
USE THE HEAT PROJECTORS FIRST--!
GIVE HIM HIS LEGAL WARNING!!!
HALT! PUT YOUR HANDS ABOVE YOUR HEAD AND FACE THE WALL!!
NO WAY--
HIT HIM WITH THE MICROWAVES!
--YOU DIDN'T SAY "SIMON SAYS"!!
HOO-HA!
THE HEAT GUNS AREN'T HAVING ANY AFFECT ON HIM!!
MISSILE AND GRENADE LAUNCHER TEAMS, FRONT AND CENTER!!
GOOD LORD, JAMESO
BACK OFF KAFKA--TH IS MY SHOW NOW!

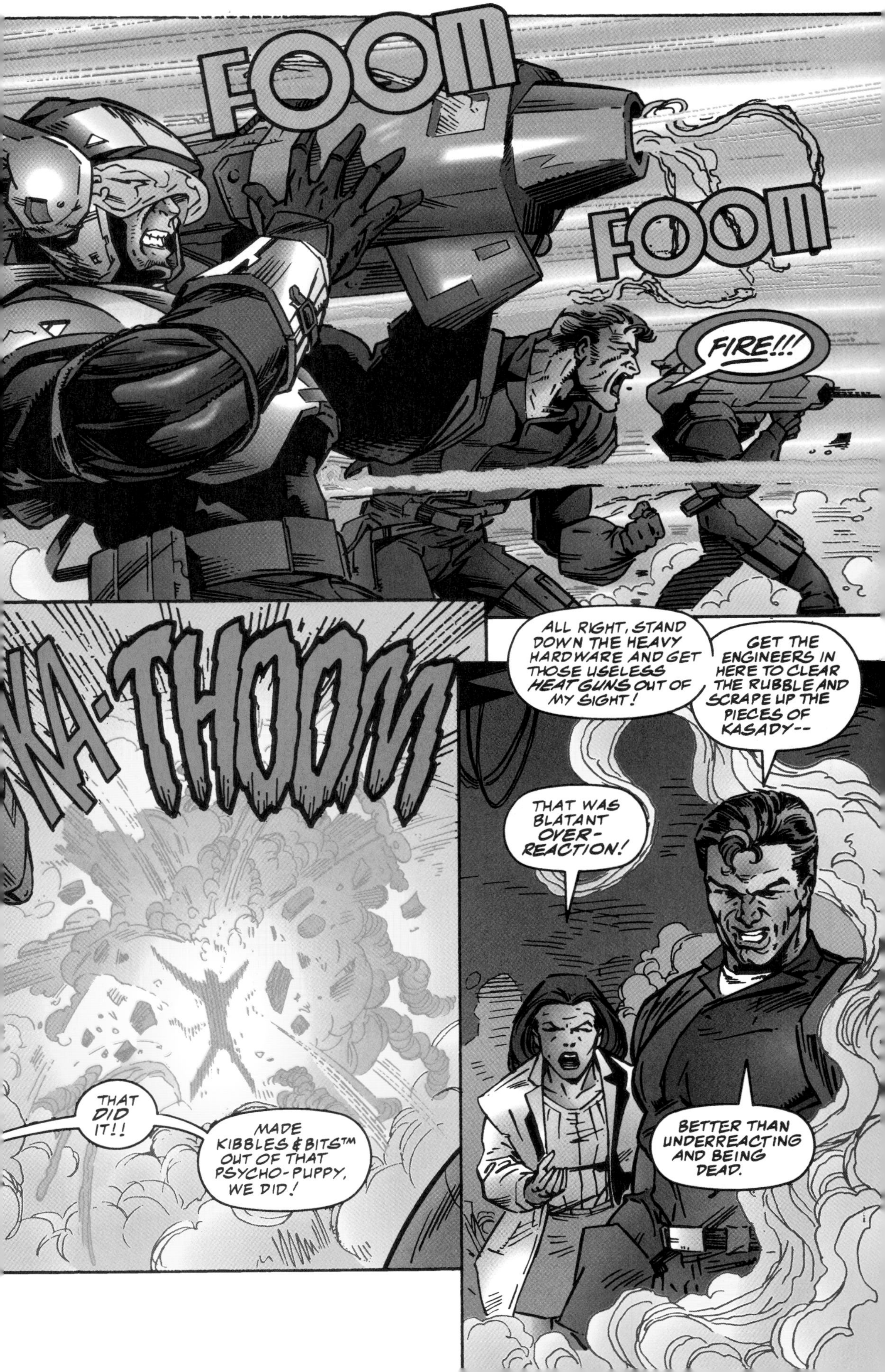
FOOM
FOOM
FIRE!!!
KA-THOOM
THAT DID IT!!
MADE KIBBLES & BITS™ OUT OF THAT PSYCHO-PUPPY, WE DID!
ALL RIGHT, STAND DOWN THE HEAVY HARDWARE AND GET THOSE USELESS HEAT GUNS OUT OF MY SIGHT!
GET THE ENGINEERS IN HERE TO CLEAR THE RUBBLE AND SCRAPE UP THE PIECES OF KASADY--
THAT WAS BLATANT OVER-REACTION!
BETTER THAN UNDERREACTING AND BEING DEAD.

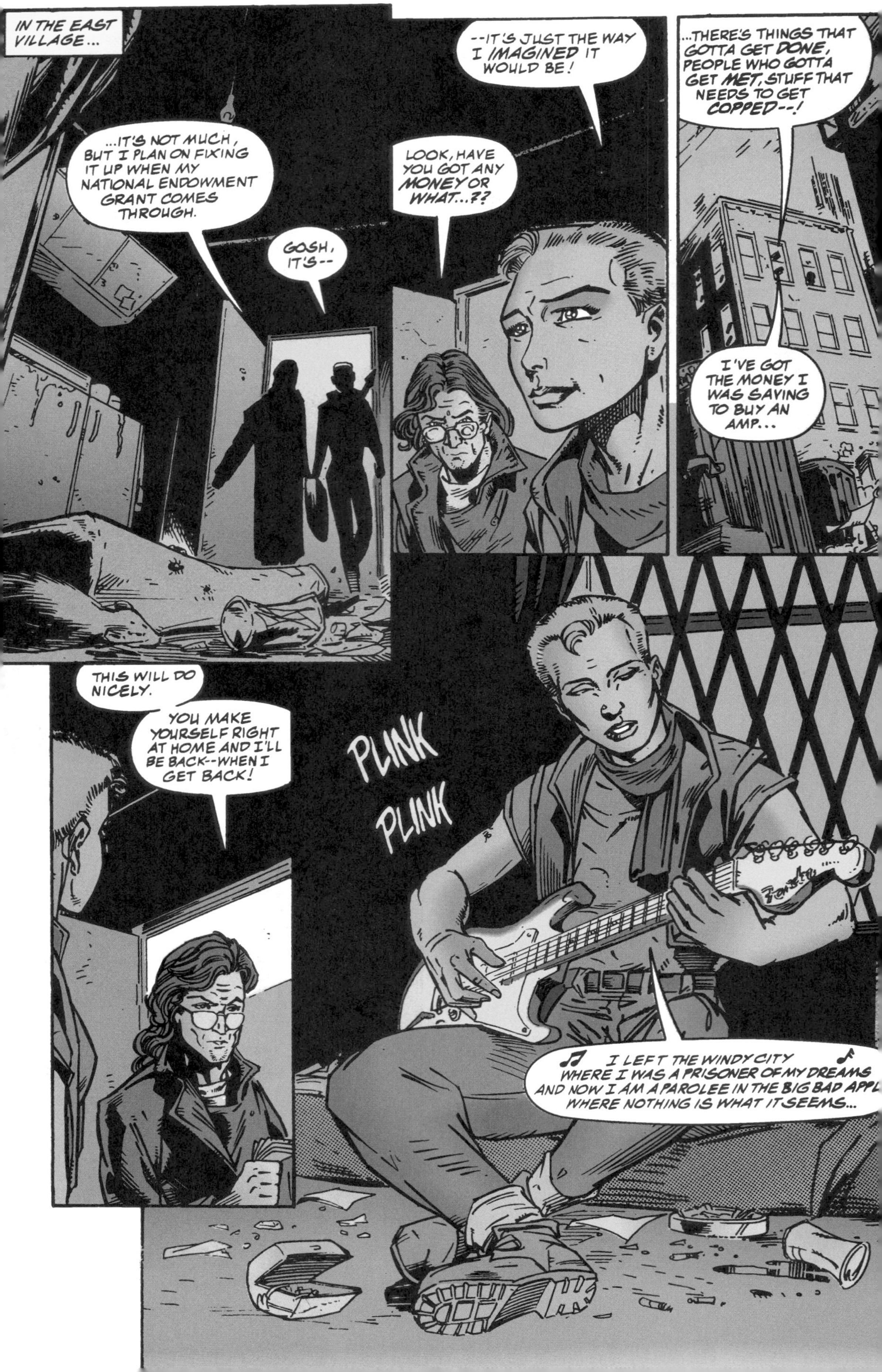

IN THE EAST VILLAGE...
...IT'S NOT MUCH, BUT I PLAN ON FIXING IT UP WHEN MY NATIONAL ENDOWMENT GRANT COMES THROUGH.
GOSH, IT'S--
--IT'S JUST THE WAY I IMAGINED IT WOULD BE!
LOOK, HAVE YOU GOT ANY MONEY OR WHAT...??
...THERE'S THINGS THAT GOTTA GET DONE, PEOPLE WHO GOTTA GET MET, STUFF THAT NEEDS TO GET COPPED--!
I'VE GOT THE MONEY I WAS SAVING TO BUY AN AMP...
THIS WILL DO NICELY.
YOU MAKE YOURSELF RIGHT AT HOME AND I'LL BE BACK--WHEN I GET BACK!
PLINK
PLINK
♫ I LEFT THE WINDY CITY ♪ WHERE I WAS A PRISONER OF MY DREAMS AND NOW I AM A PAROLEE IN THE BIG BAD APPL WHERE NOTHING IS WHAT IT SEEMS...

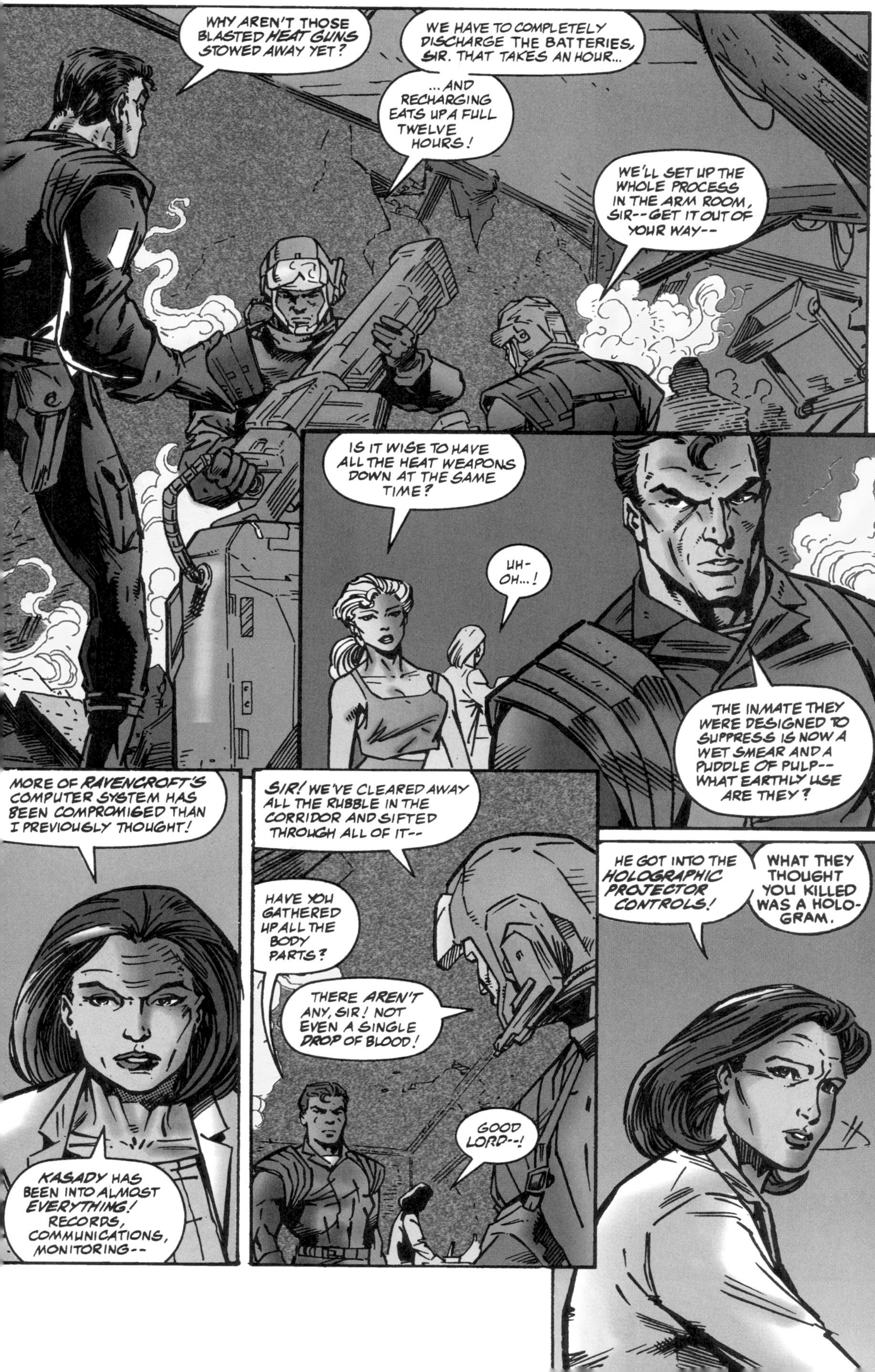
WHY AREN'T THOSE BLASTED HEAT GUNS STOWED AWAY YET?
WE HAVE TO COMPLETELY DISCHARGE THE BATTERIES, SIR. THAT TAKES AN HOUR...
...AND RECHARGING EATS UP A FULL TWELVE HOURS!
WE'LL SET UP THE WHOLE PROCESS IN THE ARM ROOM, SIR--GET IT OUT OF YOUR WAY--
IS IT WISE TO HAVE ALL THE HEAT WEAPONS DOWN AT THE SAME TIME?
UH-OH...!
THE INMATE THEY WERE DESIGNED TO SUPPRESS IS NOW A WET SMEAR AND A PUDDLE OF PULP--WHAT EARTHLY USE ARE THEY?
MORE OF RAVENCROFT'S COMPUTER SYSTEM HAS BEEN COMPROMISED THAN I PREVIOUSLY THOUGHT!
KASADY HAS BEEN INTO ALMOST EVERYTHING! RECORDS, COMMUNICATIONS, MONITORING--
SIR! WE'VE CLEARED AWAY ALL THE RUBBLE IN THE CORRIDOR AND SIFTED THROUGH ALL OF IT--
HAVE YOU GATHERED UP ALL THE BODY PARTS?
THERE AREN'T ANY, SIR! NOT EVEN A SINGLE DROP OF BLOOD!
GOOD LORD--!
HE GOT INTO THE HOLOGRAPHIC PROJECTOR CONTROLS!
WHAT THEY THOUGHT YOU KILLED WAS A HOLOGRAM.

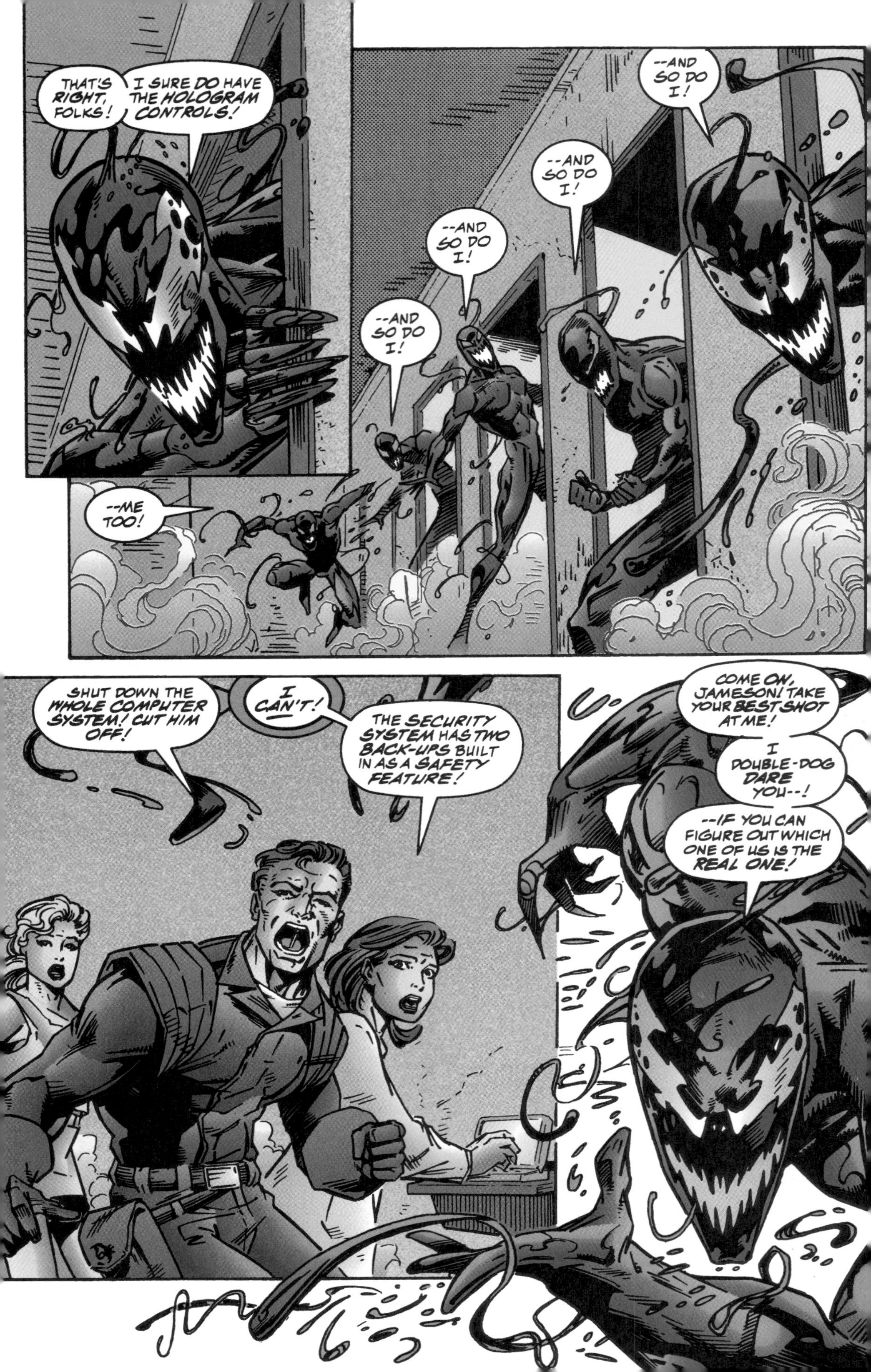
THAT'S RIGHT, FOLKS!
I SURE DO HAVE THE HOLOGRAM CONTROLS!
--AND SO DO I!
--AND SO DO I!
--AND SO DO I!
--AND SO DO I!
--ME TOO!
SHUT DOWN THE WHOLE COMPUTER SYSTEM! CUT HIM OFF!
I CAN'T!
THE SECURITY SYSTEM HAS TWO BACK-UPS BUILT IN AS A SAFETY FEATURE!
COME ON, JAMESON! TAKE YOUR BEST SHOT AT ME!
I DOUBLE-DOG DARE YOU--!
--IF YOU CAN FIGURE OUT WHICH ONE OF US IS THE REAL ONE!

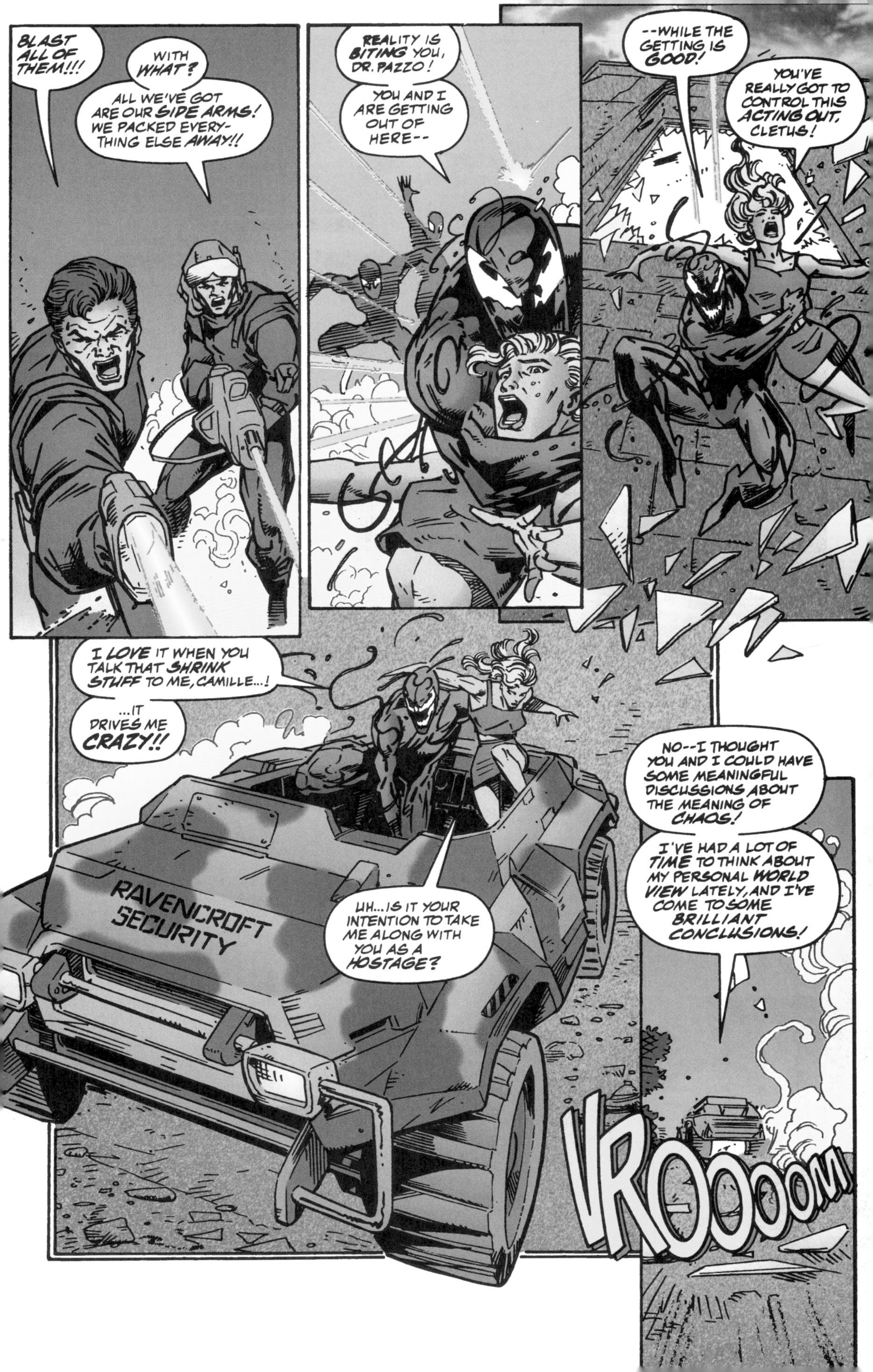
BLAST ALL OF THEM!!!
WITH WHAT?
ALL WE'VE GOT ARE OUR SIDE ARMS! WE PACKED EVERY-THING ELSE AWAY!!
REALITY IS BITING YOU, DR. PAZZO!
YOU AND I ARE GETTING OUT OF HERE--
--WHILE THE GETTING IS GOOD!
YOU'VE REALLY GOT TO CONTROL THIS ACTING OUT, CLETUS!
I LOVE IT WHEN YOU TALK THAT SHRINK STUFF TO ME, CAMILLE...!
...IT DRIVES ME CRAZY!!
RAVENCROFT SECURITY
UH...IS IT YOUR INTENTION TO TAKE ME ALONG WITH YOU AS A HOSTAGE?
NO--I THOUGHT YOU AND I COULD HAVE SOME MEANINGFUL DISCUSSIONS ABOUT THE MEANING OF CHAOS!
I'VE HAD A LOT OF TIME TO THINK ABOUT MY PERSONAL WORLD VIEW LATELY, AND I'VE COME TO SOME BRILLIANT CONCLUSIONS!
VROOOOOM

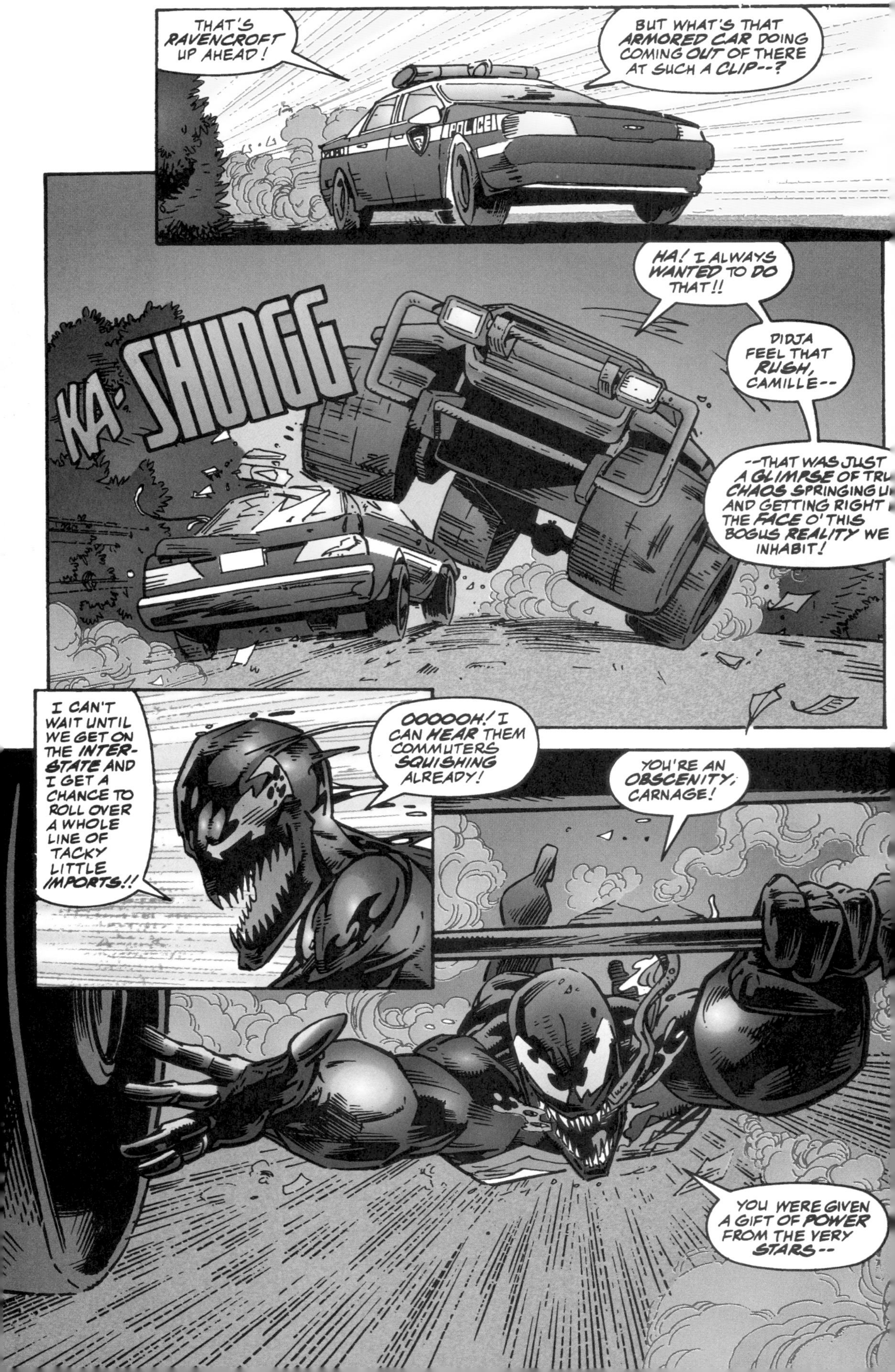
THAT'S RAVENCROFT UP AHEAD!
BUT WHAT'S THAT ARMORED CAR DOING COMING OUT OF THERE AT SUCH A CLIP--?
POLICE
KA-SHUNGG
HA! I ALWAYS WANTED TO DO THAT!!
DIDJA FEEL THAT RUSH, CAMILLE--
--THAT WAS JUST A GLIMPSE OF TRU CHAOS SPRINGING U AND GETTING RIGHT THE FACE O' THIS BOGUS REALITY WE INHABIT!
I CAN'T WAIT UNTIL WE GET ON THE INTER-STATE AND I GET A CHANCE TO ROLL OVER A WHOLE LINE OF TACKY LITTLE IMPORTS!!
OOOOOOH! I CAN HEAR THEM COMMUTERS SQUISHING ALREADY!
YOU'RE AN OBSCENITY, CARNAGE!
YOU WERE GIVEN A GIFT OF POWER FROM THE VERY STARS--

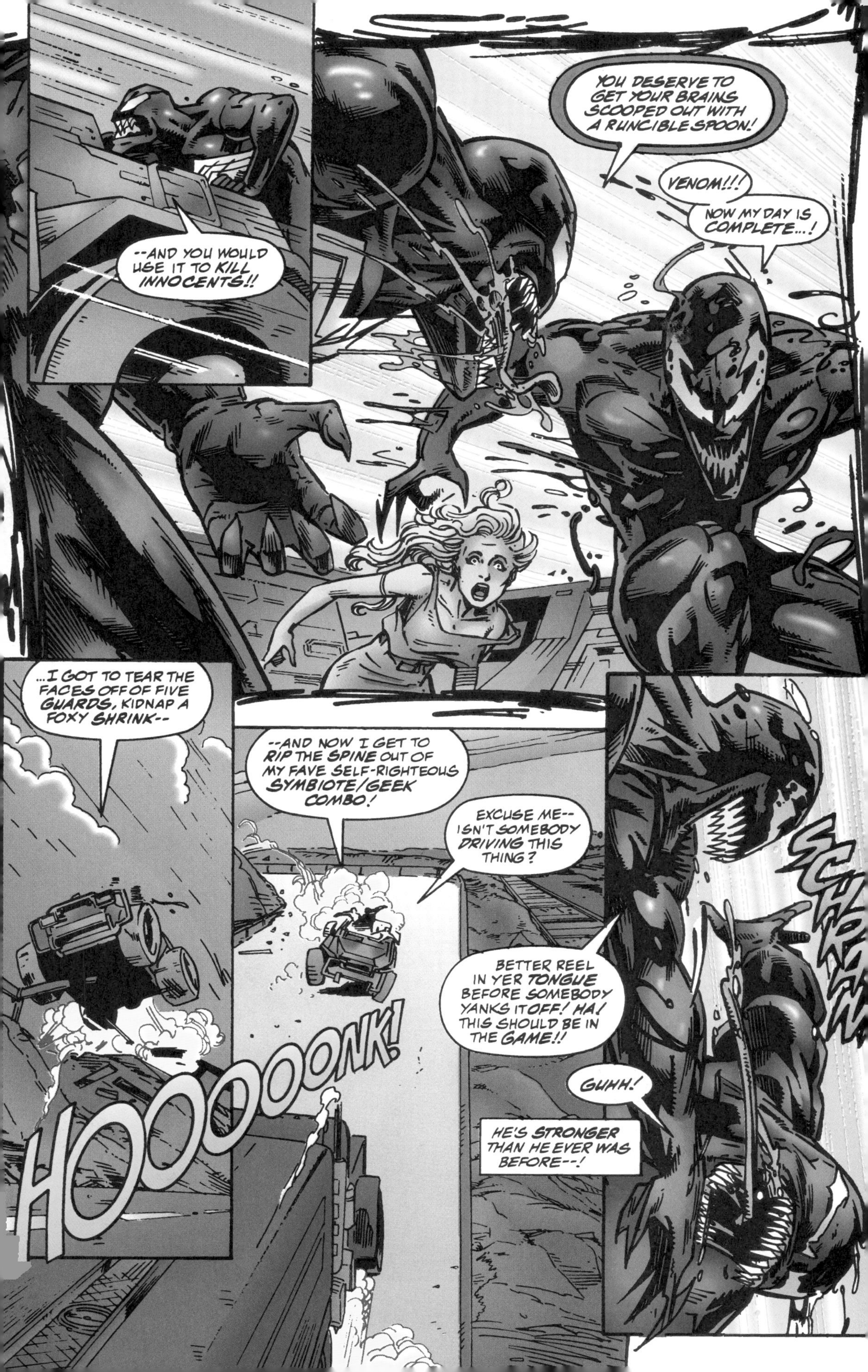
--AND YOU WOULD USE IT TO KILL INNOCENTS!!
YOU DESERVE TO GET YOUR BRAINS SCOOPED OUT WITH A RUNCIBLE SPOON!
VENOM!!!
NOW MY DAY IS COMPLETE...!
...I GOT TO TEAR THE FACES OFF OF FIVE GUARDS, KIDNAP A FOXY SHRINK--
HOOOOOONK!
--AND NOW I GET TO RIP THE SPINE OUT OF MY FAVE SELF-RIGHTEOUS SYMBIOTE/GEEK COMBO!
EXCUSE ME-- ISN'T SOMEBODY DRIVING THIS THING?
BETTER REEL IN YER TONGUE BEFORE SOMEBODY YANKS IT OFF! HA! THIS SHOULD BE IN THE GAME!!
GUHH!
HE'S STRONGER THAN HE EVER WAS BEFORE--!
SCHRAAK

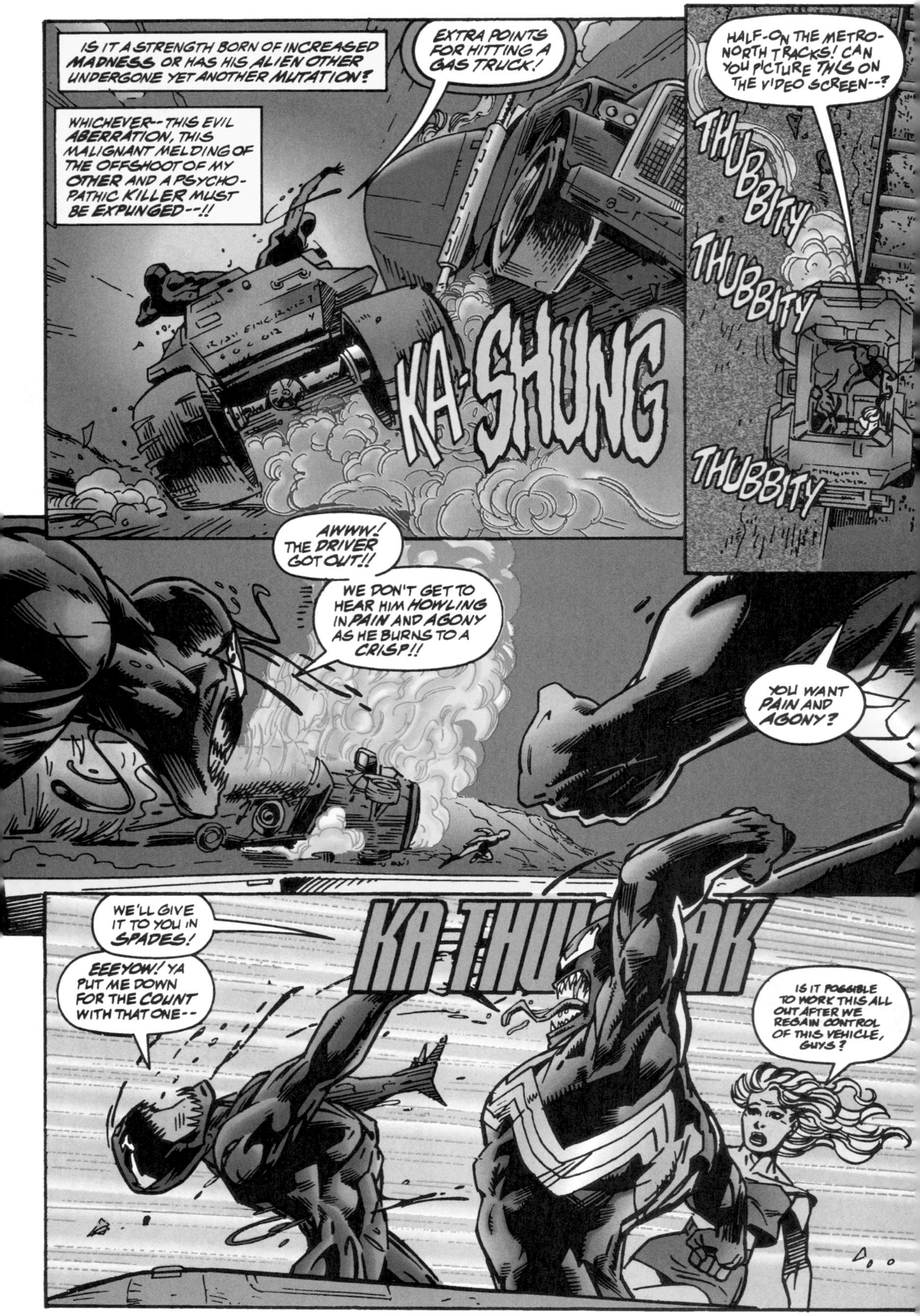
IS IT A STRENGTH BORN OF INCREASED MADNESS OR HAS HIS ALIEN OTHER UNDERGONE YET ANOTHER MUTATION?
WHICHEVER-- THIS EVIL ABERRATION, THIS MALIGNANT MELDING OF THE OFFSHOOT OF MY OTHER AND A PSYCHO-PATHIC KILLER MUST BE EXPUNGED--!!
EXTRA POINTS FOR HITTING A GAS TRUCK!
KA-SHUNG
HALF-ON THE METRO-NORTH TRACKS! CAN YOU PICTURE THIS ON THE VIDEO SCREEN--?
THUBBITY
THUBBITY
THUBBITY
AWWW! THE DRIVER GOT OUT!!
WE DON'T GET TO HEAR HIM HOWLING IN PAIN AND AGONY AS HE BURNS TO A CRISP!!
YOU WANT PAIN AND AGONY?
WE'LL GIVE IT TO YOU IN SPADES!
EEEYOW! YA PUT ME DOWN FOR THE COUNT WITH THAT ONE--
IS IT POSSIBLE TO WORK THIS ALL OUT AFTER WE REGAIN CONTROL OF THIS VEHICLE, GUYS?

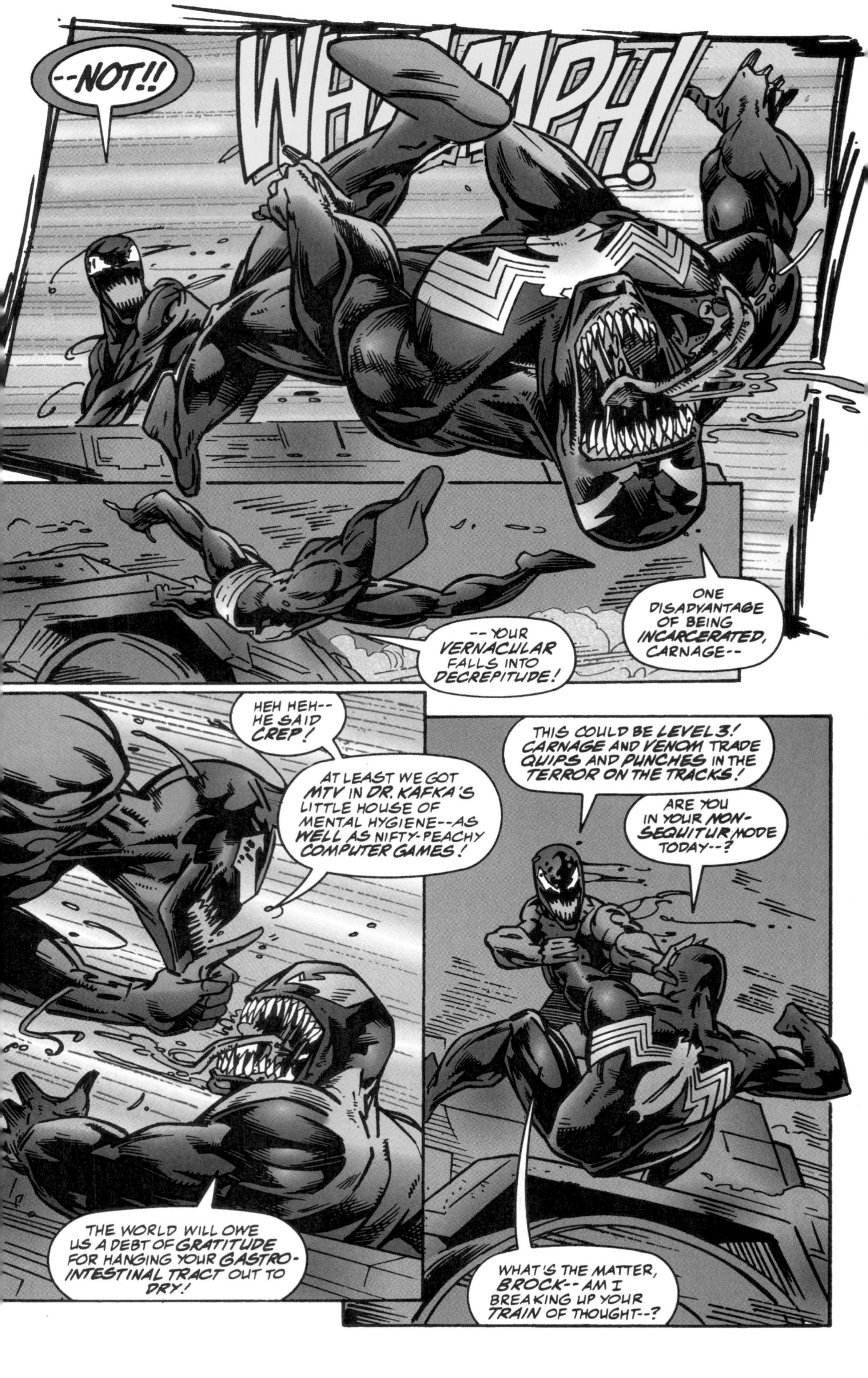
--NOT!!
WHAMMPH!
ONE DISADVANTAGE OF BEING INCARCERATED, CARNAGE--
--YOUR VERNACULAR FALLS INTO DECREPITUDE!
HEH HEH--HE SAID CREP!
AT LEAST WE GOT MTV IN DR. KAFKA'S LITTLE HOUSE OF MENTAL HYGIENE--AS WELL AS NIFTY-PEACHY COMPUTER GAMES!
THE WORLD WILL OWE US A DEBT OF GRATITUDE FOR HANGING YOUR GASTRO-INTESTINAL TRACT OUT TO DRY!
THIS COULD BE LEVEL 3! CARNAGE AND VENOM TRADE QUIPS AND PUNCHES IN THE TERROR ON THE TRACKS!
ARE YOU IN YOUR NON-SEQUITUR MODE TODAY--?
WHAT'S THE MATTER, BROCK--AM I BREAKING UP YOUR TRAIN OF THOUGHT--?

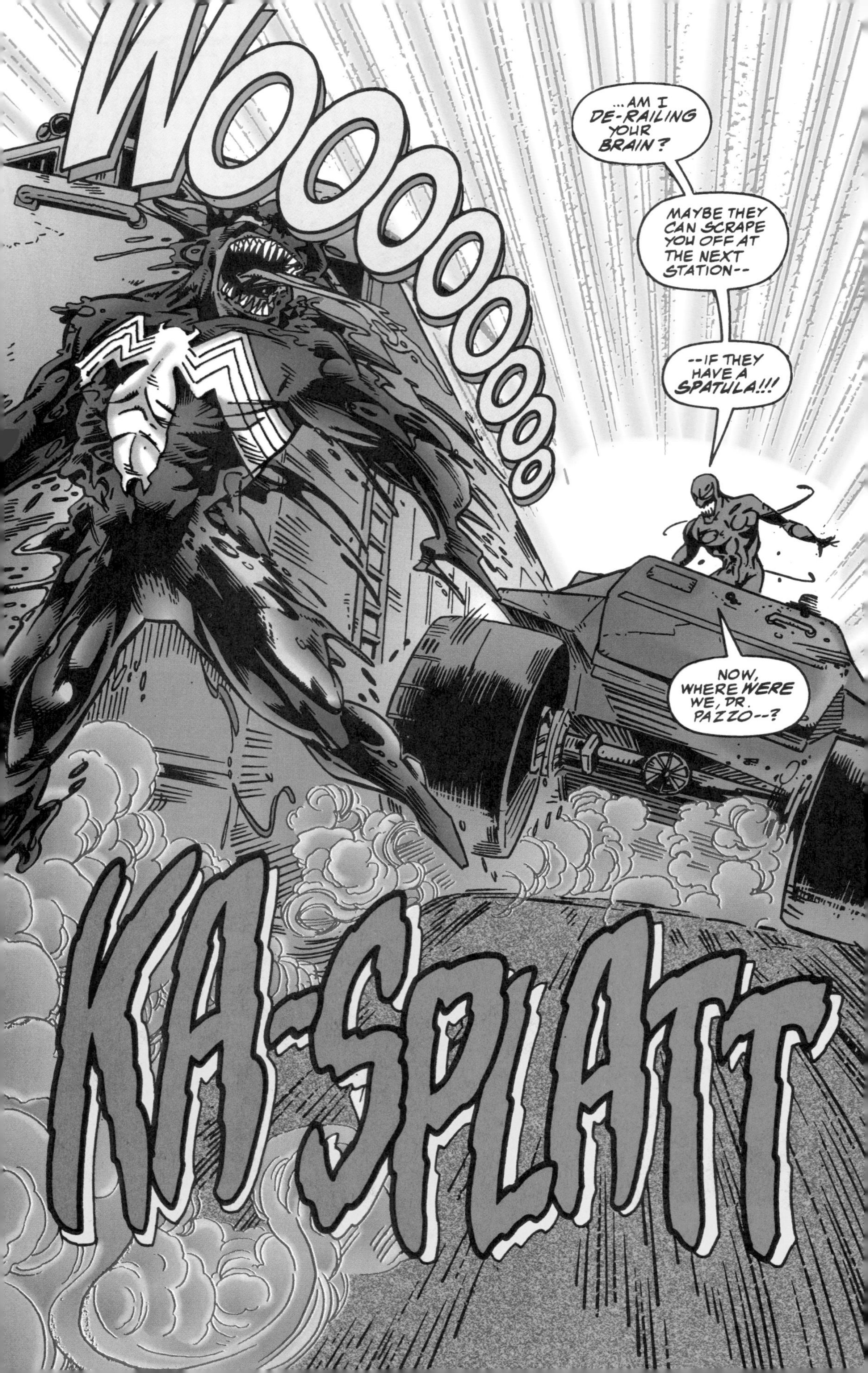
WOOOOOOOOOOOO
...AM I DE-RAILING YOUR BRAIN?
MAYBE THEY CAN SCRAPE YOU OFF AT THE NEXT STATION--
--IF THEY HAVE A SPATULA!!!
NOW, WHERE WERE WE, DR. PAZZO--?
KA-SPLATT

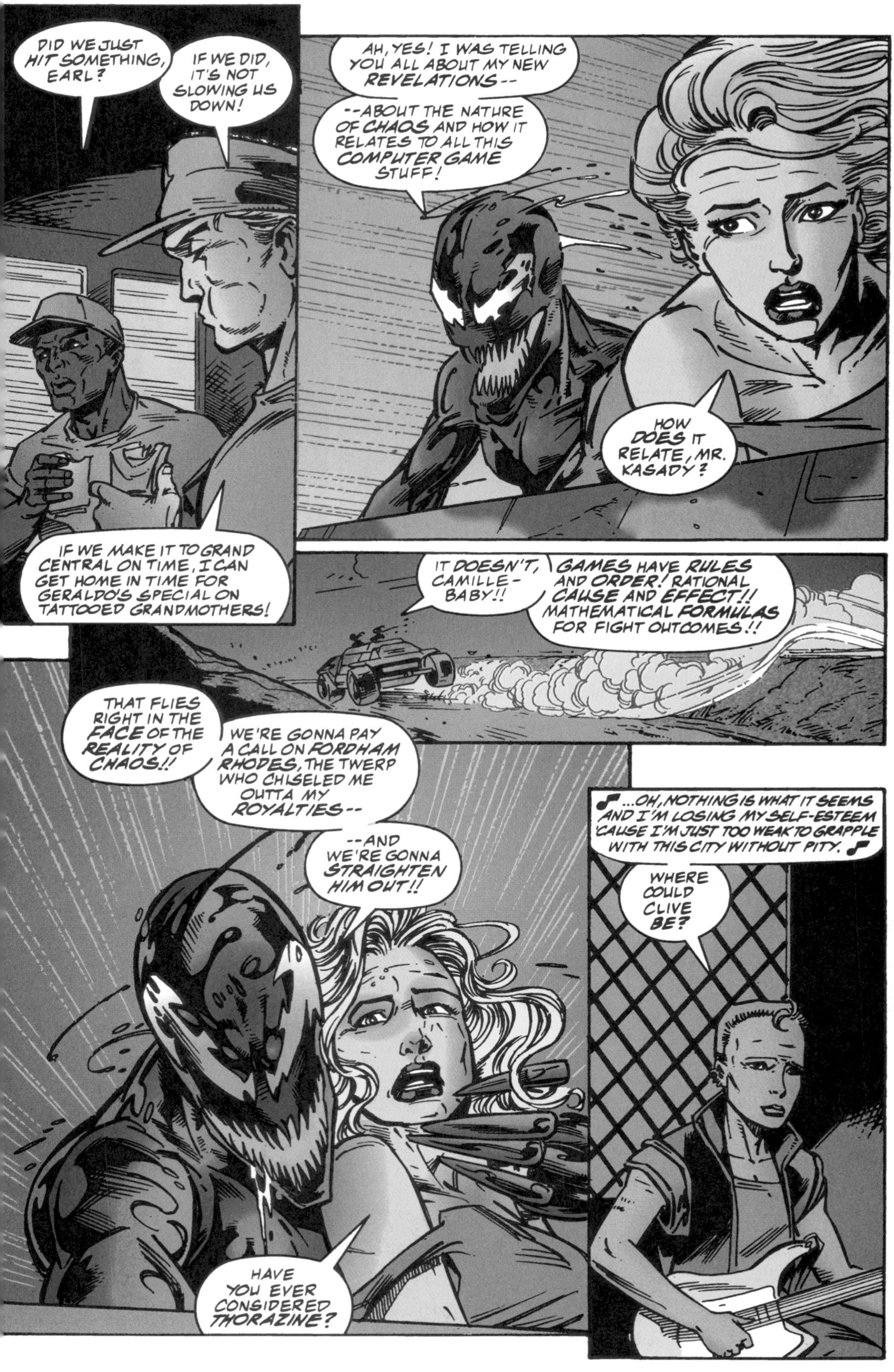
DID WE JUST HIT SOMETHING, EARL?
IF WE DID, IT'S NOT SLOWING US DOWN!
IF WE MAKE IT TO GRAND CENTRAL ON TIME, I CAN GET HOME IN TIME FOR GERALDO'S SPECIAL ON TATTOOED GRANDMOTHERS!
AH, YES! I WAS TELLING YOU ALL ABOUT MY NEW REVELATIONS--
--ABOUT THE NATURE OF CHAOS AND HOW IT RELATES TO ALL THIS COMPUTER GAME STUFF!
HOW DOES IT RELATE, MR. KASADY?
IT DOESN'T, CAMILLE-BABY!!
GAMES HAVE RULES AND ORDER! RATIONAL CAUSE AND EFFECT!! MATHEMATICAL FORMULAS FOR FIGHT OUTCOMES!!
THAT FLIES RIGHT IN THE FACE OF THE REALITY OF CHAOS!!
WE'RE GONNA PAY A CALL ON FORDHAM RHODES, THE TWERP WHO CHISELED ME OUTTA MY ROYALTIES--
--AND WE'RE GONNA STRAIGHTEN HIM OUT!!
HAVE YOU EVER CONSIDERED THORAZINE?
♪ ...OH, NOTHING IS WHAT IT SEEMS AND I'M LOSING MY SELF-ESTEEM 'CAUSE I'M JUST TOO WEAK TO GRAPPLE WITH THIS CITY WITHOUT PITY. ♪
WHERE COULD CLIVE BE?

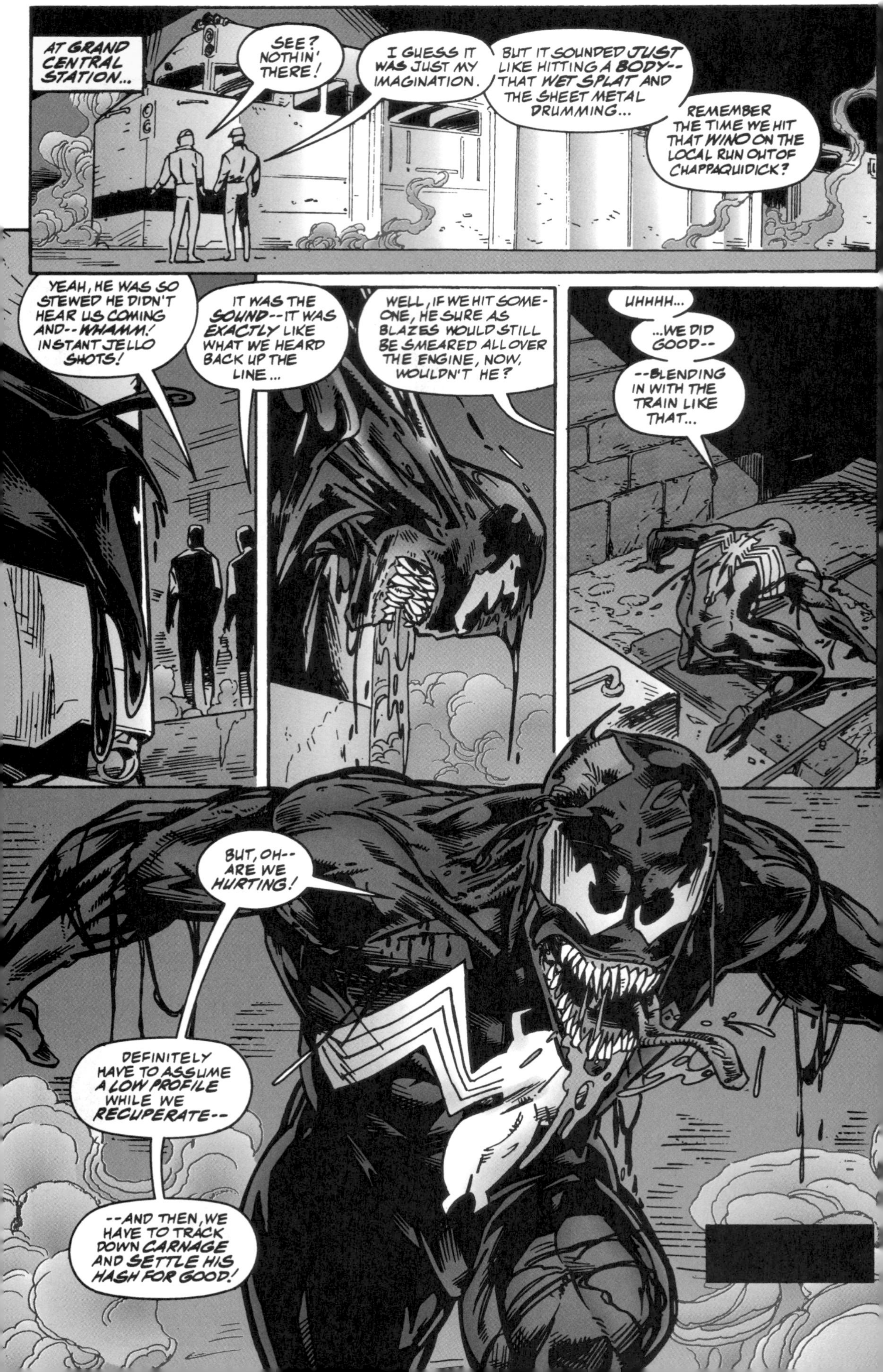
AT GRAND CENTRAL STATION...
SEE? NOTHIN' THERE!
I GUESS IT WAS JUST MY IMAGINATION.
BUT IT SOUNDED JUST LIKE HITTING A BODY-- THAT WET SPLAT AND THE SHEET METAL DRUMMING...
REMEMBER THE TIME WE HIT THAT WINO ON THE LOCAL RUN OUT OF CHAPPAQUIDICK?
YEAH, HE WAS SO STEWED HE DIDN'T HEAR US COMING AND--WHAMM! INSTANT JELLO SHOTS!
IT WAS THE SOUND--IT WAS EXACTLY LIKE WHAT WE HEARD BACK UP THE LINE...
WELL, IF WE HIT SOMEONE, HE SURE AS BLAZES WOULD STILL BE SMEARED ALL OVER THE ENGINE, NOW, WOULDN'T HE?
UHHHH...
...WE DID GOOD--
--BLENDING IN WITH THE TRAIN LIKE THAT...
BUT, OH-- ARE WE HURTING!
DEFINITELY HAVE TO ASSUME A LOW PROFILE WHILE WE RECUPERATE--
--AND THEN, WE HAVE TO TRACK DOWN CARNAGE AND SETTLE HIS HASH FOR GOOD!
[redacted]

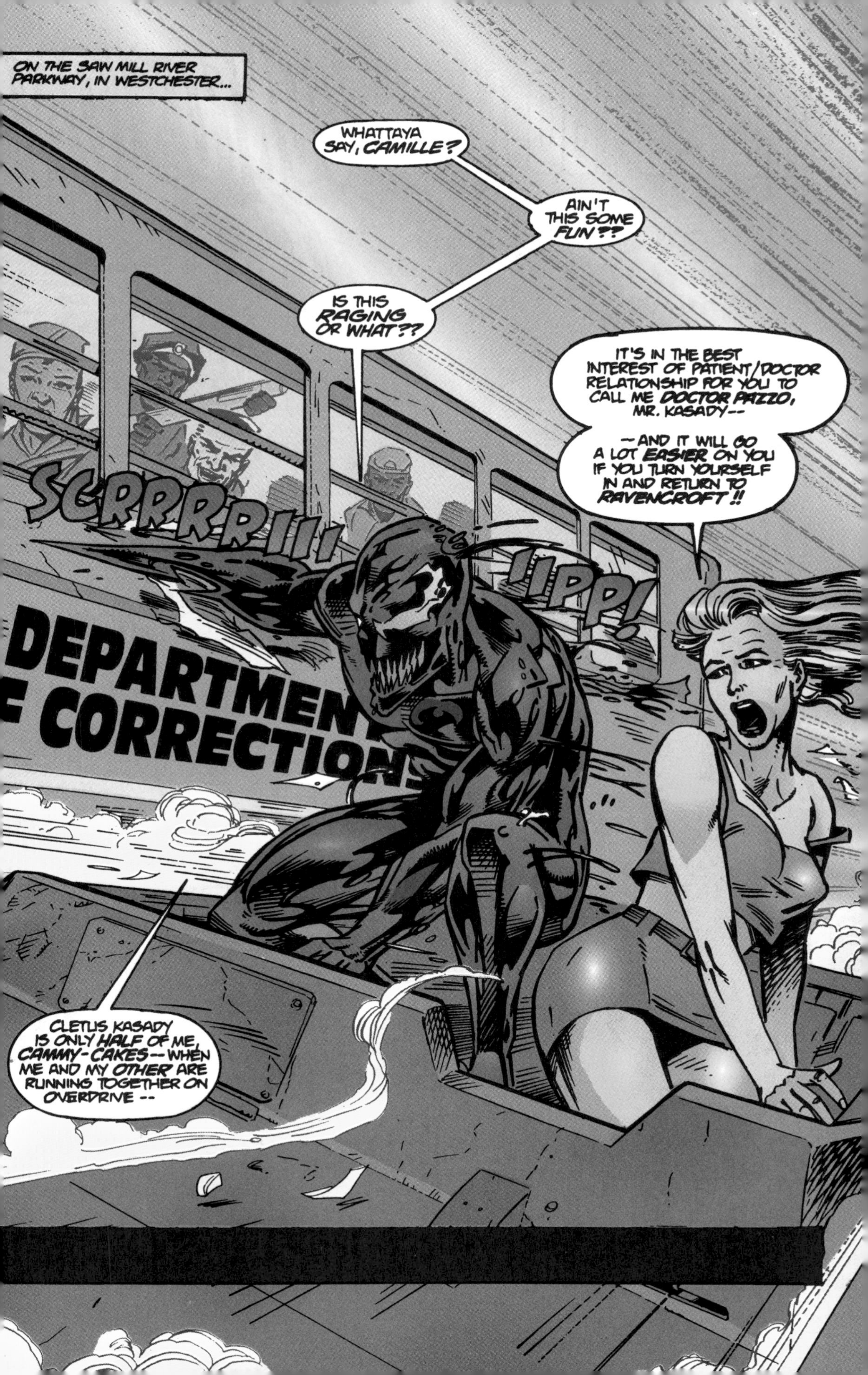
ON THE SAW MILL RIVER PARKWAY, IN WESTCHESTER...
WHATTAYA SAY, CAMILLE?
AIN'T THIS SOME FUN??
IS THIS RAGING OR WHAT??
IT'S IN THE BEST INTEREST OF PATIENT/DOCTOR RELATIONSHIP FOR YOU TO CALL ME DOCTOR PAZZO, MR. KASADY--
--AND IT WILL GO A LOT EASIER ON YOU IF YOU TURN YOURSELF IN AND RETURN TO RAVENCROFT!!
SCRRRRIII
IPP!
DEPARTMENT
CORRECTION
CLETUS KASADY IS ONLY HALF OF ME, CAMMY-CAKES--WHEN ME AND MY OTHER ARE RUNNING TOGETHER ON OVERDRIVE --

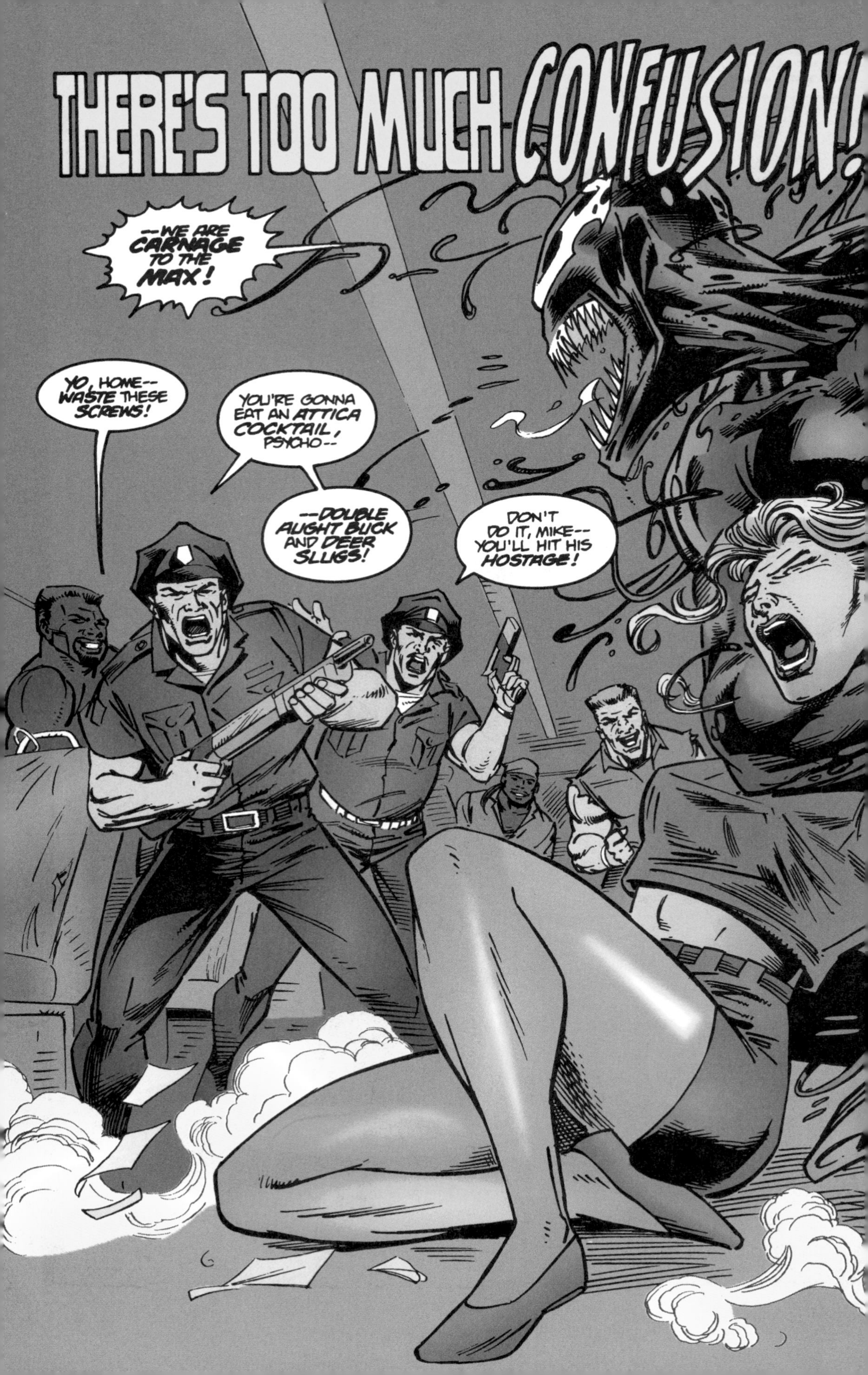
THERE'S TOO MUCH CONFUSION!
--WE ARE CARNAGE TO THE MAX!
YO, HOME-- WASTE THESE SCREWS!
YOU'RE GONNA EAT AN ATTICA COCKTAIL, PSYCHO--
--DOUBLE AUGHT BUCK AND DEER SLUGS!
DON'T DO IT, MIKE-- YOU'LL HIT HIS HOSTAGE!

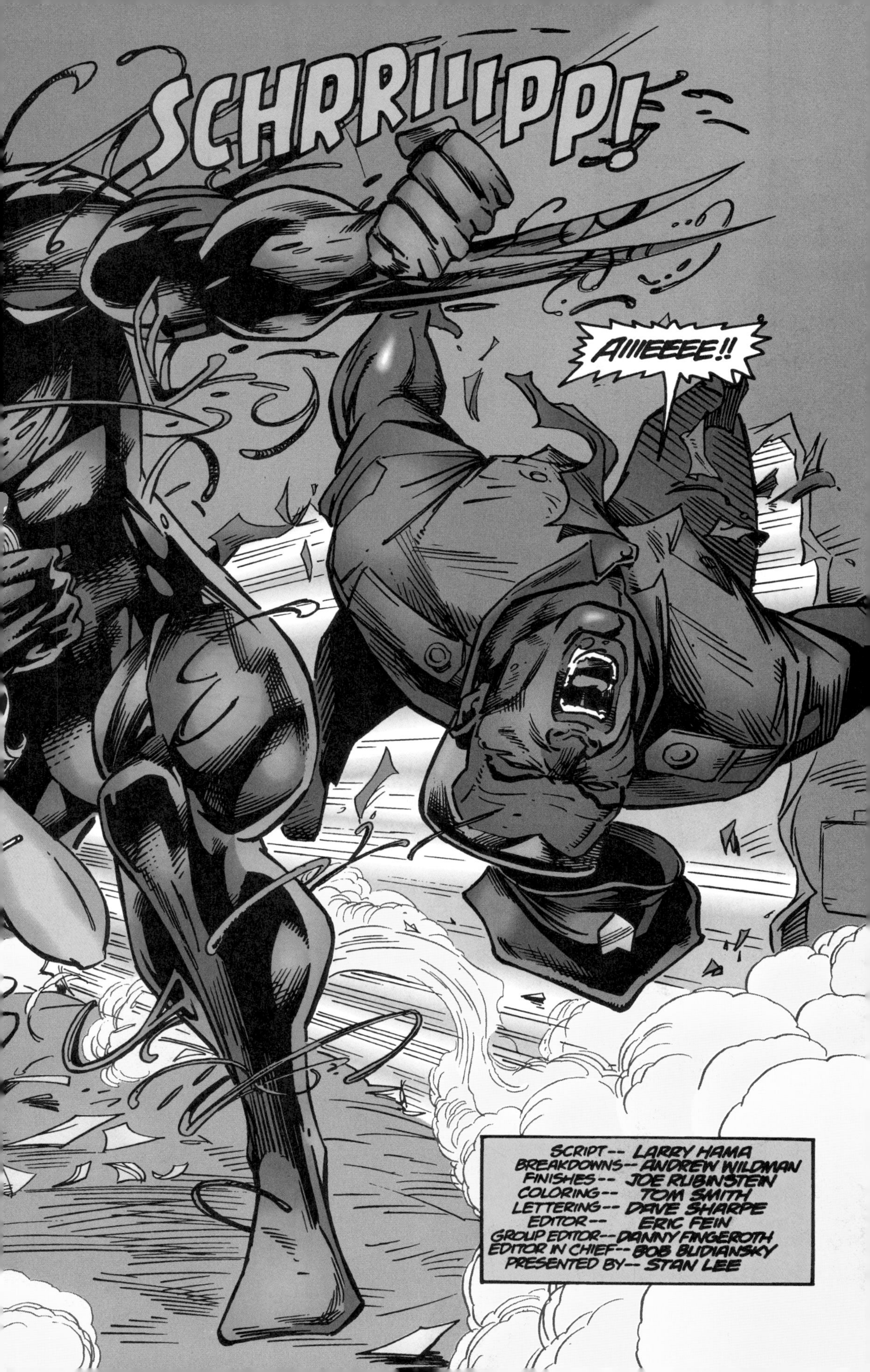
SCHRI'IPP!
AIIIEEEEE!!
SCRIPT-- LARRY HAMA
BREAKDOWNS-- ANDREW WILDMAN
FINISHES-- JOE RUBINSTEIN
COLORING-- TOM SMITH
LETTERING-- DAVE SHARPE
EDITOR-- ERIC FEIN
GROUP EDITOR-- DANNY FINGEROTH
EDITOR IN CHIEF-- BOB BUDIANSKY
PRESENTED BY-- STAN LEE

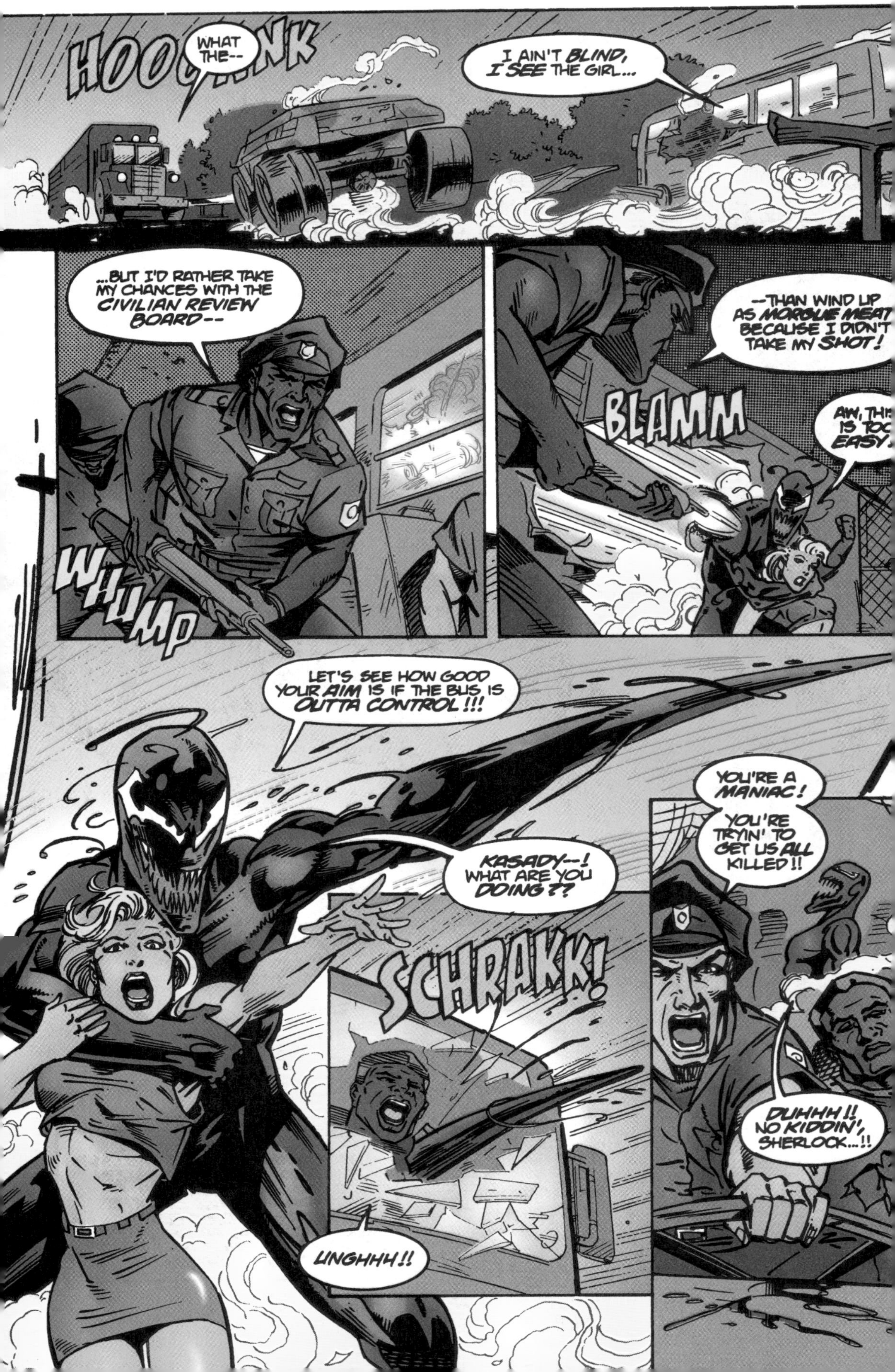
HOOONK
WHAT THE--
I AIN'T BLIND, I SEE THE GIRL...
...BUT I'D RATHER TAKE MY CHANCES WITH THE CIVILIAN REVIEW BOARD--
WHUMP
--THAN WIND UP AS MORGUE MEAT BECAUSE I DIDN'T TAKE MY SHOT!
BLAMM
AW, THIS IS TOO EASY!
LET'S SEE HOW GOOD YOUR AIM IS IF THE BUS IS OUTTA CONTROL!!!
KASADY--! WHAT ARE YOU DOING??
SCHRAKK!
UNGHHH!!
YOU'RE A MANIAC!
YOU'RE TRYIN' TO GET US ALL KILLED!!
DUHHH!! NO KIDDIN', SHERLOCK...!!

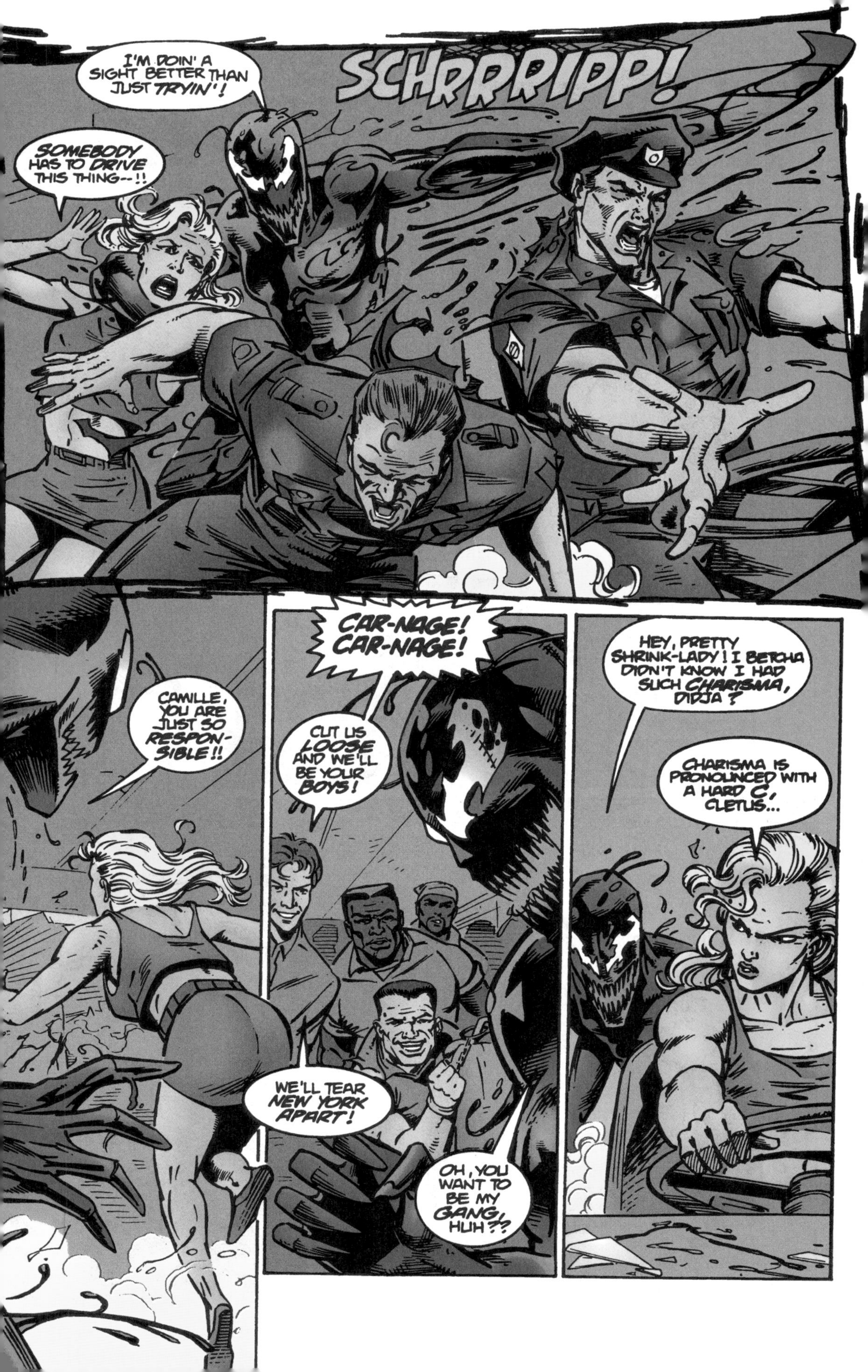
I'M DOIN' A SIGHT BETTER THAN JUST TRYIN'!
SCHRRRIPP!
SOMEBODY HAS TO DRIVE THIS THING--!!
CAMILLE, YOU ARE JUST SO RESPON-SIBLE!!
CAR-NAGE! CAR-NAGE!
CUT US LOOSE AND WE'LL BE YOUR BOYS!
WE'LL TEAR NEW YORK APART!
OH, YOU WANT TO BE MY GANG, HUH??
HEY, PRETTY SHRINK-LADY! I BETCHA DIDN'T KNOW I HAD SUCH CHARISMA, DIDJA?
CHARISMA IS PRONOUNCED WITH A HARD C, CLETUS...

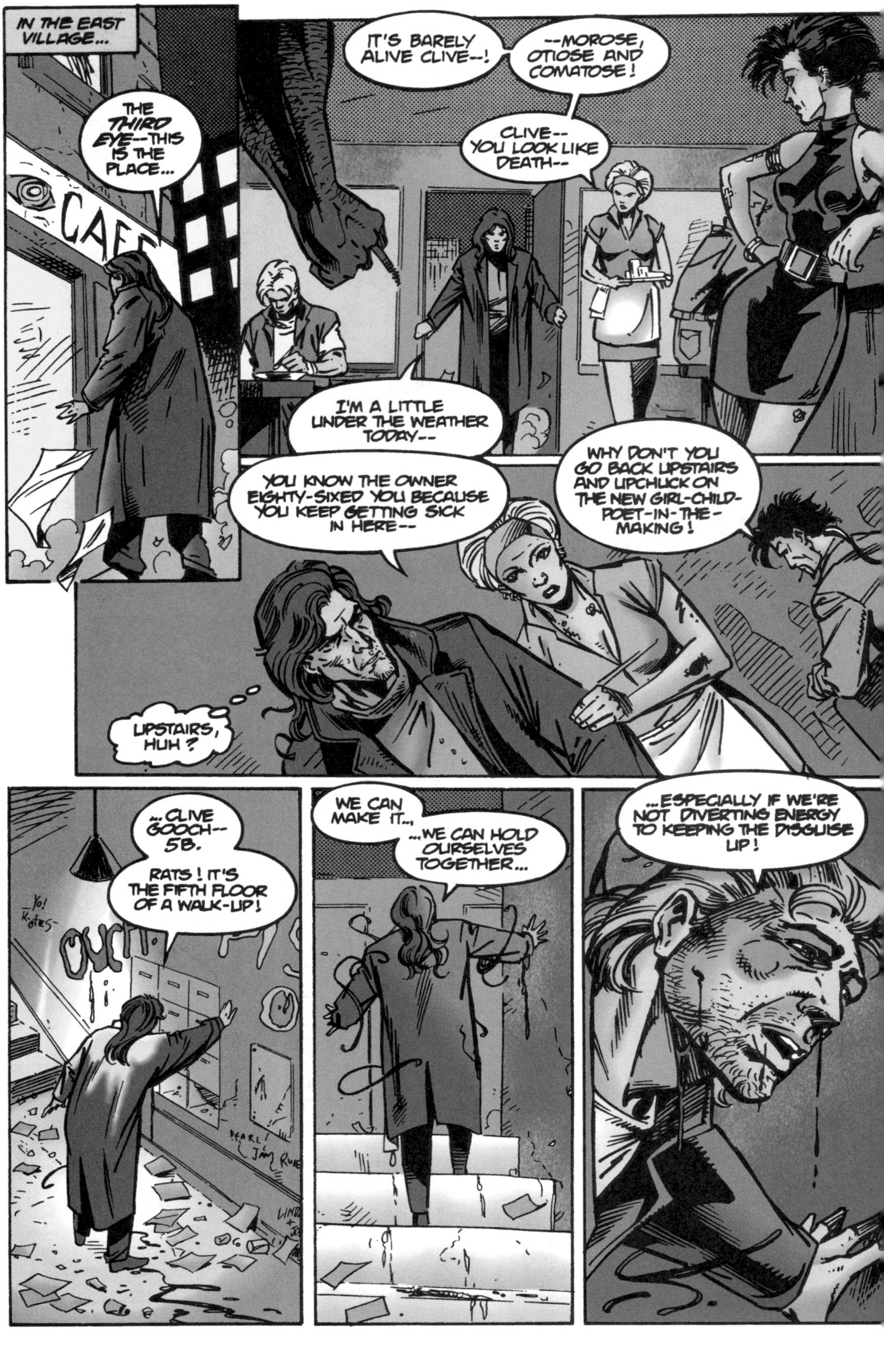
IN THE EAST VILLAGE...
THE THIRD EYE--THIS IS THE PLACE...
IT'S BARELY ALIVE CLIVE--!
--MOROSE, OTIOSE AND COMATOSE!
CLIVE-- YOU LOOK LIKE DEATH--
I'M A LITTLE UNDER THE WEATHER TODAY--
YOU KNOW THE OWNER EIGHTY-SIXED YOU BECAUSE YOU KEEP GETTING SICK IN HERE--
WHY DON'T YOU GO BACK UPSTAIRS AND UPCHUCK ON THE NEW GIRL-CHILD-POET-IN-THE-MAKING!
UPSTAIRS, HUH?
...CLIVE GOOCH-- 5B.
RATS! IT'S THE FIFTH FLOOR OF A WALK-UP!
WE CAN MAKE IT...
...WE CAN HOLD OURSELVES TOGETHER...
...ESPECIALLY IF WE'RE NOT DIVERTING ENERGY TO KEEPING THE DISGUISE UP!

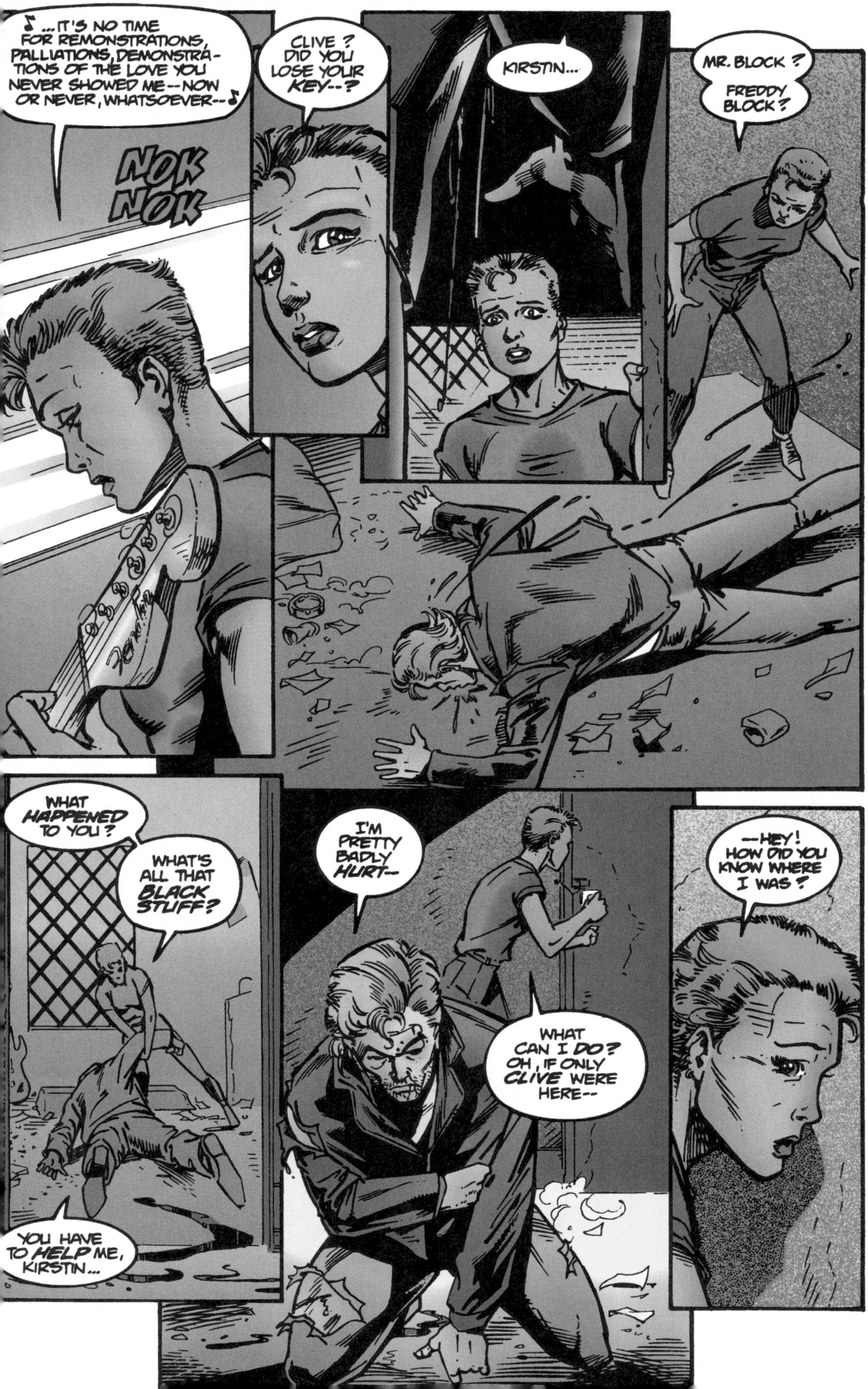
♪ ...IT'S NO TIME FOR REMONSTRATIONS, PALLIATIONS, DEMONSTRATIONS OF THE LOVE YOU NEVER SHOWED ME--NOW OR NEVER, WHATSOEVER--♪
NOK NOK
CLIVE? DID YOU LOSE YOUR KEY--?
KIRSTIN...
MR. BLOCK?
FREDDY BLOCK?
WHAT HAPPENED TO YOU?
WHAT'S ALL THAT BLACK STUFF?
YOU HAVE TO HELP ME, KIRSTIN...
I'M PRETTY BADLY HURT--
WHAT CAN I DO? OH, IF ONLY CLIVE WERE HERE--
--HEY! HOW DID YOU KNOW WHERE I WAS?

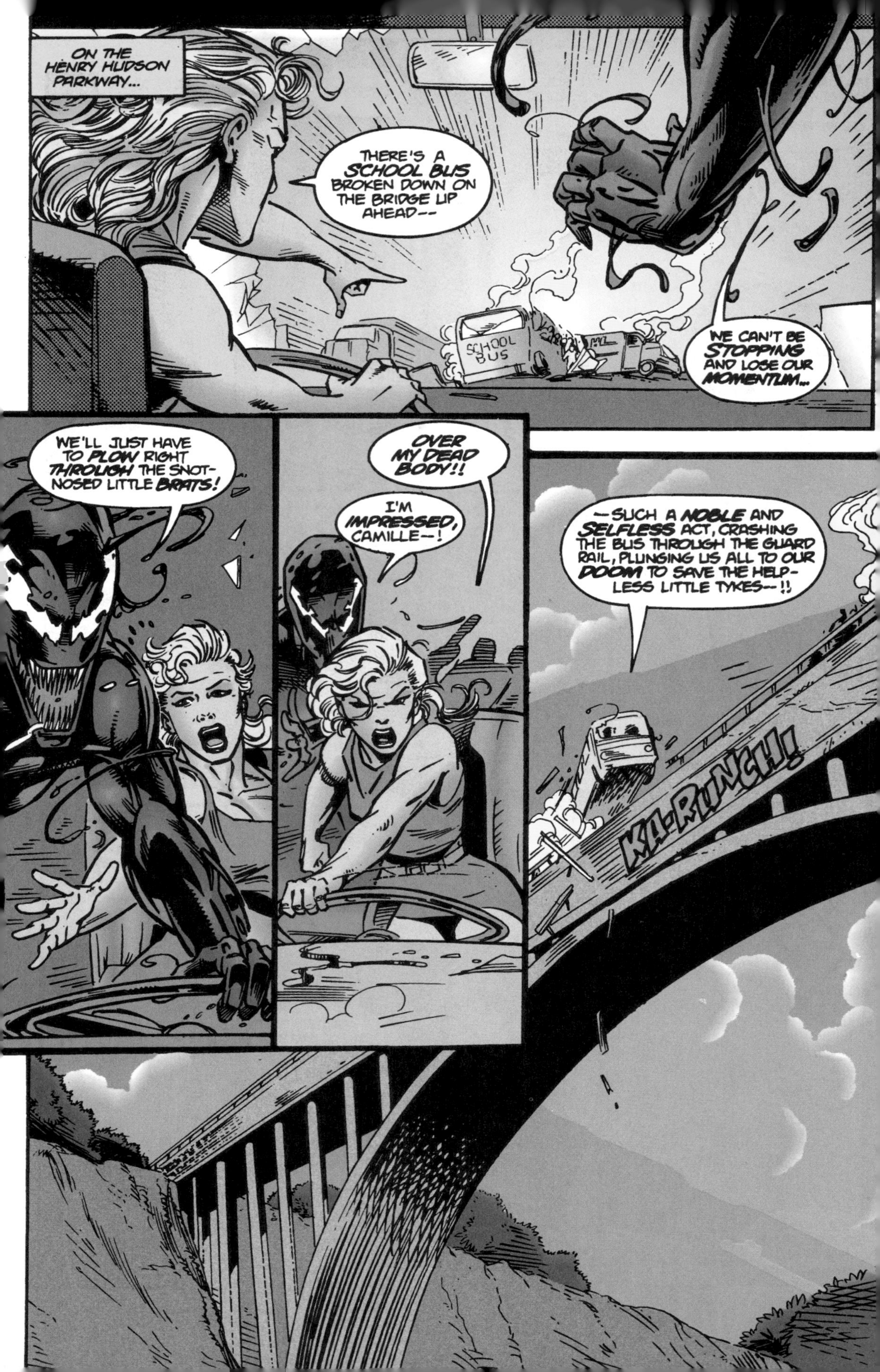
ON THE HENRY HUDSON PARKWAY...
THERE'S A SCHOOL BUS BROKEN DOWN ON THE BRIDGE UP AHEAD--
SCHOOL BUS
WE CAN'T BE STOPPING AND LOSE OUR MOMENTUM...
WE'LL JUST HAVE TO PLOW RIGHT THROUGH THE SNOT-NOSED LITTLE BRATS!
OVER MY DEAD BODY!!
I'M IMPRESSED, CAMILLE--!
--SUCH A NOBLE AND SELFLESS ACT, CRASHING THE BUS THROUGH THE GUARD RAIL, PLUNGING US ALL TO OUR DOOM TO SAVE THE HELP-LESS LITTLE TYKES--!!
KA-RUNCH!

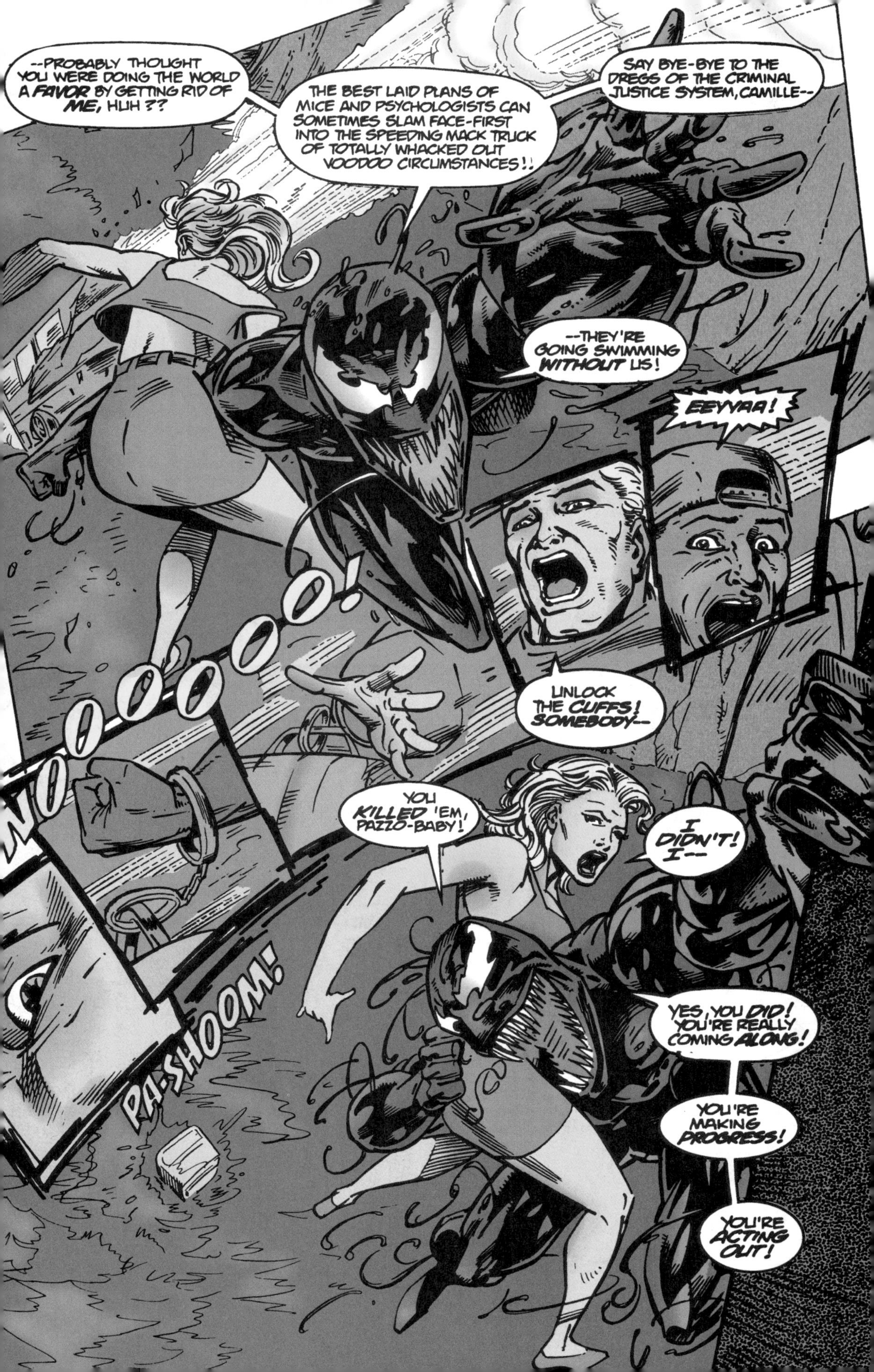
--PROBABLY THOUGHT YOU WERE DOING THE WORLD A *FAVOR* BY GETTING RID OF *ME*, HUH ??
THE BEST LAID PLANS OF MICE AND PSYCHOLOGISTS CAN SOMETIMES SLAM FACE-FIRST INTO THE SPEEDING MACK TRUCK OF TOTALLY WHACKED OUT VOODOO CIRCUMSTANCES!!
SAY BYE-BYE TO THE DREGS OF THE CRIMINAL JUSTICE SYSTEM, CAMILLE--
--THEY'RE GOING SWIMMING *WITHOUT* US!
EEYYAA!
NOOOOOOOO!
UNLOCK THE *CUFFS!* *SOMEBODY*--
YOU *KILLED* 'EM, PAZZO-BABY!
I *DIDN'T!* I--
PA-SHOOM!
YES, YOU *DID!* YOU'RE REALLY COMING *ALONG!*
YOU'RE MAKING *PROGRESS!*
YOU'RE *ACTING OUT!*

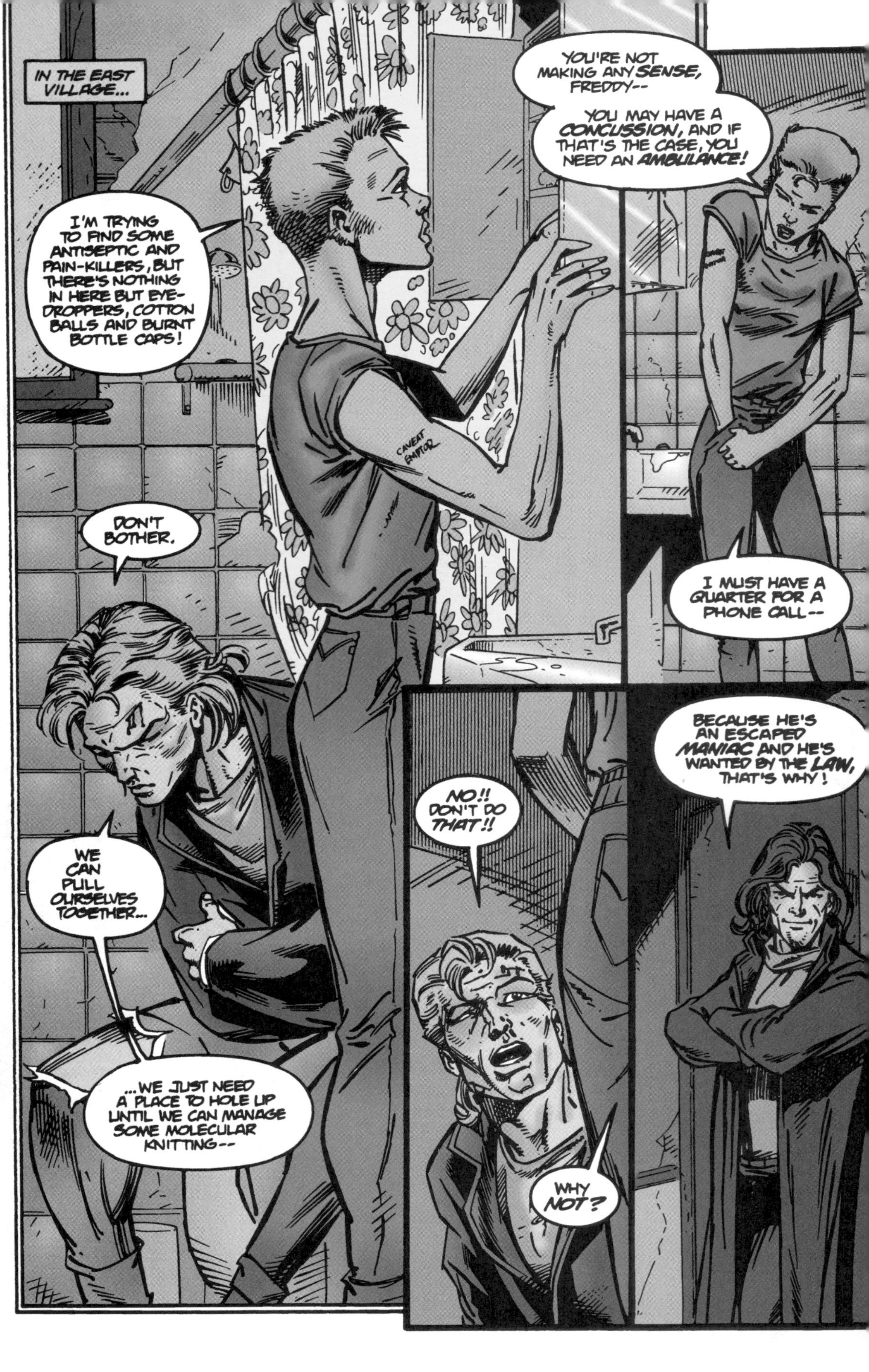
IN THE EAST VILLAGE...
I'M TRYING TO FIND SOME ANTISEPTIC AND PAIN-KILLERS, BUT THERE'S NOTHING IN HERE BUT EYE-DROPPERS, COTTON BALLS AND BURNT BOTTLE CAPS!
CAVEAT EMPTOR
DON'T BOTHER.
WE CAN PULL OURSELVES TOGETHER...
...WE JUST NEED A PLACE TO HOLE UP UNTIL WE CAN MANAGE SOME MOLECULAR KNITTING--
YOU'RE NOT MAKING ANY SENSE, FREDDY--
YOU MAY HAVE A CONCUSSION, AND IF THAT'S THE CASE, YOU NEED AN AMBULANCE!
I MUST HAVE A QUARTER FOR A PHONE CALL--
NO!! DON'T DO THAT!!
WHY NOT?
BECAUSE HE'S AN ESCAPED MANIAC AND HE'S WANTED BY THE LAW, THAT'S WHY!

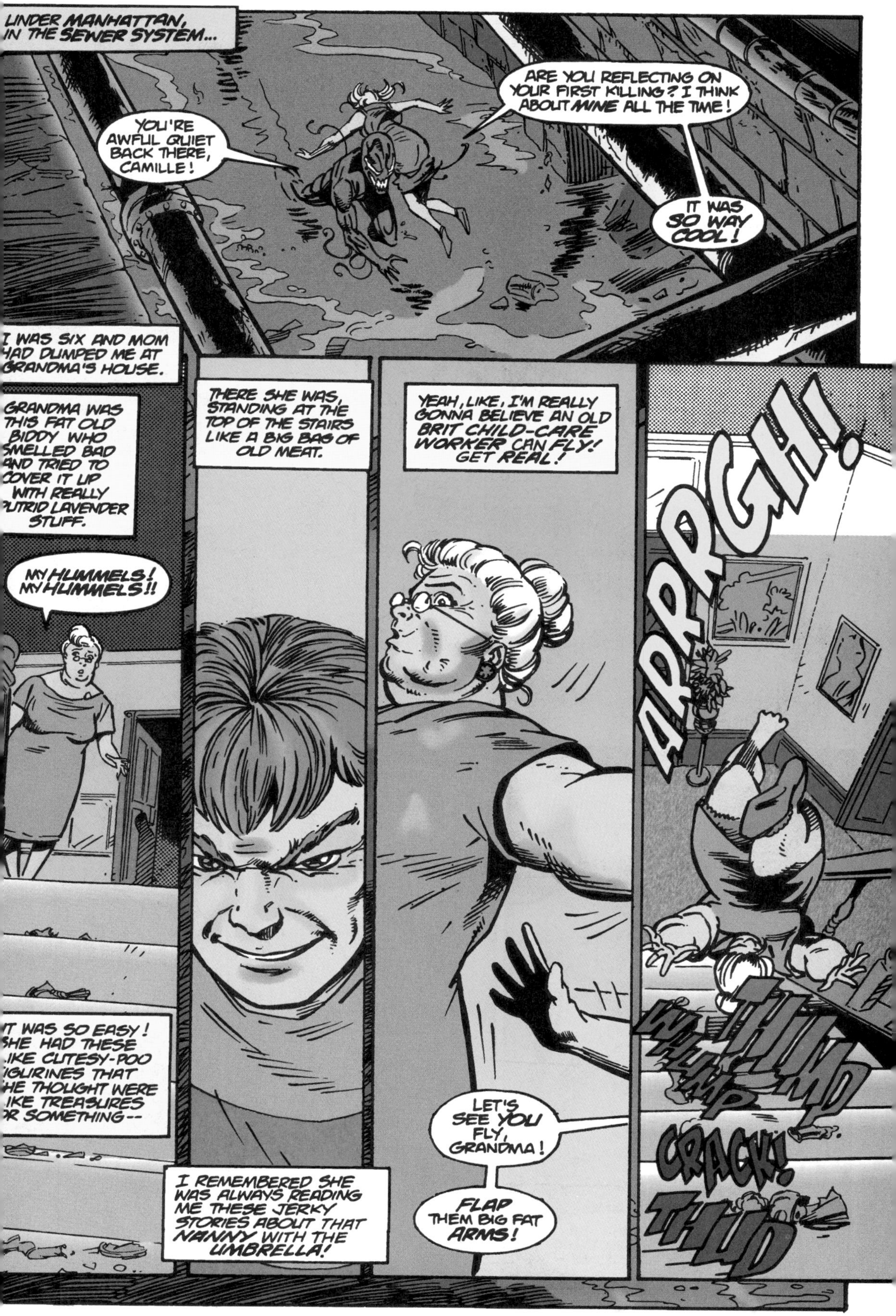
UNDER MANHATTAN, IN THE SEWER SYSTEM...
YOU'RE AWFUL QUIET BACK THERE, CAMILLE!
ARE YOU REFLECTING ON YOUR FIRST KILLING? I THINK ABOUT MINE ALL THE TIME!
IT WAS SO WAY COOL!
I WAS SIX AND MOM HAD DUMPED ME AT GRANDMA'S HOUSE.
GRANDMA WAS THIS FAT OLD BIDDY WHO SMELLED BAD AND TRIED TO COVER IT UP WITH REALLY PUTRID LAVENDER STUFF.
MY HUMMELS! MY HUMMELS!!
IT WAS SO EASY! SHE HAD THESE LIKE CUTESY-POO FIGURINES THAT SHE THOUGHT WERE LIKE TREASURES OR SOMETHING--
THERE SHE WAS, STANDING AT THE TOP OF THE STAIRS LIKE A BIG BAG OF OLD MEAT.
I REMEMBERED SHE WAS ALWAYS READING ME THESE JERKY STORIES ABOUT THAT NANNY WITH THE UMBRELLA!
YEAH, LIKE, I'M REALLY GONNA BELIEVE AN OLD BRIT CHILD-CARE WORKER CAN FLY! GET REAL!
LET'S SEE YOU FLY, GRANDMA!
FLAP THEM BIG FAT ARMS!
ARRGH!!
THUMP
WHUMP
CRACK!
THUD

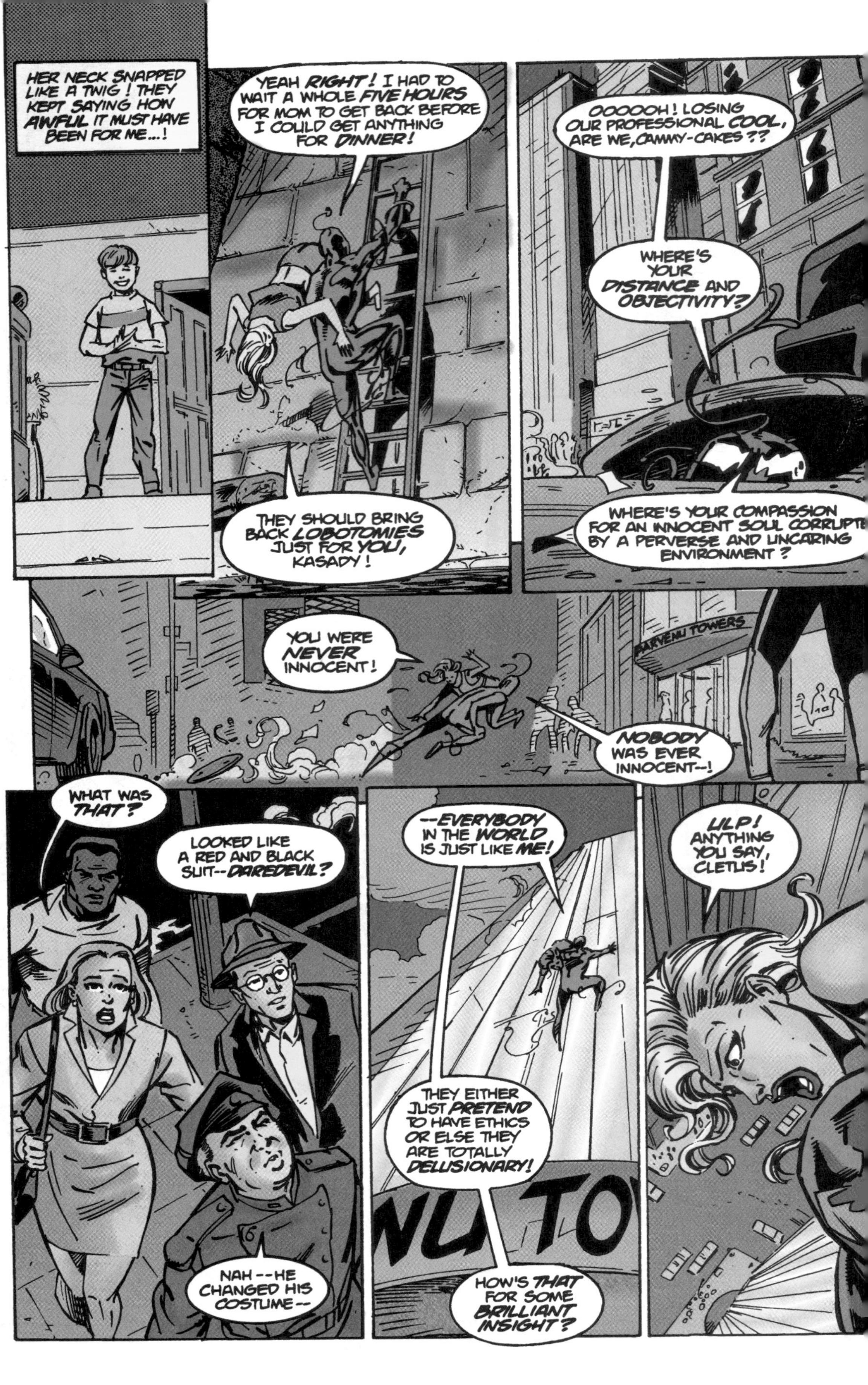
HER NECK SNAPPED LIKE A TWIG! THEY KEPT SAYING HOW AWFUL IT MUST HAVE BEEN FOR ME...!
YEAH RIGHT! I HAD TO WAIT A WHOLE FIVE HOURS FOR MOM TO GET BACK BEFORE I COULD GET ANYTHING FOR DINNER!
THEY SHOULD BRING BACK LOBOTOMIES JUST FOR YOU, KASADY!
OOOOOH! LOSING OUR PROFESSIONAL COOL, ARE WE, CAMMY-CAKES??
WHERE'S YOUR DISTANCE AND OBJECTIVITY?
WHERE'S YOUR COMPASSION FOR AN INNOCENT SOUL CORRUPTE BY A PERVERSE AND UNCARING ENVIRONMENT?
YOU WERE NEVER INNOCENT!
PARVENU TOWERS
NOBODY WAS EVER INNOCENT--!
WHAT WAS THAT?
LOOKED LIKE A RED AND BLACK SUIT--DAREDEVIL?
NAH--HE CHANGED HIS COSTUME--
--EVERYBODY IN THE WORLD IS JUST LIKE ME!
THEY EITHER JUST PRETEND TO HAVE ETHICS OR ELSE THEY ARE TOTALLY DELUSIONARY!
NU TO
HOW'S THAT FOR SOME BRILLIANT INSIGHT?
ULP! ANYTHING YOU SAY, CLETUS!

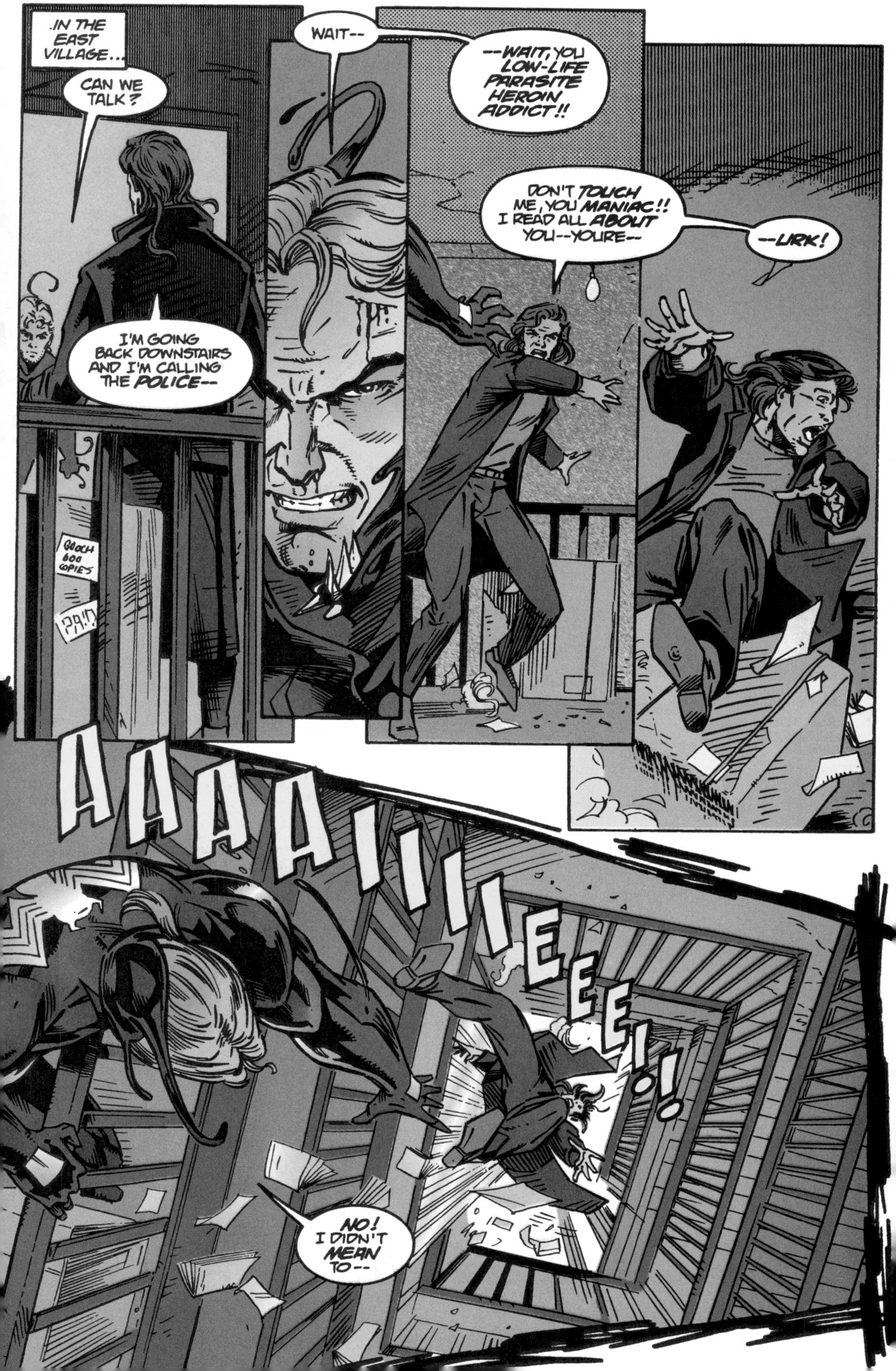

.IN THE EAST VILLAGE...
CAN WE TALK?
I'M GOING BACK DOWNSTAIRS AND I'M CALLING THE POLICE--
QOOCH 600 COPIES
PAID
WAIT--
--WAIT, YOU LOW-LIFE PARASITE HEROIN ADDICT!!
DON'T TOUCH ME, YOU MANIAC!! I READ ALL ABOUT YOU--YOURE--
--URK!
AAAAIIIIEEEE!!!
NO! I DIDN'T MEAN TO--

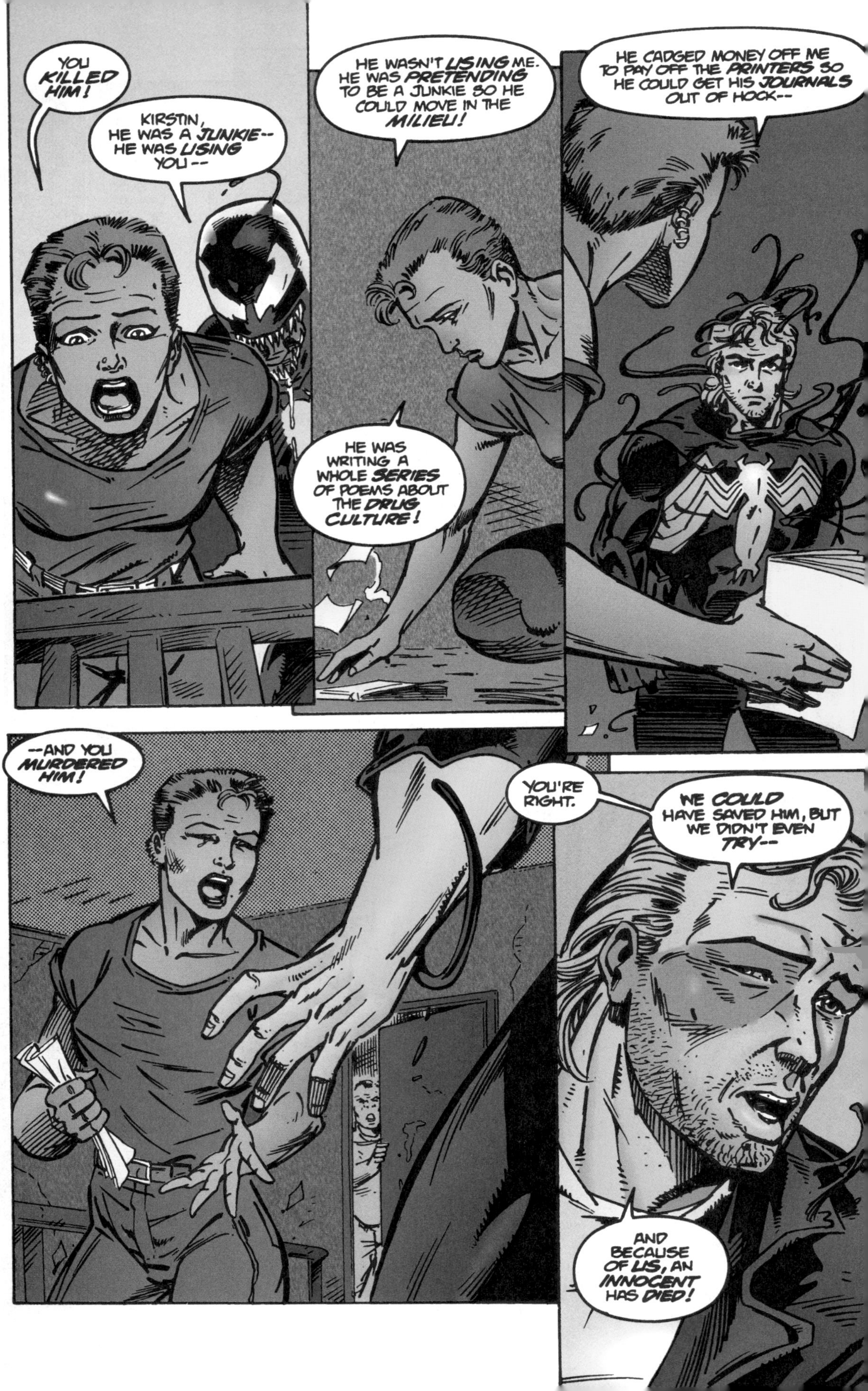
YOU KILLED HIM!
KIRSTIN, HE WAS A JUNKIE-- HE WAS USING YOU--
HE WASN'T USING ME. HE WAS PRETENDING TO BE A JUNKIE SO HE COULD MOVE IN THE MILIEU!
HE WAS WRITING A WHOLE SERIES OF POEMS ABOUT THE DRUG CULTURE!
HE CADGED MONEY OFF ME TO PAY OFF THE PRINTERS SO HE COULD GET HIS JOURNALS OUT OF HOCK--
--AND YOU MURDERED HIM!
YOU'RE RIGHT.
WE COULD HAVE SAVED HIM, BUT WE DIDN'T EVEN TRY--
AND BECAUSE OF US, AN INNOCENT HAS DIED!

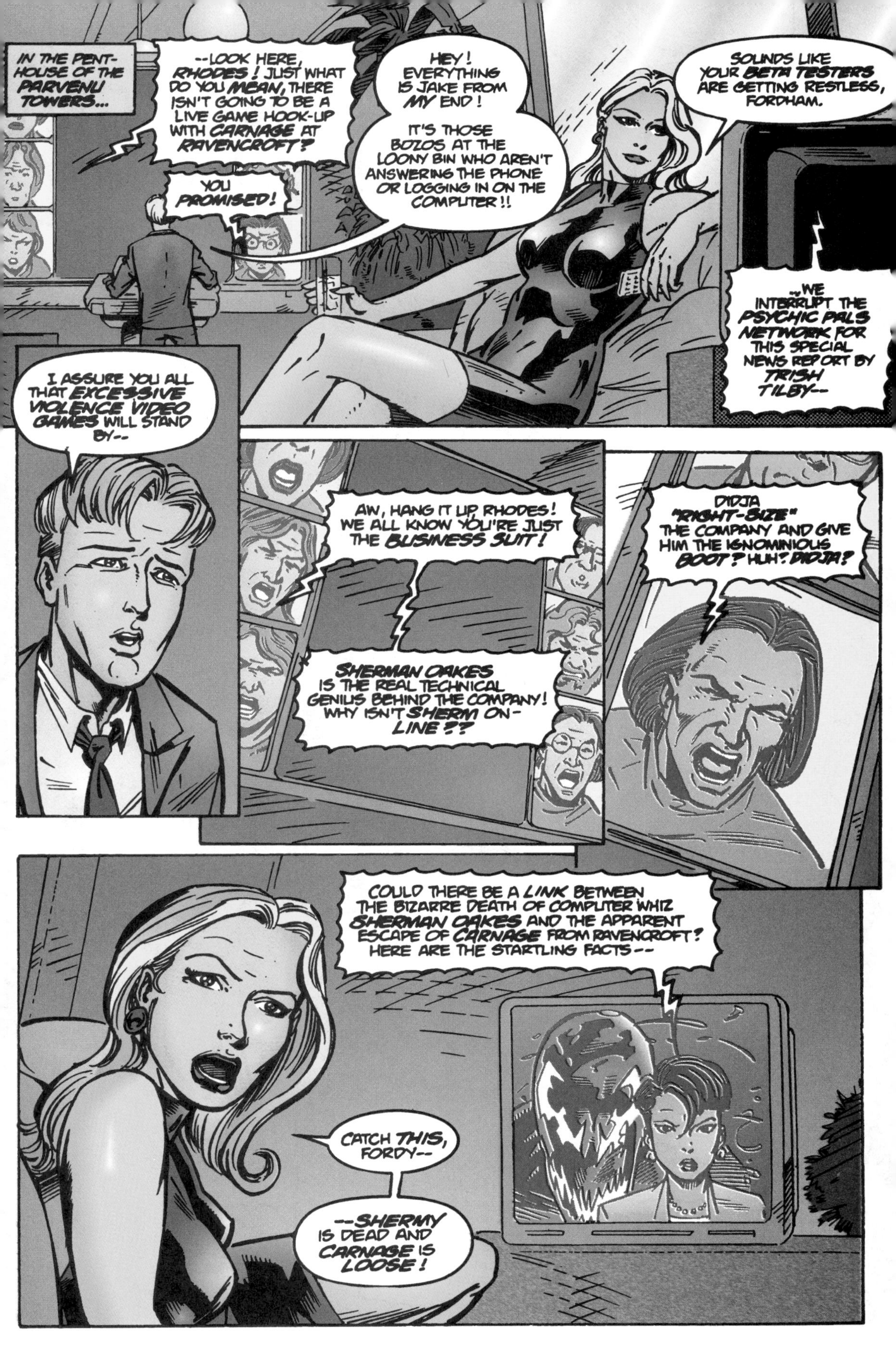
IN THE PENT-HOUSE OF THE PARVENU TOWERS...
--LOOK HERE, RHODES! JUST WHAT DO YOU MEAN, THERE ISN'T GOING TO BE A LIVE GAME HOOK-UP WITH CARNAGE AT RAVENCROFT?
YOU PROMISED!
HEY! EVERYTHING IS JAKE FROM MY END!
IT'S THOSE BOZOS AT THE LOONY BIN WHO AREN'T ANSWERING THE PHONE OR LOGGING IN ON THE COMPUTER!!
SOUNDS LIKE YOUR BETA TESTERS ARE GETTING RESTLESS, FORDHAM.
...WE INTERRUPT THE PSYCHIC PALS NETWORK FOR THIS SPECIAL NEWS REPORT BY TRISH TILBY--
I ASSURE YOU ALL THAT EXCESSIVE VIOLENCE VIDEO GAMES WILL STAND BY--
AW, HANG IT UP RHODES! WE ALL KNOW YOU'RE JUST THE BUSINESS SUIT!
SHERMAN OAKES IS THE REAL TECHNICAL GENIUS BEHIND THE COMPANY! WHY ISN'T SHERM ON-LINE??
DIDJA "RIGHT-SIZE" THE COMPANY AND GIVE HIM THE IGNOMINIOUS BOOT? HUH? DIDJA?
COULD THERE BE A LINK BETWEEN THE BIZARRE DEATH OF COMPUTER WHIZ SHERMAN OAKES AND THE APPARENT ESCAPE OF CARNAGE FROM RAVENCROFT? HERE ARE THE STARTLING FACTS--
CATCH THIS, FORDY--
--SHERMY IS DEAD AND CARNAGE IS LOOSE!

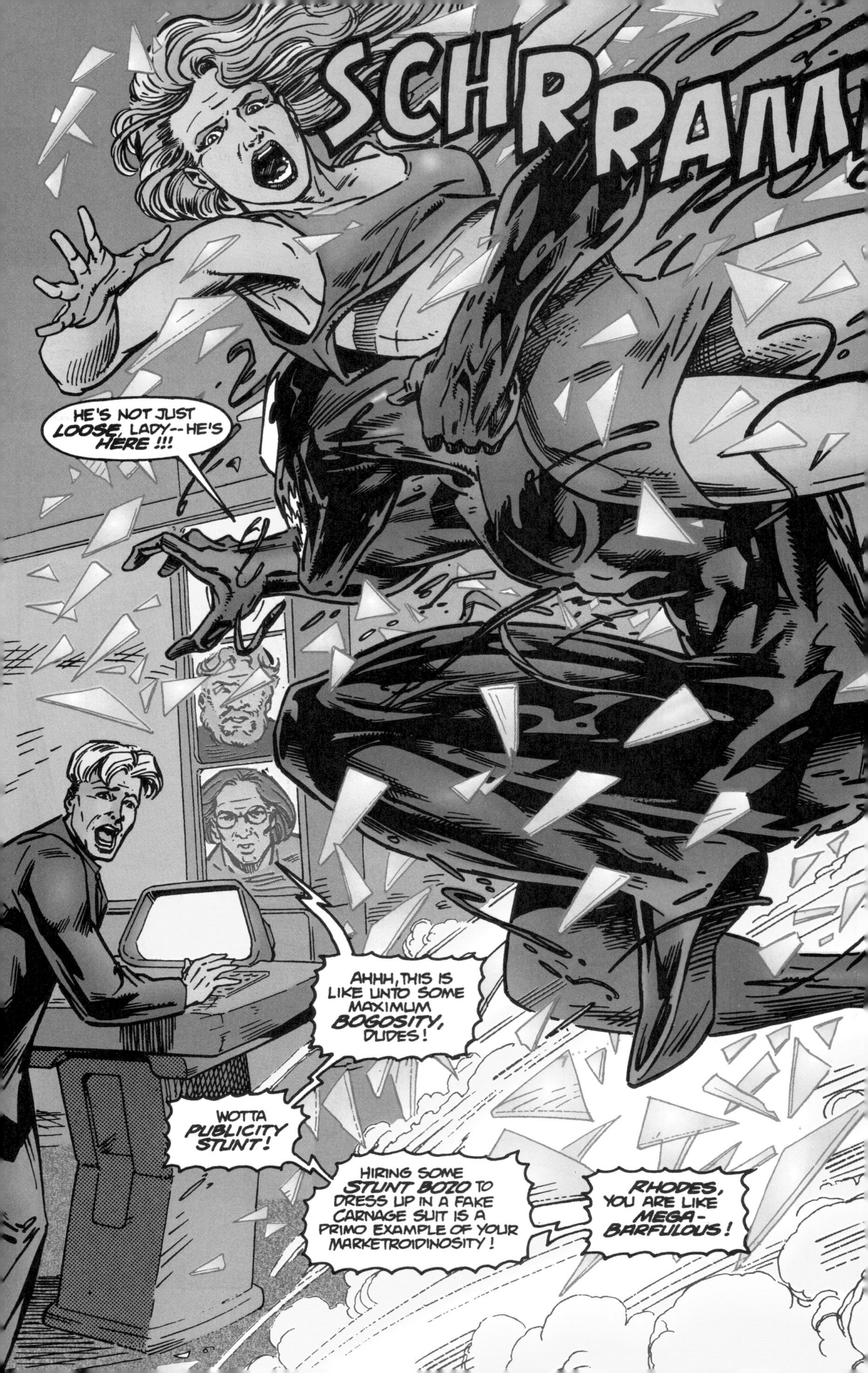
SCHRRAM!
HE'S NOT JUST LOOSE, LADY--HE'S HERE !!!
AHHH, THIS IS LIKE UNTO SOME MAXIMUM BOGOSITY, DUDES!
WOTTA PUBLICITY STUNT!
HIRING SOME STUNT BOZO TO DRESS UP IN A FAKE CARNAGE SUIT IS A PRIMO EXAMPLE OF YOUR MARKETROIDINOSITY!
RHODES, YOU ARE LIKE MEGA-BARFULOUS!

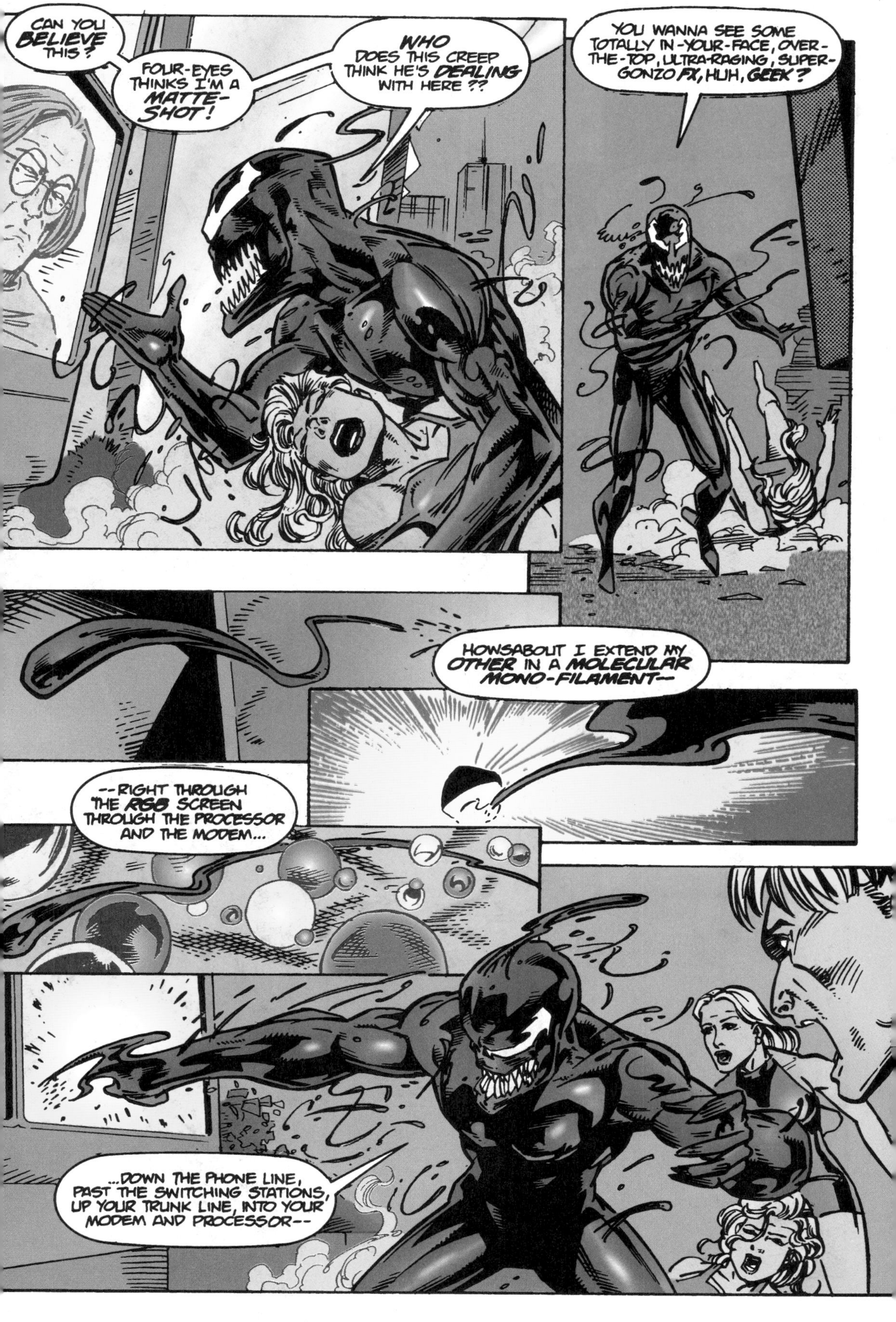
CAN YOU BELIEVE THIS?
FOUR-EYES THINKS I'M A MATTE-SHOT!
WHO DOES THIS CREEP THINK HE'S DEALING WITH HERE??
YOU WANNA SEE SOME TOTALLY IN-YOUR-FACE, OVER-THE-TOP, ULTRA-RAGING, SUPER-GONZO FX, HUH, GEEK?
HOWSABOUT I EXTEND MY OTHER IN A MOLECULAR MONO-FILAMENT--
--RIGHT THROUGH THE RGB SCREEN THROUGH THE PROCESSOR AND THE MODEM...
...DOWN THE PHONE LINE, PAST THE SWITCHING STATIONS, UP YOUR TRUNK LINE, INTO YOUR MODEM AND PROCESSOR--

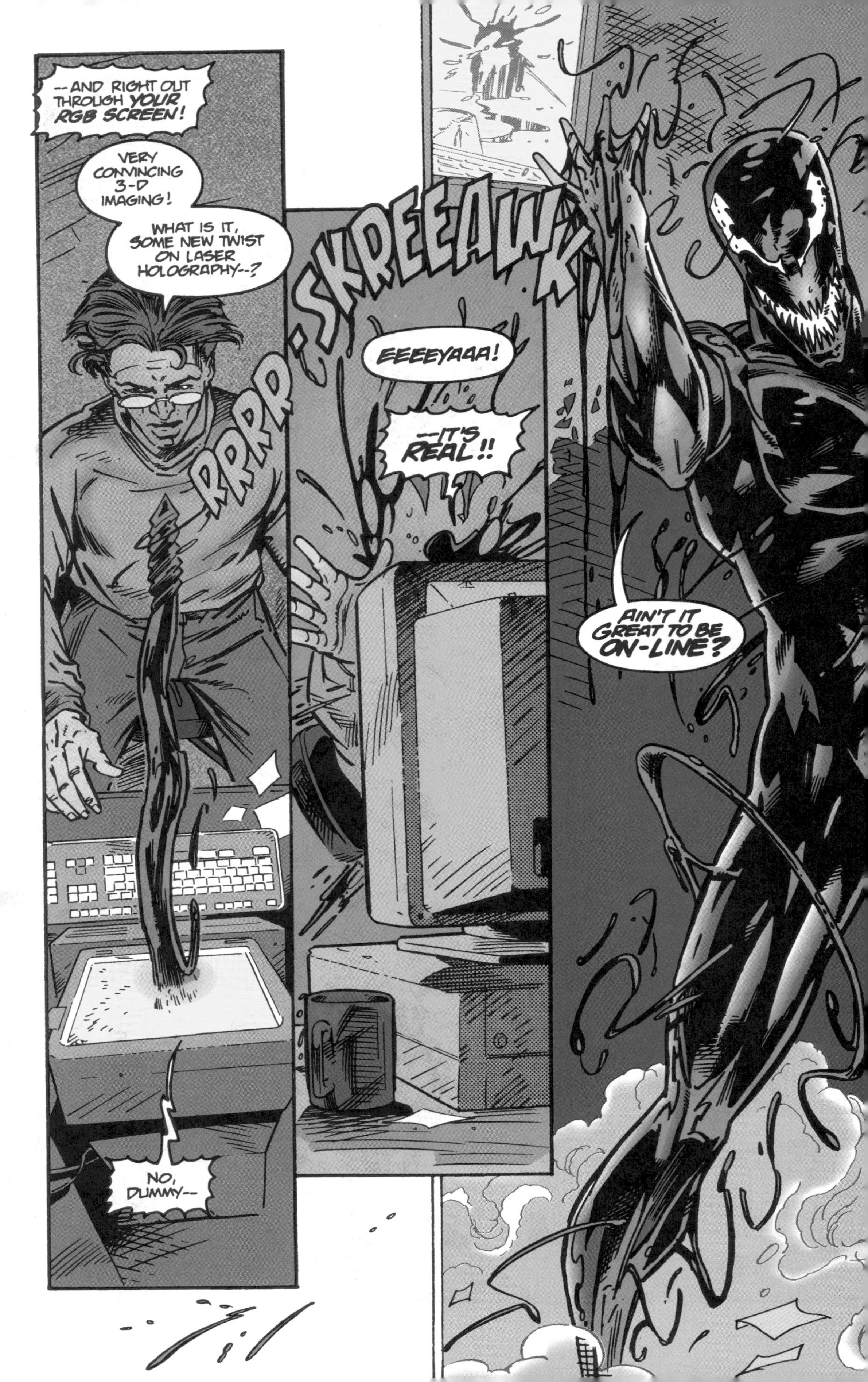

--AND RIGHT OUT THROUGH YOUR RGB SCREEN!
VERY CONVINCING 3-D IMAGING!
WHAT IS IT, SOME NEW TWIST ON LASER HOLOGRAPHY--?
NO, DUMMY--
RRRRP-SKREEAWK
EEEEYAAA!
--IT'S REAL!!
AIN'T IT GREAT TO BE ON-LINE?

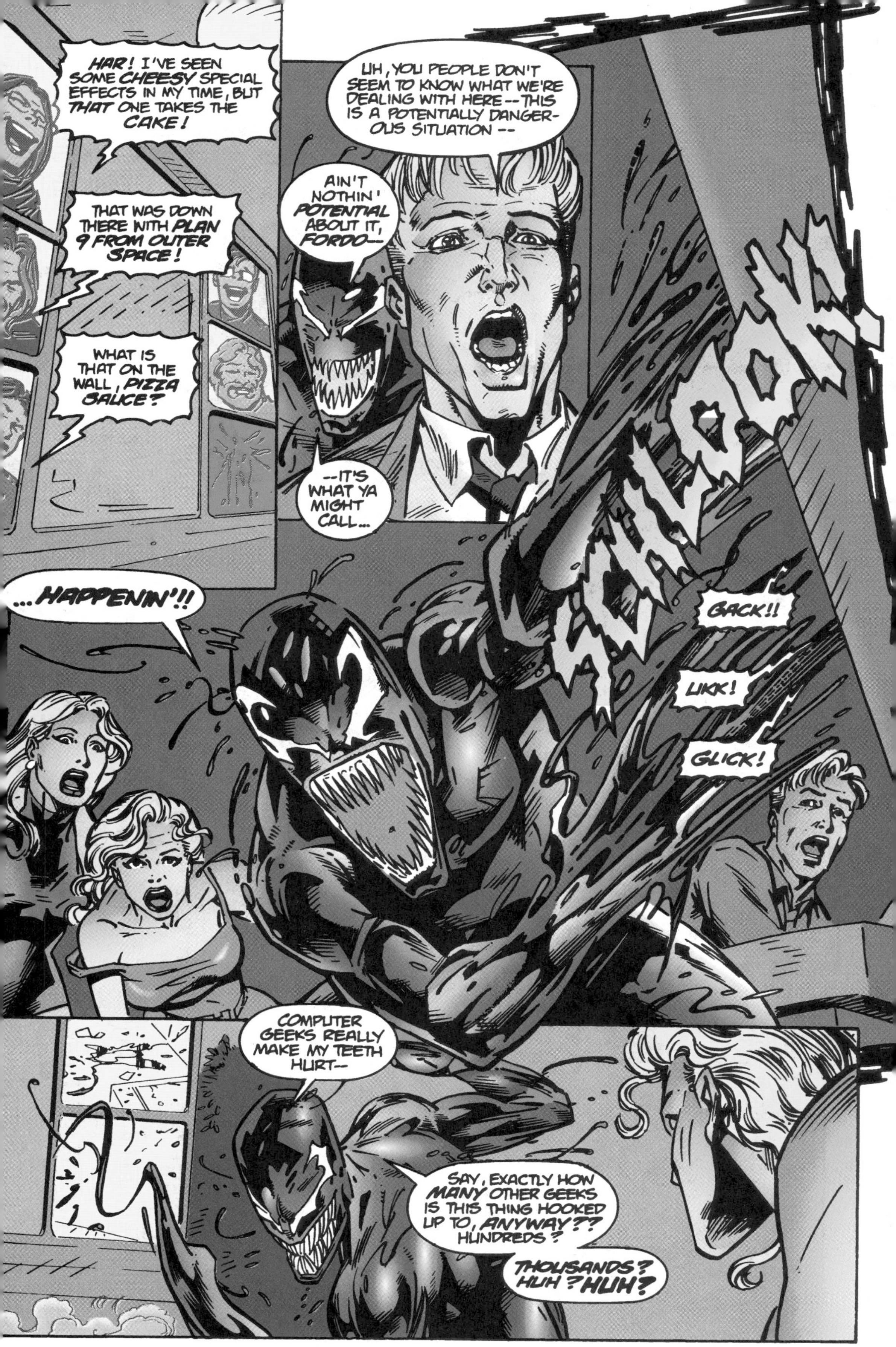
HAR! I'VE SEEN SOME CHEESY SPECIAL EFFECTS IN MY TIME, BUT THAT ONE TAKES THE CAKE!
THAT WAS DOWN THERE WITH PLAN 9 FROM OUTER SPACE!
WHAT IS THAT ON THE WALL, PIZZA SAUCE?
UH, YOU PEOPLE DON'T SEEM TO KNOW WHAT WE'RE DEALING WITH HERE -- THIS IS A POTENTIALLY DANGER-OUS SITUATION --
AIN'T NOTHIN' POTENTIAL ABOUT IT, FORDO--
--IT'S WHAT YA MIGHT CALL...
...HAPPENIN'!!
GACK!!
UKK!
GLICK!
COMPUTER GEEKS REALLY MAKE MY TEETH HURT--
SAY, EXACTLY HOW MANY OTHER GEEKS IS THIS THING HOOKED UP TO, ANYWAY?? HUNDREDS?
THOUSANDS? HUH? HUH?

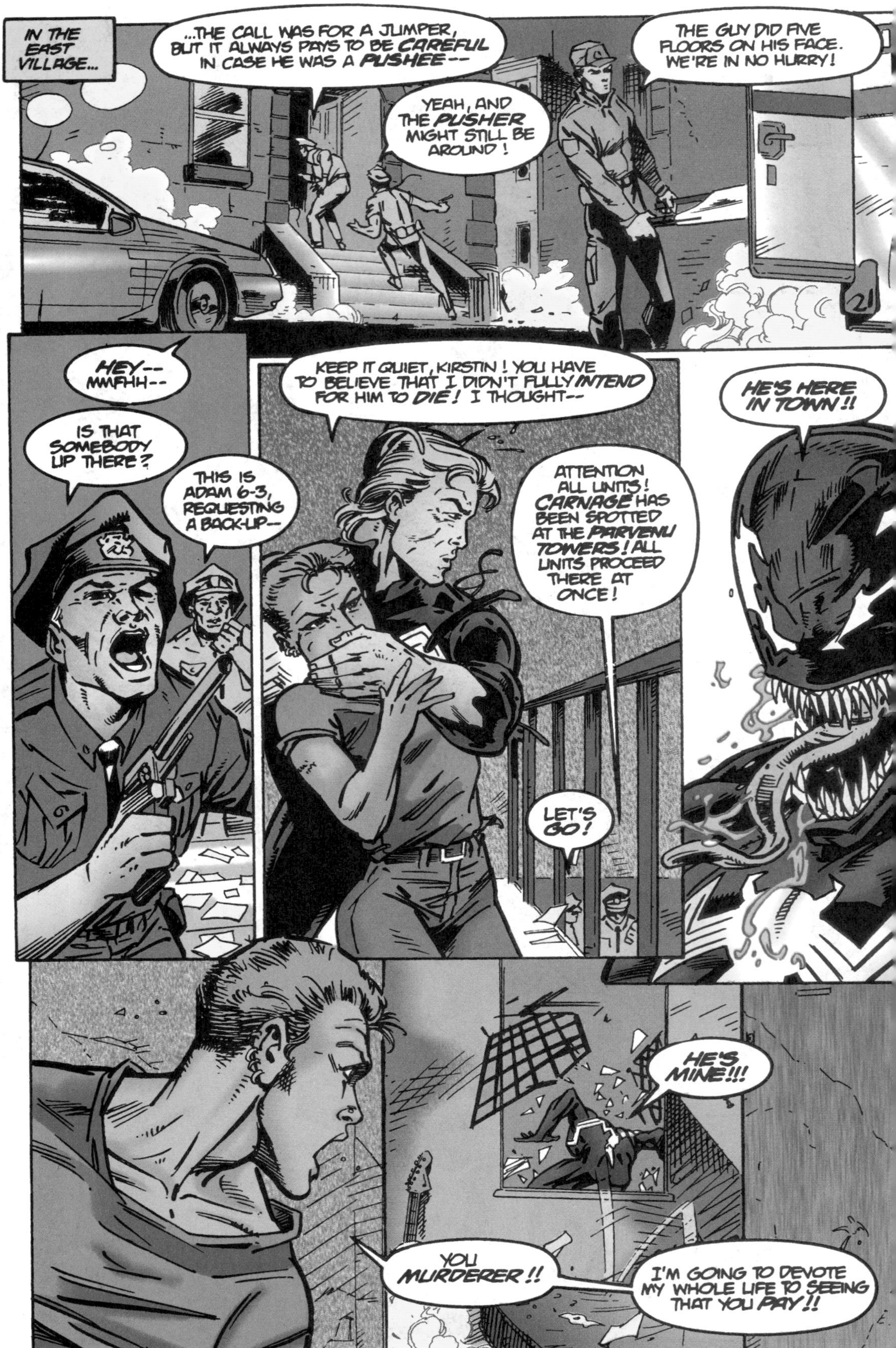
IN THE EAST VILLAGE...
...THE CALL WAS FOR A JUMPER, BUT IT ALWAYS PAYS TO BE CAREFUL IN CASE HE WAS A PUSHEE--
YEAH, AND THE PUSHER MIGHT STILL BE AROUND!
THE GUY DID FIVE FLOORS ON HIS FACE. WE'RE IN NO HURRY!
HEY-- MMFHH--
IS THAT SOMEBODY UP THERE?
THIS IS ADAM 6-3, REQUESTING A BACK-UP--
KEEP IT QUIET, KIRSTIN! YOU HAVE TO BELIEVE THAT I DIDN'T FULLY INTEND FOR HIM TO DIE! I THOUGHT--
ATTENTION ALL UNITS! CARNAGE HAS BEEN SPOTTED AT THE PARVENU TOWERS! ALL UNITS PROCEED THERE AT ONCE!
LET'S GO!
HE'S HERE IN TOWN!!
HE'S MINE!!!
YOU MURDERER!!
I'M GOING TO DEVOTE MY WHOLE LIFE TO SEEING THAT YOU PAY!!

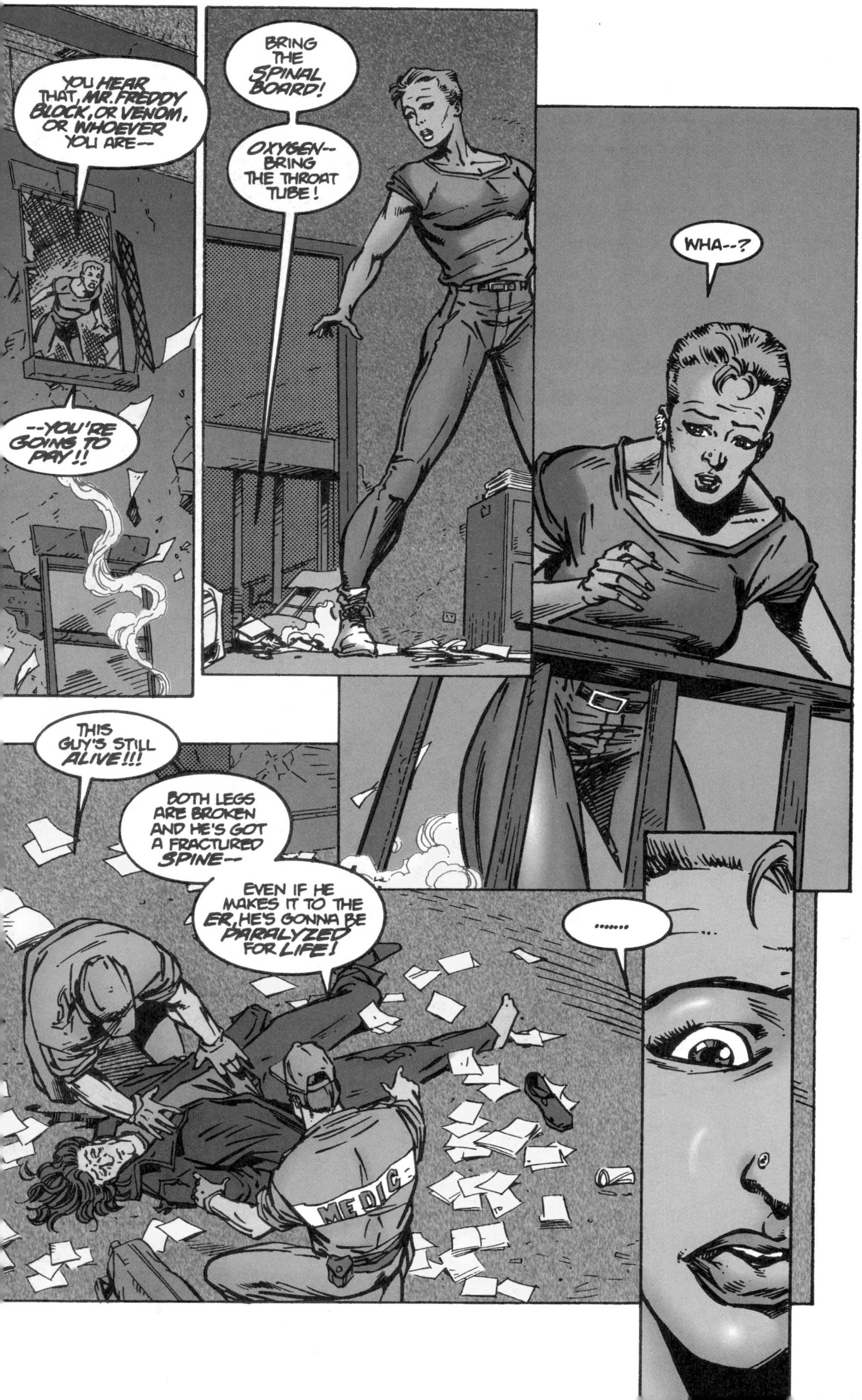
YOU HEAR THAT, MR. FREDDY BLOCK, OR VENOM, OR WHOEVER YOU ARE--
--YOU'RE GOING TO PAY!!
BRING THE SPINAL BOARD!
OXYGEN-- BRING THE THROAT TUBE!
WHA--?
THIS GUY'S STILL ALIVE!!!
BOTH LEGS ARE BROKEN AND HE'S GOT A FRACTURED SPINE--
EVEN IF HE MAKES IT TO THE ER, HE'S GONNA BE PARALYZED FOR LIFE!
....
MEDIC

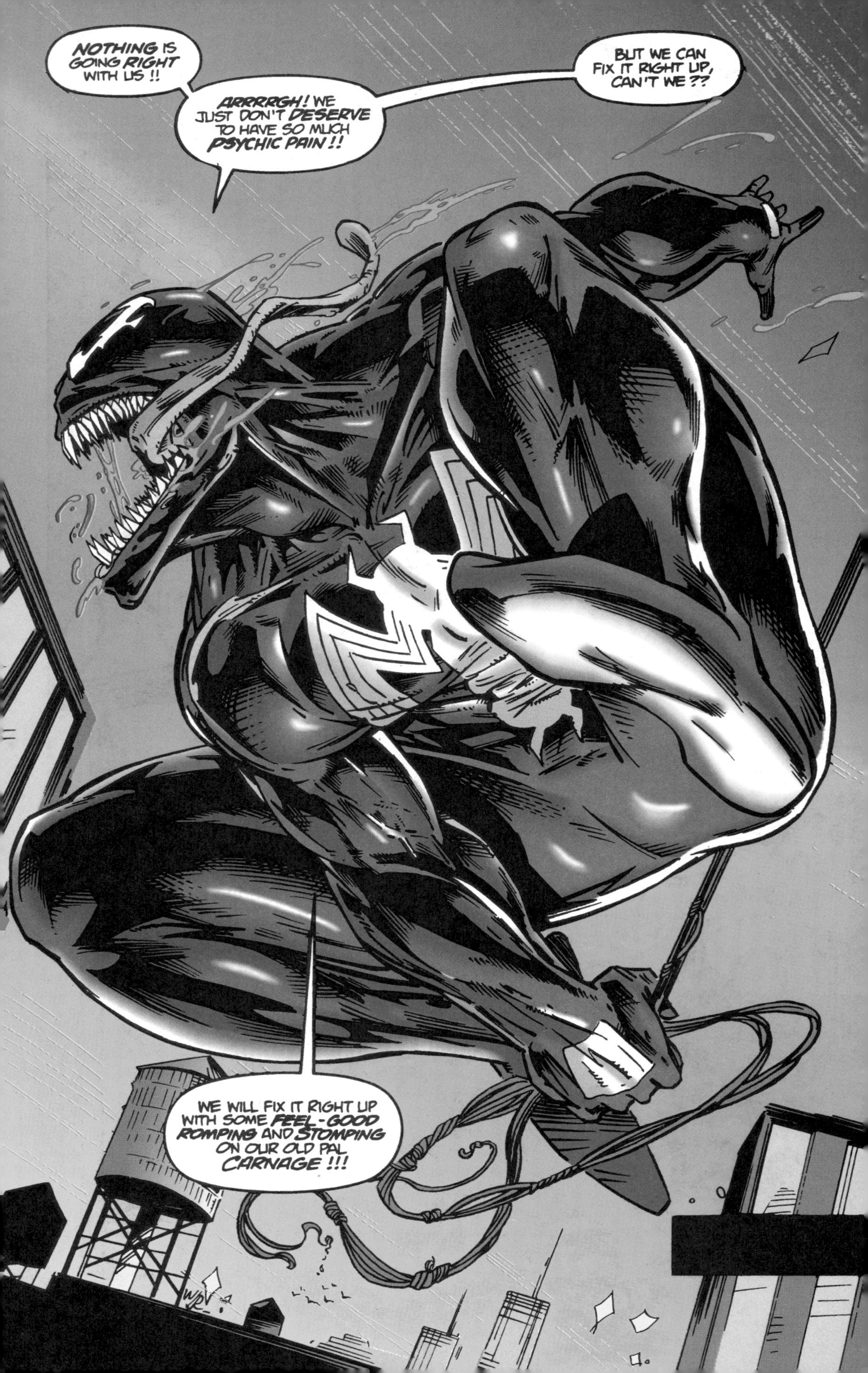
NOTHING IS GOING RIGHT WITH US !!
ARRRRGH! WE JUST DON'T DESERVE TO HAVE SO MUCH PSYCHIC PAIN !!
BUT WE CAN FIX IT RIGHT UP, CAN'T WE ??
WE WILL FIX IT RIGHT UP WITH SOME FEEL-GOOD ROMPING AND STOMPING ON OUR OLD PAL CARNAGE !!!

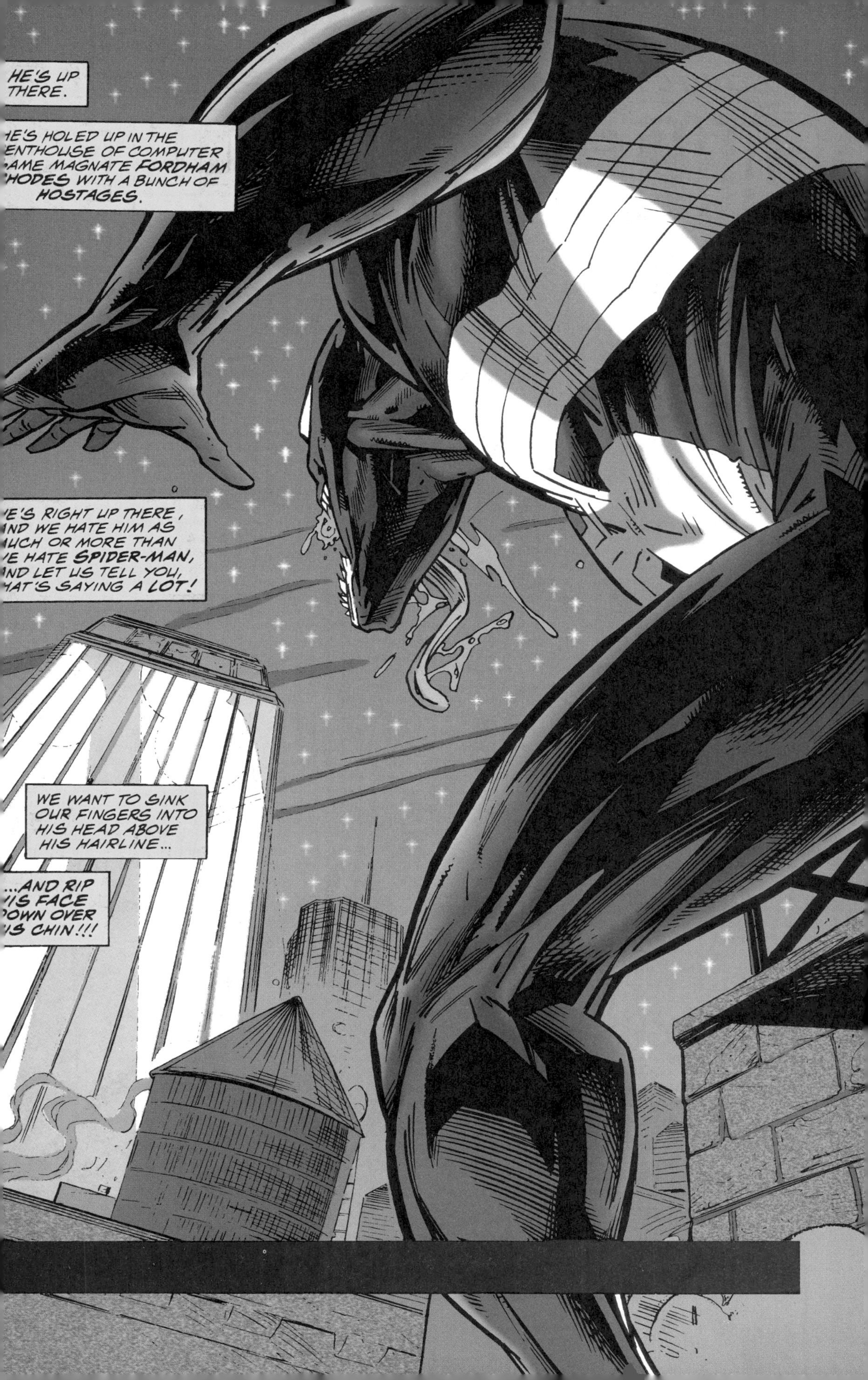

HE'S UP THERE.
HE'S HOLED UP IN THE ENTHOUSE OF COMPUTER AME MAGNATE FORDHAM HODES WITH A BUNCH OF HOSTAGES.
E'S RIGHT UP THERE, ND WE HATE HIM AS UCH OR MORE THAN E HATE SPIDER-MAN, ND LET US TELL YOU, HAT'S SAYING A LOT!
WE WANT TO SINK OUR FINGERS INTO HIS HEAD ABOVE HIS HAIRLINE...
...AND RIP IS FACE OWN OVER IS CHIN!!!

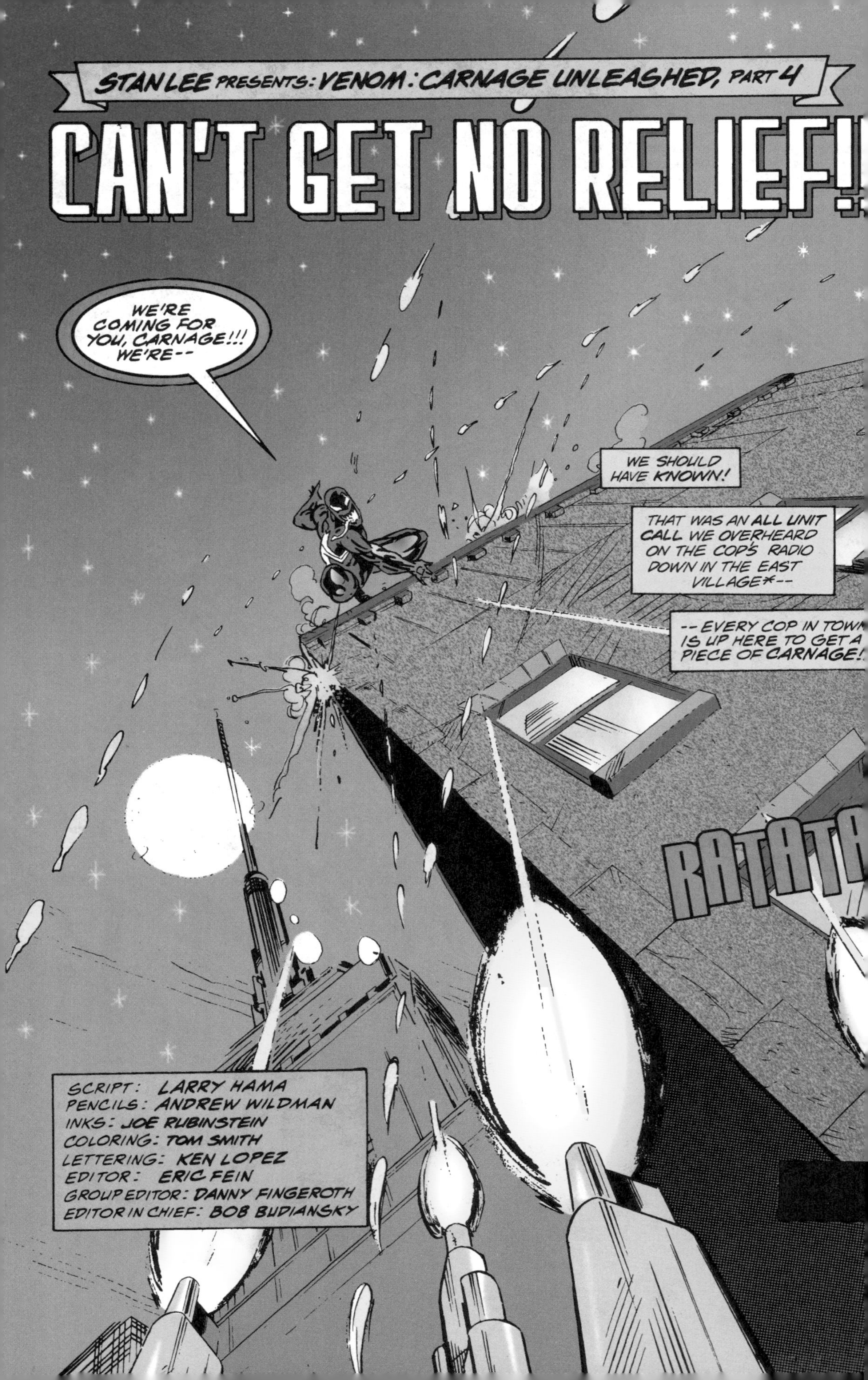
STAN LEE PRESENTS: VENOM: CARNAGE UNLEASHED, PART 4
CAN'T GET NO RELIEF!!
WE'RE COMING FOR YOU, CARNAGE!!! WE'RE--
WE SHOULD HAVE KNOWN!
THAT WAS AN ALL UNIT CALL WE OVERHEARD ON THE COP'S RADIO DOWN IN THE EAST VILLAGE*--
-- EVERY COP IN TOWN IS UP HERE TO GET A PIECE OF CARNAGE!
RATATA
SCRIPT: LARRY HAMA
PENCILS: ANDREW WILDMAN
INKS: JOE RUBINSTEIN
COLORING: TOM SMITH
LETTERING: KEN LOPEZ
EDITOR: ERIC FEIN
GROUP EDITOR: DANNY FINGEROTH
EDITOR IN CHIEF: BOB BUDIANSKY

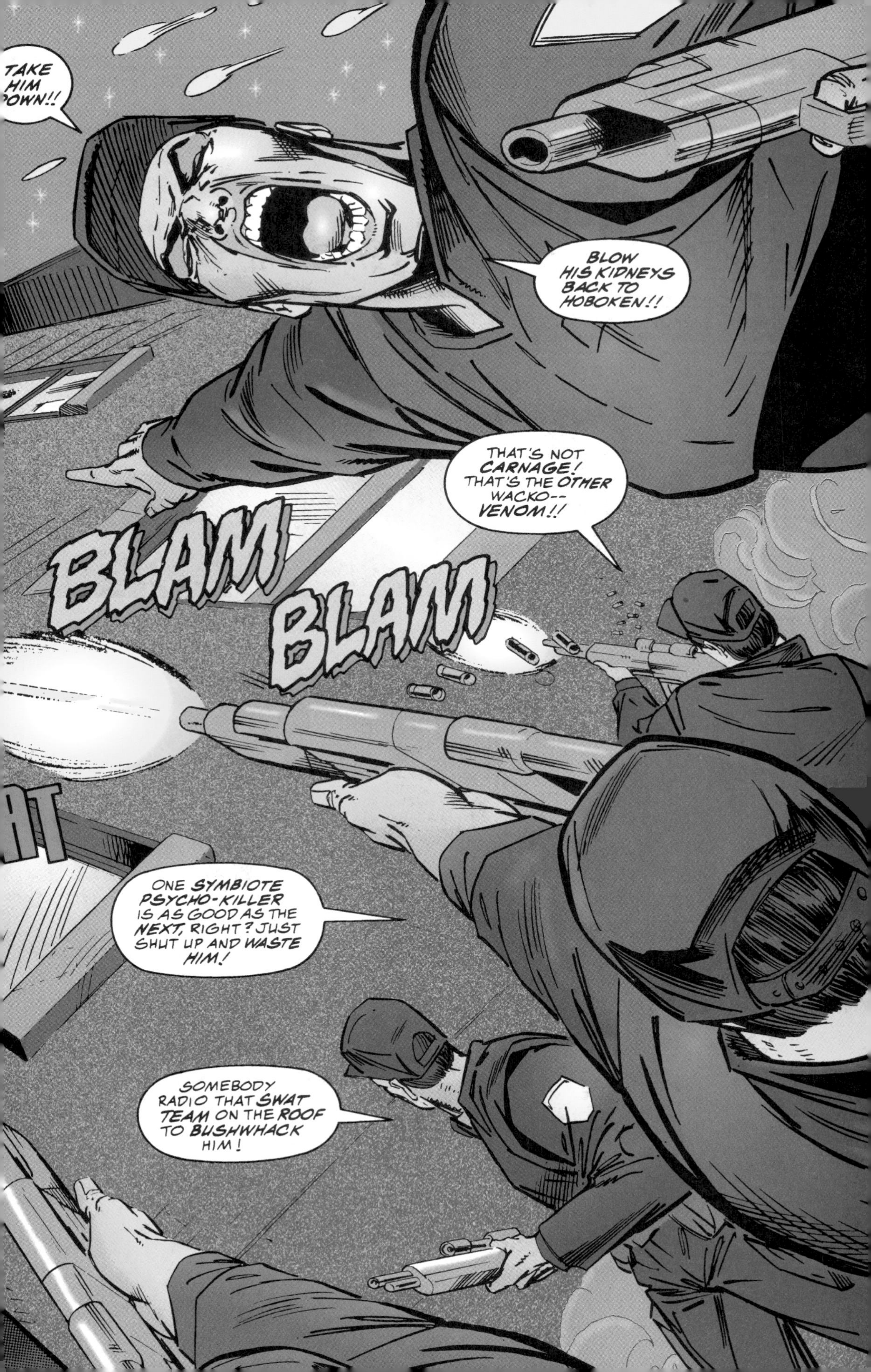
TAKE HIM DOWN!!
BLOW HIS KIDNEYS BACK TO HOBOKEN!!
THAT'S NOT CARNAGE! THAT'S THE OTHER WACKO-- VENOM!!
BLAM
BLAM
ONE SYMBIOTE PSYCHO-KILLER IS AS GOOD AS THE NEXT, RIGHT? JUST SHUT UP AND WASTE HIM!
SOMEBODY RADIO THAT SWAT TEAM ON THE ROOF TO BUSHWHACK HIM!

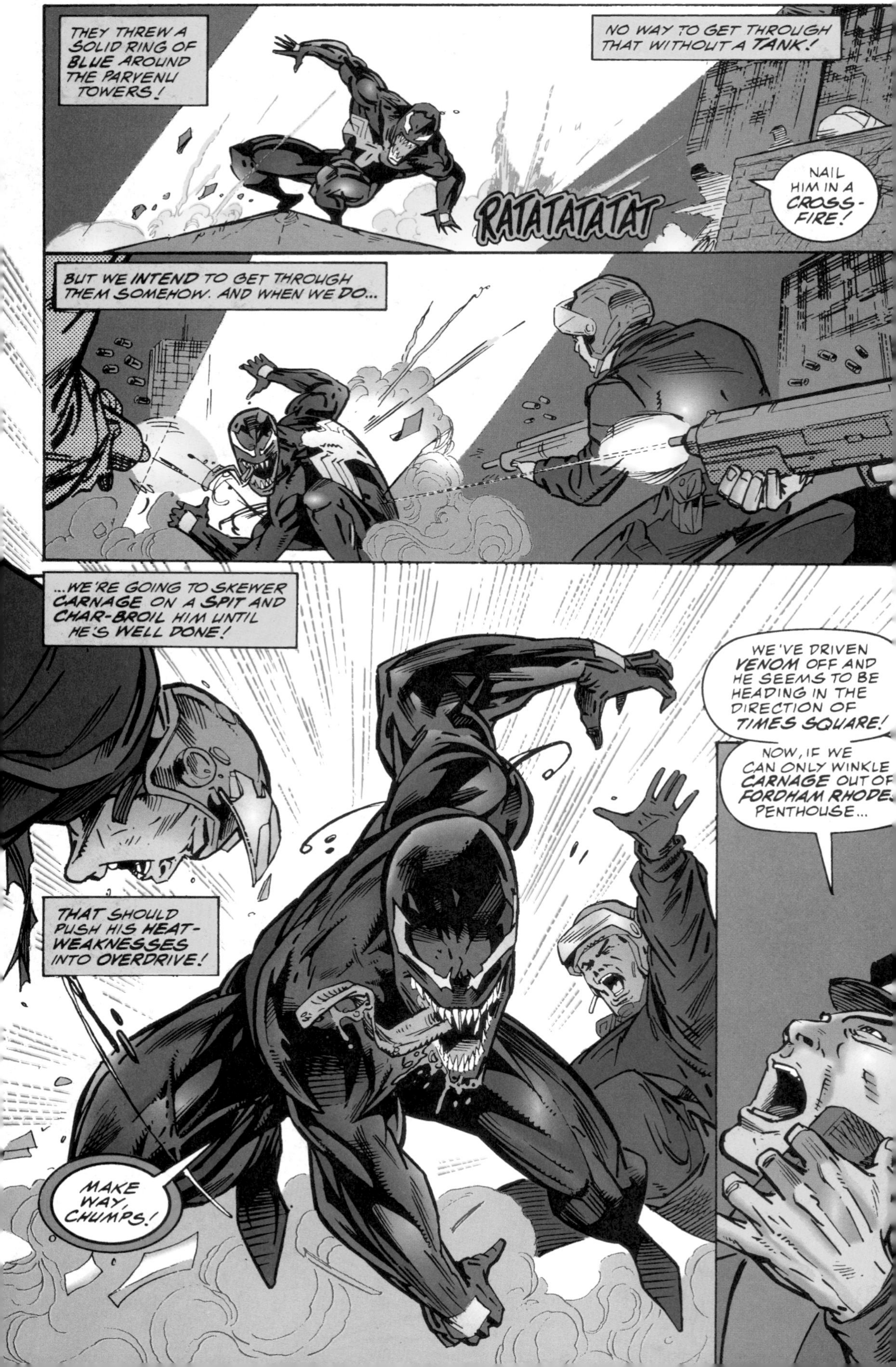
THEY THREW A SOLID RING OF BLUE AROUND THE PARVENU TOWERS!
NO WAY TO GET THROUGH THAT WITHOUT A TANK!
RATATATATAT
NAIL HIM IN A CROSS-FIRE!
BUT WE INTEND TO GET THROUGH THEM SOMEHOW. AND WHEN WE DO...
...WE'RE GOING TO SKEWER CARNAGE ON A SPIT AND CHAR-BROIL HIM UNTIL HE'S WELL DONE!
THAT SHOULD PUSH HIS HEAT-WEAKNESSES INTO OVERDRIVE!
MAKE WAY, CHUMPS!
WE'VE DRIVEN VENOM OFF AND HE SEEMS TO BE HEADING IN THE DIRECTION OF TIMES SQUARE!
NOW, IF WE CAN ONLY WINKLE CARNAGE OUT OF FORDHAM RHODES PENTHOUSE...

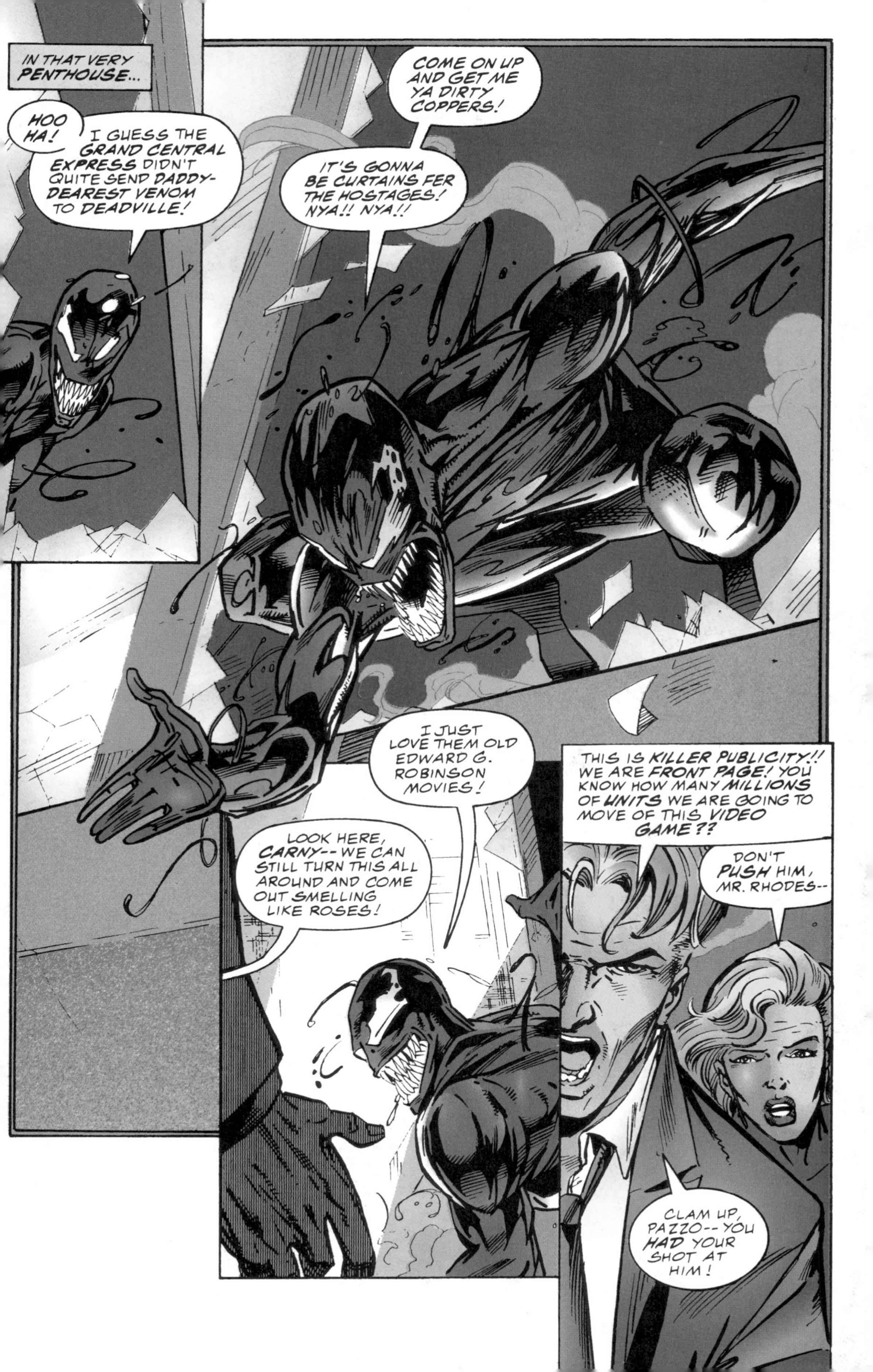
IN THAT VERY PENTHOUSE...
HOO HA!
I GUESS THE GRAND CENTRAL EXPRESS DIDN'T QUITE SEND DADDY-DEAREST VENOM TO DEADVILLE!
COME ON UP AND GET ME YA DIRTY COPPERS!
IT'S GONNA BE CURTAINS FER THE HOSTAGES! NYA!! NYA!!
I JUST LOVE THEM OLD EDWARD G. ROBINSON MOVIES!
LOOK HERE, CARNY-- WE CAN STILL TURN THIS ALL AROUND AND COME OUT SMELLING LIKE ROSES!
THIS IS KILLER PUBLICITY!! WE ARE FRONT PAGE! YOU KNOW HOW MANY MILLIONS OF UNITS WE ARE GOING TO MOVE OF THIS VIDEO GAME??
DON'T PUSH HIM, MR. RHODES--
CLAM UP, PAZZO-- YOU HAD YOUR SHOT AT HIM!

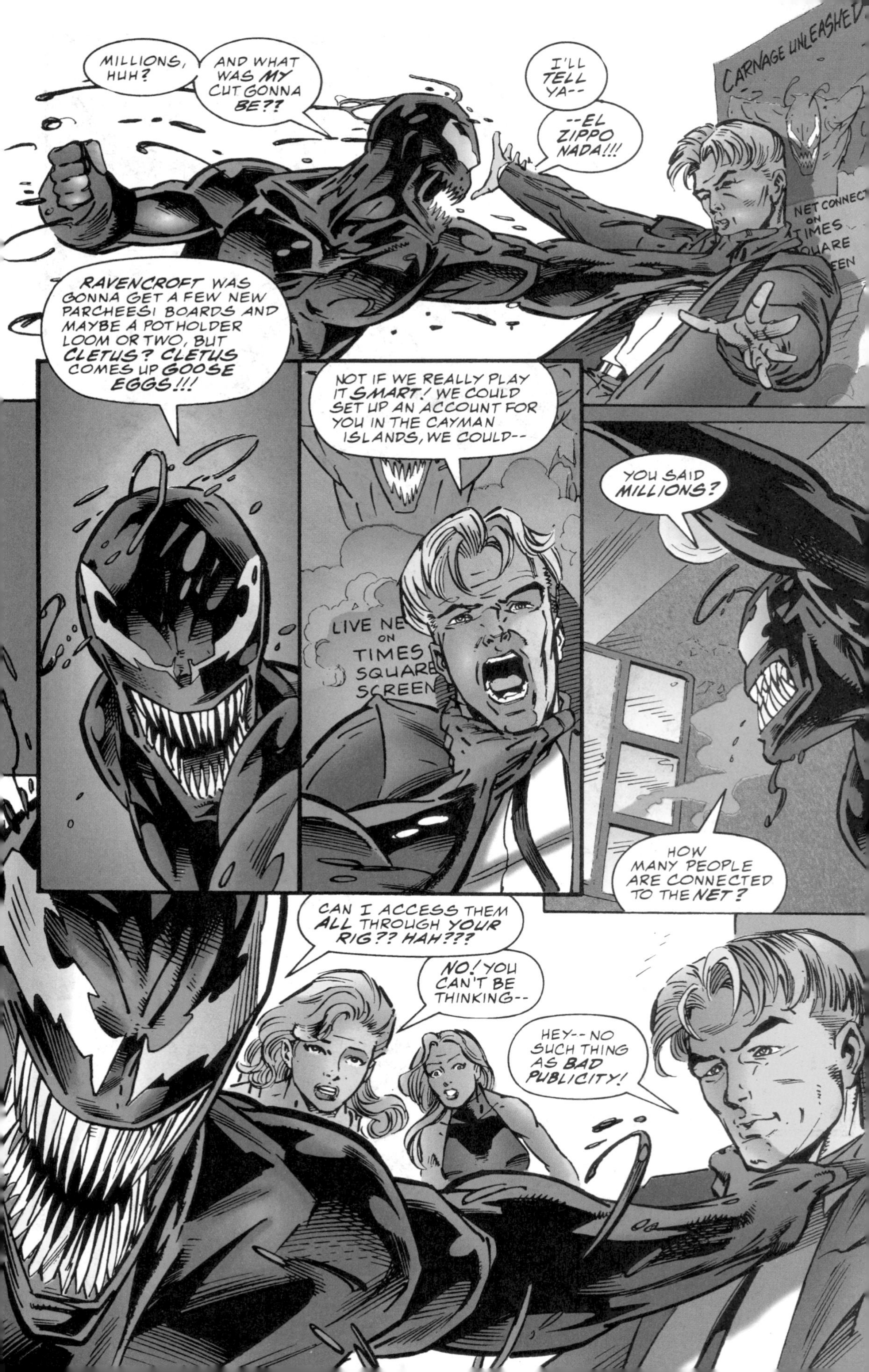
CARNAGE UNLEASHED
MILLIONS, HUH?
AND WHAT WAS MY CUT GONNA BE??
I'LL TELL YA--
--EL ZIPPO NADA!!!
NET CONNECT ON TIMES SQUARE SCREEN
RAVENCROFT WAS GONNA GET A FEW NEW PARCHEESI BOARDS AND MAYBE A POTHOLDER LOOM OR TWO, BUT CLETUS? CLETUS COMES UP GOOSE EGGS!!!
NOT IF WE REALLY PLAY IT SMART! WE COULD SET UP AN ACCOUNT FOR YOU IN THE CAYMAN ISLANDS, WE COULD--
LIVE NE ON TIMES SQUARE SCREEN
YOU SAID MILLIONS?
HOW MANY PEOPLE ARE CONNECTED TO THE NET?
CAN I ACCESS THEM ALL THROUGH YOUR RIG?? HAH???
NO! YOU CAN'T BE THINKING--
HEY-- NO SUCH THING AS BAD PUBLICITY!

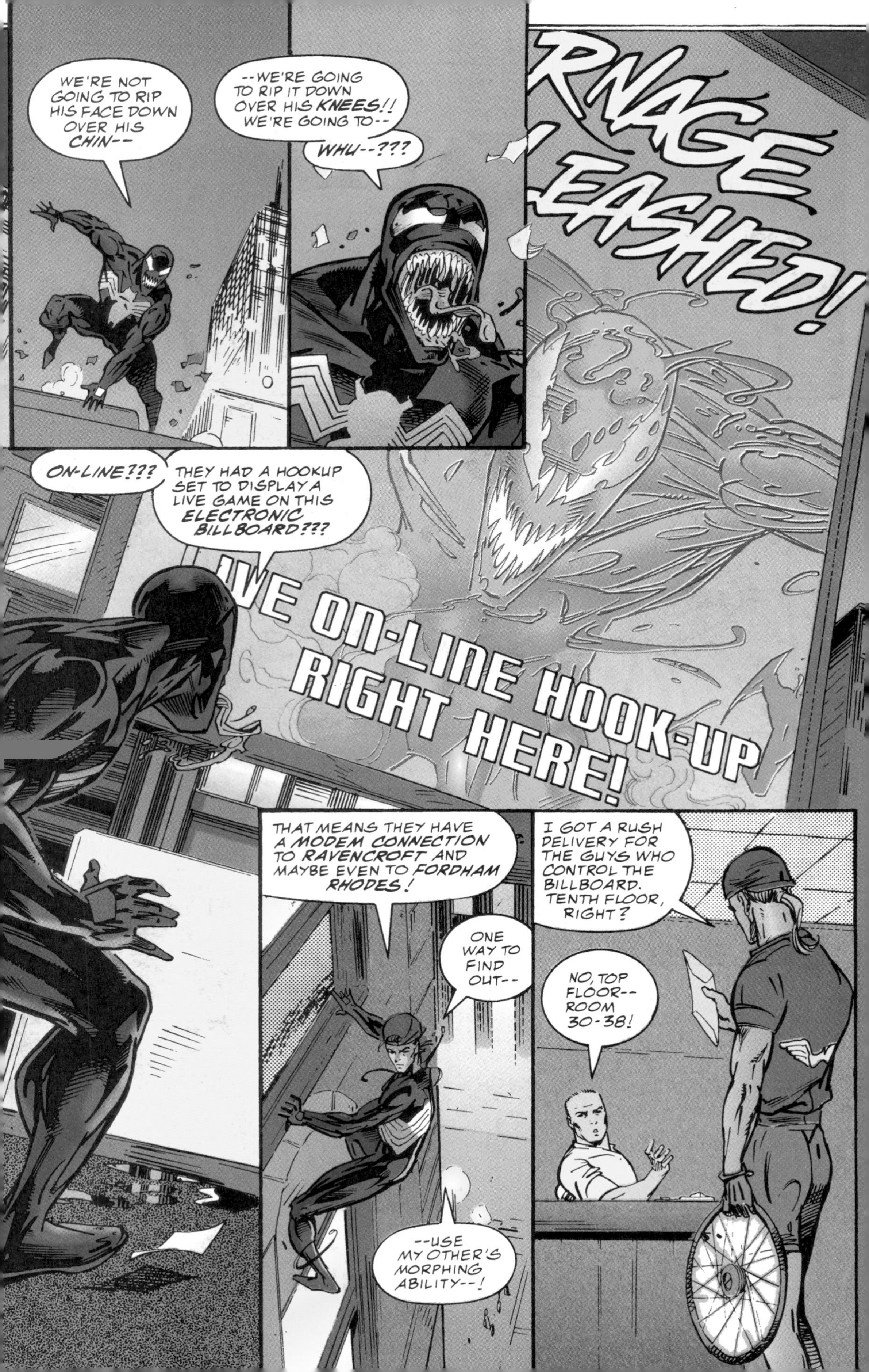
WE'RE NOT GOING TO RIP HIS FACE DOWN OVER HIS CHIN--
--WE'RE GOING TO RIP IT DOWN OVER HIS KNEES!! WE'RE GOING TO--
WHU--???
RNAGE
LEASHED!
ON-LINE???
THEY HAD A HOOKUP SET TO DISPLAY A LIVE GAME ON THIS ELECTRONIC BILLBOARD???
WE ON-LINE HOOK-UP RIGHT HERE!
THAT MEANS THEY HAVE A MODEM CONNECTION TO RAVENCROFT AND MAYBE EVEN TO FORDHAM RHODES!
ONE WAY TO FIND OUT--
--USE MY OTHER'S MORPHING ABILITY--!
I GOT A RUSH DELIVERY FOR THE GUYS WHO CONTROL THE BILLBOARD. TENTH FLOOR, RIGHT?
NO, TOP FLOOR--ROOM 30-38!

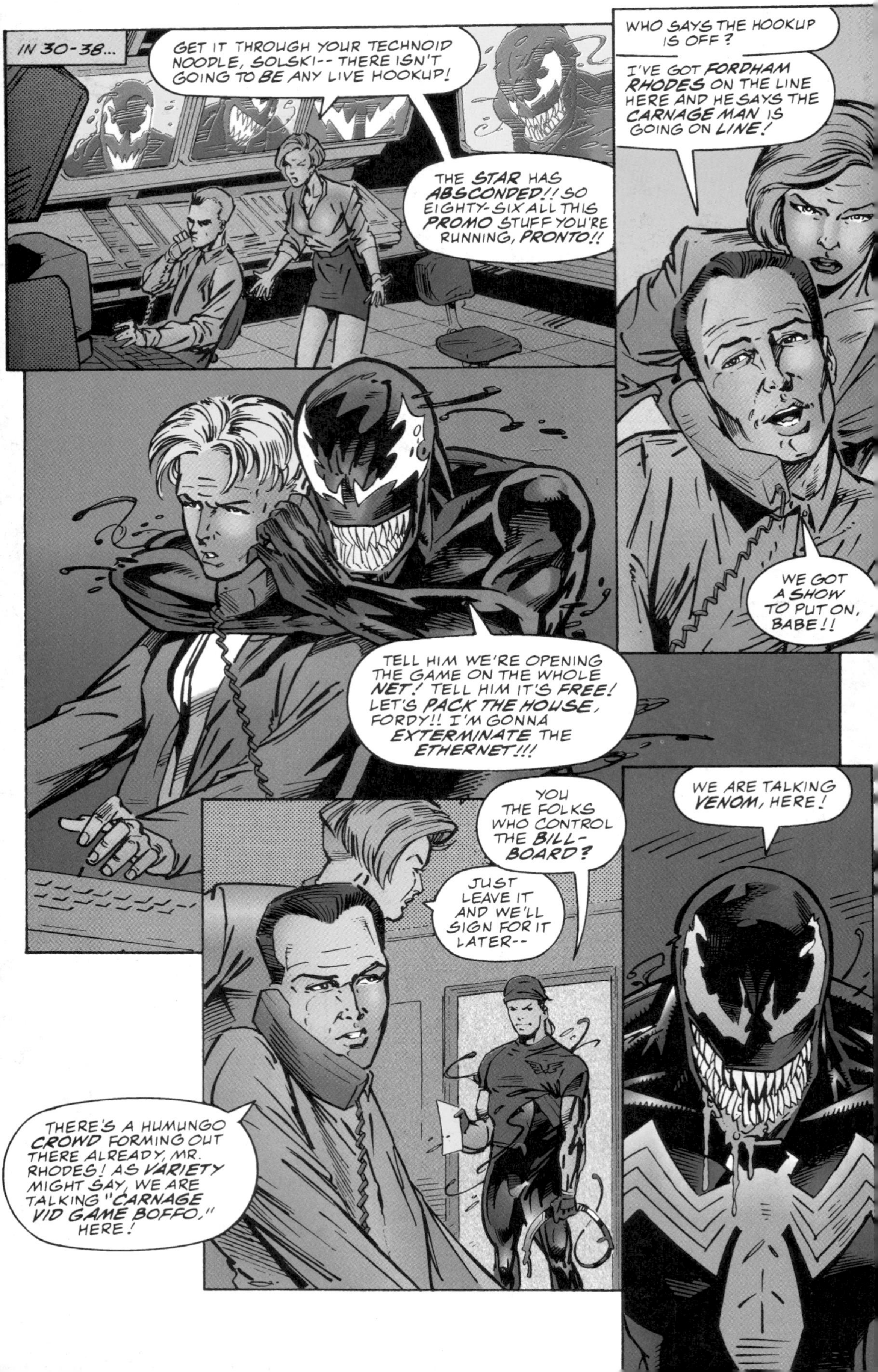
IN 30-38...
GET IT THROUGH YOUR TECHNOID NOODLE, SOLSKI-- THERE ISN'T GOING TO BE ANY LIVE HOOKUP!
THE STAR HAS ABSCONDED!! SO EIGHTY-SIX ALL THIS PROMO STUFF YOU'RE RUNNING, PRONTO!!
TELL HIM WE'RE OPENING THE GAME ON THE WHOLE NET! TELL HIM IT'S FREE! LET'S PACK THE HOUSE, FORDY!! I'M GONNA EXTERMINATE THE ETHERNET!!!
WHO SAYS THE HOOKUP IS OFF?
I'VE GOT FORDHAM RHODES ON THE LINE HERE AND HE SAYS THE CARNAGE MAN IS GOING ON LINE!
WE GOT A SHOW TO PUT ON, BABE!!
YOU THE FOLKS WHO CONTROL THE BILL-BOARD?
JUST LEAVE IT AND WE'LL SIGN FOR IT LATER--
THERE'S A HUMUNGO CROWD FORMING OUT THERE ALREADY, MR. RHODES! AS VARIETY MIGHT SAY, WE ARE TALKING "CARNAGE VID GAME BOFFO," HERE!
WE ARE TALKING VENOM, HERE!

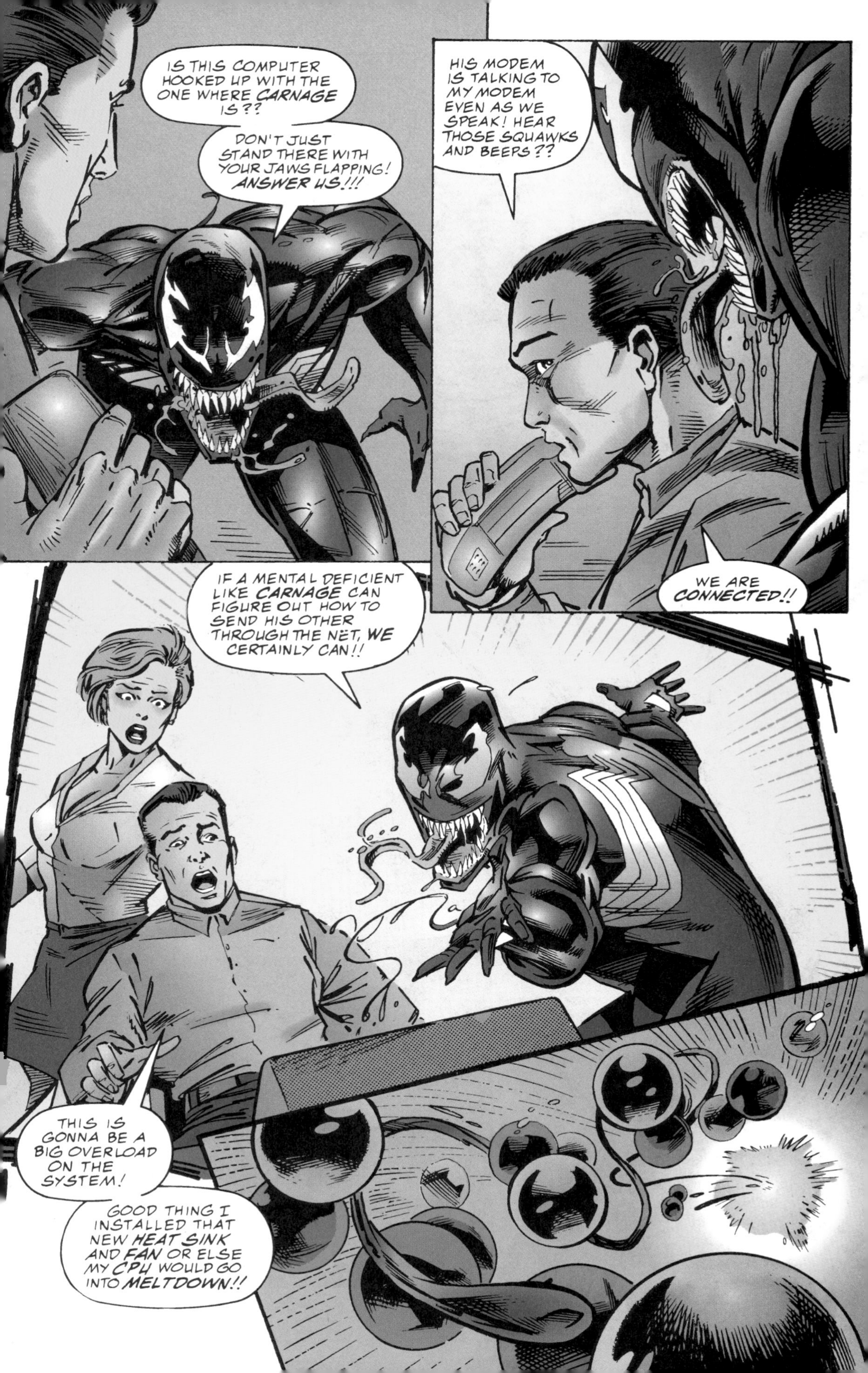
IS THIS COMPUTER HOOKED UP WITH THE ONE WHERE CARNAGE IS??
DON'T JUST STAND THERE WITH YOUR JAWS FLAPPING! ANSWER US!!!
HIS MODEM IS TALKING TO MY MODEM EVEN AS WE SPEAK! HEAR THOSE SQUAWKS AND BEEPS??
WE ARE CONNECTED!!
IF A MENTAL DEFICIENT LIKE CARNAGE CAN FIGURE OUT HOW TO SEND HIS OTHER THROUGH THE NET, WE CERTAINLY CAN!!
THIS IS GONNA BE A BIG OVERLOAD ON THE SYSTEM!
GOOD THING I INSTALLED THAT NEW HEAT SINK AND FAN OR ELSE MY CPU WOULD GO INTO MELTDOWN!!

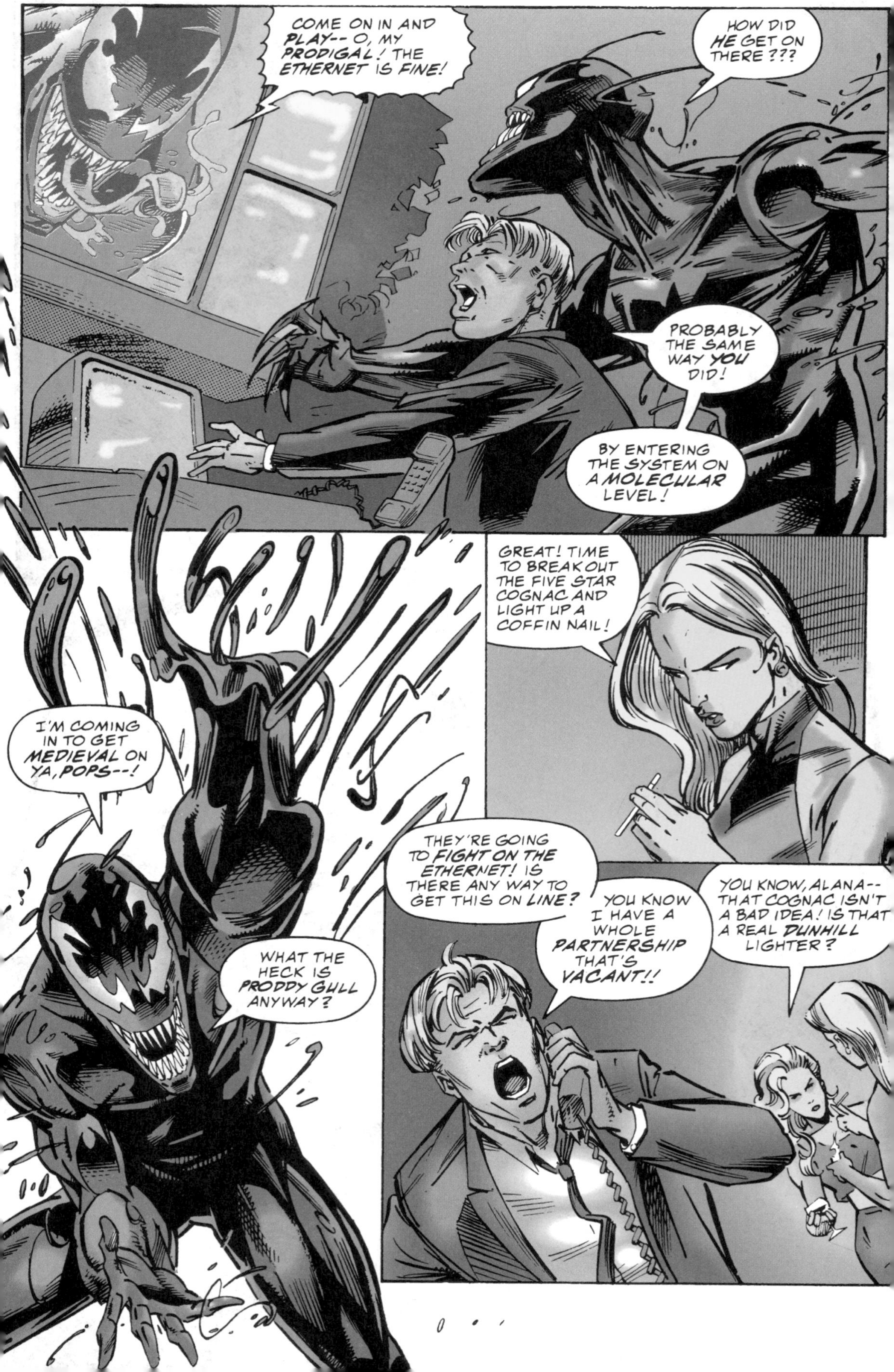
COME ON IN AND PLAY-- O, MY PRODIGAL! THE ETHERNET IS FINE!
HOW DID HE GET ON THERE???
PROBABLY THE SAME WAY YOU DID!
BY ENTERING THE SYSTEM ON A MOLECULAR LEVEL!
I'M COMING IN TO GET MEDIEVAL ON YA, POPS--!
WHAT THE HECK IS PRODDY GULL ANYWAY?
GREAT! TIME TO BREAK OUT THE FIVE STAR COGNAC AND LIGHT UP A COFFIN NAIL!
THEY'RE GOING TO FIGHT ON THE ETHERNET! IS THERE ANY WAY TO GET THIS ON LINE?
YOU KNOW I HAVE A WHOLE PARTNERSHIP THAT'S VACANT!!
YOU KNOW, ALANA-- THAT COGNAC ISN'T A BAD IDEA! IS THAT A REAL DUNHILL LIGHTER?

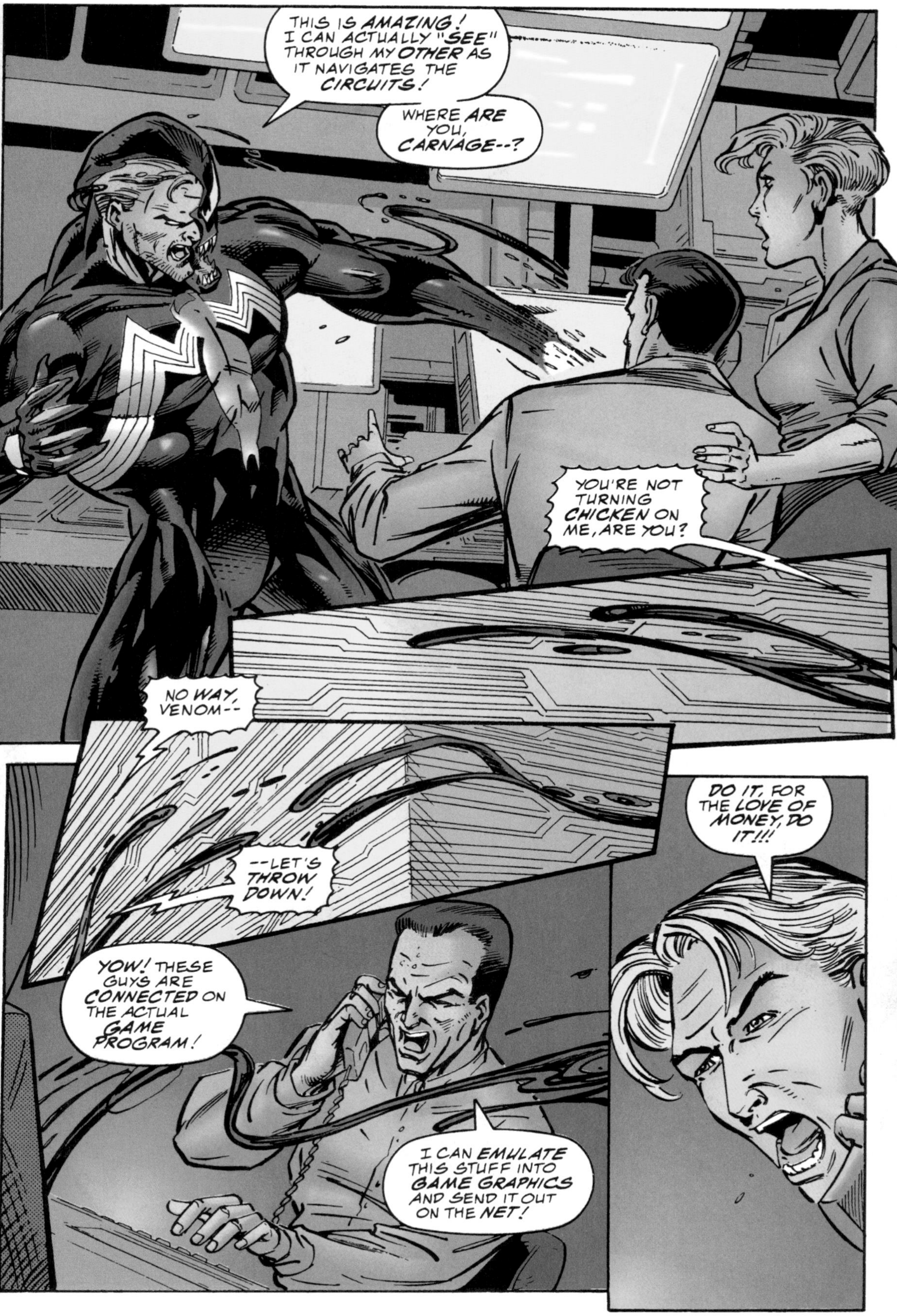
THIS IS AMAZING! I CAN ACTUALLY "SEE" THROUGH MY OTHER AS IT NAVIGATES THE CIRCUITS!
WHERE ARE YOU, CARNAGE--?
YOU'RE NOT TURNING CHICKEN ON ME, ARE YOU?
NO WAY, VENOM--
--LET'S THROW DOWN!
YOW! THESE GUYS ARE CONNECTED ON THE ACTUAL GAME PROGRAM!
I CAN EMULATE THIS STUFF INTO GAME GRAPHICS AND SEND IT OUT ON THE NET!
DO IT, FOR THE LOVE OF MONEY, DO IT!!!

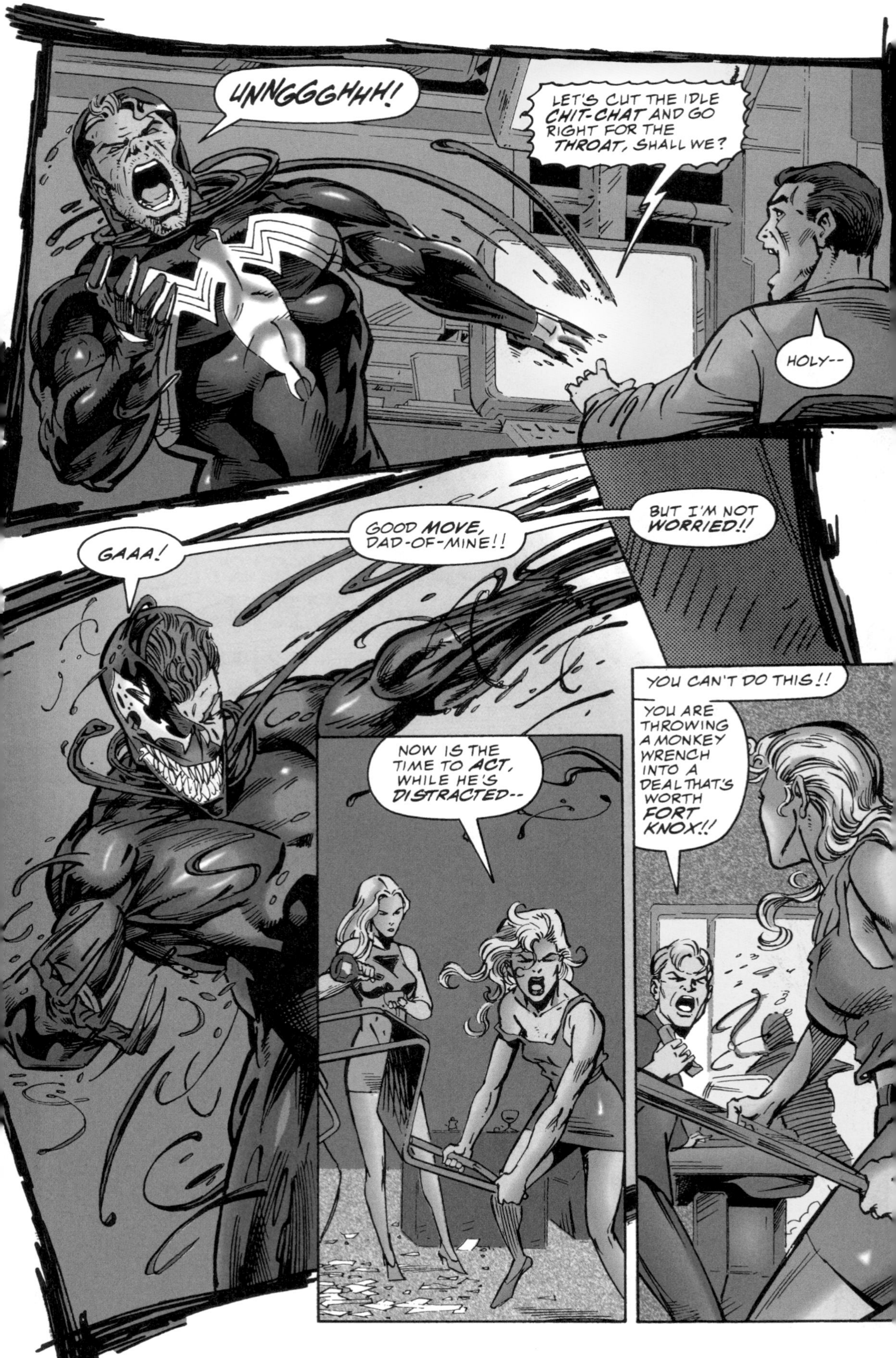
UNNGGGHHH!
LET'S CUT THE IDLE CHIT-CHAT AND GO RIGHT FOR THE THROAT, SHALL WE?
HOLY--
GAAA!
GOOD MOVE, DAD-OF-MINE!!
BUT I'M NOT WORRIED!!
NOW IS THE TIME TO ACT, WHILE HE'S DISTRACTED--
YOU CAN'T DO THIS!!
YOU ARE THROWING A MONKEY WRENCH INTO A DEAL THAT'S WORTH FORT KNOX!!

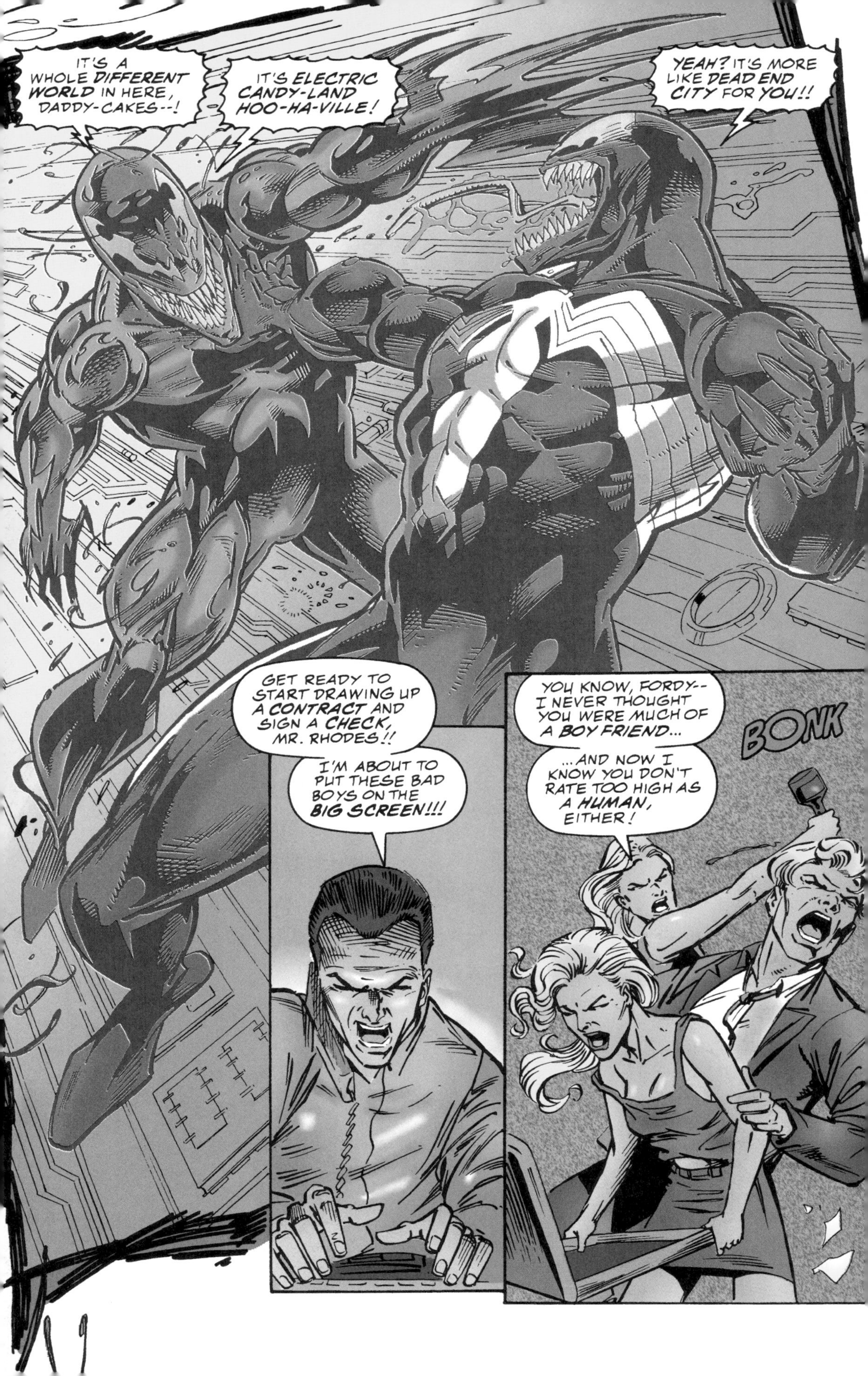

IT'S A WHOLE DIFFERENT WORLD IN HERE, DADDY-CAKES--!
IT'S ELECTRIC CANDY-LAND HOO-HA-VILLE!
YEAH? IT'S MORE LIKE DEAD END CITY FOR YOU!!
GET READY TO START DRAWING UP A CONTRACT AND SIGN A CHECK, MR. RHODES!!
I'M ABOUT TO PUT THESE BAD BOYS ON THE BIG SCREEN!!!
YOU KNOW, FORDY-- I NEVER THOUGHT YOU WERE MUCH OF A BOY FRIEND...
...AND NOW I KNOW YOU DON'T RATE TOO HIGH AS A HUMAN, EITHER!
BONK

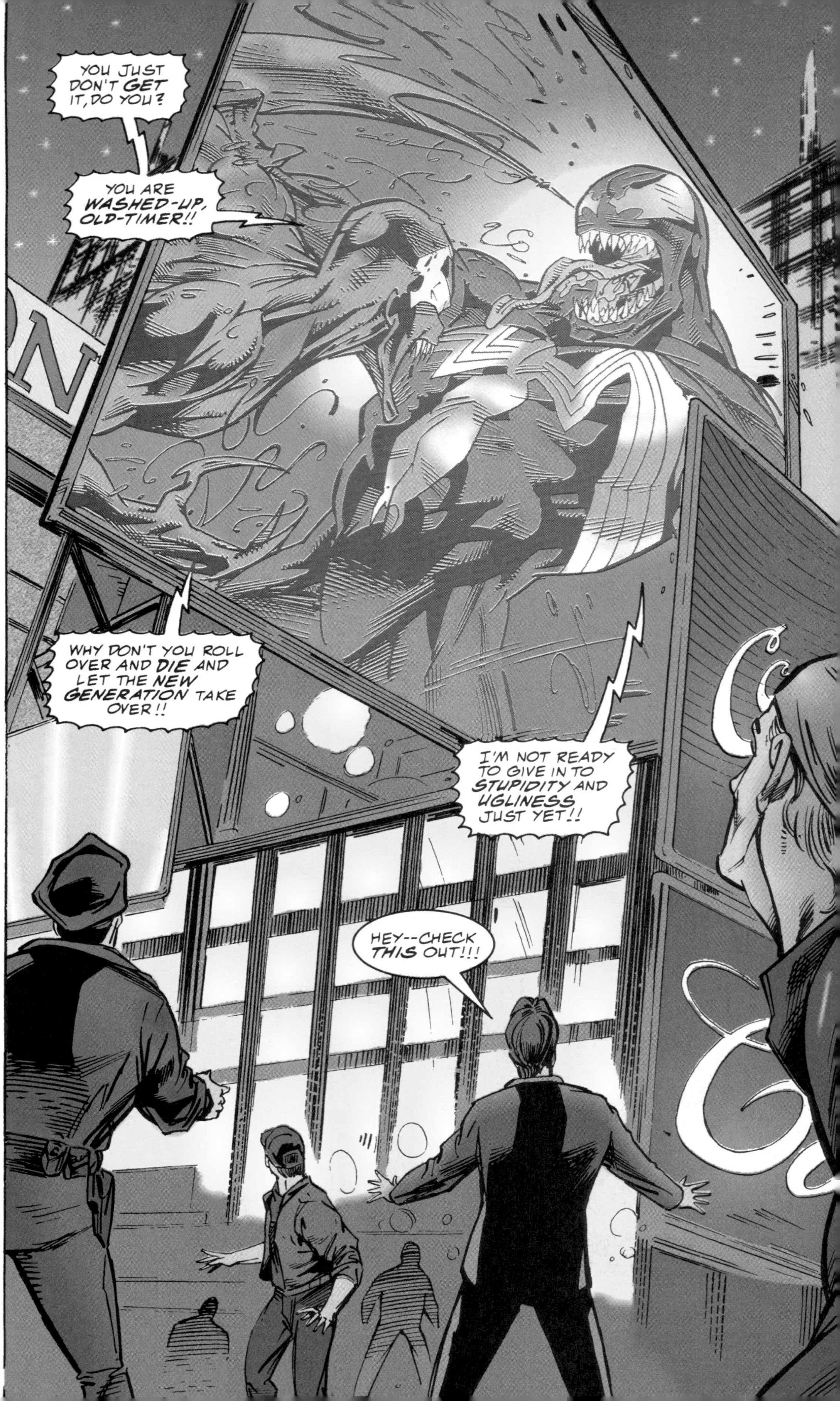
YOU JUST DON'T GET IT, DO YOU?
YOU ARE WASHED-UP, OLD-TIMER!!
WHY DON'T YOU ROLL OVER AND DIE AND LET THE NEW GENERATION TAKE OVER!!
I'M NOT READY TO GIVE IN TO STUPIDITY AND UGLINESS JUST YET!!
HEY--CHECK THIS OUT!!!

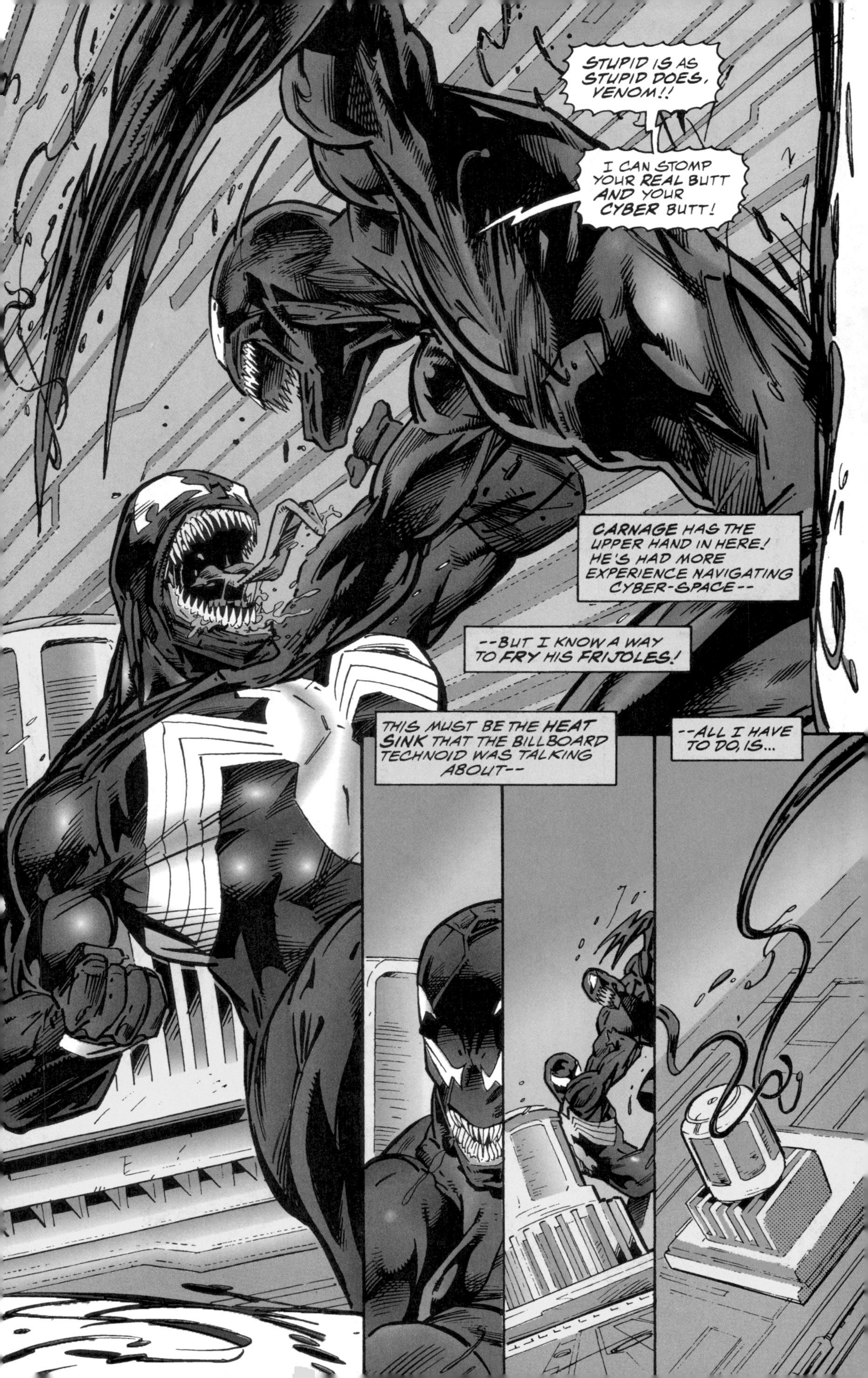
STUPID IS AS STUPID DOES, VENOM!!
I CAN STOMP YOUR REAL BUTT AND YOUR CYBER BUTT!
CARNAGE HAS THE UPPER HAND IN HERE! HE'S HAD MORE EXPERIENCE NAVIGATING CYBER-SPACE--
--BUT I KNOW A WAY TO FRY HIS FRIJOLES!
THIS MUST BE THE HEAT SINK THAT THE BILLBOARD TECHNOID WAS TALKING ABOUT--
--ALL I HAVE TO DO, IS...

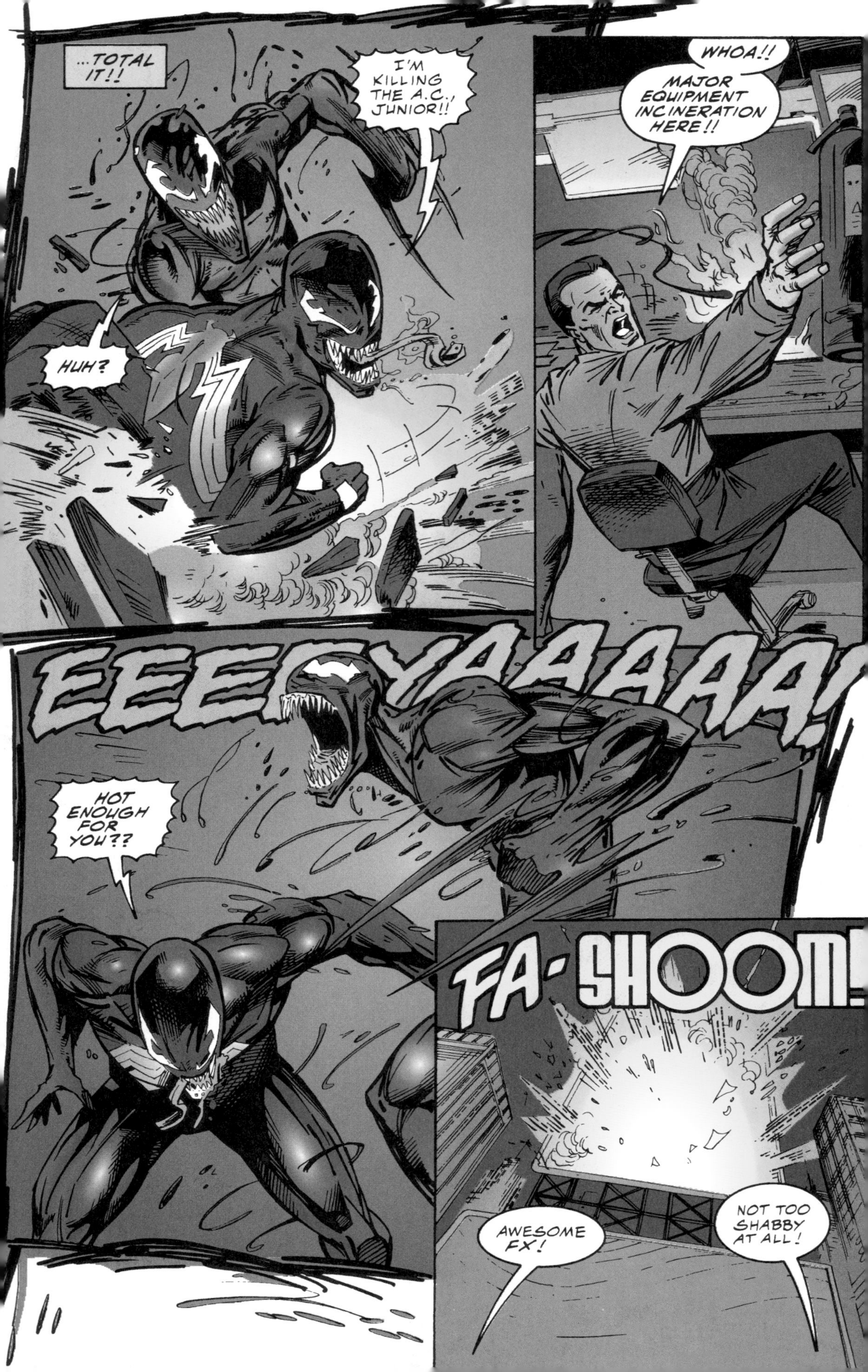
...TOTAL IT!!
I'M KILLING THE A.C., JUNIOR!!
HUH?
WHOA!!
MAJOR EQUIPMENT INCINERATION HERE!!
EEEEYAAAAAA!
HOT ENOUGH FOR YOU??
FA-SHOOOM!
AWESOME FX!
NOT TOO SHABBY AT ALL!

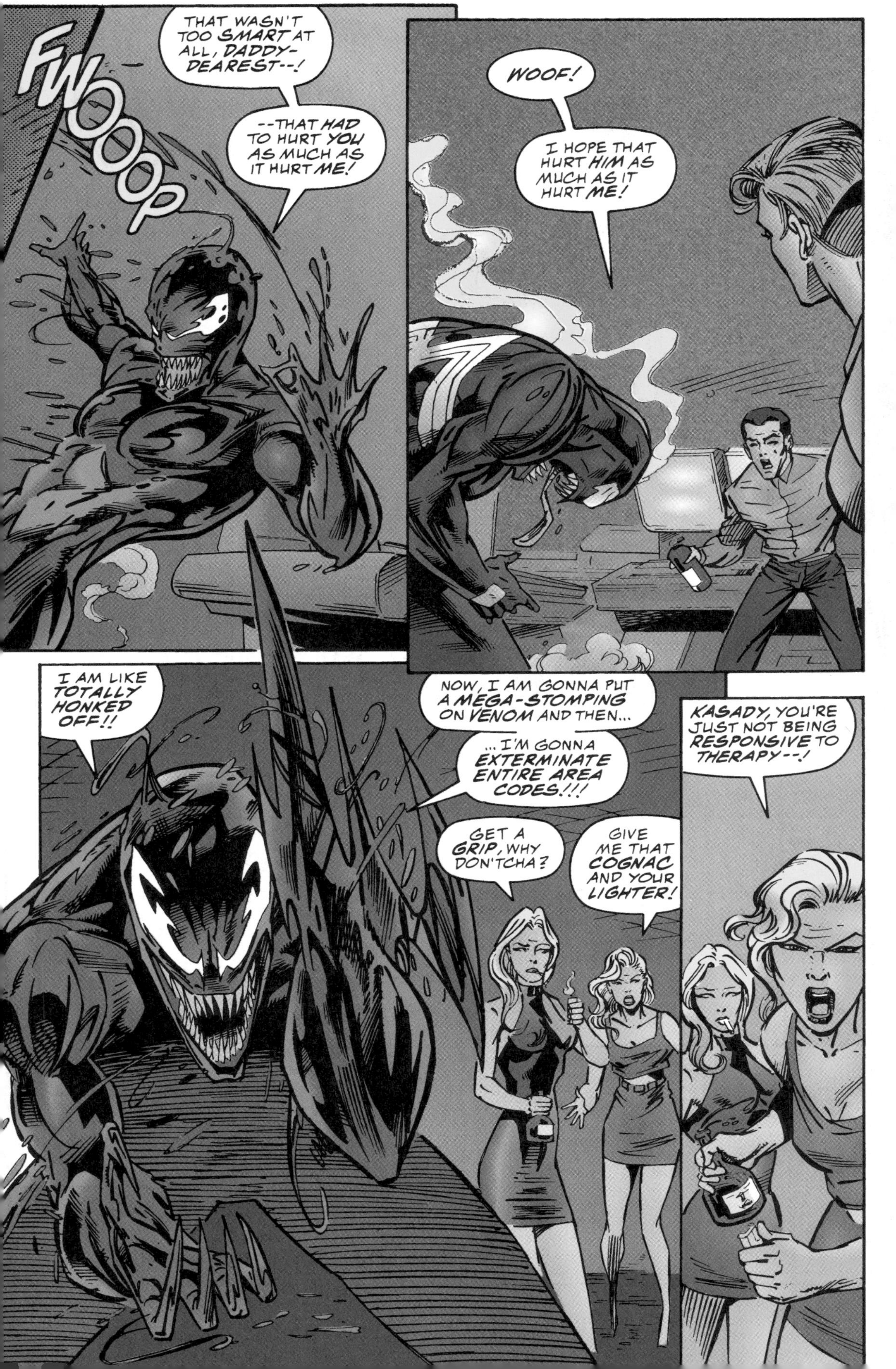
FWOOOP
THAT WASN'T TOO SMART AT ALL, DADDY-DEAREST--!
--THAT HAD TO HURT YOU AS MUCH AS IT HURT ME!
WOOF!
I HOPE THAT HURT HIM AS MUCH AS IT HURT ME!
I AM LIKE TOTALLY HONKED OFF!!
NOW, I AM GONNA PUT A MEGA-STOMPING ON VENOM AND THEN...
... I'M GONNA EXTERMINATE ENTIRE AREA CODES!!!
GET A GRIP, WHY DON'TCHA?
GIVE ME THAT COGNAC AND YOUR LIGHTER!
KASADY, YOU'RE JUST NOT BEING RESPONSIVE TO THERAPY--!

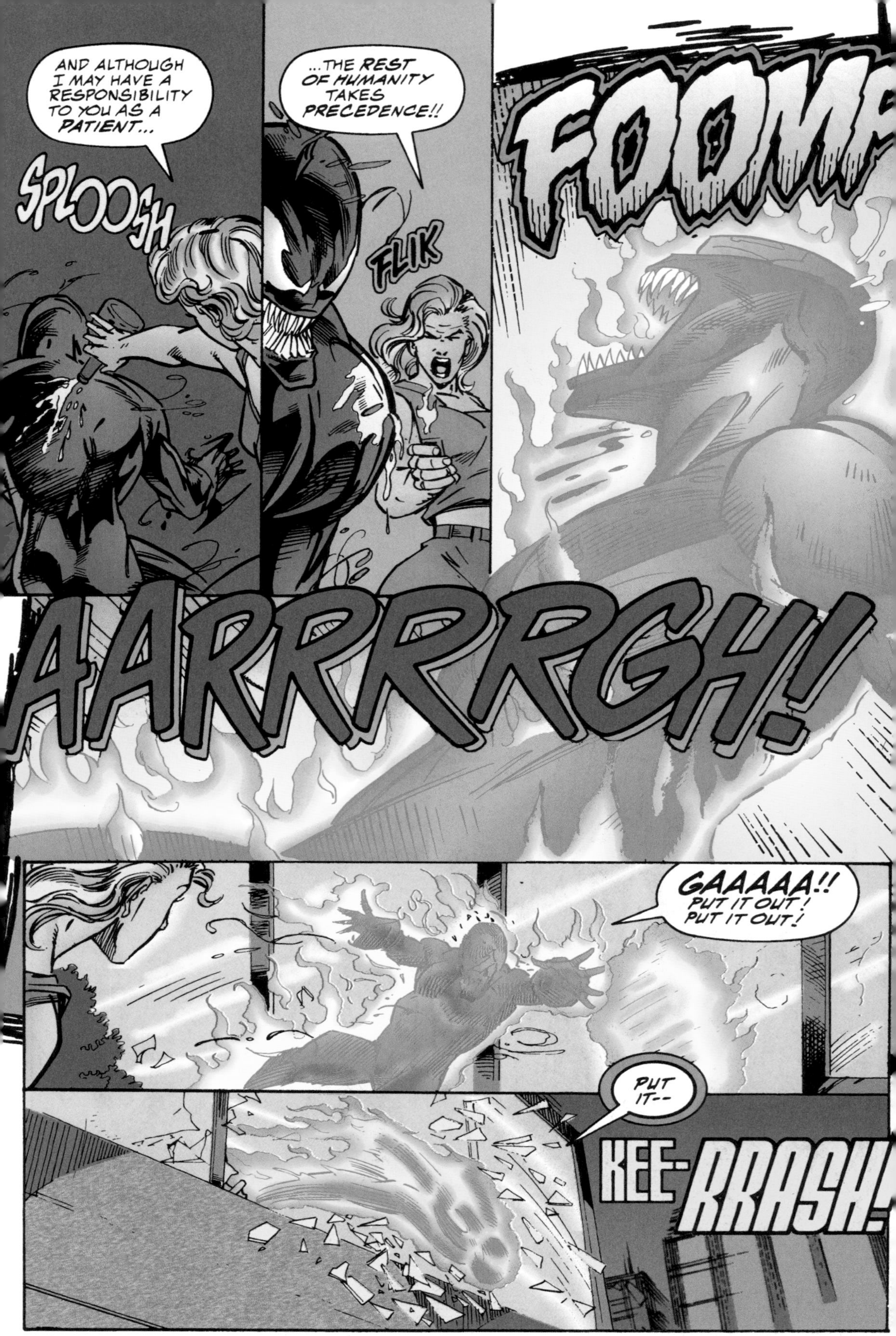
AND ALTHOUGH I MAY HAVE A RESPONSIBILITY TO YOU AS A PATIENT...
SPLOOSH
...THE REST OF HUMANITY TAKES PRECEDENCE!!
FLIK
FOOM
AARRRRGH!
GAAAAA!! PUT IT OUT! PUT IT OUT!
PUT IT--
KEE-RRASH!

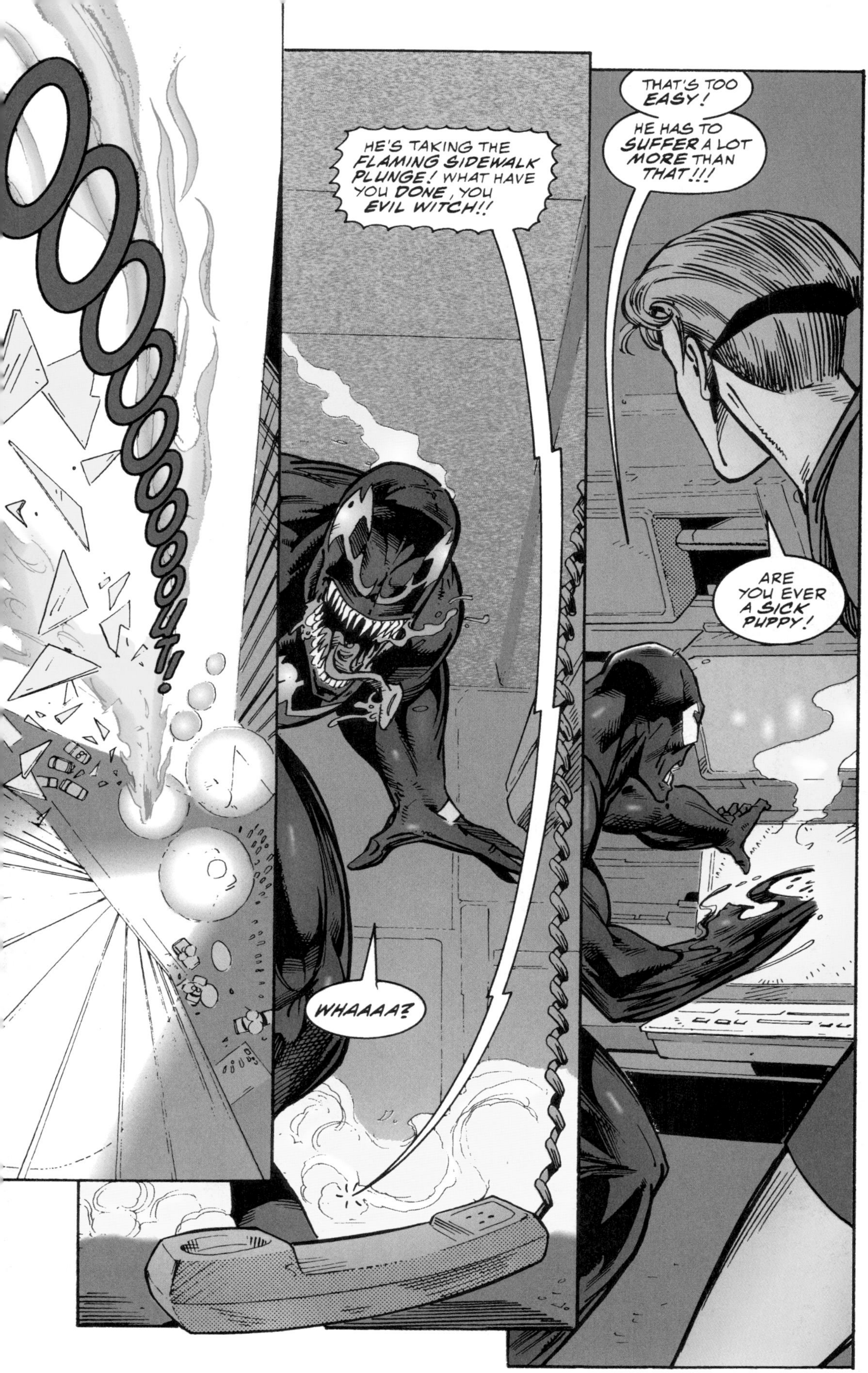
OOOOOOOOOOUT!
HE'S TAKING THE FLAMING SIDEWALK PLUNGE! WHAT HAVE YOU DONE, YOU EVIL WITCH!!
WHAAAA?
THAT'S TOO EASY!
HE HAS TO SUFFER A LOT MORE THAN THAT!!!
ARE YOU EVER A SICK PUPPY!

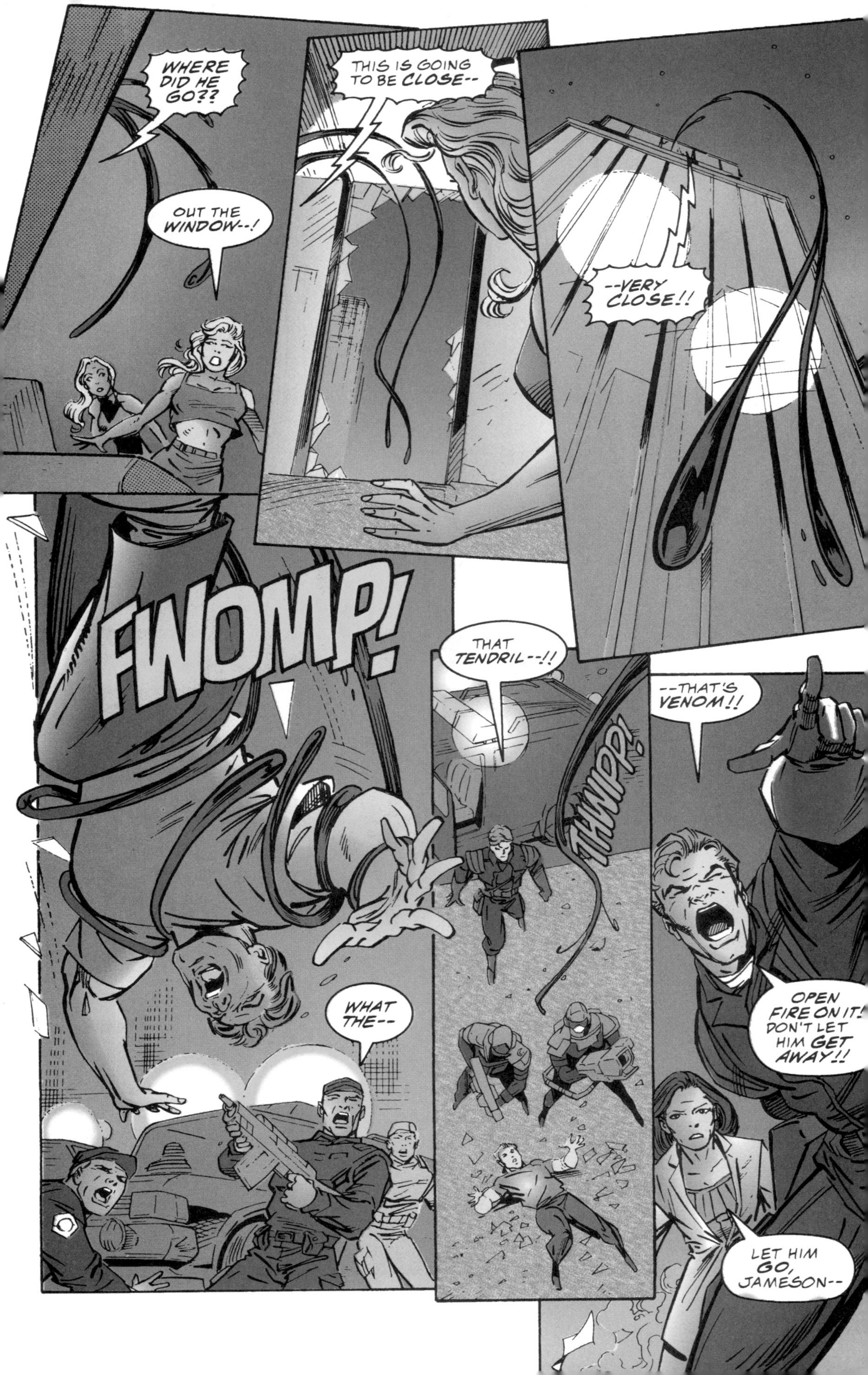
WHERE DID HE GO??
OUT THE WINDOW--!
THIS IS GOING TO BE CLOSE--
--VERY CLOSE!!
FWOMP!
WHAT THE--
THAT TENDRIL--!!
THWIPP!
--THAT'S VENOM!!
OPEN FIRE ON IT! DON'T LET HIM GET AWAY!!
LET HIM GO, JAMESON--

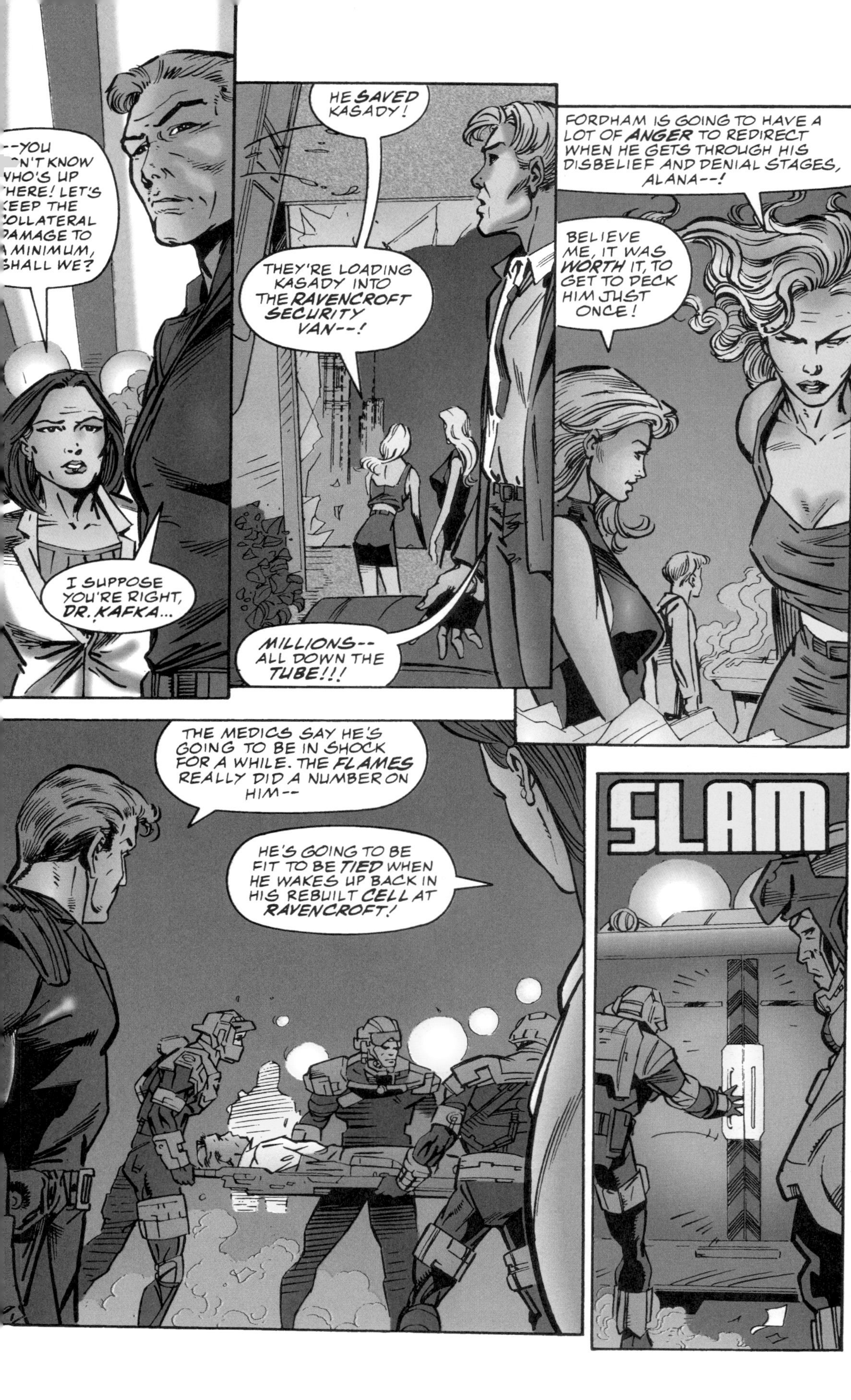
--YOU
N'T KNOW
WHO'S UP
THERE! LET'S
KEEP THE
COLLATERAL
DAMAGE TO
A MINIMUM,
SHALL WE?
I SUPPOSE YOU'RE RIGHT, DR. KAFKA...
HE SAVED KASADY!
THEY'RE LOADING KASADY INTO THE RAVENCROFT SECURITY VAN--!
MILLIONS-- ALL DOWN THE TUBE!!!
FORDHAM IS GOING TO HAVE A LOT OF ANGER TO REDIRECT WHEN HE GETS THROUGH HIS DISBELIEF AND DENIAL STAGES, ALANA--!
BELIEVE ME, IT WAS WORTH IT, TO GET TO DECK HIM JUST ONCE!
THE MEDICS SAY HE'S GOING TO BE IN SHOCK FOR A WHILE. THE FLAMES REALLY DID A NUMBER ON HIM--
HE'S GOING TO BE FIT TO BE TIED WHEN HE WAKES UP BACK IN HIS REBUILT CELL AT RAVENCROFT!
SLAM

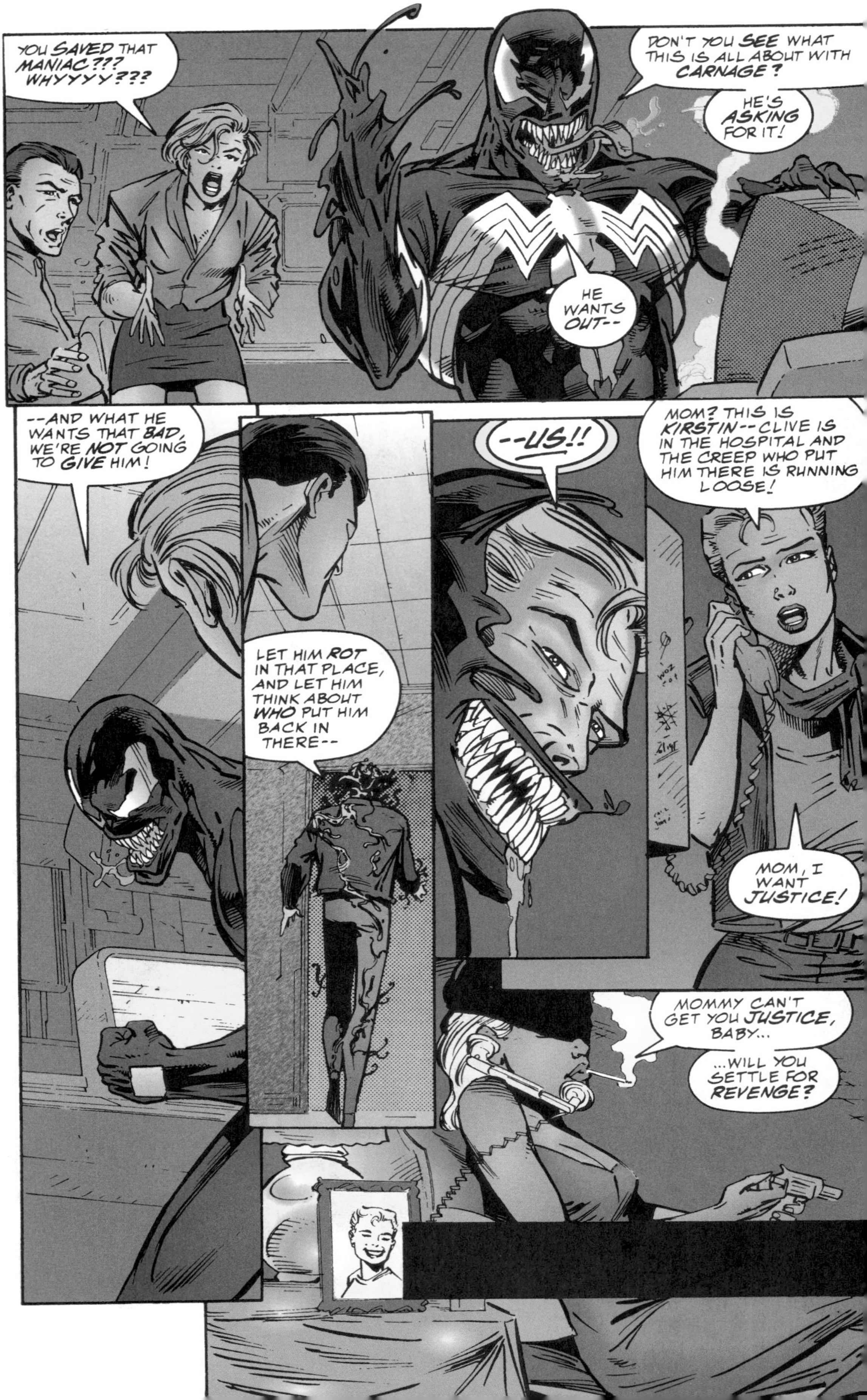
YOU SAVED THAT MANIAC??? WHYYYY???
DON'T YOU SEE WHAT THIS IS ALL ABOUT WITH CARNAGE?
HE'S ASKING FOR IT!
HE WANTS OUT--
--AND WHAT HE WANTS THAT BAD, WE'RE NOT GOING TO GIVE HIM!
LET HIM ROT IN THAT PLACE, AND LET HIM THINK ABOUT WHO PUT HIM BACK IN THERE--
--US!!
MOM? THIS IS KIRSTIN--CLIVE IS IN THE HOSPITAL AND THE CREEP WHO PUT HIM THERE IS RUNNING LOOSE!
MOM, I WANT JUSTICE!
MOMMY CAN'T GET YOU JUSTICE, BABY...
...WILL YOU SETTLE FOR REVENGE?

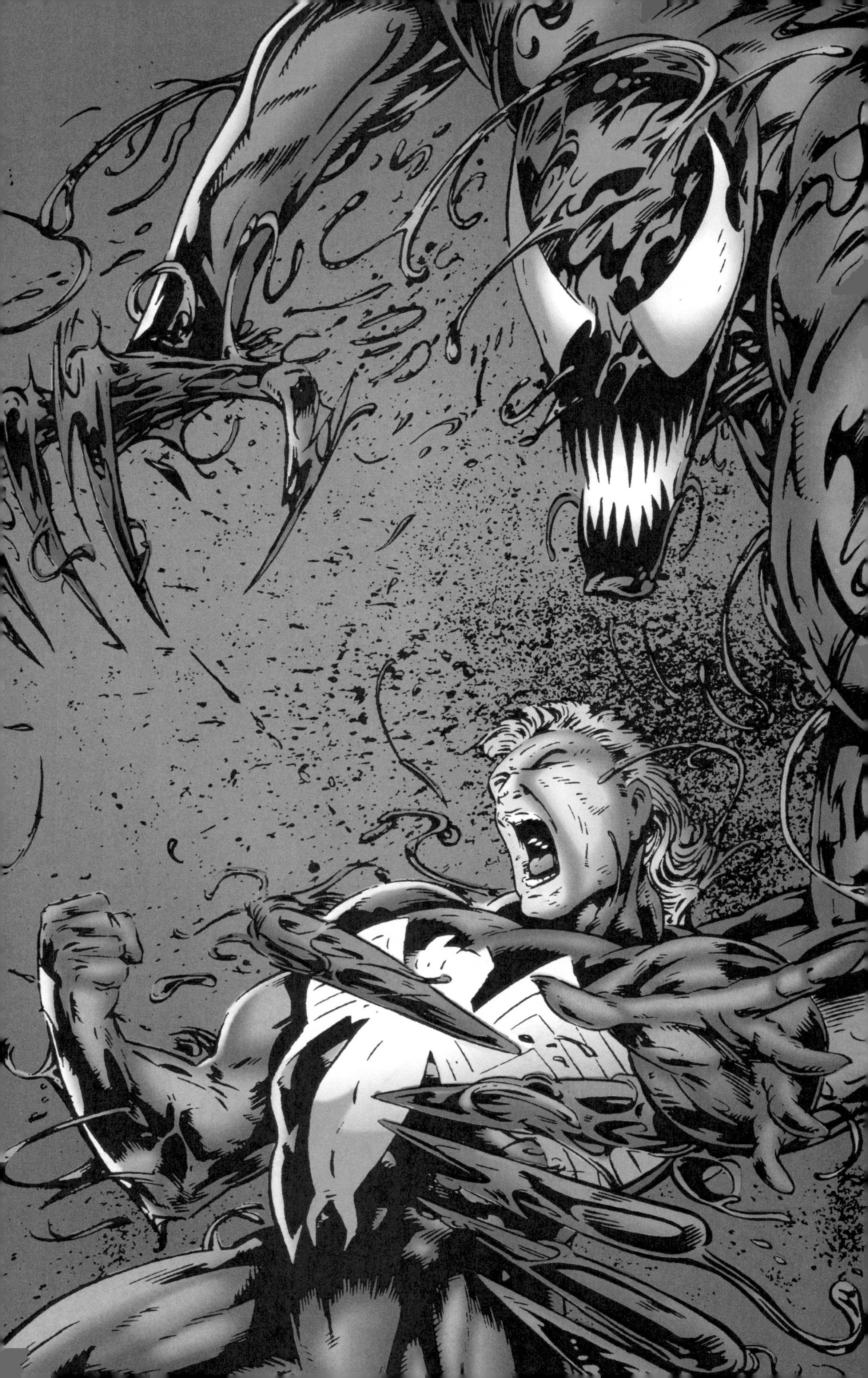

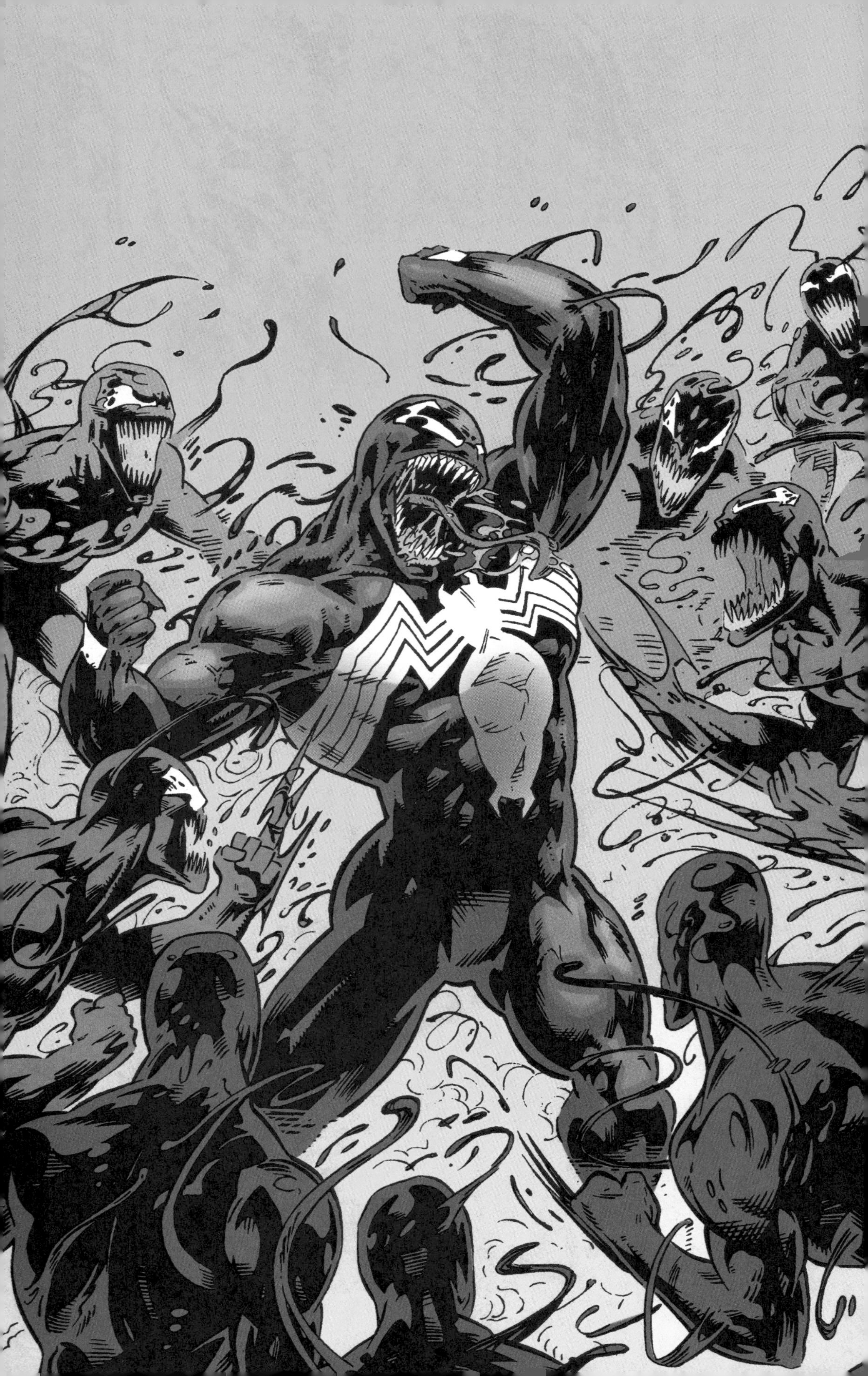

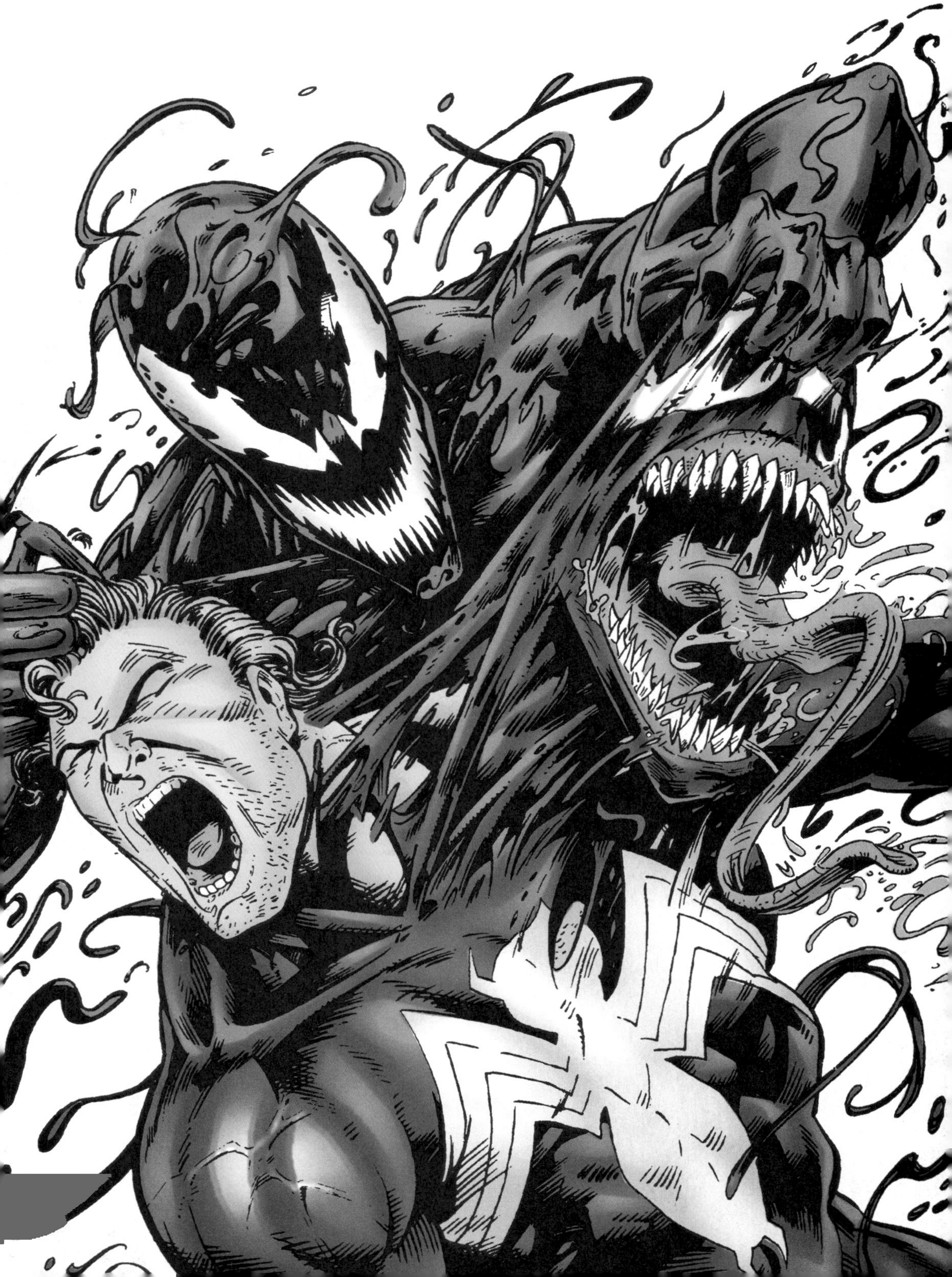

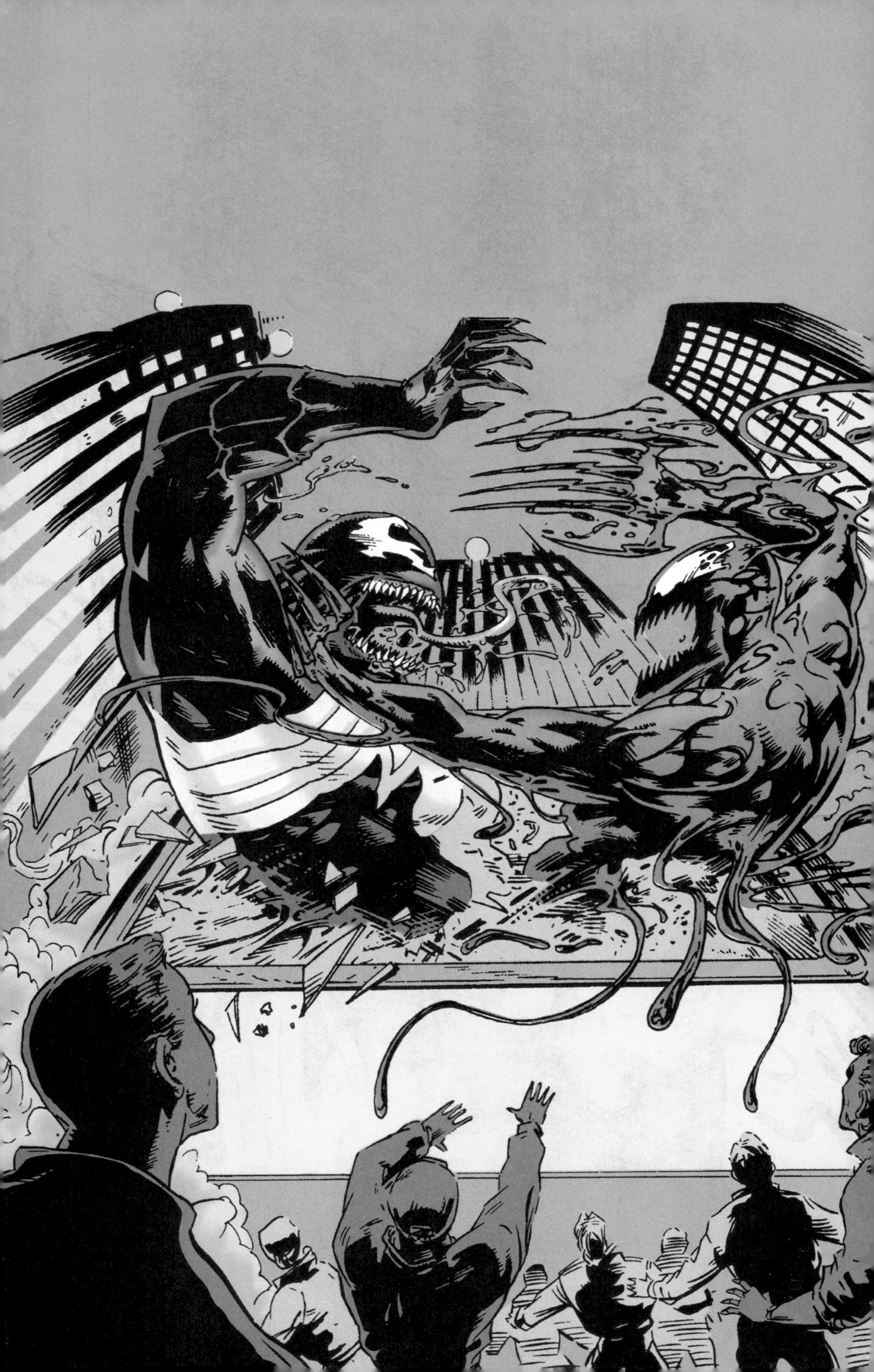